ALSO BY GEORGE MACDONALD FRASER

Mr. American
The Pyrates
The Candlemass Road
Black Ajax

SHORT STORIES
The General Danced at Dawn
McAuslan in the Rough
The Sheikh and the Dustbin

HISTORY
The Steel Bonnets: The Story of the Anglo-Scottish Border Reivers

AUTOBIOGRAPHY
Quartered Safe Out Here
The Hollywood History of the World

THE FLASHMAN PAPERS
Flashman
(BRITAIN, INDIA, AND AFGHANISTAN, 1839–42)
Royal Flash
(ENGLAND 1842–43, GERMANY 1847–48)
Flashman's Lady
(ENGLAND, BORNEO, AND MADAGASCAR, 1842–45)
Flashman and the Mountain of Light
(INDIA PUNJAB 1845–46)
Flash for Freedom!
(ENGLAND, WEST AFRICA, U.S.A., 1848–49)
Flashman and the Redskins
(U.S.A. 1849–50 AND 1875–76)
Flashman at the Charge
(ENGLAND, CRIMEA, AND CENTRAL ASIA, 1854–55)
Flashman in the Great Game
(SCOTLAND, INDIA, 1856–58)
Flashman and the Angel of the Lord
(INDIA, SOUTH AFRICA, U.S.A., 1858–59)
Flashman and the Dragon
(CHINA, 1860)

Flashman and the Tiger

Flashman and the Tiger

and other extracts from

THE FLASHMAN PAPERS

edited and arranged by

George MacDonald Fraser

Alfred A. Knopf   *New York*   2000

THIS IS A BORZOI BOOK
PUBLISHED BY ALFRED A. KNOPF

www.aaknopf.com

Originally published in Great Britain by HarperCollins Publishers,
London, in 1999.

Knopf, Borzoi Books, and the colophon are
registered trademarks of Random House, Inc.

Library of Congress Cataloging-in-Publication Data
Fraser, George MacDonald.
Flashman and the tiger / by George MacDonald Fraser. — 1st American ed.
p.   cm.
ISBN 0-375-41024-4
1. Flashman, Harry Paget (Fictitious character)—Fiction.   I. Title.
PR6056.R287   F725   2000
823'.914—dc21   00-020435

Manufactured in the United States of America
First American Edition

For Kath, a memento of Ischl and the salt-mine

FLASHMAN, Harry Paget, brigadier-general, V.C., K.C.B., K.C.I.E.: Chevalier, Legion of Honour; Order of Maria Theresa, Austria; Order of the Elephant, Denmark (temporary); U.S. Medal of Honor; San Serafino Order of Purity and Truth, 4th class; b. May 5, 1822, s. of H. Buckley Flashman, Esq., Ashby, and Hon. Alicia Paget; m. Elspeth Rennie Morrison, d. of Lord Paisley, one s., one d. Educ. Rugby School. 11th Hussars, 17th Lancers. Served Afghanistan 1841–2 (medals, thanks of Parliament); chief of staff to H.M. James Brooke, Rajah of Sarawak, Batang Luper expedn, 1844; milit. adviser with unique rank of sergeant-general to H.M. Queen Ranavalona of Madagascar, 1844–5; Sutlej campaign, 1845–6 (Ferozeshah, Sobraon, envoy extraordinary to Maharani Jeendan, Court of Lahore); polit. adviser to Herr (later Chancellor Prince) von Bismarck, Schleswig-Holstein, 1847–8; Crimea, staff (Alma, Sevastopol, Balaclava), prisoner of war, 1854; artillery adviser to Atalik Ghazi, Syr Daria campaign, 1855; India, Sepoy Mutiny, 1857–8, dip. envoy to H.R.H. the Maharani of Jhansi, trooper 3rd Native Cavalry, Meerut, subseq. att. Rowbotham's Mosstroopers, Cawnpore (Lucknow, Gwalior, etc., V.C.); adjutant to Captain John Brown, Harper's Ferry, 1859; China campaign 1860, polit. mission to Nanking, Taiping Rebellion, polit. and other services, Imperial Court, Pekin; U.S. Army (major, Union forces, 1862, colonel (staff), Army of the Confederacy, 1863); a.d.c. to H.I.M. Maximilian, Emperor of Mexico, 1867; interpreter and observer Sioux campaign, U.S., 1875–6 (Camp Robinson conference, Little Big Horn, etc.); Zulu War, 1879 (Isandhlwana, Rorke's Drift); Egypt 1882 (Kassassin, Tel-el-Kebir); personal bodyguard to H.I.M. Franz-Josef, Emperor of Austria, 1883; Sudan 1884–5 (Khartoum); Pekin Legations, 1900. Travelled widely in military and civilian capacities, among them supercargo, merchant marine (West Africa), agriculturist (Mississippi valley), wagon captain and hotelier (Santa Fe Trail); buffalo hunter and scout (Oregon Trail); courier (Underground Railroad); majordomo (India), prospector (Australia); trader and missionary (Solomon Islands, Fly River, etc.), lottery supervisor (Manila), diamond broker and horse coper (Punjab), dep. marshal (U.S.), occasional actor and impersonator. Hon. mbr of numerous societies and clubs, including Sons of the Volsungs (Strackenz), Mimbreno Apache Copper Mines band (New Mexico), Khokand Horde (Central Asia), Kit Carson's Boys (Colorado), Brown's Lambs (Maryland), M.C.C., White's and United Service (London, both resigned), Blackjack (Batavia). Chmn, Flashman and Bottomley, Ltd; dir. British Opium Trading Co.; governor, Rugby School; hon. pres. Mission for Reclamation of Reduced Females. Publications: Dawns and Departures of a Soldier's Life; Twixt Cossack and Cannon; The Case Against Army Reform. Recreations: oriental studies, angling, cricket (performed first recorded "hat trick," wickets of Felix, Pilch, Mynn, for 14 runs, Rugby Past and Present v. Kent, Lord's 1842; five for 12, Mynn's Casuals v. All-England XI, 1843). Add: Gandamack Lodge, Ashby, Leics.

CONTENTS

Explanatory Note

When Sir Harry Flashman, V.C., the celebrated Victorian soldier, scoundrel, amorist, and self-confessed poltroon, began to write his memoirs early in the present century, he set to work with a discipline remarkable in one whose life and conduct were, to put it charitably, haphazard and irregular. Disdaining chronology, he adopted a random method, selecting episodes in his adventurous life and shaping them into complete, self-contained narratives, in the fashion of a novelist rather than an autobiographer. This was of immense help to me when the Flashman Papers, which were still unpublished at Sir Harry's death in 1915, turned up as a collection of packets in a tea-chest at a Midlands sale-room in 1966, and were entrusted to me, as editor, by Flashman's executor, the late Mr. Paget Morrison of South Africa.

In accordance with his strict instructions, I dealt with the packets one at a time and found that, thanks to Sir Harry's methodical approach, only a minimum of editing—correcting his occasional spelling mistakes and providing footnotes—was necessary to render the work fit for publication. Each packet contained a book almost ready-made, and soon the public, who until then had been aware of Flashman only as the cowardly bully of Thomas Hughes's *Tom Brown's Schooldays,* were in possession of his illuminating and often scandalous accounts of the First Afghan

War, the Schleswig-Holstein Question, the African-American slave trade, and the Crimean War.

It was with the fifth packet that the pattern changed. Along with his account of the Indian Mutiny, Sir Harry had enclosed a separate brief narrative on an entirely different subject which he plainly felt did not call for extended treatment. Since it was too short for separate publication, and its inclusion with the Mutiny memoir would have made for an unwieldy book, I put it by, hoping the later packets would yield similar fragments which, with the first, might make a full volume.

Since then, two other such pieces have come to light, and the result is this collection of minor episodes in the career of an eminent if disreputable Victorian. One deals with a hitherto-unknown European crisis which, but for Flashman's reluctant intervention, might well have advanced the outbreak of the First World War by three decades, with incalculable consequences. Since it is by far the longest fragment, presents a picture of a great monarch, involves if only at a distance many leading statesmen of the time, and finds Flashman in alliance with the shade of an old adversary, I have given it priority. The second piece clears up at last one of the most puzzling mysteries of the Victorian era, the notorious Baccarat Scandal in which the Prince of Wales was an unhappy actor. The third extract touches briefly on two of the most spectacular military actions of the century, and sees Flashman pitted against one of the great villains of the day, and observing, with his usual jaundiced eye, two of its most famous heroes. As this extract was the first to come to light, more than twenty years ago, and its known existence has caused some speculation among students of the Papers, I have given its title to the full volume.

G.M.F.

THE ROAD TO CHARING CROSS

(1878 AND 1883–4)

Chapter 1

You don't know Blowitz, probably never heard of him even, which is your good luck, although I dare say if you'd met him you'd have thought him harmless enough. I did, to my cost. Not that I bear him a grudge, much, for he was a jolly little teetotum, bursting with good intentions, and you may say it wasn't his fault that they paved my road to Hell—which lay at the bottom of a salt-mine, and it's only by the grace of God that I ain't there yet, entombed in everlasting rock. Damnable places, and not at all what you might imagine. Not a grain of salt to be seen, for one thing.

Mind you, when I say 'twasn't Blowitz's fault, I'm giving the little blighter the benefit of the doubt, a thing I seldom do. But I liked him, you see, in spite of his being a journalist. Tricky villains, especially if they work for *The Times*. He was their correspondent in Paris thirty years ago, and doubtless a government agent—show me the *Times* man who wasn't, from Delane to the printer's devils—but whether he absolutely knew what he was about, or was merely trying to do old Flashy a couple of good turns, I ain't sure. It was certainly his blasted pictures that led me astray: photographs of two lovely women, laid before my unsuspecting middle-aged eyes, one in '78, t'other in '83, and between 'em they landed me in the strangest pickle of my misspent life.

Not the worst, perhaps, but bad enough, and deuced odd. I don't think I understand the infernal business yet, not altogether.

It had its compensations along the way, though, among them the highest decoration France can bestow, the gratitude of two Crowned Heads (one of 'em an out-and-out stunner, much good may it do me), the chance to serve Otto Bismarck a bad turn, and the favours of that delightful little spanker, Mamselle Caprice, to say nothing of the enchanting iceberg Princess Kralta. No . . . I can't think too much ill of little Blowitz at the end of the day.

He was reckoned the smartest newsman of the time, better than Billy Russell even, for while Billy was the complete hand at dramatic description, thin red streaks and all, and the more disastrous the better, Blowitz was a human ferret with his plump little claw on every pulse from Lisbon to the Kremlin; he knew everyone, and everyone knew him—and trusted him. That was the great thing: kings and chancellors confided in him, empresses and grand duchesses whispered him their secrets, prime ministers and ambassadors sought his advice, and while he was up to every smoky dodge in his hunt for news, he never broke a pledge or betrayed a confidence—or so everyone said, Blowitz loudest of all. I guess his appearance helped, for he was nothing like the job at all, being a five-foot butterball with a beaming baby face behind a mighty moustache, innocent blue eyes, bald head, and frightful whiskers a foot long, chattering nineteen to the dozen (in several languages), gushing gallantly at the womenfolk, nosing up to the elbows of the men like a deferential gun dog, chuckling at every joke, first with all the gossip (so long as it didn't matter), a prime favourite at every Paris party and reception—and never missing a word or a look or a gesture, all of it grist to his astounding memory; let him hear a speech or read a paper and he could repeat it, pat, every word, like Macaulay.

Aye, and when the great crises came, and all Europe was agog for news of the latest treaty or rumour of war or collapsing ministry, it was to the *Times'* Paris telegrams they looked, for Blowitz was a past master at what the Yankee scribblers call "the scoop." At the famous Congress of Berlin (of which more anon), when the doors were locked for secret session, Bismarck looked under the table, and when D'Israeli asked him what was up, Bismarck said he wanted to be sure Blowitz wasn't there. A great compliment, you may say—and if you don't, Blowitz did, frequently.

It was through Billy Russell, who you may know was also a *Times* man and an old chum from India and the Crimea, that I met this tubby prodigy at the time of the Franco-Prussian farce in '70, and we'd taken to each other straight off. At least, Blowitz had taken to me, as folk often do, God help 'em, and I didn't mind him; he was a comic little card, and amused me with his Froggy bounce (though he was a Bohemian in fact), and tall tales about how he'd scuppered the Commune uprising in Marseilles in '71 by leaping from rooftop to rooftop to telegraph some vital news or other to Paris while the Communards raged helpless below, and saved some fascinating Balkan queen and her beautiful daughter from shame and ruin at the hands of a vengeful monarch, and been kidnapped when he was six and fallen in love with a flashing-eyed gypsy infant with a locket round her neck— sounded deuced like *The Bohemian Girl* to me, but he swore it was gospel, and part of his "Destiny," which was a great bee in his bonnet.

"You ask, what if I had slipped from those Marseilles roofs, and been dashed to pieces on the cruel cobbles, or torn asunder by those ensanguined terrorists?" cries he, swigging champagne and waving a pudgy finger. "What, you say, if that vengeful monarch's agents had entrapped me—*moi*, Blowitz? What if the gypsy kidnappers had taken another road, and so eluded pursuit? Ah, you ask yourself these things, *cher* 'Arree—"

"I don't do anything o' the sort, you know."

"But you do, of a certainty!" cries he. "I see it in your eye, the burning question! You consider, you speculate, you! What, you wonder, would have become of Blowitz? Or of France? Or the *Times*, by example?" He inflated, looking solemn. "Or Europe?"

"Search me, old Blowhard," says I rescuing the bottle. "All I ask is whether you got to grips with that fascinating Balkan bint and her beauteous daughter, and if so, did you tackle 'em in tandem or one after t'other?" But he was too flown with his fat-headed philosophy to listen.

"I did not slip, me—I could not! I foiled the vengeful monarch's ruffians—it was inevitable! My gypsy abductors took the road determined by Fate!" He was quite rosy with triumph. "*Le destin*, my old one—destiny is immutable. We are like the planets, our courses preordained. Some of us," he admitted, "are comets, vanishing and reappearing, like the geniuses of the past. Thus Moses is reflected in Confucius, Caesar in Napoleon, Attila in Peter the Great, Jeanne d'Arc in . . . in . . ."

"Florence Nightingale. Or does it have to be a Frog? Well, then, Madame du Barry—"

"Jeanne d'Arc is yet to reappear, perhaps. But you are not serious, my boy. You doubt my reason. Oh, yes, you do! But I tell you, everything moves by a fixed law, and those of us who would master our destinies—" he tapped a fat finger on my knee "—we learn to divine the intentions of the Supreme Will which directs us."

"Ye don't say. One jump ahead of the Almighty. Who are you reincarnating, by the way—Baron Munchausen?"

He sat back chortling, twirling his moustache. "Oh, 'Arree, 'Arree, you are *incorrigible*! Well, I shall submit no more to your scepticism *méprisant*, your *dérision Anglaise*. You laugh, when I tell you that in our moment of first meeting, I knew that our fates were bound together. 'Regard this man,' I thought. 'He is part of your destiny.' It is so, we are bound, I, Blowitz, in whom Tacitus lives again, and you . . . ah, but of whom shall I say you are a reflection? Murat, perhaps? Your own Prince Rupert? Some great *beau sabreur,* surely?" He twinkled at me. "Or would it please you if I named the Chevalier de Seingalt?"

"Who's he when he's at home?"

"In Italy they called him Casanova. Aha, that marches! You see yourself in the part! Well, well, laugh as you please, we are destined, you and I. You'll see, *mon ami.* Oh, you'll see!"

He had me weighed up, no error, and knew that on my infrequent visits to Paris, which is a greasy sort of sink not much better than Port Moresby, the chief reason I sought him out was because he was my passport to society salons and the company of the female gamebirds with whom the city abounds—and I don't mean your poxed-up opera tarts and can-can girls but the quality traffic of the smart *hôtels* and embassy parties, whose languid *ennui* conceals more carnal knowledge than you'd find in Babylon. My advice to young chaps is to never mind the Moulin Rouge and Pigalle, but make for some diplomatic *mêlée* on the Rue de Lisbonne, catch the eye of a well-fleshed countess, and ere the night's out you'll have learned something you *won't* want to tell your grandchildren.

In spite of looking like a plum duff on legs, Blowitz had an extraordinary gift of attracting the best of 'em like flies to a jam-pot. No doubt they thought him a harmless buffoon, and he made them laugh, and flattered them something monstrous—and, to be sure, he had the stalwart Flashy in tow, which was no disadvantage, though I say it myself. I suppose you could say he pimped for me, in a way—but don't imagine for a moment that I despised him, or failed to detect the hard core inside the jolly little *flâneur.* I always respect a man who's good at his work, and I bore in mind the story (which I heard from more than one good source) that Blowitz had made his start in France by paying court to his employer's wife, and the pair of them had heaved the unfortunate cuckold into Marseilles harbour from a pleasure-boat, left him to drown, and trotted off to the altar. Yes, I could credit that. Another story, undoubtedly true, was that when the *Times,* in his early days on the paper, were thinking of sacking him, he invited the manager to dinner—and there at the table was every Great Power ambassador in Paris. That convinced the *Times*, as well it might.

So there you have M. Henri Stefan Oppert-Blowitz,' and if I've told you a deal about him and his crackpot notions of our "shared destiny," it's because they were at the root of the whole crazy business, and dam' near cost me my life, as well as preventing a great European war—which will happen eventually, mark my words, if this squirt of a Kaiser ain't put firmly in his place. If I were Asquith I'd have the little swine took off sudden; plenty of chaps would do it for ten thou' and a snug billet in the Colonies afterwards. But that's common sense, not politics, you see.

That by the way. It was at the back end of '77 that the unlikely pair of Blowitz and Sam Grant, late President of the United States, put me on the road to disaster, and (as is so often the case) in the most innocent-seeming way.

Like all retired Yankee bigwigs, Sam was visiting the mother country as the first stage of a grand tour, which meant, he being who he was, that instead of being allowed to goggle at Westminster and Windermere in peace, he must endure adulation on every hand, receiving presentations and the freedom of cities, having fat aldermen and provosts pump his fin, which he hated of all things, listening to endless boring addresses, and having to speechify in turn (which was purgatory to a man who spoke mostly in grunts), with crowds huzzaing wherever he went, the nobility lionising him in their lordly way, and being beset by admiring females from Liverpool laundresses to the Great White Mother herself.

Hard sledding for the sour little bargee, and by the time I met him, at a banquet at Windsor to which I'd been bidden as his old comrade of the war between the states, I could see he'd had his bellyful. Our last encounter had been two years earlier, when he'd sent me to talk to the Sioux and lost me my scalp at Greasy Grass,* and his temper hadn't improved in the meantime.

"It won't do, Flashman!" barks he, chewing his beard and looking as though he'd just heard that Lee had taken New York. "I've had as much ceremony and attention as I can stand. D'you know they're treating me as *royalty?* It's true, I tell you! Lord Beaconsfield has ordained it—well, I'm much obliged to him, I'm sure, but I can't take it! If I have to lay another cornerstone or listen to another artisans' address or have my hand tortured by some worthy burgess bent on wrestling me to the ground . . ." He left off snarling to look round furtive-like in case any of the Quality were in earshot. "At least your gracious Queen doesn't shake hands as though she purposed to break my arm," he added grudgingly. "Not like the rest of 'em."

"Price of fame, Mr. President."

"Price of your aunt's harmonium!" snaps he. "And it'll be worse in Europe, I'll be bound! Dammit, they embrace you, don't they?" He glared at me, as though daring me to try. "Here, though—d'you speak French? I know you speak Siouxan, and I seem to recollect Lady Flashman extolling your linguistic accomplishments. Well, sir—do you or don't you?"

I admitted that I did, and he growled his satisfaction.

"Then you can do me a signal favour . . . if you will. They tell me I must meet Marshal Macmahon in Paris, and he hasn't a word of English—and my French you could write on the back of a postal stamp! Well, then," says he, thrusting his beard at me, "will you stand up with me at the Invalids or the Tooleries or wherever the blazes it is, and play interpreter?" He hesitated, eyeing me hard while I digested this remarkable proposal, and cleared his throat before adding: "I'd value it, Flashman . . . having a friendly face at my elbow 'stead of some damned diplomatic in knee-britches."

* See *Flashman and the Redskins*

Ulysses S. Grant never called for help in his life, but just then I seemed to catch a glimpse, within the masterful commander and veteran statesman, of the thin-skinned Scotch yokel from the Ohio tanyard uneasily adrift in an old so-superior world which he'd have liked to despise but couldn't help feeling in awe of. No doubt Windsor and Buck House had been ordeal enough, and now the prospect of standing tongue-tied before the French President and a parcel of courtly supercilious Frogs had unmanned him to the point where he was prepared to regard *me* as a friendly face. Of course I agreed straight off, in my best toady-manly style; I'd never have dared say no to Grant at any time, and I wouldn't have missed watching him and Macmahon in a state of mutual bewilderment for all the tea in China.

So there I was, a few weeks later, in a gilded salon of the Elysée, when Grant, wearing his most amiable expression, which would have frightened Geronimo, was presented to the great Marshal, a grizzled old hero with a leery look and eyebrows which matched his moustache for luxuriance—a sort of Grant with garlic, he was. They glowered at each other, and bowed, and glowered some more before shaking hands, with Sam plainly ready to leap away at the first hint of an embrace, after which silence fell, and I was just wondering if I should tell Macmahon that Grant was stricken speechless by the warmth of his welcome when Madame Macmahon, God bless her, inquired in English if we'd had a good crossing.

She was still a charmer at sixty, and Sam was so captivated in relief that he absolutely talked to her, which left old Macmahon standing like a blank file. Blowitz, who as usual was to the fore among the attendant dignitaries and crawlers, came promptly to the rescue, introducing me to the Marshal as an old companion-in-arms, sort of, both of us having served in Crimea. This seemed to cheer the old fellow up: ah, I was that Flashman of Balaclava, was I? And I'd done time in the Legion Étrangère also, had I?

Why, he was an old Algeria hand himself; we both had sand in our boots, *n'est-ce pas,* ho-ho! Well, this was *formidable,* to meet, in an English soldier of all people, a *vieille moustache* who had woken to the cry of *"Au jus!"* and marched to the sausage music.[2] Blowitz said that wasn't the half of it: *le Colonel* Flashman had been a distinguished ally of France in China; Montauban would never have got to Pekin without me. Macmahon was astonished; he'd had no notion. Well, there weren't many of us left; decidedly we must become better acquainted.

The usual humbug, though gratifying, but pregnant of great effects, as the lady novelists put it. For early in the following May, long after Grant had gone home (having snarled his way round Europe and charmed the Italians by remarking that Venice would be a fine city if it were drained), and I was pursuing my placid way in London, I was dumfounded by a letter from the French Ambassador informing me that the President of the Republic, in recognition of my occasional services to France, wished to confer on me the Legion of Honour.

Well, bless the dear little snail-eaters, thinks I, for while I've collected a fair bit of undeserved tinware in my time, you can't have too much of it, you know. I didn't suspect it, but this was Blowitz at work, taking advantage of my meeting with old Macmahon to serve ends of his own. The little snake had discovered a use for me, and decided to put me in his debt—didn't know Flash too well, did he? At all events, he'd dropped in Macmahon's ear the suggestion that I was ripe for a Frog decoration, and Macmahon was all for it, apparently, so back to Paris I went in my best togs, had the order (fourth or fifth class, I forget which) hung round my unworthy neck, received the Marshal's whiskery embrace, and was borne off to Voisin's by Blowitz to celebrate—and be reminded that I owed my latest glorification to him, and our shared "destiny."

"What joy compares itself to advancing the fortunes of an

old friend to whom one is linked by fate?" beams he, tucking his napkin under his several chins and diving into his soup. "For in serving him, do I not serve myself?"

"That's my modest old Blow," says I. "What d'ye want?"

"Ah, *sceptique*! Did I speak of obligation, then? It is true, I hope to interest you in a small affair of mine—oh, but an affair after your own heart, I think, and to our mutual advantage. But first, let us do honour to the table—champagne, my boy!"

So I waited while he gorged his way through half a dozen overblown courses—why the French must clart decent grub with glutinous sauces beats me—and when the waiters had cleared and we were at the brandy and cigars he sighed with repletion, patted his guts, and fished a mounted picture from his pocket.

"It is a most amusing intrigue, this," says he, and presented it with a flourish. "*Voilà!*"

I'm rather a connoisseur of photography, and there was a quality about the present specimen which took my attention at once. It may have been the opulence of the setting, or the delicacy of the hand-colouring, or the careful composition which had placed two gigantic blackamoors with loincloths and scimitars among the potted palms, or the playful inclusion of the parakeet and tiny monkey on either side of the oriental couch on which lounged a lovely odalisque clad only in gold turban and ankle-fetters, her slender body arched to promote jutting young bumpers which plainly needed no support, her lips parted in a sneer which promised unimaginable depravities. A caption read "La Petite Caprice"; well, it was a change from Frou-Frou . . . I tore my eyes away from the potted palms, a mite puzzled. As I've said, Blowitz had put me in the way of Society gallops, but never a professional.

"*Très appétissante, non?*" says he.

I tossed it back to him. "Which convent is she advertising?"

He clucked indignantly. "She is not what you suppose! This is a theatrical picture, made when she was employed at the Folies—from necessity, let me tell you, to finance her studies—serious studies! Such pictures are *de rigueur* for a Folies comedienne."

"Well, I could see she hated posing for it—"

"Would it surprise you," says he severely, "to learn that she is a trained criminologist, speaks fluently four languages, rides, fences and shoots, and is a valued member of the *département secret* of the Ministry of the Interior, at present in our Berlin Embassy . . . where I was influential in placing her? Ah, you stare! Do I interest you, my friend?"

"*She* might, if she was on hand. But since she ain't, and posing for lewd pictures belies her stainless purity—"

"Did I say that? No, no, my boy. She is no *demi-mondaine, la belle* Caprice, but she is . . . a woman of the world, let us say. That is why she is in Berlin."

"And what's she to do with this small affair after my own heart to our mutual advantage?"

He sat back, lacing his tubby fingers across his pot. "As I recall, you were at one time intimate with the German Chancellor, Prince Bismarck, but that you hold him in no affection—"

I choked on my brandy. "Thank'ee for the dinner and the Legion of Honour, old Blow," says I, preparing to rise. "I don't know where you're leading, but if it's to do with him, I can tell you that I wouldn't go near the square-headed bastard with the whole Household Brigade—"

"But, my friend, be calm, I beg! Resume the seat, if you please! It is not necessary that you . . . go near his highness! No such thing . . . he figures only, how shall I say—at a distance?"

"That's too bloody close!" I assured him, but he protested that I must hear him out; our destinies were linked, he insisted, and he would not dream of a proposal distasteful to me, death of his life—quite the reverse, indeed. So I sat down, and put myself right with a brandy; mention of Bismarck always unmans me, but the fact was I was curious, not least about the delectable Mamselle Caprice.

"*Eh bien,*" says Blowitz, and leaned forward, plainly bursting to unfold his mystery. "You are aware that in a few weeks' time a great conference is to take place at Berlin, of all the Powers, to amend this ridiculous Treaty of San Stefano made by Russia and Turkey?" I must have looked blank, for he blew out his cheeks. "At least you know they have recently been at war in the Balkans?"

"Absolutely," says I. "There was talk of us having a second Crimea with the *moujiks,* but I gather that's blown over. As for . . . San Stefano, did you say? Greek to me, old son."

He shook his head in despair. "You have heard of the Big Bulgaria, surely?"

"Not even of the little 'un."

He seemed ready to weep. "Or the Sanjak of Novi Bazar?"

"Watch your tongue, if you please. We're in a public place."

"*Incroyable!*" He threw up his hands. "And it is an educated Englishman, this, widely travelled and of a military reputation! Europe may hang on the brink of catastrophe, and you . . ." He smote his fat forehead. "My dear 'Arree, will you tell me, then, what events of news you *have* remarked of late?"

"Well, let's see . . . our income tax went up tuppence . . . baccy and dog licences, too . . . some woman or other has sailed round the world in a yacht . . ." He was going pink, so just to give him his money's worth I added: "Elspeth's bought one of these phonographs that are all the rage . . . oh, aye, and Gilbert and Sullivan have a new piece, and dam' good, too; the jolliest tunes. 'I am an Englishman, be-hold me!' . . . as you were just saying—"[3]

"Enough!" He breathed heavily. "I see I must undertake your political education *sur-le-champ.* Gilbert and Sullivan, *mon dieu!*"

And since he did, and I'll lay odds that you, dear reader, know no more about Big Bulgaria and t'other thing than I did, I'll set it out as briefly as can be. It's a hellish bore, like all diplomat-icking, but you'd best hear about it—and then you can hold your own with the wiseacres at the club or tea-table.

First off, the Balkans . . . you have to understand that they're full of people who'd much rather massacre each other than not, and their Turkish rulers (who had no dam' business to be in Europe, if you ask me) were incapable of controlling things, what with the disgusting inhabitants forever revolting, and Russia and Austria trying to horn in for their own base ends. By and large we were sympathetic to the Turks, not because we liked the brutes but because we feared Russian expansion towards the Mediterranean (hence the Crimean War, where your correspon-dent won undying fame and was rendered permanently flatulent by Russian champagne).*

At the same time we were forever nagging the Turks to be less monstrous to their Balkan subjects, with little success, Turks being what they are, and when, around '75, the Bulgars revolted and the Turks slaughtered 150,000 of them to show who was mas-ter, Gladstone got in a fearful bait and made his famous remark about the Turks clearing out, bag and baggage. He had to sing a different tune when the Russians invaded Ottoman territory and handed the Turks a handsome licking; we couldn't have Ivan lording it in the Balkans, and for a time it looked as though we'd have to tackle the Great Bear again—we sent warships to the Dardanelles and Indian regiments to Malta, but the crisis passed when Russia and Turkey made peace, with the San Stefano Treaty.

The trouble was that this treaty created what was called "Big Bulgaria," which would clearly be a Russian province and stepping-stone to the Mediterranean and the Suez Canal. The Austrians, with their own ambitions in the Balkans, were also leery of Russia, so to keep the peace Bismarck, the "honest bro-

* See *Flashman at the Charge*

ker" (ha!), called the Congress of Berlin to amend San Stefano to everyone's satisfaction, if possible.[4]

"Everyone will be there! *Tout le monde!*" Blowitz was fairly gleaming with excitement. "Prince Bismarck will preside, with your Lord Salisbury and Lord Beaconsfield—as we must learn to call M. D'Israeli—Haymerle and Andrassy from Austria, Desprez and Waddington from France, Gorchakov and Shuvalov from Russia—oh, and so many more, from Turkey and Italy and Germany . . . it will be the greatest conference of the Powers since the Congress of Vienna, with the fate of Europe—the world, even—at stake!"

I could see it was just his meat; but what, I wondered, did it have to do with me. He became confidential, blowing garlic at me.

"A new treaty will emerge. The negotiations will be of the most secret. No word of what passes behind those closed doors will be permitted to escape—until the new treaty is published, no doubt by Prince Bismarck himself." His voice sank to a whisper. "It will be the greatest news story of the century, my friend—and the correspondent who obtains it *beforehand* will be hailed as the first journalist of the world!" The round rosy face was set like stone, and the blue eyes were innocent no longer. "*The Times* will have that story . . . First! Alone! Exclusive!" His finger rapped the table on each word, and I thought, aye, you could have heaved your wife's former husband into the drink, no error. Then he sat back, beaming again. "More brandy, my boy!"

"Got an embassy earwig, have you? How much are you paying him?"

He winked, like a conspiring cherub. "Better than any 'earwig,' dear 'Arree, I shall have the *entrée* to the mind of one of the principal parties . . . and he will not even know it!" He glanced about furtively, in case Bismarck was hiding behind an ice-bucket.

"The Russian Ambassador to London, Count Peter Shuvalov, will be second only to Prince Gorchakov in his country's delegation. He is an amiable and experienced diplomat—and the most dedicated lecher in the entire *corps diplomatique*.⁵ Oh, but a satyr, I assure you, who consumes women as you do cigars. And with a mistress who knows how to engage his senses, he is . . . oh, *qui ne s'en fait pas* . . . how do you say in English—?"

"Easy-going?"

"*Précisément!* Easy-going . . . to the point of indiscretion. I could give numerous instances—names which would startle you—"

"Gad, you get about! Ever thought of writing your recollections? You'd make a mint!"

He waved it aside. "Now, this Congress will dance, like any other, and it is inevitable that M. Shuvalov will encounter, at a party, the opera, perhaps on his evening promenade on the Friederichstrasse, the enchanting Mamselle Caprice of the French Embassy. What then? I will tell you. He will be captivated, he will pursue, he will overtake . . . and his enjoyment of her charms will be equalled only by the solace he will find in describing the labours of the day to such a sympathetic listener. I know him, believe me." He sipped a satisfied Chartreuse. "And I know her. No doubt she will be the adoring *ingénue,* and M. Shuvalov will leak like an old samovar."

I had to admire him. "Crafty little half-pint, ain't you, though? Here, give us another squint at that picture . . . by Jove, lucky old Shovel-off! But hold on, Blow—she may romp each day's doings out of him, but she can't get you the treaty word for word—and that's what you want, surely?"

"*Mais certainement!* Am I an amateur, then? No . . . I absorb her reports by the day, and only when all is concluded, and the treaty is being drafted, do I approach a certain minister who holds me in some esteem. I make it plain that I am *au fait* with the entire negotiation. He is aghast. 'You know it all?' he cries. 'A matter of course,' I reply with modesty, 'and now I await only the text of the treaty itself.' He is amazed . . . but convinced. This Blowitz, he tells himself, is a wizard. And from that, *cher* 'Arree," says he, smiling smugly, "it is but a short step to the point where he gives me the treaty himself. Oh, it is a technique, I assure you, which never fails."

It's true enough; there's no surer way of getting a secret than by letting on you know it already. But I still couldn't see why he was telling me.

"Because one thing only is lacking. It is out of the question that Caprice should communicate with me directly, for I shall be jealously observed at all times, not only by competitors, but by diplomatic eyes—possibly even by the police. It is the price of being Blowitz." He shrugged, then dropped his voice. "So it is vital that I have what you call a go-between, *n'est-ce pas?*"

So that was it, and before I could open my mouth, let alone demur, his paw was on my sleeve and he was pattering like a Yankee snake-oil drummer.

" 'Arree, it can only be you! I knew it from the first—have I not said our fates are linked? To whom, then, should I turn for help in the greatest *coup* of my career? And it will be without inconvenience—indeed, to your satisfaction rather—"

"So that's why you wangled me the Order of the Frog!"

"Wangle? What is this wangle? Oh, my best of friends, that was a bagatelle! But this what I beg of you . . . ah, it imports to me beyond anything in the world! And I would trust no other— my destiny . . . *our* destiny, would forbid it. You will not fail Blowitz?"

When folk yearn and sweat at me simultaneous, I take stock. "Well, now, I don't know, Blow . . ."

"Shall I give you reasons? One, I shall be forever in your debt. Two, my *coup* will enrage Prince Bismarck . . . that pleases, eh? And three . . ." he smirked like a lascivious Buddha ". . . you will make the acquaintance . . . the intimate acquaintance, of the delicious Mamselle Caprice."

At that, it wasn't half bad. It was safe, and I could picture

Bismarck's apoplexy if his precious treaty was published before he could make his own pompous proclamation. I took another slant at the photograph lying between us . . . splendid potted palms they were, and while her pose of wanton invitation might be only theatrical, as Blowitz had said, I couldn't believe she wasn't enjoying her work.

"Well . . . what would I have to do?"

D'you know, the little villain had already reserved me a Berlin hotel room for the duration of the conference? Confidence in destiny, no doubt. "It is in the name of Jansen . . . Dutch or Belgian, as you prefer, but not, I think, English." He had it all pat: I would rendezvous with Caprice at her apartment near the French Embassy, and there, in the small hours of each morning, when she had sent Shuvalov on his exhausted way, she would give me her reports, writ small on rice paper.

"Each day you and I will lunch—separately and without recognition, of course—at the Kaiserhof, where I shall be staying. You will have concealed Mamselle's report in the lining of your hat, which you will hang on the rack at the dining-room door. When we go our respective ways, I shall take your hat, and you mine." This kind of intrigue was just nuts to him, plainly. "They will be identical in appearance, and I have already ascertained that our sizes are much the same. We repeat the performance each day . . . *eh, voilà!* It is done, in secrecy the most perfect. Well, my boy, does it march?"

The only snag I could see was being first wicket down with the lady after she'd endured the attentions of blasted Shovel-off, and would be intent on writing her reports. Happy thought: being a mere diplomat, his performance might well leave her gnawing her pretty knuckles for some real boudoir athletics—in which case the reports could wait until after breakfast.

Well, if I'd had any sense, or an inkling of what lay years ahead, or been less flown with Voisin's arrack, I'd have given the business the go-by—but you know me: the promise of that photograph, and the thought of dear Otto smashing the chandelier in his wrath, were too much for my ardent boyish nature. And it never hurts to do the press a good turn.

So it was with a light heart and my hat on three hairs that I found myself strolling under the famous lime trees to the Brandenburg Thor a few weeks later, taking a long slant at the Thier Garten in the June sunshine, and marvelling at the Valkyrian proportions of German women—which awoke memories of my youthful grapplings with that blubbery baroness in Munich . . . Pech-something, her name was, a great whale of a woman with an appetite to match.

That had been thirty years ago, and I hadn't visited Germany since, with good reason. When you've been entrapped, kidnapped, forced to impersonate royalty, shanghaied into marriage, half-hung by Danish bandits, crossed swords in dungeons with fiends like Rudi von Starnberg, drowned near as dammit, and been bilked of a fortune . . . well, Bognor for a holiday don't look so bad.* Thank God, it was far behind me now; Rudi was dead, and lovely Lola, and even Bismarck had probably given up murder in favour of war . . . not that he'd done much in that line for a few years. Mellowing with age, like enough. Still, I'd steer well clear of their Congress: Otto aside, I'd no wish to have D'Israeli inveigling me into a game of vingt-et-un.† Nor had I any great desire to "do" Berlin; it may have the finest palaces in Germany, and the broadest streets, which is capital if you enjoy miles of ornamented stucco and don't mind tumbling into drains which are mostly uncovered, but it also has the disadvantage of being full of Germans, most of 'em military. They say there's a garrison of 20,000 (in a town no bigger than Glasgow) and it seemed to me the whole kit-boodle of 'em were on Unter den Linden—

* See *Royal Flash*
† See *Flash for Freedom!*

sentries presenting arms at every door and the pavements infested by swaggering Junkers with plumed helmets and clanking medals, still full of Prussian bounce because they'd licked the Frogs eight years before, as though that mattered.

The Congress was to begin on the 13th, and it was on the evening of the 12th that I left my modest hotel on the Tauben Strasse and walked the short distance to the discreet, pleasant little court off the Jager Strasse where Mamselle had her apartment—both of us quietly tucked away (trust Blowitz) but convenient for Unter den Linden, and the Wilhelmstrasse where the Congress was to sit. Blowitz had fixed the time, and primed her; his note awaiting me at my hotel had hinted delicately that she knew I wasn't a puritan, exactly, and would expect to be paid in kind for my services, so I was in excellent fettle as I knocked at her door. My one doubt was that, being used to coupling for her country (or, in this case presumably, for *The Times*), she might be a dutiful icicle with one eye on the clock and her mind elsewhere, in which case I'd just have to jolly the sparkle into her eyes.

I needn't have fretted; it was there from the first in the mouth-watering vision who opened the door determined to practise her art on Flashy. Like all good actresses, she'd decided exactly how to play her part, and dressed according in a *déshabillé* of frothy black lace clinging to a petite hourglass shape which recalled the Maharani Jeendan of intoxicating memory. Without her turban, her hair showed light auburn, cut in a fetching schoolgirl fringe above a lovely impudent face whose smile of invitation would have melted Torquemada. For an instant it faded on "Herr . . . Jansen?" only to return as I made my gallant bow.

"Oh, *pardon*!" she exclaimed. "I was expecting someone . . . much older!"

"Mamselle," says I, saluting her dainty fingertips, "you and I will get along famously! May I return the compliment by saying that your photograph don't do you justice?"

"Ah, that photograph!" She made a pretty *moue* and rolled

her eyes. "How I blushed to see it outside the theatre . . . but now, it has its uses, *non?*" She didn't wink, but her voice did, and her smile, as she closed the door and looked me up and down, was pure sauce. "Stefan tells me it brought you to Berlin . . . *oui?*"

"Stefan has a reputation for accuracy, *oui*," says I, and now that the courtesies had been observed, and she was French anyway, I slipped my hands under her delectable stern, hoisted her up, and kissed her soundly. She gave a muffled squeak for form's sake before thrusting her tongue between my lips, but just as I was casting about for a convenient settee she disengaged, giggling, and said I must put her down, and we should have an *aperitif*, and then I must explain something to her.

"No explanation necessary," growls I, but she wriggled clear, rolling her rump, and checking my pursuit with a shaken finger— and if you'd seen that bouncy little bundle, pouting mischievous reproof and absolutely crying, "Non-non-la-la!" like the maid in a French farce, you'd have been torn between bulling her on the spot and brushing away a sentimental tear. I did neither; I enjoy a good performance as well as the next licentious rascal, and never mind playing wait-a-bit with a coquette who knows her business. So I sat on the couch while she filled two glasses, pledged me with a flashing smile, and then sauntered artlessly into the sunlight from the window to give me the benefit of her transparent *négligée*. There followed as eccentric a conversation as I can recall— and I've been tête-à-tête with Mangas Colorado Apache, remember, and the lunatic leader of the Taiping rebellion.

> MAMSELLE (solicitous): You are comfortable? *Eh bien*, you must rest quietly a moment, and be *courtois* . . . what you call proper, correct . . . until you have explained what I wish to know.
> FLASHY (slavering with restraint): Good as gold. Fire away.

M (handing him an illustrated journal): So tell me, then, what is so *très amusant* about *that?*

F: Good God, it's *Punch!* One of last month's.

M (ever so serious): If I am to be perfect in English, I must understand your humour, *n'est-ce pas?* So, instruct me, if you please.

F: What, this cartoon here? Ah, let's see . . . two English grooms in Paris, and one is saying there ain't no letter "W" in French, and t'other says: "Then 'ow d'yer spell 'wee'?" Just so . . . well, the joke is that the second chap doesn't know how to spell "oui," you see . . .

M: And one is to laugh at that?

F: Well, I can't say I did myself, but—

M: *Pouf!* And this other, then? (Sits by F, taps page with dainty scarlet nail, regards him wide-eyed)

F (aware that only a wisp of gauze lies between him and the delightful meat): Eh? Oh, ah, yes! Well, here's a stout party complaining that the fish she bought yesterday was "off," and the fishmonger retorting that it's her own fault for not buying it earlier in the week . . .

M (bee-stung lips breathing perfume): What then?

F: Gad, that's sweet! . . . Ah, well, I guess that the joke is that *he's* blaming *her,* don't you know, when in fact he's been selling the stuff after it's started to stink.

M (bewildered, nestling chin on F's shoulder): So *le poissonier* is a thief. That amuses, does it?

F: See here, I don't write the damned jokes . . . (Attempts to fondle her starboard tit)

M (parrying deftly): Good as gold, *méchant*!
Now, this page here, the lady in harlequin costume . . . ah, *très chic*, her hat and veil *trop fripon*,
and her figure exquisite, *mais voluptueuse*! (Sits
bolt upright, inspired to imitation)

F: God love us!

M (swaying out of reach): . . . but her expression
is severe, and she carries a baton—to chastise?
She is perhaps a *flagellatrice*? *Formidable!* But this
also is humourous?

F: Certainly not. This picture is intended to be
ogled by lewd men. Speaking as one myself . . .

M: No, no, be still, you promised! What is
"ogled"?

F: What people did at your Folies photograph, as
well you know! Enjoyed posing for it, didn't
you?—dammit, you're enjoying *this*!

M (wickedly): *Mais certainement!* (Nestles again,
nibbling F's ear) *Et vous aussi?* No-no-no-wait!
One last question . . . ah, but only one . . . these
words, above this article . . . what do they mean?

F (reading): "Hankey Pankey" . . . (As she bursts
out laughing) I knew it, bigod! You understand *Punch*'s beastly jokes as well as I do, don't
you? Well, just for that, young woman, I shan't
tell you what Hankey Pankey means . . . I'll show
you! (Demonstrates, *avec élan et espièglerie*
and lustful roarings, to delighted squeals and
sobs from Mamselle. Ecstatic collapse of both
parties.)[6]

Afterwards, as I lay blissfully tuckered, with that splendid
young body astride of me, moist and golden in the fading sunlight, her eyes closed in a satisfied smirk, I found myself won-

dering idly if the French secret service ran an École de Galop to train their female agents in the gentle art of houghmagandie, as Elspeth calls it—and if so, were there any vacancies for visiting professors? Anyway, Mamselle Caprice must have been the Messalina Prizewoman of her year; no *demi-mondaine* perhaps, according to Blowitz, but as expert an amateur as I'd ever struck, with the priceless gift of fairly revelling in her sex, and using it with joyous abandon . . . and considerable calculation, as I was about to learn.

She stretched across to the nearby table for a gilt-tipped cigarette, lighting it from a tiny spirit lamp, and I couldn't resist another clutch at those firm pointed poonts overhead. She squirmed her bottom in polite response, trickling smoke down her shapely nostrils as she studied me, head on one side; then she leaned down, murmuring in my ear.

"If you were Count Shuvalov . . . would you be ready to confide in me now?" She gave a little chuckle, and nibbled.

"I'll be damned! Been using me for net practice, have you?" I couldn't help laughing. "Experimenting on me, you little trollop—of all the sauce!"

"Why not?" says the shameless baggage, sitting up again and drawing on her scented weed. "If I am to learn his secrets, it is well I should know what . . . beguiles men of his age. After all, you and he are no longer boys, but mature, possibly of similar tastes . . ."

"A couple of ageing libertines, you mean? Well, thank'ee, my dear, I'm obliged to you—as I'm sure Count Shovel-off will be, and if you pay him the kind of loving attention you've just shown me, I dare say he'll be sufficiently captivated to gas his fat head off—"

"Oh, he is captivate' already," says she airily. "He has admired the notorious photograph . . . and we have met, and he has begged an assignation for tomorrow night."[7]

"Has he, now? That's brisk work." Highly professional,

too . . . by Blowitz? . . . by the French secret department? Certainly by the brazen little bitch sitting cool as a trout athwart my hawse, sporting her boobies and blowing smoke-rings while she mused cheerfully on how best to squeeze the juice out of her Russian prey.

"You see," says she, "to captivate, to seduce, is nothing . . . he is only a man." She gave the little shrug that is the Frenchwoman's way of spitting on the pavement. "But afterwards . . . to make him tell what I wish to know . . . ah, that is another thing. Which is why I ask you, who are experienced in secret affairs, Blowitz says. You know well these Russians, you have made the intrigues, you have made love to many, many women, and I am sure they have—how do you say?—practised their nets on you." She smiled sleepy seductive-like, and leaned down again to flicker the tip of her tongue against my lips. "So, tell me . . . which of them most appealed, to win your confidence? The fool? The task-mistress? The slave? *L'ingénue?* Or perhaps *la petite farceuse* who teases you with foolish jokes, and then . . ." She wriggled, stroking her bouncers across my chest. "To which would you tell your secrets?"

"My, you've studied your subject, haven't you?" I eased her gently upright. "Well, the answer, my artful little seductress, is . . . to none of 'em—unless I wanted to. But I ain't Shovel-off, remember. From what I hear he's the kind of vain ass who can't resist showing off to every pretty woman he meets, so it don't matter a rap whether you play the innocent or Delilah or Gretchen the Governess. Get him half-tipsy, pleasure him blind, and listen to him blather . . . but don't try to come round him with jokes from *Punch*, 'cos they'd be lost on him. Tease him with a few funny bits from Tolstoy, if you like, or the latest wheezes from Ivan the Terrible's Guffawgraph—"

"Oh, *idiot!*" She slapped me smartly on the midriff, giggling. "You are not serious, you! I ask advice, and you make game of me!"

"Advice, my eye—mocking a poor old man, more like."

"Old? Ha!" exclaims she, rolling her eyes—she could pay a neat compliment, the minx.

"As if there was anything I could teach you about bewitching a man!" I can pay a compliment, too. She gave a complacent toss of the head, arms akimbo.

"Oh, one can always learn, from a wise teacher . . . I think," says she, assuming the depraved sneer she had worn in her photograph, "that since I do not like M. Shuvalov, I should prefer to be Gretchen the Governess, *très implacable, sans remords!*" She made growling noises, flourishing an imaginary whip. "Ah, well, we shall see! And now," she hopped nimbly down, "I make supper!"

Which she did, very tasty: an omelette that was like a soufflé, for lightness, with toast and a cold Moselle, fruits soaked in kirsch, and coffee Arabi style—black as night, sweet as love, hot as hell. Listening to her cheery prattle and bubbling laughter across the table, I found myself warming to Mamselle Caprice, and not only 'cos she was a little stunner and rode like a starving succubus and cooked rather well. I liked her *style:* no humbug, just Jezebel with a sassy twinkle and a fifth-form fringe, lightly touched by the crazy gods—as many politicals are; Georgie Broadfoot was daft as a brush. In her case it might have been a mask, a brass front over inner hurt; she was in a dirty business, and no doubt her male colleagues, being proper little Christian crooks, would make it plain that they regarded her as no better than a whore—I did myself, but I wasn't fool enough to damp her amorous ardour by showing it. But no, 'twasn't a mask; as we talked, I recognised her as one of these fortunate critters who (like yours truly) are simply without shame, and wouldn't know Conscience if they tripped over it in broad day. She was fairly gloating at the prospect of wringing Shuvalov dry for the sheer fun of it—and the handsome fee Blowitz had promised her.

"A hundred golden pounds!" cries she gleefully. "You see, it is not a secret department matter, but personal to Stefan and his paper. And since he has friends in high places . . . behold, I am in Berlin!"

"And that's all that matters to me, my little *Punch*-fancier," says I, nuzzling her neck as we repaired to the couch. "As an Asian princess once said to me: 'Lick up the honey, stranger, and ask no questions.' "

"An Asian princess!" She clapped her hands. "Ah, but I must hear of this! Was she beautiful? Did you carry her off? Were you her slave?" and so on, so I told her all about Ko Dali's dreadful daughter, and how she'd rescued me from a Russian dungeon, and filled me with hasheesh unawares, and dam' near had me blown to bits, and was surpassingly beautiful (at which Caprice pouted "Pouf!") but bald as an egg (which sent her into peals of delight). Whether she believed me, God knows, but she demanded particulars of a most intimate nature, inviting comparison between the Silk One and herself, and that inevitably led to another glorious thrashing-match which restored her *amour-propre* and left me in what I once heard a French naval officer describe as a condition of swoon.

Only when I was taking my leave did we return to the subject of Shuvalov. His assignation with her was for eight the following evening, after the first day of the Congress, and she expected to have him off the premises by midnight, whereafter I would roll up to see that all was well, she would write her report, and we would enjoy a late supper and whatever else came to mind before I left with her despatch in my hat for transfer to Blowitz later in the day.

She hadn't counted on Shovel-off's appetite for jollity, though. The clocks were chiming twelve when I sauntered up the Jager Strasse in the warm dark of the next night, and turned into her court only to see that her curtain was still closed—the signal we'd agreed if the Russian buffoon was still infesting her quarters. I took a turn up and down, thankful that it wasn't winter; Berlin in June evidently went home with the milk, and there were open carriages carrying merry-makers up the Mauer Strasse to the Linden, sounds of gaiety and music came from the Prinz Carl Palace across the way, and beyond it I could see lights burning in the great ministries on the Wilhelmstrasse: understrappers of the Congress still hard at it while their betters waltzed and junketed—aye, and rogered away the diplomatic night, if Shuvalov was anything to go by. It was close on two, and I was in a fine fume, when a cloaked and tile-hatted figure emerged at last from Caprice's court, taking the width of the pavement, damn him, and a moment later I was being admitted to her apartment by a furious hareem houri clad only in a gold turban with a slave-fetter on one ankle, fairly spitting blood while she filled an antique bath-tub with hot water; the air was thick with steam and Gallic oaths which I hadn't heard outside a Legion barrack-room.

Count Shuvalov, she informed me, was a sacred perverted beast, a savage and a mackerel and a swine of tastes indescribable. He professed to have been so enraptured by her photograph that he had brought the turban and shackles for her to wear, describing himself as Haroun al-Raschid and demanding from her an Arabian Nights performance which I doubt even Dick Burton had ever heard of. He had also insisted that they smear each other all over with quince jam, to which he was partial, and while much of it had been removed in the ensuing frolic, I noticed that she still had a tendency to attract fluff and other light debris as she raged to and from the kitchen with hot kettles for her bath.

"And for a hundred pounds I endure this!" cries she, kicking her fettered foot and fetching herself a crack on the shin with the chain. "Ah, *merde*, it will not come off—and I shall never be clean again! Oh, but it is not only this disgusting *confiture*, this . . . this *ordure collant*, but his loathsome touch, his foul body and vile breath, his hideous tongue upon me . . . ugh! Muscovite ape! Oh, do not look at me—I cannot bear to be seen!" In fact she looked adorable, if you can imagine an Alma Tadema beauty striking passionate poses while picking feathers off her bottom.

I soothed her by undoing the ankle-chain, lifting her into the bath, and lovingly soaping her from head to foot while murmuring endearments. I'm a dab hand at this, having trained under Queen Ranavalona, so to speak, and after a while her plaintive cursing gave way to little sighs and whimpers, her eyes closed and her mouth trembled, and when I suggested I could do with a sluicing myself she responded with an enthusiasm that would have done credit to those poor little Kashmiri sluts who bathed me so devotedly at Lahore, the night the ceiling fell in.* Aye, I've wallowed in some odd spots in my time, but nowhere more happily than Berlin, with that delightful mermaid performing as though Shovel-off had never existed, and the floor ankle-deep in suds. Heaven knows what the charwoman had to say in the morning.

It cheered Caprice up no end, and by the time we'd dried off and drowsed a little and made an early breakfast of coffee and rolls, she was her vivacious self again, even making fun of Shovel-off's amorous peculiarities. Her first report for Blowitz was a brief one, the Galloping Cossack having been too intent on his muttons for much conversation, but having taken his measure she was sure she could make him sing in due course. "A shallow fool, *mais pompeux*, and his brain is in his —" was her charming verdict. "Also, he is jealous of his leader, the Prince Gorchakov." She lowered an eyelid. "Let me touch that key, and he will boast everything he knows!"

And I guess he did. Having sampled her myself, and marked her A1 at Flashy's, I'd still wondered if she could keep Shuvalov in thrall for the whole Congress—it lasted a month, you know— but damme if she didn't. Not that he saddled her up every night, you understand, but more often than not, and whether she was ringing the changes, Pride o' the Hareem one night, Gretchen the Governess the next, or was tempting him with different flavours

* See *Flashman and the Mountain of Light*

of jam, I didn't inquire. She kept him happy, I had my ration of her, and for the rest, Blowitz's arrangements went like clockwork: there he was every day, browsing at the Kaiserhof while I lunched at t'other side of the room, never a glance between us, and each picking up the other's tile when we left.

We had one scare, when an idiot diner by mistake went off with my hat containing Caprice's report. My first thought was, oh lor', we're rumbled, and I was ready to make for the long grass till I saw that Blowitz was on the q.v., but instead of leaping up with screams of "*Ah, voleur! Rende₂ le chapeau!*" as you'd expect from a Bohemian Frog, he quietly despatched a waiter in pursuit, the apologetic diner replaced my roof on its peg—and no attention had been drawn to Blowitz or to me. My opinion of little fat Stefan went up another rung; he was a cool hand—and even, it seemed to me, sometimes a reckless one.

It was about halfway through the Congress, when the other correspondents were all in a frenzy at the absolute lack of news from the secret sessions, that he broke cover with an item that was plainly from the horse's mouth. Gorchakov had made some speech *in camera,* and there was the gist of it in *The Times* two days later. Diplomatic Berlin was in uproar at once; who could have leaked the news? It was after this that Bismarck, who took the breach as a personal affront, looked under the table to see if Blowitz was roosting there. His fury was even greater soon after, when *The Times* had the news that Disraeli had threatened to leave Berlin over some wrangle that had arisen, and then decided to stay after all.

Of course the blabberer in both cases had been Shuvalov, as I learned from Caprice, who had passed the glad tidings on to Blowitz via my tile. I was fearful that Shovel-off might twig he was being milked, but she "Pouf!"-ed it away; he was too dull and besotted to know what he was saying after she'd put him over the jumps, and depend upon it, says she, Stefan knew what he was about.

She was right, too. The little fox had been angling, like every other scribbler, for an interview with Bismarck—and after the column about Dizzy appeared, hanged if he didn't get one! Otto, you see, was so piqued and mystified that his precious Congress was being blown upon, that he invited Blowitz to dinner, no doubt hoping to learn what his source had been. Fat chance. Blowitz came away with a five-hour interview, leaving the Iron Chancellor none the wiser and fit to be tied, *The Times* triumphed yet again, and the rest of the press gang could only gnash their teeth.

What between helping to spoil Bismarck's digestion and whiling away the golden afternoons with Caprice (for we'd abandoned our nocturnal meetings, and I was collecting her reports in the mornings) I was in pretty bobbish form, and took to promenading about the town in search of amusement. I didn't find it on one day at least, when chance took me down the Wilhelmstrasse past the Congress hall, and who should I meet face to face but dear Otto himself; he was with a group of his bag-carriers and other reptiles, coming down the steps to his carriage, and for one blood-freezing instant our eyes met—as they had not done since that day at Tarlenheim thirty years before when he'd launched me unsuspecting into his ghastly Strackenz murder plot. I'd never have recognised him if I hadn't seen his mug in the papers, for the nasty young Norse God had turned into a jowly sausage-faced old buffer whose head seemed to grow straight out of his collar without benefit of neck. Just for a second he stared, and I thought bigod he remembers me, but there ain't a thing he can do, so why don't I exclaim: "Well, Otto, old sport, there you are, then! Drowned any Danish princelings lately?" It's the kind of momentary madness that sometimes takes me, but thank God I tipped my tile instead, he did likewise, frowning, and a moment later he was clambering aboard and I was legging it in search of a gallon or two of brandy. Quite a turn he'd given me—but then, he always did. Bad medicine, Bismarck; bad man.

I kept clear of the official cantonment thereafter, and by the last week of the Congress was beginning to be infernally bored, even with Caprice; when I found myself knocking at her door in the expectation of having it opened by Elspeth, smiling blonde and beautiful, I realised it was time for the train home. Oddly enough, if I'd cut out then it wouldn't have mattered, for Blowitz no longer needed her reports, although he continued to change hats with me at the Kaiserhof.

The fact was his stock had risen so high with his three "scoops" that he was being fed information by the bushel, the embassy fawns being anxious to stand well with him; he even put it about, very confidential-like, that Bismarck had promised to give him the treaty before it was published, which wasn't true, but made them toad-eat him harder than ever. I knew nothing of this, of course, and on the penultimate day of the Congress, a Friday, as I was strolling home enjoying the morning after a strenuous late breakfast with Caprice, I was taken flat aback by Blowitz's moon face goggling at me from the window of a drosky drawn up near my hotel.

"In! In!" hisses he, whipping down the blind, so I climbed aboard, demanding what the devil was up, and before I was seated he was hammering on the roof and bawling to the coachee to make for the station with all speed.

"We leave on the 12:30 for Cologne!" cries he. "Fear not, your bill is paid and your baggage awaits at the train!"

"The dooce it does! But the Congress don't end till tomorrow—"

"Let it end when it will! It is imperative that I leave Berlin at once—that I am *seen* to leave, mortified and *en colère!*" He was red with excitement—and beaming. "*Regardez-moi*—do I look sufficiently enraged, then?"

"You sound sufficiently barmy. But what about the treaty—I thought t'wasn't to be finished until this evening?"

He pulled back the lapel of his coat, chuckling, whipped out a bulky document, waved it at me, and thrust it away again. "A treaty of sixty-four articles—approved, printed, *fini*! What d'you say to that, my boy? Nothing remains but the preamble and a few extra clauses to be adopted at today's session." He rubbed his hands, squirming with delight. "It is done, dear friend, it is done! Blowitz triumphs! He is exalted! Ah, and you, my brave one, my accomplice extraordinary, I could embrace you—"

"Keep your dam' distance! Look here, if you've got the thing, what are you in such an infernal hurry for?"

He smote his forehead. "Ah, forgive me—in my joy I go too fast. Let me explain." He was licking his lips at his own cleverness. "You remember I told you in Paris how I would persuade some diplomat of eminence to give me an advance copy of the treaty? *Eh bien*, this morning I received it. I rejoice, knowing that no other journalist will see the treaty until after the signing ceremony tomorrow. But in the meantime a crisis has raised itself. Since my interview with Prince Bismarck the German press has been in jealous agitation, and to pacify them he has let it be known that he will give them the treaty *this evening*! When I learn this, I am thunderstruck!" He assumed a look of horror. "Of what use to me to have the treaty in my pocket if it is to appear in the Berlin journals tomorrow? Where then is my exclusive account, my priority over my rivals?"

"Down the drain, I'd say. So why are you exalted?"

"Because I see at once how to frustrate them. I go to Prince Hohenlohe, the German Minister, and demand that as a reward for my services to the Congress—and because I am Blowitz—Prince Bismarck should give the treaty only to me, so that I may publish it in *The Times* tomorrow. Hohenlohe consults Bismarck, who refuses (as I knew he would). He says I must wait until it is signed. But," he raised a pudgy finger, "I know Bismarck. He is one for strict justice. Having said I must wait until tomorrow, he will now make the German papers wait also. So, in effect, I have gained a postponement . . . you see?"

I don't know if Macchiavelli was a fat little cove with long whiskers, but he should have been.

"When Prince Hohenlohe tells me my request is refused, I play my part. I am affronted. My disgust knows no bounds. I tell him I am leaving Berlin at once in protest. If Blowitz is to be treated with such contempt, they may keep their Congress and their treaty. Hohenlohe is dismayed, but I am adamant. I take my leave in what you call the dudgeon—and word flies from mouth to mouth that Blowitz is beaten, that he sulks like a spoiled child, my rivals rejoice at my failure—and breathe sighs of relief . . . and all the time the treaty is here—" he tapped his breast, chortling "—and tomorrow it will appear in *The Times* and in no other paper in the world!"

He paused to draw breath and gloat; you never saw smugness like it, so I pointed to the one fly I saw in his ointment.

"But you haven't got the preamble or the clauses they're adopting today."

He gave a lofty wave. "*Soit tranquil,* my 'Arree. From Hohenlohe I go *tout suite* to M. de St. Vallier, the French Ambassador—who I know has a copy of the preamble. In confidence I show him the treaty. He is staggered, he goes pale, but when I ask for the preamble and clauses, he throws up the hands, crying why not, since already I have so much? He cannot give me his copy of the preamble, but he reads it aloud, page upon page, and now it is here—" he tapped his brow "—and will be dictated to my secretary after we board the train."

I ain't given to expressions of admiration, as you know, but looking at that grinning cherub with his baby peepers and daft whiskers I confess I put a finger to my hat brim. "Though I still don't see why you're in such an almighty sweat to leave. Can't you telegraph your story to London?"

"From Berlin? Oh, my boy, you want to laugh! Where my every action is watched, my movements followed—why, let a telegraph clerk catch a glimpse of my message and I should be in a police cell!" He grew earnest. "But it is not the authorities I fear—it is envious rivals. My little charade of pique will deceive the many, but not all. Some, knowing Blowitz, will suspect me still. They may board the train. They would rob me if they could. That," says he, clapping a hand on my knee, "is why I bring you with me. I am small, you are large. Who knows what they may attempt between here and Paris? But what have I to fear," cries he, with a great idiot laugh, "when the bravest soldier of the British Army, the partner of my fate, is by my side?"

A great deal, I could have told him, if Bismarck's bullies were after him; he'd find himself relying on the communication cord. But no, that wasn't likely; even Otto wouldn't dare. Blowitz's brother journalists were another matter, as I saw when we reached the station, and they were on the platform to see him off with covert grins and ironic tile-doffing; I hadn't realised what respect and jealousy my stout friend attracted. He bustled down the train looking like an angry frog in his great fur coat and felt hat, ignoring their greetings, and I played up by taking his arm and wearing my most threatening scowl.

The secretary and Blowitz's colleague, Wallace, were already aboard, and when we pulled out punctually on 12:30, Blowitz told the secretary to get out his book, folded his hands across his paunch, closed his eyes, and recited steadily for half an hour. It was fearful stuff, all in German, with an occasional phrase in French or English by way of explanation, and he didn't even pause; once, when the train clanked to an unexpected halt and we were almost jolted from our seats, he forged right ahead with his dictation, and when it was done he sat drooping like a limp doll, and then went straight off to sleep. For concentration and power of mind, I don't recall his equal.

Sure enough, there were fellows from the other papers on the train. Wallace spotted two Germans and an Italian in the next carriage, but once one of 'em had tried to look in on us, and I'd sent him about his business, they let us alone. They followed us when we alighted for refreshment at Cologne, but we baffled 'em by each taking a different way back to the train, so that they had to separate, one dogging Blowitz, another behind me, the third after the secretary—and no one at all to watch Wallace, who was lurking in the W.C. with treaty, preamble and all inside his shirt, until the time came for him to board another train to Brussels, where he would telegraph the whole thing to London. Wallace had wondered if the Belgians would accept such an important document; Blowitz told him that if there was any difficulty he was to send for the superintendent, tell him *The Times* was thinking of setting up (and paying handsomely for) a daily line to London, and that this despatch was by way of a test. Of course, if Brussels didn't want the business . . .'nuff said.

So next morning, Saturday, July 13, 1878, before the leading statesmen of Europe had even penned their signatures on the treaty, Otto Bismarck was goggling apoplectically at a telegram from London informing him that the whole sixty-four articles, preamble, etc., were in that day's *Times*—with an English translation. Talk about a "scoop"! Blowitz was drunk with glory, conceit, and gratitude when I managed to tear myself from his blubbering embrace in Paris, and I wasn't displeased myself. T'isn't every day you play a part in one of the great journalistic coups, and whenever I see some curmudgeon at the club cursing at the labour of cutting open his *Times* and then complaining that there's no news in the dam' thing, I think, aye, you should see what goes to the making of those paragraphs that you take for granted, my boy. My one regret as I tooled back to London was that I hadn't been able to bid a riotous farewell to Caprice; she'd been worth the trip, ne'er mind spoking Otto's wheel, and I found myself smiling fondly as I thought of *Punch* and the gauzy lace clinging to that houri shape in the sunlight . . . Ah well, there would doubtless be more where that came from.

In case you don't know, the great Berlin Treaty panned out to general satisfaction—for the time being anyway. "Big Bulgaria" was cut in two; Roumania, you'll be charmed to learn, became independent; Austria won the right to occupy Bosnia and Herzegovina (which only an idiot would want to do, in my opinion, but then I ain't the Emperor Franz-Josef); Russia got Bessarabia, wherever that may be; the Turks remained a power in the Balkans, more or less, and by some strange sleight of hand we managed to collar Cyprus (no fool, D'Israeli, for all he dressed like a Pearly King). There had been a move at one stage (this is gospel, though you mayn't credit it) to invite my old comrade William Tecumseh Sherman, the Yankee general, to become Prince of Bulgaria, but nothing came of it. Pity; he was the kind of savage who'd have suited the Bulgars like nuts in May.

At all events, what they call "a balance" was achieved, and everyone agreed that Bismarck had played a captain's innings, hoch! hoch! und he's ein jolly good fellow. So he ought to have been content—but I can tell you something that wasn't suspected at the time, and has been known to only a handful since: the Congress left darling Otto an obsessed man. It's God's truth: the brute was bedevilled by the galling fact that little Blowitz had stolen a march on him, *and he could not figure out how it had been done*. Astonishing, eh? Here was the greatest statesman of the age, who'd just settled the peace of Europe for a generation and more, and still that trifle haunted him over the years. Perhaps 'twas the affront to his dignity, or his passion for detail, but he couldn't rest until he knew how Blowitz had got hold of that treaty. How do *I* know, you may ask? Well, I'm about to tell you—and I'm not sure that Bismarck's mania (for that's what it amounted to) wasn't the strangest part of the adventure that befell me five years later, and which had its origins in my meetings with Grant and Macmahon, Caprice's picture, and the Congress of Berlin.[8]

Chapter 2

The trouble with a reputation like mine is that you're bound to live up to it. It's damnably unfair. Take General Binks or Colonel Snooks, true-blue military muttonheads, brave as bedamned, athirst for glory, doing their dutiful asinine bit in half a dozen campaigns, but never truly catching the public eye, and at last selling out and retiring from obscurity to Cheltenham with a couple of wounds and barely enough to pay the club subscription, foot the memsahib's whist bill, send Adolphus to a crammer 'cos the Wellington fees are beyond them, and afford a drunken loafer to neglect the garden of Ramilles or Quatre Bras or whatever they choose to call their infernal villas. That's Snooks and Binks; profitable labour to the grave, and no one notices.

And then take Flashy, born poltroon and wastrel, pitchforked against his will into the self-same expeditions and battles, scared out of his wits but surviving by shirking, turning tail, pretence, betrayal, and hiding behind better men—and emerging at the end o' the day, by blind luck and astonishing footwork, with a V.C., knighthood, a string of foreign decorations as long as Riley's crime sheet, a bloody fortune in the bank, and a name and fame for derring-do that's the talk of the Empire. Well now, Flash old son, says you, that's compensation surely, for all the horrors *un*manfully endured—and don't forget that along the road you've had enough assorted trollop to fill Chelsea Barracks, with an annexe at Aldershot. And Elspeth, the most undeserved benefit of all.

Furthermore, you've walked with the great ones of the earth, enjoy the admiring acquaintance of your gracious Queen and half a dozen other royalties and presidents, to say nothing of ministers and other prominent rabble, and are blessed (this is the best of it) with grandlings and great-grandlings too numerous to count . . . so what the devil have you to complain of? Heavens, man, Binks and Snooks would give their right arms (supposing they haven't already left 'em in the Punjab or Zululand or China, from which *you* escaped with a pretty whole skin) for one-fiftieth of your glory and loot. And you've never been found out . . . a few leery looks here and there, but no lasting blemishes, much. So *chubbarao*,* Flashy, and count yourself lucky.

Well, I do; damned lucky. But there's been a price to pay, and I don't mean in terror and agony and suffering. Not at all. My cavil is that having bought it cruel hard, I wasn't left to enjoy it in peace, like Binks and Snooks. They could run up to Town to get their hair cut and drop in at the club at a moment of national crisis, and no one paid them any heed, much less expected 'em to race round to Horse Guards applying to be let loose against the Ashantis or the Dervishes or whatever other blood-drinking heathen were cayoodling round the imperial outposts. Retired, gone to grass, out of reckoning absolutely, that was Colonel Snooks and General Binks.

Ah, but Flashy was a different bag of biltong altogether. Let some daft fakir start a rising in a godforsaken corner you never heard of, or the British lion's tail be tweaked anywhere between Shanghai and Sudan, and some journalistic busybody would be sure to recall that 'twas in that very neck of the woods that the gallant Flashy, Hector of Afghanistan, defender of Piper's Fort, leader of the Light Brigade, won his spurs or saved the day or

* Be quiet! (Hind.)

committed some equally spectacular folly (with his guts dissolving and praying for the chance to flee or surrender, if only they knew it). "The hour demands the man, and who better to uphold Britannia's honour in her present need than the valiant veteran of Lucknow and Balaclava . . ." and so forth. They were never rash enough to suggest I should have command, but seemed to have in mind some auxiliary post of Slaughterer-General, as befitting my desperate reputation.

Not that the ha'penny press matters—but the United Service and Pall Mall *do*, with their raised eyebrows and faintly critical astonishment. "Ah, Flashman, lamentable business in Egypt, what? Goin' with Wolseley, I dare say . . . No? You surprise me." Dash it, you can see them thinking, man of his reputation, prime of life, don't he know his duty, good God? If I'd had the belly of Binks or Snooks's gout (both of 'em younger than I) I'd not be thought of, but when you've a lancer figure and barely a touch of grey in your whiskers and the renown of Bayard, you're expected to be clamouring for service. And when your sovereign lady regards you pop-eyed over the tea-cups with a bland "I expect, dear Sir Harry, that you will be accompanying Sir Garnet to Egypt," you can hardly remind her that you're past sixty and disinclined, especially when the idiot you married in an evil hour is assuring Her Majesty that you're champing at the bit. (Wanted me away, I suspect, so that she could cuckold me in comfort.) All round it's a case of "No show without Flashy," and before you can say God-help-us you're in the desert listening to "Cock o' the North" and trying to look as though you're itching to come to grips with twice your weight in angry niggers.

It is, I repeat, damnably unfair, and by the autumn of '83 I'd had enough of it. In the five years since Otto's Congress I'd been well in the public eye, chiefly because of my supposed heroics in South Africa in '79—a place I'd have shunned like the plague but for Elspeth's insatiable fondness for money, as if old Morrison's million wasn't enough without bothering her empty head over her cousin's supposed mine (but I'll record that disgusting episode another day). Then in '82 there had been the Egyptian garboil I mentioned a moment ago; Joe Wolseley had asked for me point-blank, and with the press applauding and the Queen approving and Elspeth bursting into tears as I rogered her farewell, what the blazes could I do but fall in?

In the event it wasn't the worst campaign I've seen, not by a mile; at least it was short. We only went in with great reluctance (when did Gladstone ever show anything else?) to help the Khedive quell his rebellious army, who were slaughtering Christians and vowing to drive all foreigners from the country—bad news for our Suez Canal investors (44 per cent, what?) and our lifeline to India. Joe brought 'em to heel smartly enough at Tel-el-Kebir, where the kilties massacred everything in sight, and my only bad scare was when I found myself perforce charging with the Tin Bellies at Kassassin, but by gallantly turning aside to help Baker Russell when his horse was shot, and so arriving when the golliwog infantry were already taking to their heels, I missed the worst of it, cursing my bad luck and Baker for holding me up. A good glare and loud roar, sabre in hand, work wonders; Joe said I'd been an inspiration to the Household riders, and wanted me to stay on at Cairo, but I muttered that he didn't need me now that peace was breaking out, and his staff wallopers grinned at each other and said wasn't that old Flashy, just?[9]

I was mighty glad to be home by Christmas of '82, I can tell you, for while Egypt was quiet enough by then, I could guess it was liable to be hot enough presently, and not just with the sun. After we'd brought the Khedive's troops back to their allegiance, the idea was that we'd withdraw, but that was all my eye (we're there yet, have you noticed?), for down south, in the Sudan, the war drums were already beating, with the maniac Mahdi stirring up the Fuzzy-Wuzzies in a great *jihad* to conquer the world, with Egypt first on the list. Hell of a place the Sudan, all rock and sand and thorn and the most monstrous savages in creation; Charley

Gordon, my China acquaintance, had governed it in the '70s, and spent most of his time poring over the Scriptures and chasing slavers before retiring to Palestine to watch rocks and contemplate the Infinite. Mad as a cut snake, he was, but the Sudan had gone to pot entirely after he left, and was now going to need attention—from guess who? From the Khedive's army, led by soldiers of the Queen, that was who, whether Gladstone liked it or not, and I was shot if I was going to be one of 'em.

So I came home, along of Joe and Bimbashi Stewart and others, having served my turn—but would you believe it, in '83 when that immortal ass Hicks was given command of the Khedive's army, half of whom had been our enemies a few months earlier, and told to deal with the Sudan, there were those at Horse Guards with the brazen cheek to suggest that I should go out *again,* to serve on his staff? Since he was my junior, I was able to scotch that flat, but when word came in September that he'd gone off Mahdi-hunting at last, blowed if one of the gutter rags didn't come out with a leaderette regretting "that the task has fallen to an officer of comparative inexperience, while such distinguished soldiers as Lord Wolseley, Major-General Gordon, and Sir Harry Flashman, men thoroughly familiar with the country and the enemy, remain at home or unemployed."

It was the mention of Gordon's name, more than my own, that brought the sweat out on my brow, for while no one in his senses would suggest that *I* should replace Hicks, there was a strong shave in the clubs that Cracked Charley would be recalled and given the job, and I knew that if he was, Flashy would be the first he'd want to enlist.[10] China had given him the misguided notion that I was the devil's own fire-eater, and just the chap to have on hand when Fuzzy charged the square. Well, soldiering under Joe Wolseley had been bad enough, but at least he was sane. Gordon? I'd as soon go to war with the town drunk. The man wasn't safe—sticking forks in people and scattering tracts from railway carriages and accosting perfect strangers to see if they'd met Jesus lately, I ask you! No, a holiday abroad was indicated, before the Mad Sapper came recruiting.

And I'd just reached that conclusion when Blowitz's letter, bearing that fateful second photograph, landed on the breakfast table. It couldn't have come more pat. This is what he wrote, with more underlinings and points of admiration than Elspeth at her worst—not *Times* style at all:

> Dearest Friend!
>
> I write to you <u>by Royal Command</u>—what do you think of that!! It is true—a PRINCESS, no less! And such a Princess, *plus belle et elegant,* whose most Ardent Desire is <u>to meet the gallant and renowned</u> Sir H.F.—for reasons which I shall explain when we meet.
>
> Come to Paris no later than October the fourth, my dear Harry. I promise you will be enchanted and oblige your best of friends and loyal comrade in destiny
>
> Stefan O-B.
>
> P.S. Recalling your <u>interest in photography</u>! I enclose a portrait of Her Royal Highness. *A bientôt!*

Well, wasn't this the ticket? Elspeth was in Scotland enduring her sisters, and here was the ideal billet where I could lurk incog. while Gordon beat the bushes—and enjoy some good carnal amusement, to judge from the photograph. Not that Her Highness was an outstanding beauty, but her picture grew on me as I studied it. It showed a tall, imposing female standing proud in a splendid gown of state, a coronet on her piled blond hair, one gloved hand resting on the arm of a throne, the other holding a plumed fan, the sash of a jewelled order over her bare shoulders, and enough *bijouterie* disposed about her stately person to start a bazaar. She was in profile, surveying the distance with a chilling contempt which sat perfectly on a rather horsy face with a curved high-bridged nose. Minor Mittel European royalty to the life, with the same stench-in-the-nostrils look as my darling little Irma of Strackenz, but nowhere near as pretty. Striking, though, and there were promising signs: she'd be about forty and properly saddle-broken, with the full mouth and drooping lower lip which betoken a hearty appetite, and a remarkable wasp waist between a fine full rump and upper works which would have made Miss Marie Lloyd look positively elfin. I could imagine stripping her down and watching her arrogance diminish with each departing garment. And she had an Ardent Desire to meet the gallant Sir H.F. I reached for Bradshaw.

Reading the letter again later, it struck me that there was something familiar about it; an echo of the past which I couldn't place—until a couple of days later, the afternoon of October the third to be precise, when I was ensconced in my smoker on the Continental Mail Express, and suddenly I knew what I'd been reminded of: that doom-laden summons that had taken me to Lola Montez in Munich, oh, so long ago. There was the same slightly eccentric wording (though Blowitz's English was a cut above that of Lola's Chancellor—what had his name been? Aye, Lauengram) and the purport was uncannily similar: an invitation from an exotic titled woman of mystery, for reasons unstated, with a strong hint of fleshly pleasures in prospect . . . and what besides? In Lola's case there had been a nightmare of terror, intrigue, imposture, and deadly danger from which I'd barely escaped with my life—oh, but that had been a Bismarck plot in the bad old days; this was jolly little Blowitz, and a doubtless spoiled and jaded piece of aristocracy in search of novelty and excitement . . . but how had she heard of me (Blowitz cracking me up, to be sure) and why was I worth fetching across the Channel? Odd, that—and for no reason I remembered Rudi Starnberg's voice across the years: "She brought *me* all the way from Hungary," and found myself shivering. And why no later than October the fourth?

Aye, odd . . . but not fishy, surely? It's the curse of a white liver that it has you starting at shadows, imagining perils where none exist. On t'other hand, it's been a useful storm signal over the years, and it was still at work ever so little when we pulled into the Gare du Nord.

At the sight of Blowitz on the platform, my cares dissolved. He was a trifle plumper in the cheek, a shade greyer in the whisker, but still the same joyful little bonhomme, rolling forward waving his cane with glad cries, fairly leaping up to embrace me and dam' near butting me under the chin, chattering nineteen to the dozen as he led me out to a fiacre, and not letting me get a word in until we were seated at the self-same table in Voisin's, when he had to leave off to attend to the *maître*. I couldn't help grinning at him across the table, he looked so confounded cheery.

"Well, it's famous to see you again, old Blow," says I, when he'd ordered and filled our glasses. "Here's to you, and to this mysterious lady. Now—who is she . . . and what does she want?"

He drank and wiped his whiskers, business-like. "The Princess Kralta. But of blood the most ancient in Europe, descended from Stefan Bathory, Arnulf of Carinthia, Barbarossa . . . name whom you will, she is *de la royauté la plus royale*—and landless, as the best monarchs are. But rich, to judge from the state she keeps—oh, and received everywhere, on terms with the highest. She is befriended of the German Emperor, for example, and—" he shot me a quizzy look "—of our old acquaintance Prince Bismarck. No-no-no," he added hastily, "her intimacy with him is of a . . . how shall I say? . . . of an unconventional kind."

"I've met some of his unconventional intimates, and I didn't take to 'em a bit. If she's one of his—"

"She is not one of anyone's! I mention Bismarck only because when I first met the Princess she brought me a friendly message from him. *C'est vrai, absolument!* Can you guess what it was? That he bears me no ill will for my activities at the Congress of Berlin!" He shook his head, chuckling. "Can you believe it, eh?"

"No—and neither will you if you've any sense. That bastard never forgave or forgot in his life. Very well, ne'er mind him— what more about this Princess? Is she married?" It's always best to know beforehand.

"There is a husband." He shrugged. "But he does not figure."

"Uh-huh . . . so, what does she want with me?"

He gave a little snort of laughter. "What do women ever want with you? Ah, but there is something else also." He leaned forward to whisper, looking droll. "She wishes to know a secret . . . a secret that she believes only you can tell her."

He sat back as the food arrived, with a cautioning gesture in case I made some indiscreet outcry, I suppose. Since I knew the little blighter's delight in mysterious hints I just waded into the grub.

"You do not ask what it is?" he grumbled. "Ah, but of course—*le flegme Britannique*! Never mind, you will raise a brow when you hear, I promise!"

And I did, for I never heard an unlikelier tale in my life—all of it true, for I saw it confirmed in the little blighter's memoirs a few years ago, and why should he lie to posterity? But even at the time I believed it because, being a crook myself, I can spot a straight tongue, and Blowitz had one.

He'd met the Princess Kralta at a diplomatic dinner, and plainly fallen head over heels—as he often did, in his harmless romantic way—and she had equally plainly given him every encouragement. "You have seen her likeness, but believe me, it tells you nothing! How to describe her . . . her *magnétisme*, the light of charm in those great blue eyes, the little toss of her silky blonde hair as she smiles, revealing the brilliancy of her small teeth—you found her portrait forbidding, *non?* My friend, when you see those queenly features melt into the tenderest of expressions, the animation of her darting glances, the melodious quality of her voice . . . ah, *mais ravissante*—"

"Whoa, steady lad, mind the cutlery. Liked her, did you?"

"My friend, I was enchanted!" He sighed like a ruptured poodle. "I confess it, I who have encountered the charms of the loveliest women in Europe, that the Princess Kralta wove a spell about me. And it is not only her person that allures, her exquisite elegance, her divinity of shape and movement—"

"Aye, she's well titted out, I noticed."

"—but the beauty of her nature, her frank friendliness and ease of deportment, the candour of her confidences . . ."

He babbled through the next two courses, but don't suppose that I despised his raptures—there are women like that, and as often as not they're not the ones of perfect feature. Angie Burdett-Coutts was no radiant looker, but she'd have caused a riot in the College of Cardinals simply by walking by, whereas the Empress of Austria, of whom more presently, was perfection of face and figure and quite as exciting as a plate of mashed turnip. I'd seen enough of la Kralta in her picture to believe that she might well have the magic, February face or no.

She'd gone out of her way to captivate Blowitz over a period of months, doing him little kindnesses, making friends with his wife, and trusting him with her most intimate confidences— which is the surest way a woman has of getting a man under her dainty thumb. Once or twice she spoke of the Berlin Congress, and Bismarck's curiosity as to how Blowitz had got his "scoop"— it had irritated Otto that he couldn't fathom that, and he'd told her he was determined to find out some day.

"Indeed, my friend," says Blowitz to me as he plunged into his dessert, "she confessed to me that she had promised the Prince she would use all her womanly wiles to wring the secret from me. I admired her honesty in admitting as much, but assured her that

I never, under any persuasion, betray my sources. She laughed, and told me playfully that she would continue to try to beguile the truth from me."

"And did she succeed?"

"No—but I was content that she should try. One does nothing to discourage the attention of a lady of such fascination. I am not vain of my attractions," sighs he, glancing ruefully at the balding little tub with ghastly whiskers reflected in the long glass on Voisin's wall, "and I know when I am being . . . how would you say? . . . worked upon. I enjoy it, and my affection and regard for the lady are not diminished. Rather they increase as she continues to confide in me with a candour which suggests that her friendship and interest in me are true, and not merely assumed. Listen, and judge for yourself."

And he launched into a piece of scandal which I'd have said no woman in her right mind would have confided to a journalist— not if she valued her reputation, as presumably this Kralta female did. Yet she'd confessed it, says Blowitz, to convince him how deeply she trusted him.

This was her story: she'd been staying at some fashionable spa where the German Emperor, an amiable dotard with whom, as Blowitz had said, she was on friendly terms, had sent for her in great agitation. Would she do him a favour—a service to the state and to the peace of the world? At your service, Majesty, says loyal Kralta. The Emperor had then confessed that he was damnably worried about Bismarck: the Chancellor was in a distracted state, nervous, irritable, complaining about everyone, suspicious that the Great Powers were plotting mischief against Germany, moody, obstinate, and off his oats entirely. Even now he was alone on his estate, sunk in the brooding dumps, and unless something was done he'd go to pieces altogether; international complications, possibly even war, would follow.

What Otto needed to set him to rights, said the Emperor, was an amusement, something to divert him from vexatious affairs of state—and Princess Kralta was just the girl to provide it. She must visit Bismarck's estate in perfect secrecy, taking only her maid and enough clothing for a week's stay; anonymous agents would drive her to the station, put her in a reserved compartment, meet her, arrange delivery of her luggage, and take care of all expenses. Her husband would have been got out of the way before her departure: the Emperor would send him to Berlin on a mission which would keep him there until after Kralta had returned to the spa. No word of her visit must be spoken; the Emperor's part must never be mentioned.

Blowitz paused. "She agreed, without hesitation."

"Hold on there!" says I. "Are you telling me that the German Emperor, the All-Highest Kaiser of the Fatherland, pimped for Otto Bismarck? Get away with you!"

"I am telling you," says Blowitz primly, "precisely what the Princess told me. No more, no less, *c'est tout*."

"Well, dammit, what she's saying is that she was sent— where, Schonhausen?—to grind Otto into a good humour!"

"I do not know 'grind.' And she did not mention Schonhausen. May I continue?"

"Oh, pray do! I'm all attention!"

"She goes to Bismarck. He asks, 'Did the Emperor send you?' She says he did not, and that she has come to see how such a great man will receive 'a giddy little person who ventures into the lion's solitude'—those were her very words to me. The Chancellor laughs, hopes it will not be a short visit, and then," says Blowitz, poker-faced, "assists her to unpack her 'frills and furbelows'— her own words again—expressing gay amusement as he does so." He shrugged and sat back, helping himself to brandy.

"Well, come on, man! What else did she tell you?"

"Only that at the end of her visit the Chancellor saw her to her landau saying: 'I have been delighted to forget the affairs of the world for a time.' The Princess returns to her watering-place, her husband is summoned back from Berlin, and the Emperor thanks her joyfully for saving the peace of Europe." Blowitz swilled and sniffed his brandy. "And that, my boy, is all the lady's tale."

"Well, I'll be damned! That's one you wouldn't send to *The Times*! D'you believe her?"

"Without doubt. What woman would invent such a story? Also, I know when I am being deceived."

I didn't disbelieve it myself—although the Emperor's part took a little swallowing. And yet . . . if he truly believed that a week's rogering with a royal flashtail would put Otto in trim and keep the ship of state on a smooth course, why not? Bismarck would be all for it—he'd been the town bull around Schonhausen in his young days, and would be just as randy in his sixties. Well, it was an interesting piece of gossip, and confirmed that the haughty Princess Kralta was partial to mutton—come to think of it, Blowitz had a gift for encountering females who were patriotic riders, hadn't he just? And of introducing 'em to me, bless him. Well, well. I returned to the point—which had suddenly become clear to me.

"Well, Blow, I'm grateful to you for rehearsing the lady's character for me," says I. "Very instructive, possibly useful. Of course," I went on carelessly, "the secret which she believes she can learn only from me is the one that Bismarck's dying to know—how you got the Berlin Treaty in advance. That's it, ain't it?"

For once he was taken flat aback. His blue eyes popped, his jaw dropped, and then he burst out laughing.

"Oh, but you should have been a journalist!" cries he. "And I hoped to amaze you with my *dénouement*! How did you guess?"

"Come, now, what other secret do I have that she could want to know? But if you're willing to let her have it, why not tell her yourself?" I nearly added that he could have charged her a delightful price for it (as I fully intended to, given the chance), but I knew that wasn't his style. Odd fish, Blowitz; ready and willing to put me in the way of fleshly delights, as he'd shown in the past, but strict Chapel himself. He regarded me seriously.

"I shall tell you," says he slowly. "The Princess's confession to me of her visit to Prince Bismarck moved me deeply. *En fait*, she was saying to me: 'Here is my trust, *ma confiance*, my honour as a woman; I place it in your hands, Blowitz.' Oh, my dear 'Arree, *quel geste*! What trust, what proof of devoted affection!" So help me, he was starting to pipe his eye. "From such a woman, so worldly, so intelligent, so *sensible*, it could not fail to awaken in me emotions of gratitude and obligation. It gave her the right to demand from me an equal proof of my friendship, my trust in her. You, my friend, will see that, I know."

Well, I didn't, in fact, but I ain't a besotted Bohemian. He sighed, long and solemn, like an old horse farting.

"When she renews her request that I divulge my secret, I feel I can no longer refuse. It means much to her, since it will enable her to gratify Prince Bismarck, and it can bring no harm to me. I resolve, then, to tell her."

He took another gulp of brandy, leaned towards me, and became dramatic, as though he were telling a ghost story in whispers.

"We are in her salon, seated upon a sofa that stands against a great mirror covering the wall behind us. The salon is dim, the curtains drawn, the only light comes from a candelabrum on the table before us. As I prepare to speak, I see one of the candles flicker. I am astonished. All doors and windows are closed, so whence comes this draught? I move myself on the sofa—and a zephyr from the direction of the mirror fans my cheek. What can it mean, I ask myself. And then—I know!"

You never saw such desperate bad acting—hands raised, eyes and mouth agog, worse than Irving hearing the bells. Then he glared like a mad marmoset, one finger outthrust.

"I realise I am the victim of treachery, which I hate above all else in the world! I closely scrutinise the mirror! What do I see but that a gap has opened in the glass! So! One stands behind the mirror, a witness to take down what I say! I rise, pointing to the flickering flame, then to the cloven mirror, just as the Princess puts out a hand to remove the candlestick. I address her in a voice which I vainly strive to render calm. 'Too late, madame!' I cry. 'I have understood!' She touches an electric button, a door opens, a butler enters, and without a word the Princess indicates to me the way to the door. I bow. I withdraw. I leave the house."

He dried up there abruptly, looking expectant, so I said that after such a thrilling tale I was surprised that five masked chaps with stilettoes hadn't leaped on him in the hall. He said stiffly that they hadn't, and the mortification he felt at her duplicity had been keener than any stab wounds. I said that I gathered he was still on terms with the lady, though, and he blew out his cheeks in resignation.

"*Que voulez-vous?* Am I one to bear a grudge against a beautiful woman? True, our relationship cooled for a time—until a few weeks ago, in effect, when she begged me to visit her, and pleaded that the importance she had attached to learning my secret had made it imperative that she have a witness. Her contrition was expressed with such charm and sincerity that I forgave her at once, and she then confessed that she had a favour to ask of me. I had once told her, had I not, that among my friends I numbered the celebrated Sir Harry Flashman? I replied that you were my best of friends, and she sighed—oh, such a sigh!—and cried out, 'Ah, that hero! What I would give to meet him!' I assured her that it could be arranged—and then," he twinkled mischievously, "it occurred to me that here was an opportunity to repay you, *cher* 'Arree, for your great service to me in Berlin. 'It happens,' I told her, 'that Sir Harry also possesses the secret of the Congress treaty. No doubt he could be persuaded to divulge it to one so charming as yourself.' My friend, she was overjoyed, and urged me to effect an introduction without delay." He beamed at me, stroking his whiskers. "You see my thought—while I do not doubt your ability to captivate a lady who already holds you in the warmest regard, it will do no harm if you are also in a position to answer a question to which she attaches such importance. It will amuse you to be . . . persuaded, *non*?"

I studied the innocent-cunning face, wondering. "Subtle little devil, ain't you, Blow? Why are you so obliging? You know how I'll make her pay for the secret—are you using me as a penance for her sins, by any chance?"

"My dear friend! Ah, but that is unkind! When I have no thought but to amuse you! Oh, perhaps I am also taking my little revenge on *la Grande Princesse* by making her a suppliant to one less foolishly sympathetic than Blowitz. But who knows," he tittered, "it may end by amusing her also!"

"If you mean that she'll find me a welcome change from Otto Bismarck, I'm flattered," says I, and asked when I'd meet the lady. He became mysterious again, saying it would be for tomorrow night, but wouldn't tell me where. "Be patient, my friend. I wish your rendezvous to be a surprise, what you call a treat—my *petit cadeau* to you. Believe me, it will be a most novel meeting-place—oh, but romantic! You will be delighted, I promise, and I will have made you a trifling repayment towards the debt I owe you for Berlin."

So I humoured him, and agreed to be at my hotel, the Chatham, the following evening, with my valise all packed. His mention of Berlin had reminded me of Caprice, but he had not seen her in two years. "After the Congress I heard of her in Rome and Vienna, but nothing since, and I do not inquire, since I suppose her work is of a secret nature still. Ah, but she had the true gift of intrigue, *la petite Caprice*! Decidedly she must marry an ambassador of promise; then her talents will have full play, eh?"

Chapter 3

Looking back, I guess Blowitz's "treat" was a sight to see. The first of anything usually is, and the inauguration which took place in Paris that Sunday night was historic, in a Froggy sort of way. If I wasn't unduly impressed, Blowitz himself was partly to blame; one evening of his company was always about my limit, and his enthusiasm for his *"petit cadeau"* was such that I was quite put off beforehand, and a day spent loafing in the hotel hadn't raised my spirits. The small unease that had been in my mind on the Channel crossing had returned, as it always does when I ain't quite sure what I'm being pushed into, or why, and when Blowitz collected me from the Chatham as dusk was falling, I was carrying a decided hump—all the greater 'cos common sense told me I'd no reason for it.

Blowitz was in a fine excitement, greeting me exuberantly, telling the cabby to make all haste to the Place de Strasbourg, and parrying my inquiries with a waggishness which set my teeth on edge: all would be revealed presently; yes, we had a small journey to our rendezvous with Princess Kralta, but everything was arranged, and I would be transported in more ways than one—this with a hysterical giggle as he bounced up and down on his seat, urging the driver to hurry. I fought down an urge to kick the little chatterbox out of the cab, and consoled myself with the thought that presently I'd be having my wicked way with that fine piece of blue-blooded batter; the vision of her imperious figure-head and strapping form had been in my mind all day, competing with my vague unease, and now that the reality was in prospect, I was becoming a mite impatient.

Shortly before seven we pulled up at the canopied entrance of the Gare de l'Est, Blowitz clamouring for porters and hurrying me into the concourse—so our "small journey" was to be by rail, which meant, I supposed, that Madame's mansion lay in one of the fashionable districts outside the city.

The station seemed uncommon busy for a Sunday night. There was a great crowd milling under the electric lamps, but Blowitz bustled through like a tug before a liner, flourishing a token and announcing himself with his usual pomposity to a blue-coated minion who conducted us through a barrier to a less-crowded platform where knots of passengers and uniformed railway officials were waiting beside a train. All eyes were turned to it, and I have to say it looked uncommon smart and polished, gleaming blue and gold under the lights, but otherwise ordinary enough, the steam hissing up from beneath the engine with that pungent railway smell, the porters busy at the five long coaches, on one of which the curtains were drawn back to reveal the glowing pink interior of a dining salon—and yet there was an unwonted hush about the working porters, an excitement among the throng watching from the barrier, and an air of expectancy in the little groups on the platform. Blowitz stopped, clutching at my arm and staring at the train like a child in a toy shop.

"Ah, gaze upon it!" cries he. "Is it not the train of trains—the ultimate, *l'apogée, le dernier cri* of travel! Oh, my boy, who was the genius who said, 'Let the country build the railway, and the railway will build the country'? And not only a country—now a continent, a world!" He flourished a hand. "Behold that which will be called the monarch of the rails, as it prepares for its first journey!" He turned to beam up at me, his eyes glistening moistly. "Yes, this is my surprise, my treat, my *petit cadeau* to you, dearest of friends—to be one of the select band who will be the pioneers on this historic voyage! You and I, 'Arree, and a mere handful of others—we alone will share this experience, the envy of generations of travellers yet to come, the first to ride upon the magic carpet of the steel highway—*l'Express Orient!*"

The name meant nothing then, since this was only the inception of what I suppose is now the most famous train on earth— and to be honest, it still don't mean that much. I'm a steamship man, myself; they don't rattle or jolt, I don't mind the occasional heave, and the feeling of being snug and safe appeals to my poltroon nature—once aboard, the world can't get at you, and if danger threatens you can usually take to the boats or swim for it. Trains I regard as a necessary nuisance, but with Blowitz bouncing and pawing my sleeve I was bound to be civil.

"Well, much obliged, Blow," says I. "Handsome of you. It looks a capital train, as trains go—but how far *is* it going, eh?" It didn't look district line, exactly, but my question was ignored.

"Capital! As trains go!" squawks he, flinging up his hands. "*Milles tornades!* This you say of the supreme *train de luxe!* A veritable palace upon wheels, the reassertion of privilege in travel! Why, thanks to my good friend Nagelmacker, *le haute monde* may be carried to the ends of the continent in the luxury of the finest hotel, sleeping and waking in apartments of elegance and comfort, dining on the superb cuisine of a Burgundian chef, enjoying perfect service, splendid wines, everything of the best! And all this," he concluded triumphantly, "for two thousand miles, from Paris to Constantinople, in a mere ninety hours, less than—"

"What's that? You ain't getting me to Constantinople!"

He crowed with laughter, taking my arm to urge me forward. "No, no, that is for me, not for you, *cher* 'Arree! I travel on, about my business, which will be to seek interviews with ministers and crowned heads *en route*, with a grand finale in Constantinople, where I hope to obtain audience of the Sultan himself. Oh, yes, Blowitz works, while you—" he glanced roguishly from me to the train "—journey only as far as Vienna, in the company of royalty more agreeable by far. Aha, that marches, eh? A day and a night in her charming company, and then—the city of the waltz, the Tokay, of music and romance, where you may dally together by the banks of the enchanted Danube—"

I managed to stem his Cook's advertising at last. "You mean she's on the train?"

He raised a finger, glancing round and dropping his voice. "Officially, no—the sleeping coach reserved for ladies will be unoccupied until Vienna. However," he nodded towards one of the darkened coaches, "for such a distinguished passenger as Her Highness, accommodation has been found. And now, my immovable Englishman," cries he grinning all over his fat cheeks, "you will tell me at last that you are glad you came to Paris, and that Blowitz's little gift pleases you!"

Whatever I replied must have satisfied him, for he bore me off to meet the other passengers, all of whom seemed to know him, but in fact I wasn't at all sure that I liked his "*petit cadeau.*" I'd come to France to skulk and fornicate in peace, not to travel; on the other hand, I'd never visited Vienna, which in those days was reckoned first among all the capitals of Europe for immoral high jinks, and a day and a night of luxurious seclusion with Her Highness should make for an amusing journey. The last railroad rattle I'd enjoyed had been the voluptuous Mrs. Popplewell on the Baltimore line in '59, and rare fun it had been—until she pitched me off the train, and I had to hightail it for dear life with the Kuklos in hot pursuit. Still, the Three Fates were unlikely to be operating in Austria—oh, the blazes with it, what was I fretting for?* So I exchanged courtesies with the others, of whom I remember only the celebrated Nagelmacker, boss of the

---

* See *Flashman and the Angel of the Lord,* which recounts, inter alia, his adventures with the Kuklos, the forerunner of the infamous Ku Klux Klan, and its leaders, who styled themselves Atropos, Clotho, and Lachesis—the Three Fates of mythology.

line, who looked like a Sicilian bandit but was all courtesy, and a Something-or-other Effendi, a fat beard from the Turkish Embassy; there were various scribblers and a swarm of railway directors, Frog and Belgique mostly, making about two score all told.

And then there was a sudden bustle, and we were being herded aboard, with minions directing us to our compartments—I remember Blowitz and I were in Number 151, which seemed odd on such a small train—and whistles were blowing and guards shouting, and from our window we could see the mob at the barrier hurrahing and throwing up their hats, and officials on the platform were waving, and the carriage doors were closed, crash! crash! crash!, a last whistle shrilled—and then a strange silence fell over the Gare de l'Est, and I guess little Blowitz's enthusiasm must have had its effect, for I remember feeling a strange excitement as the train quivered ever so little, the steam rushed hissing past our window, there was a faint clank of buffers, a gentle rumble of wheels beneath our feet, and we were gliding away smoothly and ever so slowly, the waving figures on the platform passing from sight in succession, and then we were out of the station and I was thinking, you've been in some odd vanguards, Flashy, from the Forty-Niners to the Light Brigade, and here's another for you, and Blowitz snapped shut his hunter and shook my hand, gulping with emotion—gad, he was a sentimental little barrel.

"*Sept heures et un, précisément,*" says he reverently. "*L'Express Orient parti!*"

He was in a state of non-alcoholic intoxication if ever I saw one, exclaiming in delight over every convenience and decoration in our cabin, and inviting me to marvel at the fine upholstered furniture, the glossy panelling, the neatly-concealed little basin in a corner by the door, the array of lights and buttons, the hidden cupboards and drawers, the velvet curtains, and the rest. Every second word of his babble was "*magnifique!*" or "*superbe!*" or "*merveilleux!*" and once even "top-hole, I declare!," and I couldn't deny that it was. As it turned out, my first journey on the Orient Express was to be my last, but I remember it as the best-appointed train I ever struck, and delighted Blowitz by saying so."

"You will find no more splendid accommodation in Vienna!" cries he. "Which reminds me, you should stay at the Golden Lamb on the Praterstrasse, rather than the Archduke Charles; give my name to Herr Hauptmann and you will receive every attention. And his table is all that could be desired—*ah, mais écoutez!* Even as I speak, *le diner est servi! Allons, mettons-nous!*"

That was another score for the Orient Express: we were hardly out of Paris before we had the nosebags on, and I have to concede that there was nothing wrong with the grub on offer in the opulent dining salon with its little pink shades and snowy cloths and silver and crystal and swift service. Blowitz almost burst into tears of gluttony at the sight of it, and stuffed himself to ecstasy, going into raptures at each arriving course, and reproaching me for my apparent lack of appetite; in fact I was sharp-set, but ate and drank in moderation, for my mind was on the ladies' sleeping-coach where I supposed la Kralta would be dining in anonymous seclusion; you don't want to be bloated when the charge is sounded. The food and wine had its effect, though; my blues had vanished, and I was beginning to enjoy the luxurious comfort. Presently, when Blowitz had engulfed his last *marron glacé* and staggered afoot, gasping blessings on the chef, we made our way to the little observation platform for a smoke before going our separate ways. He had given me the number of Madame's *voiture* in the ladies' car, and said with knowing chuckles that he imagined he would have No. 151 to himself for the night.

"You will hardly wish to join the excursion at Strasbourg, which we reach at five o'clock in the morning," sniggers he. "Oh, yes, I shall take it—no rest for *le pauvre* Blowitz—and I confess

I am still too excited to sleep anyway! Oh, my friend, what a journey! I can hardly believe it! Strasbourg, Vienna, Budapest, Bucharest . . . we glide through them all, the jewels of Europe, and at last the Bosphorus, the Golden Horn! I cannot prevail on you to make the whole journey? No, well, it may be best that you alight with Her Highness at Vienna—only Nagelmacker's trusted few know of her presence, but it could hardly be secret after other ladies join us, and we wish no gossip, eh?" He tapped his booze-enriched nose. "My boy, I wish you joy of your adventure . . . ah, but one thing! In divulging our little secret, you will make no mention of La Caprice by name; that must remain confidential always. Now, to my arms!" He embraced me as closely as his pot-belly permitted. "We shall meet again before Vienna. *A bientôt!*"

He toddled off rejoicing to the salon, and I finished my cigar, watching the dark woods and fields flow past at thirty miles an hour. Then I made my leisurely way back through the salon, where Blowitz and the boys were plainly intent on making a night of it; from the laughter and jollity I guessed they'd be singing ere long. In our sleeping coach the attendants were making up the berths, one above t'other as on shipboard; whether Blowitz or Nagelmacker had warned them to look the other way, I don't know, but none of 'em gave me so much as a glance as I passed through the communicating door to the ladies' coach, closed it behind me, and found myself in the long empty corridor which ran past the doors of the untenanted compartments to the front baggage car.

It was quieter here, with only the rumble of wheels and the faint creak of coachwork. The number on the nearest door suggested that Madame's cabin was at the far end, and I paused beneath the dim night-light over the attendant's empty stool to consider my tactics. It was a novel situation, you see, even for as practised a ram as yours truly: how d'you set about a proud beauty who's probably ready to ride in return for information, but whom you've never met? Question of etiquette, really, and I couldn't recall a similar case. I might approach her à la cavalier, all courtly grace and Flash gallantry, giving her the chance to pretend (?) willing surrender, thus respecting the conventions and prolonging the fun; or I could stride in with "Evening, ma'am, fine weather, what? Strip away!" which had answered splendidly with little Duchess Irma . . . not that she was a total stranger; we'd met at our wedding. But recalling the haughty mien and fine proportions of Princess Kralta, I suspected that jollying her into action might be a bore, while on t'other hand she was too big to wrestle into submission in the confines of a sleeping berth . . . Quite a dilemma, and I was getting monstrous randy just thinking about it, so I decided to play the bowling as it came, strode down the swaying corridor, and knuckled the walnut.

"*Wer ist es?*" says a female voice, and, not knowing the German for Roger the Lodger I said it was Flashman, ein Englander und ein Edelman, and a pal of Blowitz's. At this there was a bustle within, murmured question and brisk reply, a sudden almighty clattering of crockery, a blistering rebuke in Mittel European, and finally out popped a pert little giggler of a lady's maid bearing a tray of dinner dishes. As she emerged, a slim be-ringed hand reached from behind the door, deftly removing a bottle from the tray, the door closed, the maid shot me a smirk and scurried into the next cabin, and I was just interpreting these as excellent omens when the rebuking voice started to call "*Herein!*" but changed it to "Enter!," I tooled in, and there she stood, Her Extremely Royal Highness the Princess Kralta as ever was, clad in regal dignity and a magnificent coat of sables which covered her to the floor.

I might have thought it an odd rig at that time of night if I'd had eyes for anything except the long pale equine face framed by unbound blonde hair flowing to her shoulders, the cold blue eyes looking disdainfully down her noble nose, the full haughty mouth, the white hand clasping the coat beneath her rather pointed chin while she extended the other imperiously, slim fingers drooping to be kissed—it was as though some highly superior Norse goddess was condescending to notice an unusually dirty worm of a mortal. I nuzzled dutifully, deciding that while she couldn't compare for beauty to Montez or Elspeth or Yehonala or a dozen others, Blowitz had been right: she had "magnétisme" by the bucket, enough to inspire worship in him and his like—why, for a moment I felt awed myself . . . and that was enough to put me on guard, thinking 'ware this one, lad, she's too good to be true, and likely false as a two-bob diamond for all her grand air and queenly poise; watch her like a hawk . . . but rejoice in the droop of the plump nether lip and the wanton way she lets you make a meal of her fingers—sure signs that with proper management she'll romp like a demented stoat. (I can always spot 'em; it's a gift.)

"Enchanted, highness," says I, retaining her hand, and for a moment we weighed each other before she withdrew it to indicate the lower berth, which was made up as a bed. "You come unannounced, sir. I was about to retire. I had not expected you tonight." She spoke perfect English with that soft Danube accent that is so attractive in men and women both.

"Your highness is gracious to expect me at all," says Galahad Flashy. "If I am inopportune, my excuse is that having seen your picture I could not wait to view the reality."

She arched an eyebrow. "Indeed? But as we left Paris more than two hours ago, I take it you have restrained your eagerness long enough to dine?" Smiling ever so cool, the smart bitch. Very good, my lass, brace yourself.

"Sparingly, your highness," says I, "and with mounting impatience. Had I known how far your beauty outshines the image of the photographer, I'd have gone without dessert, possibly even without the *poulet aux truffes*. From the evidence of your dinner tray I gather you enjoyed them both, so you may judge the depth of my sincerity." I moved a step closer, sighed deeply, and regarded her solemnly. "But what am I saying? The truth is that for one glance from those glorious eyes, one gleam of the golden cascade of your hair, I'd have made do with a cheese sandwich and a pint of stout."

It took her flat aback, small wonder, and for an instant she stiffened and I received the freezing Queen Bess stare, and then to my astonishment her lips trembled into a smile, and then a chuckle, and suddenly she was laughing outright, bless her—I'd been right, she was human beneath the ice, and I warmed to her in that moment, and not only out of lust, although I wondered if a swift Flashman cross-buttock (tit in one hand, arse in t'other) mightn't be in order, but decided to observe the niceties a little longer. Make 'em laugh and you're halfway to bed anyway. She was regarding me now with an odd look, quarter amused, three parts wary.

"The *poulet* was passable; the *crêpe chantilly* . . ." She shrugged. "And I begin to see that M. Blowitz spoke no more than the truth when he said that Sir Harry Flashman was a quite unusual man. *Très amusant, très beau*, he told me . . . and *très galant*." Now the cool smile on the fine horse face was haughty-coquettish as she looked me up and down. "Quite overpoweringly *galant*."

"It's these tiny compartments; chaps my size tend to loom, rather," says I, happy to continue bantering now that I was sure of her, and curious to see how she'd play the game—after all, she was the one who wanted something. "Perhaps if your highness would deign to be seated . . ." I indicated the only chair, and she gave me a sidelong look and disposed herself gracefully, an elbow on the chair arm, a finger along her cheek, but still keeping the fur carefully about her.

"Yes . . . certainly unusual," says she. "That is very well. I am unconventional myself. I think that we shall understand each other." She smiled again, which strangely enough didn't improve her looks, for while her teeth were like pearls, they protruded slightly—breeding, no doubt. "In spite of your tendency to talk charming nonsense. Golden cascades and sandwiches of cheese! Is that how you approach all your ladies?"

"Only if I'm sure it'll be appreciated. But don't misunderstand me, highness—it may be nonsense, but I meant every word of it." I took a step forward and hunkered down in front of her, eyeing her with ardour. "You're what we call an absolute stunner, you know. Aye . . . the most desirable woman I've seen since—"

"—since we left the Gare de l'Est?" says she coolly. "Even that is not true. My maid is prettier by far than I . . . as I am sure you noticed."

"Pretty's ten a penny, I said desirable. Anyway, she's only a maid, not a princess . . . and she don't want anything from me."

She sat farther back in her chair, considering me as she toyed with her hair. "And I do," says she. "In fact, Sir Harry, each of us wants something from the other, do we not?" She glanced at the bottle she'd taken from the tray, standing above the basin. "Shall we begin our . . . negotiation with a glass of wine?"

I rose to fill a couple of glasses, and when we'd sipped she set hers on the little stand by the window, crossed her legs beneath the coat, tossed back her golden mane, and looked me in the eye, no longer smiling, but not unfriendly either. I hunkered down again—believe it or not, it puts you at an advantage; women don't care to have a great hairy man crouched at their feet, prepared to spring.

"Stefan Blowitz tells me that you hold a secret which I wish to know," says she, "and that you are willing to—"

"Pardon, highness . . . a secret Prince Bismarck wants to know."

"Very true." She inclined her head. "By the way, I expect 'highness' from inferiors. To friends, I am Kralta."

"Honoured, I'm sure—I'm Harry. So first, tell me—why should busy Otto, with the cares of the world on his back, want to know an old secret that ain't worth a button?"

"I do not know," says she simply. "He did not tell me. And he is not a man of whom one asks reasons."

"Not even if one is on intimate terms with him?" She didn't even blink, let alone blush. "Come now, Kralta, we both know Bismarck and his fine clockwork mind. He don't ask damfool questions—and this one couldn't be sillier—without an excellent reason. Can't you even guess what it might be?"

She took a sip of wine. "You have said it yourself . . . Harry. His fine clockwork mind. He must know all. If he has another reason I do not know it."

And wouldn't tell if she did. Well, it made no odds now, as I contemplated the perfect buttermilk skin and silken tresses. It was time to get to the meat of the matter.

"Well, it don't signify. But I beg your pardon—I interrupted. You were saying, about Blowitz . . . ?"

"He said that if I asked you how the Berlin Treaty was obtained . . . you could tell me."

"Absolutely. Happy to oblige. "

It surprised her. "Now?"

"Well, presently. Let's say . . . in Vienna."

"On your word of honour?"

"Cross my heart. Never fear, I'm an authority on honour."

She hesitated. "And in the meantime?" I just grinned at her, wicked-Flashy-like, and she sat back in her chair, giving me a long look with a pout to her lower lip that set my mouth watering. "I see. There is a price."

"Fair exchange, I'd call it," says I, enjoying myself, and to avoid meeting my eye she turned her head aside, displaying the imperious brood-mare profile. Her voice was calm and quiet.

"You think it fair . . . to exact a price? To take advantage of a helpless woman? Perhaps you are one of those men—I suppose I must call them that—who enjoy forcing a woman to humiliate herself—"

"Aye, I'm a cruel swine, ain't I just? And you're about as helpless as the Prussian Army."

"But I am expected to ask your terms, to plead, perhaps—"

"D'you need to ask them?"

She was still for a moment, and then she sighed, rose from her chair, still clasping the fur collar beneath her chin, and looked down at me with that cool superior smile.

"Not for a moment," says she, and turning her back she shrugged the coat to the floor and stood there bare as a babe. I overbalanced and sat staring at the long shapely legs, the plump buttocks, the wasp waist, and the alabaster perfection of the smooth strong back, all revealed so unexpected. She stirred her rump, and as I reached out, clutching joyfully, she glanced complacently over her shoulder.

"A fair exchange, *n'est-ce pas?*"

And I have to own that it was. That sudden shedding of her clobber just when she'd been pretending that she'd have to be coaxed or ravished, is the kind of lecherous trick that wins my heart every time, and when we came to grips she behaved like the demented stoat aforesaid. Not as skilful as many, perhaps (though you must make allowances for the limited space in a sleeping berth), but a good bruising rough-rider, full of running, and as heartily selfish as royal fillies invariably are, intent on nothing but their own pleasure, which suits me admirably: there's nothing like voracity in the fair sex, especially when she's as strong as a bullock, which Kralta was. Not unlike that gigantic Chinese brigandess who half-killed me on the road to Nanking, but civilised, you understand, and willing to chat afterwards, in a frank, easy way which you'd not have expected from her lofty style and figurehead.

I guess I just like contrary women, and Kralta was one. Crooked as a Jesuit's conscience, as I was to discover, but with a spirit and quality that made you feel it was almost a privilege to mount her—but then, I've remarked before that royal breeding tells, and no doubt I'm as impressionable as the next horny peasant. She was a born adventuress, too—aye, the very archetype of all those subtle sirens whom romantic writers love to imagine aboard the Orient Express. I'd barely disentangled myself from those muscular satin limbs, and she'd stopped gasping in what I think was Hungarian and recovered her breath, when she murmured:

"So . . . must the secret wait until Vienna?" Her long fingers stroked my stomach, careless-like. "Better there should be nothing between us, *nem*? Then we can enjoy our journey." She flirted her lips across my chest. "Why not tell me now?"

"So that you can call the guard and have me slung out as soon as you've heard it? I've known women who wouldn't think twice."

"You think I am such a one . . . after . . . ?" Her stroking hand slid downwards. "Do you not trust me, when I have trusted you . . . Harry?"

"Steady, girl! A little decorum, if you please . . . I'll tell you, princess—"

"Kralta . . ."

"Aye, well, Kralta . . . I trust folk as far as I can throw 'em, which in your case," I fondled a voluptuous handful, "ain't far, thank God. No, Vienna'll be soon enough. I ain't a modest man, but I'm not fool enough to think that you'd continue to play pretty just for the sake of my manly charms . . . d'you know?"

"How little you know of women," says she. "Or rather, how little you know of me."

"I know you're Bismarck's mistress." I couldn't resist touching this condescending madam on a raw spot—but of course it wasn't.

"Fat little Stefan has been gossiping, has he?" She sounded amused. "What did he tell you?"

"Oh, how the German Emperor persuaded you to gallop stout Otto into a cheerful frame of mind—which I'm bound to say you're well equipped to do." I gave her bottom a hearty squeeze. "I'll bet he couples like a cannibal, does he?" Coarse stuff, you see, to put her in her place, but all it provoked was a dry chuckle.

"Poor Blowitz! Either he is a bad reporter, or he was trying to protect my reputation." She eased herself up on an elbow and smiled at me bold-eyed. "In fact, His Majesty made no such suggestion; he merely poured out his fears to me, like the garrulous old woman that he is. It was I who suggested, delicately, since the Emperor is easily shocked, that I myself should . . . refresh Prince Bismarck."

Delicacy being her forte, the brazen bitch. "God's truth—d'you mean you *wanted Bismarck?* Talk about a glutton for punishment! What on earth possessed you?"

She gave a little dismissive shrug. "Amusement? Whim? What shall I call it? I am forty years old, immensely rich in my own right, titled and privileged, married to a dull nonentity . . . and bored beyond belief. It follows that I seek diversion, excitement, pleasure, and above all, novelty. When a new sensation offers, I pursue it . . . as you have discovered." She teased her lips across mine. "That is what possessed me."

"I'll be damned! You didn't tell that to the Emperor, I'll be bound! What did he say?"

"Oh, men are such hypocrites! He pretended not to understand . . . but he did everything in his power to smooth my way to Schonhausen—secret arrangements, agents to conduct me, my husband sent off on a fool's errand." She gave a well-bred sneer. "A professional procurer could have done no more! And so . . . Bismarck was, as you say, 'galloped' into a good humour, the Emperor was pleased and grateful, and I," says she, sitting up and stretching wantonly, poonts at the high port, "enjoyed the supreme gratification of having the most powerful man in the world panting for me in his shirt-tail."

See why I said it was a privilege to mount her? There ain't many women as shameless as I am—and by gum she was proud of it. Of course I was bound to ask how the most powerful man in the world had performed, and she shrugged, laughing.

"Oh, very active . . . for his age. And very Prussian, which is to say gross and greedy. An ageing bull, without refinement or subtlety." She was one to talk. "As the French philosopher said, it was an interesting experience, but not one to be repeated. Now I," her eyes narrowed and the ripe lower lip drooped as she reclined beside me again, her hands questing across my body, "am devoted to repetition, and so, I believe, are you . . . ah, but indeed you are! And since I did not decoy you from London only to find out silly secrets . . ." she slid a strapping thigh across my hips, gasped sharply in Hungarian, and began to plunge up and down ". . . oh, let us repeat ourselves, again, and again, and again . . . !"

So we did, as the Orient Express thundered on towards distant Strasbourg, myself rapturously content to lend support, so to speak, while royalty revelled in the joys of good hard work. God knows how Bismarck had stood it at his time of life, and I remember thinking that if one had wanted to assassinate him, Kralta could have given him a happier despatch than the old bastard deserved.[12]

Chapter 4

Clanks and whistles and a shocking cramp in my old thigh wound awoke me as we pulled in past the Porte de Saverne to Strasbourg station, and when I tried to move, I couldn't, because Kralta was sleeping on top of me—hence my aching limb, trapped beneath buxom royalty. That's the drawback to railroad rattling: when you've walloped yourselves to a standstill there's no room to doze off contentedly rump to rump, and you must sleep catch-as-catch-can. Fortunately she soon came awake, and I heard the rustle of her furs as she slipped out into the corridor, leaving me to knead my leg into action, sigh happily at the recollection of a rewarding night's activity, raise the blind for a peep at the station, and groan at the discovery from the platform clock that it was only ten to five.

The place was bustling even at that ungodly hour, with some sort of reception for our passengers, and I remembered Blowitz had talked of a dawn excursion. There he was, sure enough, well to the fore with Nagelmacker and a gang of tile-tipping dignitaries; he was trying to be the life and soul as usual, but looking desperate seedy after all his sluicing and guzzling, which was a cheering sight. If I'd known then that the Strasbourg river is called the Ill, I'd have called to him to have a look at it, as suiting his condition.

That reminded me that I was in urgent need of the usual

offices, and I was about to lower the blind when my eye was caught by a chap sauntering along the platform valise in hand, a tall youthful figure, somewhat of a swell with his long sheepskin-collared coat thrown back from his shoulders, stylishly tilted hat shading his face, ebony cane, a bloom in his lapel, and a black cigarette in a long amber holder. Bit of a Continental fritillary, but there was something in the cut of his jib that seemed distantly familiar as he strolled leisurely by. Couldn't be anyone I knew, and I put it down as a fleeting likeness to any one of a hundred subalterns in the past, lowered the blind, drew on shirt and trousers, and hobbled out to seek relief.

When I returned, the little maid had set out a tray of coffee, hot milk, and *petit pain,* and was plumping the pillows and smoothing the sheets of the berth. Kralta was in the chair, her robe about her, perfectly groomed and bidding me an impersonal good day as though she'd never thrashed about in ecstatic frenzy in her life.

"Early as it is, I thought a *petit déjeuner* would not be amiss," says she. "Manon has made up a berth for you in the next cabin, so that you may sleep until a more tolerable hour, as I shall." The maid poured coffee for me and milk for her mistress, and waited on us while we ate and drank in silence—Kralta poised and dignified as befitting royalty *en déshabillé,* Flashy half-conscious as usual when rousted out at 5 a.m. I was glad of the coffee, and finished the pot; worn as I was with lack of sleep and Kralta's attentions, I knew it would take more than a pint of Turkish to keep me awake.

When we'd finished, Manon removed the tray, and I was preparing to take my weary leave when Kralta stopped me with a hand on my sleeve. She said nothing, but put her hands up to my cheeks, appraising me in that shall-I-buy-the-brute-or-not style—and then she was kissing me with startling passion, mouth wide, lips working hungrily, tongue halfway to breakfast. Tuckered or not, I was game if she was, and I was delving under the fur for her fleshpots when she pulled gently away, pecked me on the cheek, murmured, "Later . . . we have Vienna," and before I knew it I was in the corridor and her lock was clicking home.

I was too tired to mind. The lower berth in the next cabin was turned down and looked so inviting that I dragged off my duds any old how and crawled in gratefully, reflecting that the Orient Express was an A1 train, and Kralta, the teasing horse-faced baggage with her splendid assets, was just the freight for it . . . and Vienna lay ahead. Even as my head touched the pillow the train gave a clank and shudder, and then we were gliding away again, and I was preparing for sleep by saying my prayers like a good boy, their purport being the pious hope that I hadn't forgotten any of the positions Fetnab had taught me on the Grand Trunk, and which I'd rehearsed with Mrs. What's-her-name in the ruined temple by Meerut, and would certainly demonstrate to Kralta as soon as we found a bed with a decentish bit of romping room in it . . .

I expected to sleep soundly, but didn't, for I was troubled by a most vivid dream, one of those odd ones in which you're sure you're awake because the surroundings of the dream are those in which you went to sleep. There I was in my berth on the Orient Express, stark beneath the coverlet, with sunlit autumn countryside going past the window, and near at hand two people were talking, Kralta and an Englishman, and I knew he was a public school man because although they spoke in German he used occasional slang, and there was no mistaking his *nil admirari* drawl. I couldn't see them, and it was the strangest conversation, in which they chaffed each other with a vulgar freedom which wasn't like Kralta at all, somehow. She said *of course* she'd made love to me, twice, and the man laughed and said she was a slut, and she said lightly, no such thing, she was a female rake, and he was just jealous. He said if he were jealous of all her lovers he'd have blown his brains out long ago, and they both seemed amused.

Then their voices were much closer, and Kralta said: "I wonder how he'll take it?," and the man said: "He'll have no choice." Then she said: "He may be dangerous," and the man said the queerest thing: that any man whose name could make Bismarck grit his teeth was liable to be dangerous. The dream ended there, and I must have slept on, for when I woke, sure enough I was still in the berth, but somehow I knew that time had gone by . . . but why was there no feeling in my legs, and who was the chap in the armchair, smoking a black gasper in an amber holder, and rising and smiling as I strove to sit up but couldn't? Of course! He was the young boulevardier I'd seen on Strasbourg station . . . but what the hell was he doing here, and what was the matter with my legs?

"Back to life!" cries he. "There now, don't stir. Be aisy, as the Irishman said, an' if yez can't be aisy, be as aisy as ye can. Here, take a pull at this." The sharp taste of spa water cleared my parched throat, if not my wits. "Better, eh? Now, now, gently does it! Who am I, and where's the delightful Kralta, and what's to do, and how's your pater, and so forth?" He chuckled. "All in good time, old fellow. I fancy you'll need somethin' stronger than spa when I tell you. Ne'er mind, all's well, and when you're up to par we'll have a bite of luncheon with her highness—I say, though, you've made a hit there! Bit of a wild beast, ain't she? Too strong for my taste, but one has to do the polite with royalty, what?" says this madman cheerfully. "Care for a smoke?"

I tried again to heave up, flailing my arms feebly, without success—and now my dream came back to me, half-understood, and I knew from the numbness of my limbs that this was no ordinary waking . . . Kralta, the bitch, must have doctored my coffee, and it had been no dream but reality, and this was the bastard she'd been talking to . . . about *me*. And Bismarck . . .

"Lie still, damn you!" cries the young spark, grinning with a restraining hand on my shoulder. "You must, you know! For one thing, your legs won't answer yet awhile, and even if they did,

you're ballock-naked and it's dam' parky out and we're doin'
forty miles an hour. And if you tried to leave the train," he added
soothingly, "I'd be bound to do somethin' desperate. See?"

I hadn't seen his hand move, but now it held a small under-
and-over pistol, levelled at me. Then it was gone, and he was
lighting a cigarette.

"So just be patient, there's a good chap, and you'll know all
about it presently. Sure you won't smoke? There's no cause for
alarm, 'pon honour. You're among friends . . . well, companions,
anyway . . . and I'm goin' to be your tee-jay and see you right,
what?"

D'you know, in all my fright and bewilderment, it was that
piece of schoolboy slang that struck home, so in keeping with his
style and speech, and yet so at odds with his looks. He couldn't
be public school, surely . . . not with those classic features that
belong east of Vienna and would be as out of place in England as
a Chinaman's. No, not with that perfect straight nose, chiselled
lips, and slightly slanted blue eyes—if this chap wasn't a Mittel
European, I'd never seen one.

"Tee-jay?" I croaked, and he laughed.

"Aye . . . guide, philosopher, and friend—showin' the new
bugs the ropes. What did you call 'em at Rugby? I'm a Wyke-
hamist, you know—and that was your doin', believe it or not!
'Deed it was!"

He blew a cloud, grinning at my stupefaction, and the feeling
that I'd seen him before hit me harder than ever—the half-jeering
smile, the whole devil-may-care carriage of him. But where?
When?

"Oh, yes, you impressed the guv'nor no end!" cries he. " 'It's
an English school for you, my son,' he told me. 'Hellish places,
by all accounts, rations a Siberian *moujik* wouldn't touch, and
less civilised behaviour than you'd meet in the Congo, but I'm
told there's no education like it—a lifetime's trainin' in knavery

packed into six years. No wonder they rule half the world. Why, if I'd been to Eton or Harrow I'd have had Flashman on toast!' That's what the guv'nor said!"

This was incredible. "The . . . the guv'nor?"

"As ever was! You and he were sparrin'-partners . . . oh, ever so long ago, before my time, ages! He wouldn't tell about it, but he thought you no end of a fellow. 'If ever you run into Flashman . . . well, try not to, but if you do, keep him covered, for he's forgotten more dodges than you'll ever know,' he told me once. 'His great trick is shammin' fear—don't you believe it, my boy, for that's when he's about to turn tiger.' I remember he fingered the scar on his brow as he said it. I say, did you give him that?" His eyes were alight with admiration, damned if they weren't. "You'll have to tell me about that, you know!"

My heart had stopped beating some time before. I could only stare at him appalled as the truth dawned.

"My God! You mean . . . you're—"

"Rupert Willem von Starnberg!" cries he, sticking out his hand. "But you must call me Bill!"

It's a backhanded tribute to the memory of the late unlamented Rudi von Starnberg that my first impulse on meeting his offspring was to look for the communication cord and bawl for help. Time was I'd ha' done both, but when you've reached your sixties you've either learned to bottle your panic, sit tight, and think like blazes . . . or you haven't reached your sixties, *mallum*?* I didn't know what the devil was afoot, or why—but I'd heard his name and his threat and seen his Derringer. No wonder he'd seemed familiar: taller, longer in the jaw, straight auburn hair instead of curls, and clean-shaven, but still unmistakable. Rudi's son . . . my God, another of him!

* understand?

That settled one thing. Whatever the ghastly plot, it didn't signify beside the urgent need to get off this infernal train in one piece, *jildi*,* and if this brute was anything like dear Papa, I'd have my work cut out. You may think his threat was ridiculous, on a civilised railroad carrying respectable passengers through the heart of peaceful Europe. I did not. I knew the family.

But I must have time to think and find out, so I let him clasp my nerveless hand, assuring me warmly that he'd wanted ever so much to meet me. That was a facer, if you like; Rudi had been as deadly an enemy as I'd ever run from, and dam' near did for me in the Jotunberg dungeons, and here was this ruffian talking as though we'd been boon companions . . . and yet, hadn't that been Rudi all over, carefree villainy with a twinkling eye, clapping your shoulder and stabbing your back together?

Playing for time, I muttered something idiotic about not knowing Rudi had married, and he laughed heartily.

"He had to, you see, when I happened along in '60. You knew Mother—Helga Kossuth, lady-in-waitin' to the Duchess of Strackenz in your time. I've heard her speak of you, but nothin' to a purpose. Kept her counsel, like the guv'nor."

They would; imposture and assassination ain't matters to beguile your infant's bed-time. I remembered Helga, a lovely red-haired creature whom Rudi had been sparking back in '48— evidently with more constancy than I'd have given him credit for. And now the result of their union was watching me with an eye like an epee as I cautiously flexed my toes, feeling the life return to my legs, weighed the distance between us, and asked what time it was.

"Just past noon; Munich in half an hour—but don't form any rash plans for gettin' out there." He eyed me mockingly. "I'm sure you wouldn't enjoy ten years in a Bavarian prison. Bad as Rugby, I shouldn't wonder. Oh, yes," he continued, enjoying

* quickly (Hind.)

himself, "I have it on excellent authority—Prince Bismarck's in fact—that a warrant still exists for the arrest of one Flashman, a British subject, on a most serious criminal charge, the rape of one Baroness Pechmann at a house in the Karolinen Platz, Munich, thirty-five years ago. Astonishin' how youthful peccadilloes come home to roost—"

"It's a lie! A damned infamous lie!" It was startled out of me in a bellow of shock and rage. "It was a trap! A vile plot by that swine Bismarck and Lola Montez and that fat lying whore—"

"So you told the examinin' magistrate . . . one Herr Karjuss." He drew a paper from his breast. "Strangely enough, he didn't believe you. Of course, there were several witnesses, includin' the victim herself, and—"

"Your forsworn rat of a father!"

"You took the words from my mouth. Yes, their signed statements are in the files, and would have been used at your trial if you hadn't absconded. Still, the case can easily be reopened."

Absconded, my God! Trepanned into that Strackenz nightmare . . . I felt as though I'd been kicked in the stomach, for it was all true, though I hadn't given it a thought in half a lifetime—true, at least, that I'd been falsely accused by those fiends, blackmailed with the threat of years in a stinking gaol. And the evidence would still be there, the only falsehood being that I'd raped that simpering sow—why, we'd barely buckled to, and she'd been fairly squealing for it—

"The Baroness, you'll be happy to know, is in excellent health and eager to testify. Did I say ten years? Strait-laced lot, the Bavarians; it could easily be life."

"You wouldn't dare! What, d'you think I'm nobody, to be railroaded by some tinpot foreign court on a trumped-up charge? By God, you'll find out different! I count for something, and if you think the British Government will stand by while your lousy, corrupt—"

"They stood by while . . ." he consulted his paper ". . . yes, while Colonel Valentine Baker went away for twelve months. He was a stalwart hero of the Empire, too, it seems, and all he'd done was kiss a girl and tickle her ankle in a railway carriage. I must say," he chuckled, "the longer I serve Bismarck the more I admire him. It's all here, you know." He tapped the paper. "How you'd bluster, I mean, and how to shut you up. I'd never heard of this Baker chap . . . dear me, flies unbuttoned on the Portsmouth line, what next? I say! We might even work up a second charge against you—indecent assault on the Orient Express, with Kralta sobbin' in the witness-box! That'd make the cheese more bindin' in court, what?" He shook his head, mock regretful. "I'm afraid, Harry my boy, you're cooked."

I'd known that, for all my noise, the moment he'd recalled the name Pechmann. They'd got me, neck and heel, this jeering ruffian and his icy bitch of an accomplice . . . and Bismarck. Who else would have thought to conjure up that ancient false charge to force my hand now . . . but for what, in God's name? I must have looked like a landed fish, for he gave me a cheery wink and slapped the edge of my berth.

"But don't fret—it ain't goin' to happen! It's the last thing we want—heavens, you'd be no good to us in clink! I only mentioned the Pechmann business to let you see where you stand if . . . But see here," says he, brisk and friendly, "why not hear what we want of you? It ain't in the least smoky, I swear. In fact, it's a dam' good deed." He came to his feet. "Now then, you're feelin' better, I can see, in body if not in spirit. Legs right as rain, eh? Oh, yes, I noticed!" He gave me that cocky Starnberg grin that shivered my spine. "So, I'll take a turn in the corridor while you put on your togs and have a sluice. No shave just yet, I'm afraid; I took the razor from your valise, just in case. Then we'll have some grub and come to biznai." He gave a cheery nod and was gone.

I can't tell you my thoughts as I rose, none too steadily, and dressed, because I don't remember. I'd been hit where I lived, and hard, and there was nothing for it but to clear my mind of fruit-less speculation, and take stock of what I knew, thus:

Starnberg and Kralta were Bismarck agents, and had trapped me, drugged me, threatened me with firearms and the certainty of years in gaol if I didn't . . . do what? "Nothing smoky . . . a dam' good deed"? I doubted that, rather . . . but on t'other hand, they hadn't shown hostile, exactly. Kralta had let me roger her as part of the trap, but I knew, from a lifetime's study of well-rattled women, that she'd taken a shine to me, too. And while Starn-berg was probably as wicked and dangerous a son-of-a-bitch as his father, he'd seemed a friendly disposed sort of blackmailing assassin . . . why, latterly he'd been almost coaxing me. I was at a loss; all I knew was that if they were about to force me into some diabolic plot, or preparing to sell me a fresh cargo of gammon, they were going a rum way about it. I could only wait, and listen, and look for the chance to cut.

So I made myself decent, took another pull at the spa, touched my toes, transferred my clasp-knife from my pocket to my boot (you should have frisked my clothes, Bill), decided I'd felt worse, and was in fair parade order when he returned, pre-ceded by Manon with a loaded tray which she set down on a little folding camp table before making brisk work of converting the berth into a sofa.

"What, not hungry?" says he, when I declined sandwiches and drumsticks. "No, I guess lay-me-down-dead ain't the best foundation for luncheon—but you'll take a brandy? Capital! Ah, and here is her highness! A glass of champagne, my sweet, and the armchair. 'It is well done, and fitting for a princess,' as my Stratford namesake has it. She is a real princess, you know, Harry—and I'm a count, and you're a belted what-d'ye-call-it, so we're rather a select company, what?"

It might have been Rudi himself, chattering gaily and keep-ing between me and the door as he bowed in Kralta, very elegant in a fur-trimmed travelling dress and matching Cossack cap. She gave me her cool stare, and then to my surprise held out her hand with a little smile, asking courteously if I'd slept well, damn her impudence. But I took her hand as a little gentleman ought, with a silent bow, as though she hadn't fed me puggle and we'd never played two-backed beastie in our lives. A still tongue and sharp eyes and ears were my line until I knew what was afoot—after which I'd be even stiller and sharper.

"All glasses charged?" cries Starnberg. "Capital! To our happy association, then!" He lighted one of his cigarettes and settled on the sofa corner by the door; I was seated by the window.

"Now then . . . biznai," says he. "First off, Chancellor Prince Bismarck presents his compliments, apologises for any inconvenience caused, and invites your assistance in preservin' the peace of Europe. And that's no lie," he added. "It's in the balance, and if things go wrong we'll have the bloodiest mess since Bonaparte." He'd stopped smiling, and Kralta was watching me intently.

"Why *your* assistance?" he went on. "Freak of chance, nothing more. You've been told that for five years Bismarck wondered how Blowitz got hold of the Berlin Treaty; that's true, tho' it didn't keep him awake. Then a few months ago, idly enough, he suggested to Kralta that she might worm it out of little Stefan. She failed, but here's the point." He levelled his cigarette at me. "In talkin' to her about Berlin, Blowitz chanced to mention your name in passin'—you know how he gasses about the people he knows—and in reportin' her failure she, in turn, mentioned it to Bismarck. Now," says he, looking leery, "I don't know what you and Bismarck and the guv'nor were up to in Strackenz years ago, but when Bismarck heard the name Flashman, he sat up straight—didn't he, Kralta?"

She nodded. "He said: 'That man again! I was right—I *did* see him in Berlin during the Congress!' Then he laughed, and said I should trouble no more about Blowitz; he would find out the secret of the treaty for himself, through other agents."

"And didn't he just!" cries Starnberg. "All about some courtesan who wormed information out of one o' the Russians, and you passed it to Blowitz in your hat, and a French diplomat was so impressed by Blowitz's omniscience that he handed over the treaty. Who was the courtesan, Harry?" says he, with a sly glance at Kralta. "Another of your light o' loves?"

I'd kept a straight face through this revelation; now I shook my head. Since Bismarck was so dam' clever, let him find out Caprice's identity for himself, if he wanted to.

"Well, Bismarck was amused: said he admired Blowitz's ingenuity. But that was that; havin' discovered the ploy, Bismarck was content—and none of it matters now; the only important thing about Blowitz and the whole Berlin business was *that it brought your name back to Bismarck's notice,* see? So, just by that chance, you were still in his mind a few weeks ago, when he first had word of the threatenin' crisis I mentioned just now. It struck him that you would be useful—nay, essential—to him in meetin' that crisis. 'Flashman is the man,' were his very words. 'We must have him.' The question was, how to enlist you. He thought you might be reluctant." He glanced at Kralta. "Wasn't that how he put it?"

"Rather more strongly." For once there was a glimmer of humour in the cool blue eyes. "He said you would have to be compelled. So I was instructed to entice you to Paris." She paused, and Starnberg burst out laughing.

"Tell him what Bismarck said! Oh, well, if you won't, I will! He said you were a lecherous animal governed altogether by lust." He winked at Kralta. "Which made him irresistible to you, didn't it, my dear?"

She ignored this. I'd resolved to keep mum, but suddenly the chance to play parfit gentil Flashy seemed sound policy.

"Knowing your parentage, I'm not surprised by your guttersnipe manners," says I. "Get to the point, and keep your impertinences to yourself."

He crowed with delight, clapping his hands. "Why, Kralta, I

do believe you've got a champion! Bless me if you haven't won his manly heart—or some other part of his anatomy which I shan't mention, since delicacy seems to be the order of the day." He grinned from one to the other of us. "Lord, what a pair of randy hypocrites you are! The older generation . . ." He shook his head.

"As I was saying," says Kralta calmly to me, "I was the lure to attract you. As you know, I used the unsuspecting Blowitz to bring us together. He was most obliging, hinting slyly that if I still wished to know how the Berlin Treaty was obtained, you could be persuaded to tell me. Naturally, I did not tell him that we already knew that little secret, but pretended delight, and urged him to lose no time in bringing you to Paris. You may resent the deception we . . . I have practised, but I cannot regret it." The horse face was proudly serene, but with the little smile at the corner of her mouth. "For several reasons. When you have heard what Prince Bismarck proposes, you will understand one of them." She made a languid gesture to Starnberg to continue.

"Well, thank'ee, ma'am," says he sardonically, and filled my glass. "But before we come to that, we have a few questions, and 'twill save time if you answer without troublin' why we ask 'em. You'll learn, never fear. How friendly are you with the Emperor of Austria?"

"Franz-Josef? Hardly friendly . . . I've met him—"

"Yes, on his yacht off Corfu in 1868, on your return from Mexico, where you had led the unsuccessful attempt to rescue his brother Maximilian from a Juarista firin' squad. A gallant failure which earned you the imperial gratitude, as well as the Order of Maria Theresa, presented to you . . ." he cocked a quizzy eyebrow ". . . by the Empress Elisabeth, and ain't she a peach, though? I'd call that friendly."

They'd done their lessons, up to a point. The "gallant failure" had been the biggest botch since the Kabul Retreat, thanks to the idiot Maximilian, who was damned if he'd be rescued, so there, and I'd come off by the skin of my chattering teeth and the good offices of that gorgeous little fire-eater, Princess Aggie Salm-Salm, and Jesus Montero's gang of unwashed bandits who were on hand only because Jesus thought I knew where Montezuma's treasure was cached, more fool he. Another fragrant leaf from my diary, that was, and my only regret for Emperor Max was that he'd been a fairish cricketer for a novice, and might have made a half-decent batter, if he'd lived.[13] But it was true enough that Franz-Josef had been uncommon civil, for an emperor, and the beautiful Sissi (Empress Elisabeth to you) had given me the glad eye as she'd handed over the white cross. Can't think what became of it; in a drawer somewhere, I expect.

Kralta asked: "Did the Emperor Franz-Josef shake hands with you?"

A deuced odd question, and I had to think. "I believe he did . . . yes, he did, coming and going."

"Then he's certainly friendly," says Starnberg. "He only takes the paw of close relatives and tremendous swells, usually. That was the only time you met him . . . would he be pleased to see you again, d'you think? You know, hospitably inclined, stop over for a weekend, that kind of thing?"

"How the devil should I know? What on earth has this to do—?"

"Bismarck is sure he would be. Not that he's asked—but your name has been mentioned to the Emperor lately, and he spoke of you most warmly. Gratifyin', what—from such a cold fish?"

"And the Empress?" This was Kralta. "Was she well disposed towards you?"

"She was very . . . gracious. Charming. See here, this is—"

"Did you admire her?"

"Of course he did!" laughs Willem. "Who doesn't? Half Europe's in love with the beautiful Sissi!"

"You met her again, later," says Kralta. "In England."

"I hunted with her, once or twice, yes."

"Hunted, eh?" Willem's tongue was in his cheek. "Was that the only . . . exercise you took with her?"

"Yes, damn your eyes! And if that's where you've been leading with your infernal questions—"

"It had to be asked," says Kralta sharply. She stared down her nose. "Then there are no grounds at all for the Emperor to feel . . . jealousy towards you? Where his wife is concerned?"

"Or to put it tactfully," says Willem, "if you happened along, Franz-Josef wouldn't bar the door on you just because little Sissi was on the premises?" He gave the snorting little chuckle which I was beginning to detest. "Ve-ry good! D'ye know what, Kralta? Bismarck was right. 'Flashman is the man' . . . I say, Munich already! How time flies in jolly company!" He stood up and consulted his watch. "We stop only five minutes . . . but you won't do anythin' rash, Harry, will you? A German gaol wouldn't suit, you know."

He needn't have fretted. One thought alone was in my mind as we waited, looking out on the orderly bustle of Munich station: the Austrian frontier lay a bare sixty miles off, we'd cross it in two hours, and if (a large if, granted) I could give 'em the slip I'd be beyond the reach of Bavarian law in a country at loggerheads with Germany and as likely to oblige Bismarck by returning a fugitive as I was to take holy orders.

As to what he could want of me, I was no wiser. What could it matter what the Emperor and Empress of Austria thought of a mere British soldier? She had an eye for men, and it was common talk that Franz-Josef had warned her off various gallants with whom her relations had probably been innocent enough, but I hadn't been among 'em. I dare say I could have added her scalp to my belt, but I'd never tried, for good reason: everyone knew that Franz-Josef, whose ambition seemed to be to bag every chamois and woman in Austria, had given her Cupid's measles, and while the poultice-wallopers had doubtless put her in order again, you can't be too careful. And while she looked like Pallas Athene, I suspected she was half-cracked—flung herself about in gymnasiums and went on starvation diets and wrote poetry and asked for a lunatic asylum as a birthday present, so I'd been told. She and Franz-Josef hadn't dealt too well since he'd poxed her, and she'd taken to wandering Europe while he pleaded with her to forgive and forget. Royal marriages are the very devil.

I tell you this because it's pertinent to the catechism which Willem resumed as soon as we'd pulled out of Munich. He began by asking what I knew of the Austrian Empire. I retorted that they seemed to be good at losing wars and territory, having been licked lately by France, Prussia, and Italy, for heaven's sake, and that the whole concern was pretty ramshackle. Beyond that I knew nothing and cared less.

He nodded. "Aye, ramshackle enough. Fifty million folk of a dozen different nations bound together in a discontented mass under a stiff-necked autocrat who don't know how to manage 'em. He's a dull dog, Franz-Josef, whose blunders have cost him the popularity he enjoyed as the handsome boy-emperor of thirty-five years ago. But his empire's the heart and guts of Europe, and if it were to suffer any great convulsion . . . well, it better not. Know anythin' about Hungary?"

I understood it was the biggest state in the empire bar Austria itself, and that the natives were an ornery lot, but fine horsemen. He grinned.

"Proper little professor of international politics, you are! Well, I'm quarter Hungarian myself, through Mama; rest o' me's Prussian. And you're right, they're an ornery lot, and don't care above half for Austrian rule. They've declared independence in the past, risin' in revolt, and Franz-Josef made the mistake of gettin' the Tsar to put 'em down with Russian troops—they'll never forgive him that. He's been at his wits' end to keep 'em quiet, makin' concessions, havin' himself and Sissi crowned King and Queen of Hungary, but there are still plenty of Magyar nationalists who'd like to cut with Austria altogether. People like Lajos Kossuth, regular firebrand who led the uprisin', now in his eighties and exiled in Italy but still hatin' the Hapsburgs like poison and dreamin' of Free Hungary. Believe it or not, he and his nationalist pals have the sympathy of Empress Sissi and the Emperor's son and heir, Crown Prince Rudolf, who favour constitutional reform.[14] And there are others, extremists who'd like to take a shorter way."

He paused to light a cigarette, blowing out the match and watching its smoke. "Terrorists like the Holnup, which is Hungarian for 'tomorrow,' 'nuff said. They skulk in secret, plottin' bloody revolution, but most Hungarians regard 'em as a squalid gang of fanatics not to be taken seriously." He threw aside the spent match. "So did we . . . until about a month ago, when Bismarck got word, through his private intelligence service, that the Holnup were about to take the warpath in earnest. Here, let me give you another brandy."

He poured out a stiff tot, and a cloud must have passed over the sun just then, for the brightness faded from the pretty autumn colours speeding past the window, and to my nervous imagination it seemed that the shadow penetrated into the compartment, robbing the trickling brandy of its sparkle, and that even the rumble of the wheels had taken on a menacing, insistent note.

"The Holnup intend to assassinate Franz-Josef," says Willem, filling a second glass for himself. "If they succeed, there'll be civil war. Oh, pottin' royalty's nothing new, and usually there's no great harm done—various lunatics have tried for Franz-Josef before, there have been two attempts on the German Emperor, and the Tsar was blown up a couple of years ago . . . but this would be different.[15] What, Hungarians killin' the Austrian monarch, at a time when Hungary's boilin' with unrest, when it's known that Sissi supports its independence, and surrounds herself with worshippin' Magyars, and corresponds with Kossuth, and there's even been rumour of a conspiracy to bestow the crown of Hungary on Prince Rudolf, who hates Papa and is as pro-Hungarian as his beautiful idiot of a mother?" He gave a mirthless bark of laughter. "Think what use the nationalists could make of those two half-wits, willin' or not! *Casus belli*, if you like! Civil war in Austria-Hungary—and how long before France and Germany and Russia, aye, and perhaps even England, were drawn in? And that is what will happen if Franz-Josef stops a Hungarian bullet."

Kralta spoke. "It must not happen. At all costs it must be prevented."

She was intent on me, but Willem, as he handed me my glass and sat back, seemed almost amused. There was a look of mischief on the handsome face, like a practical joker about to spring his surprise.

"Fortunately," says he, "thanks to Bismarck's earwig in the Holnup, we know precisely when and how and where they intend to strike. Franz-Josef is to be murdered in his huntin'-lodge at Ischl, a charmin' but secluded resort in the Saltzkammergut, over the hills but not very far away from where we sit at this moment. They'll do it this week, by night, a small group of well-armed and expert assassins. They have it planned all to a nicety . . . and all in vain, poor souls." His smile widened as he clinked his glass against mine. "Because you and I, old son, are goin' to stop 'em."

Chapter 5

Somewhere or other that downy bird Kipling observes that the lesson of the island race is to put away all emotion and entrap the alien at the proper time.[16] I learned it in my cradle, long before he wrote it, and have practised it all my life with some success, and only this difference, that for "entrap" I prefer to substitute "escape." The putting-away-emotion business ain't always easy, but I like to think I managed it pretty well in the face of Starnberg's disgusting proposal, concealing my shocked bewilderment before that grinning young devil and his steely-eyed accomplice as they watched to see how I would respond to their bombshell.

There was no point in protest or roaring refusal. As you know, I'd been press-ganged aboard the good ship Disaster before, by legions of experts from Palmerston to Lincoln, with the likes of Colin Campbell and Alick Gardner and U. S. Grant and Broadfoot and J. B. Hickok and Raglan and God knew who else along the way, all urging hapless Flashy into the soup by blackmail and brute force, and nothing to be done about it. Ah, but this time there *was*, you see, with the Austrian border drawing nearer by the minute, so I must bide my time and delude the aliens as seemed best, listening to their lunatic notions as though I might be persuadable, and waiting my chance to cut and run. My strong card was that despite Willem's menaces, they'd made it plain that they wanted me as a willing ally; I must play on that, but not too hard. The question was, which role to adopt (ain't it always?), balancing righteous outrage at the way I'd been treated against the chivalrous impulses which they'd expect from an officer and gentleman. So now I let out a soft "Ha!" and gave Willem my most sardonic stare.

"Are we, indeed? Just the two of us, eh? Well, setting aside your optimism and impudence, perhaps you'll tell me how, precisely?"

"You mean you're game?" cries he eagerly. "You're with us?"

"Suppose you tell me why I should be."

"How can you not?" Kralta couldn't believe her ears, like a queen with a farting courtier. "With the peace of Europe in the balance, and the lives of thousands, perhaps millions, at stake?"

"Ah, but are they? Forgive me if after being hoodwinked, lied to, held against my will, and threatened with prison and pistols, I can't help wondering if this great tale of a plot is true."

"Of course it's true!" cries Willem. "Heavens, man, why should we invent it?" I gave this the shrug it deserved, and he cursed softly. "Look here, if you're in a bait 'cos you've been bobbled and made a muffin of—" he sounded like a third-form fag "—well, I don't wonder, but can't you see we had no choice? Bismarck was sure we'd have to force your hand, and that this was the only way. Havin' seen you, I ain't so sure he's right." He ran a hand through his hair, and leaned forward, looking keen. "You ask me how you and I can stop the Holnup, and I'll tell you the ins and outs presently, but in principle, now—ain't it a stunt after your own heart? As I told you, nothin' smoky, but a dam' good deed, and a rare adventure! Why, the old guv'nor would have jumped at it—and you'd ha' been the first he'd have wished to have alongside!"

"And if you cannot forgive the deceits we have practised," put in Kralta, "think of the cause we serve. You have done brave deeds for your Queen and country, but nothing nobler than this."

She hadn't the style or figurehead to look pleading, but she absolutely laid a hand on mine, and her glance had more promise than appeal in it. "For my part, if I can make any amends . . ." She ventured a toothy smile, pressing my fin. "Please . . . say you will not fail us. All depends on you."

All of which confirmed my conclusion that they were under the misapprehension which has sustained me for a lifetime—they truly believed my heroic reputation, and thought I was the kind of derring-do idiot who'd answer the call of duty and danger like a good 'un, itching to fight the good fight. Bismarck knew better, which was why I'd been threatened with violence and the law, but now blessed if they weren't appealing to my better nature. Remarkable . . . but you have to play the ball as it comes off the wicket, so . . .

"All very fine," says I. "But before I hear the ins and outs, let me tell you that so far you've made no sense. You say these Hungarian rascals are going to put paid to Franz-Josef, and you know where and when. Very well—round 'em up and string 'em up, why don't you—"

"Because it ain't that simple!" insists Willem. "Bismarck's spy in the Holnup knows their plan, but not the names of the assassins, or where they are this minute. All we're sure of is that they'll have assembled somewhere near Ischl three days from now, and will strike before the Emperor returns to Vienna on Sunday next. That means the attempt will be made this Friday or Saturday—"

"Then let him go back to Vienna tomorrow, for God's sake! Or if he's fool enough to stay, surround his place with troops! Or hasn't brilliant Otto Bismarck thought of that?"

"You do not understand." Kralta had me by the hand again. "None of these things is possible. No ordinary precautions will serve. You see, the Emperor does not know he is in danger—he must not know."

She meant it, too. I could only gape and ask: "Why not?"

"Because the Lord alone knows what he'd do if he did!" exclaims Willem. "It's this way—no one knows of this plot except Bismarck, his man in the Holnup, and a handful of his agents, like ourselves. But suppose Franz-Josef, or the imbeciles who compose his cabinet, got wind of it—he's the kind of pur-blind ass who would take it as a sure sign that all Hungary's out for his blood, and he'd act according, orderin' arrests, repressions, perhaps even executions, or some such folly! He could provoke the very upheaval Bismarck's tryin' to prevent. Hungary's a powder-keg, and an outraged Franz-Josef is the very man to set it off." He drew breath. "That's why he mustn't know."

"There is another reason," says Kralta. "The Empress and Crown Prince make no secret of their Hungarian sympathies. She is adored in Budapest, and there are those who would welcome Rudolf as king of an independent Hungary. If the Emperor learned of the Holnup plot, he might easily be led to false conclusions."

"He wouldn't be in the mood for a game of Happy Families, at any rate!" snaps Willem. "So there you have it. Now ... Franz-Josef is only at Ischl by chance; normally he comes for a summer's shootin', with a full retinue, but this week there are only the lodge servants, a couple of aides, and a file of sentries under a sergeant, more for ceremony than anything, and quite useless against assassins who know their business. There's no earthly way to make him leave early without informin' him of the plot—so Bismarck has devised a way to guard him secretly, *so that he don't know he's bein' guarded!*" He laughed at my look of derision. "Impossible, you think? Oh, come, come, you know Bismarck; why, it's nuts to him!"

"I'm waiting to hear what it is to me," I reminded him.

"Patience, I'm comin' to that. We leave the train this evening at Linz, where we spend the night, and catch the local train to Ischl in the morning, arrivin' at about noon. We spend the next thirty-six hours establishin' ourselves as tourists who've come to enjoy the attractions of the spa, browse in its boutiques, partake of the delicious confections for which its cafés are famous, and walk in the delightful countryside," says he airily. Never mind Bismarck, it was nuts to him, the jaunty ruffian.

"On Thursday morning, you and I will take a stroll in the grounds of the royal lodge, which lies a little way outside the town, refreshin' our spirits in the beautiful hilly woodland and admirin' the picturesque river meanderin' down to the town below. But now—" he spread his hands in comic dismay "—misfortune overtakes us. You slip, and sprain your ankle. I hasten to find help, and spy a gentleman out with his gun and loader—and damme, if it ain't the Emperor of Austria! And if you think that's one whale of a coincidence," says he, cocking an eyebrow, "it ain't. Franz-Josef would rather shoot chamois than eat his dinner, and is in those woods at crack of dawn every day bar Sunday. If by some mischance he's not, I'll go to the lodge, but one way or t'other he's goin' to learn that there's a foreign gentleman in distress in his bailiwick, and when he discovers that 'tis none other than Sir H. Flashman, old acquaintance and saviour (well, nearly) of Brother Max in Mexico, he'll be all concern and will undoubtedly offer him and his companion (a German count, no less) the hospitality of the royal residence for a day or two. And there, my dear Harry," chuckles he, "we shall be, honoured guests *chez* Franz-Josef, and if the Holnup can come at him while we're on the premises . . . well, they'll be smarter lads than I think they are, what?"

Taking this as a rhetorical question, and being numb and speechless anyway, I let it pass without remark. Willem rubbed his hands.

"Now for the fun. Franz-Josef is all for the simple life. He sleeps on a soldier's bedstead in a plain little room overlookin' the garden, with a single orderly on a pallet outside the door and his aides snug in their rooms down the corridor, everyone snorin' their heads off as they've done this thirty years past, and why not? What's to fear? A single sentry under the window, probably half asleep, all quiet in the garden and surrounding woods, God's in his heaven, and all's well, until . . ." he dropped his voice to a hollow whisper ". . . out of those woods the Holnup come skulkin' in the half-light before dawn . . . perhaps a single bravo, more likely two, but certainly not more than three. Say three, two to look out and cover, one to do the dirty deed . . . all creepin' unawares into our ambush." There was a glitter in his eye that took me straight back to the Jotunberg dungeons. "We'll take 'em either in the house or outside, as chance dictates. And we kill 'em. Stone dead. Every one. Follow?"

I let that pass, too, taking the advice of his Irishman and being as aisy as I could, while he lighted himself a nonchalant cigarette.

"It'll be a noisy business, of course, and there'll be a fine how-de-do when the sleepers awake to find three dead assassins and the two gallant visitors whose vigilance has saved the day. But once they've grasped what's happened, you can bet your last tizzy they'll want to keep it quiet." He grinned, pleased as Punch, tapping my knee. "There'll be no inconvenient inquiry which might result in the unhappy discovery that this was a *Hungarian* plot. Why? Because whatever folly Franz-Josef might have committed if he'd learned of the Holnup attempt *beforehand*, he'll not raise Cain when it's all past and no harm done. There'll be nothin' to show that the corpses *are* Hungarians—they may even be foreign hirelings—and whatever he may suspect, the less the public hear of it, the better. No monarch likes it to be known that he's been a target, not if it can be kept dark, and his aides won't care to have their incompetence noised abroad. So 'twill all be discreetly damped down, everyone sworn to secrecy, eternal gratitude to the two gallant saviours, perhaps even a pound out of the royal poor-box—why, if failin' to save poor old Max earned you the Maria Theresa, we ought to get a couple of Iron Crowns at least!"

"And Europe will remain at peace," says Kralta quietly.

"Aye, and we'll all live happy ever after." Willem blew a smoke-ring. "So there you have it—all of it. Now you understand what all this to-do, which you've found so puzzlin' and inconvenient, has been about . . . and why Bismarck chose you, 'cos you're the only man he could put into Franz-Josef's house and no questions asked. And you're . . . qualified for the work." He paused, contemplating his cigarette. "Well, there it is. What d'you say . . . Harry?"

The honest answer to that would have been to tell him he was stark raving mad, and if he hadn't been Rudi Starnberg's son, with a gun in his armpit and the means to railroad me on to the Bavarian rock-pile for life, I might well have given it. Since my present need was to temporise, and give the impression that I might be talked into their ghastly scheme, I played it as they would expect from the redoubtable Flashy, indignation forgotten, narrow-eyed and considering, asking shrewd questions: How could they be sure Franz-Josef would offer us bed and board? What other agents would Bismarck have at Ischl? What if our ambush went wrong? What if it couldn't be hushed up? What if, by some unforeseen twist of fate, Willem and I should find ourselves facing charges of murder?

Entirely academic questions from my point of view, but they elicited prompt answers—none of them, incidentally, concerned with the morality of butchering the would-be assassins. Willem, being a chip off the Starnberg block, wouldn't think twice, but I was interested that Kralta too apparently took bloodshed for granted—and both, you'll notice, assumed that it was all in the night's work for me. Flattering, if you like.

Willem dealt confidently with my doubts. "It's Bismarck's scheme, and he don't make mistakes. Franz-Josef is bound to take us in, but if he didn't we'd just picket his lodge and deal with the Holnup in the grounds. There'll be half a dozen stout lads in Ischl at my orders, but they won't know what's afoot and I shan't call on them unless I must. If word of the fracas gets out—well, that's

Bismarck's biznai, and he'll see to it that we're kept clear of embarrassment. Murder? What, when we've saved the Emperor of Austria? Don't be soft. Well, satisfied?"

I wasn't, but I chewed my lip, looking grim, while they watched me with mounting hope and encouraged me with occasional reminders of what a fine crusading enterprise it was, and no other way to ensure the peace of Europe and the welfare of its deserving peasantry. Kralta was particularly moving on the score of the juvenile population, I remember, while Willem appealed to what he supposed was my sense of adventure, poor fool; plainly he regarded a hand-to-hand death-struggle in the dark as no end of a lark. I responded with few words, and at last said I would sleep on it when we reached Linz. They seemed to take that as a sign that I was halfway to agreement, for Willem nodded thoughtfully and refilled my glass, while Kralta astonished me by kissing me quickly on the cheek and leaving the compartment. Willem laughed softly.

"Sentimental little thing, ain't she? Gad, what a week you'll have in Vienna when it's all over! But I," says he, fixing me with a merry eye, "ain't sentimental at all, and in case—just in case, mind you—you're as foxy as my old guv'nor made out, and have some misguided notion that you'll be able to slip away once we're on Austrian soil . . . well, don't try it, that's all. Those stout lads I spoke of will be on hand, and they can have you back in Bavaria before you can say knife." He patted his pocket. "If I haven't shot you first."

I reminded him coldly that I'd be no use to him dead, and he grinned. "You'd be even less use to yourself. But we won't dwell on that, eh? You're a practical man, and I've a notion that you'll fall in with us. Just so long as you understand that you're going to stand up with me against the Holnup, one way or t'other, what?"

So I hadn't fooled him above half, and must just wait and hope. One thing only I was sure of: he wasn't getting me within a mile of Franz-Josef and the blasted Holnup—supposing they existed, and the tale I'd been spun wasn't some huge Machia-vellian hoax conceived by Bismarck for diabolic purposes that I couldn't even guess at.

That was possible . . . but d'you know, I was inclined to believe they'd told me the truth. Not all of it, perhaps, but true so far as it went. It was wild, but no wilder than some intrigues I'd known—the Strackenz marriage for one, John Brown's raid for another. That Hungarian fanatics should be after Franz-Josef's blood was all too credible; what boggled the mind was the scheme Bismarck had designed to stop them . . . until you studied it and saw that nothing else would have answered. The threat of explo-sion in Europe had arisen suddenly, like a genie from a bot-tle, worse than '48 or Crimea or San Stefano, and faced with the apparently impossible task of ensuring the Emperor's safety while keeping him in the dark, that ice-cold brain had seen that unlikely old Flashy was the vital cog, having the entrée to Franz-Josef and being eminently blackmailable. And he'd gone calmly and swiftly to work to bring me where I now was, by the most outlandish means, using Kralta and Willem (and Blowitz?) and above all his knowledge of me. His planning had been meticu-lous . . . so far. As for what lay ahead, it remained to be seen whether the web which his perverted genius had spun over Ischl would be proof against my frantic efforts to break loose, and the hell with Franz-Josef and the peace of Europe both. Well, he'd spun a similar web over Strackenz, and I'd diddled the bastard then, hadn't I?

All very well; my immediate concern was to bolt, and with this son-of-a-bitch Starnberg half-expecting it, I'd have my work cut out. It must be soon; once he'd got me to Ischl, with his gang dogging us, I'd be sunk. Linz, where we were to stop the night, might be my best chance; I'd no doubt he was as restlessly quick on the trigger as his murderous father, but if I yelled for help in the street, or in a hotel, he'd not dare cut loose with his piece . . . would he? Yes, he would though, and take his chance, and make his excuses to Bismarck later. The local train to Ischl would be no easier to break from than the Orient Express . . . dear God, had I the nerve to spring at him now, land one solid blow, and leg it for the compartment where Blowitz and the boys would be whiling away the time and I'd be safe even from this bloody young villain . . . and as the desperate thought flashed across my mind I realised that he was drawing lazily on his cigarette, watching me with that insolent Starnberg smile on his handsome face, and my courage (what there was of it) melted like slush in a gutter.

Since I was supposed to be meditating on whether to join their frightful scheme or not, they let me be for the rest of the journey, Kralta next door and Willem reading and smoking placidly while I brooded in my corner. Once I made a half-hearted suggestion about bidding farewell to Blowitz, who expected me to get out at Vienna and might wonder where I'd got to; Willem gave me a slantendicular smile and said Kralta would send him a note.

Dusk was falling when we pulled into Linz, but no more rapidly than my spirits when we left the station, Willem close at my elbow and Kralta alongside, and I saw the closed coach by the kerb, with a couple of burly fellows in billycocks and long coats waiting to usher us aboard. One sat by the driver while the other rode inside with us; he was a beef-faced rascal with piggy little pale eyes which never left me, and great mottled hands resting on his knees—strange, I can see them yet, powerful paws with bitten nails, while the rest of that brief coach-ride has faded from memory, possibly because of the shock I received when we reached our destination, and I saw that it wasn't the expected hotel or inn, but a detached house on what I suppose were the outskirts of Linz, surrounded by a high ivy-covered wall and approached through an arched gateway which was closed behind us by the chap on the box.

That put the final touch to my despair. It wasn't only that there would plainly be no escape from here, or the sight of another brace of bullies waiting by the open front door under a flickering lantern, or the air of gloom that hung over the house itself, conjuring thoughts of bats and barred windows and Varney the Vampire doing the honours as butler; what chilled my skin was the Bismarckian efficiency of it all, the evidence of careful preparation, the smoothness with which I'd been conveyed from train to prison (for that's what it was). That was the moment when I began to doubt if there was a way out, and the nightmare sketched out by Willem changed from the frighteningly possible to the unspeakably probable.

There are chaps, I know, who when doom seems certain grit their teeth and find renewed courage in their extremity. I ain't like that at all, but my native cowardice does take on a sort of reckless frenzy, rather like those fellows who caught the Black Death and thought, oh, well, to hell with everything, we might as well carouse and fornicate to the end, 'cos at least it's more fun than repentance or prayer. It was in this spirit that I was able to roger that houri in Borneo during the Batang Lupar battle, whimpering fearfully the while, and do justice to Mrs. Popplewell while in flight from the outraged townsfolk of Harper's Ferry. It don't cast out fear, but it does take your mind off it.

In my present plight, things were made easier by Willem and Kralta, who kept up the pretence that I was a willing guest, chatting amiably as we went indoors, calling for comforts and refreshments, and when we came to a late supper in the sparsely furnished dining-room, setting themselves to put me at ease—a Herculean task, you'll allow, but they didn't shirk. Willem pattered away cheerily, and Kralta, shrewdly guessing that nothing was more likely to put me in trim than a fine display of gleaming shoulders and rampant boobies across the board, had changed into evening rig of red velveteen stuff with jewels sparkling on her bosom and in her hair. Why not, thinks I, it'll see you through a restless night at any rate. So I joined in their talk, stiff enough at first, but unbending to the extent of reminiscing about a campaign or two, and from their occasional exchange of glances I could see that they were thinking, aha, the brute's coming round after all. Nothing was said about the Ischl business until we were about to part for the night, by which time I'd drunk enough to swamp my worst fears and prime me for another bout with Kralta. She'd left us to our cigars, with a cool smile for me as I drew back her chair, and when we were alone Willem says:

"Our proposal . . . d'you still need to sleep on it?"

"Do I have a choice?" I wondered.

"Hardly. But I'd like to think you were with me willingly—for the good cause, oh, and the fun of it!" He chuckled—gad, he was like Rudi, ruthless as cold iron but treating it as a game. "Come on, Harry—what d'you say?"

"If I say 'aye'—would you trust me?"

"On your word of honour—yes." Lying bastard, but it gave me the chance to play bluff Flashy to the hilt. I sat up straight and looked him in the eye.

"Very well," says I deliberately. "I'll give it . . . in return for your word of honour that all you've told me is gospel true."

He was on his feet like a shot, hand held out, smiling eagerly. "Done!" cries he. "On my honour! Oh, this is famous! I knew you'd come round! Here, we must certainly drink to this!" So we did, neither of us believing the other for an instant, but content with the pretence. At that, I ain't sure that he didn't half-believe me, for I can sound damned true-blue when I want to. We drank, and he clapped me on the shoulder, bubbling with spirits, and delivered me to my beefy watchdog, crying "Good night, old fellow! Sweet dreams!" as I was shepherded up the stairs.

The lout saw me silently into a room, which was as I'd expected—bars on the window, lock clicking behind me, and Kralta sitting up in the great four-post bed, clad in a gauzy night-rail and a look of expectation.

"Tell me he persuaded you!" cries she.

"Not for a moment, my dear," says I, shedding my coat. "You

see, I knew his father, and I'd not trust either of 'em round the corner." The fine long face hardened in dismay, and she drew back against the pillows as I sat down on the side of the bed. "No, he has not persuaded me . . ." I leaned towards her with my wistful Flashy smile, reaching out to touch her hair ". . . but you have. You see, I'm a simple sort of chap, Kralta, always have been. I don't always know a wrong 'un when I meet one, but I do know when someone's straight." I kissed her gently on the forehead, and felt her quiver distractingly. "You're straight as a die. And while I ain't much on politics, or the smoky things these statesmen get up to, or even understand above half all the stuff that Willem told me . . . well, that don't matter, truly." I fondled a tit with deep sincerity, and felt it harden like a blown-up football. "If you think it's a worthy cause . . . well, that's good enough for me."

Ever seen a horse weep? Nor I, but having watched the tears well in those fine blue eyes and trickle down her muzzle, and heard her whinny and bare her buck teeth in a smile of glad relief, I don't need to. Her arms went round my neck.

"Oh . . . but all my deceits and lies—"

"Honourable lies, my darling, to a noble end. Why, I've told a few stretchers of that sort myself, in my time, when duty demanded it." I slipped the flimsy stuff aside to get a proper grip of the meat, and kissed her lingeringly on the mouth. She clung moistly, making small noises of contrition turning to passion, and I went to the glad work of entrapping the alien at the proper time.

Chapter 6

Ischl's a pretty little place, almost an island enclosed on three sides by the rivers Traun and Ischl, and lying at the heart of some of the finest scenery in Europe, forest country and lakes and the mountains of the Saltzkammergut. Bad Ischl they call it nowadays, and I believe it's become a favourite resort of the square-head quality, but even in '83 the Emperor's patronage had made it fashionable, and there was more of Society about than you'd have expected, come to take the waters, inhabit the fine villas along the Traun, drive in the woods and on the river boulevards, promenade in the gardens of the New Casino, and throng the more elegant shops and cafés, of which there were a surprising number. The townsfolk were stout and prosperous, and the inevitable peasantry in their awful little black pants and suspenders seemed to know their place, and gave the scene an air of picturesque gaiety.

Which didn't reflect my mood, exactly. Willem, I think, reckoned I was reluctant still, but would be bound to go through with his ghastly scheme; Kralta, on t'other hand, having a romantic and patriotic heart beneath her glacial exterior, and being partial to pork, was convinced I'd seen the light. She'd taken to me, no error, and *wanted* to trust me, you see. That was fine, but left me no nearer to finding a means of escape. The journey from Linz had afforded no chance at all, with Willem close on hand, and his four thugs in the next compartment, and at Ischl, where we were installed at the Golden Ship, in a side-street off the Marktplatz, they never let me out of their sight. That very first day, when we'd settled in and got our bearings in the town, strolling by the Traun, admiring the casino gardens, taking coffee in an opulent *pâtisserie,* and generally idling like well-bred little tourists, Willem stuck like a burr, and my beefy scoundrel lurked in the background.

How they'd act if I suddenly darted to the nearest copper, yelling that I was being kidnapped, I couldn't guess and didn't dare find out. Set aside that Willem might well have put a slug in my spine and faded out of sight, you're at the deuce of a disadvantage being a foreigner, even if you speak the lingo. The authorities ain't inclined to believe you, not in the face of explanations from an imposing lady of quality and her Junker escort, backed by four worthy cabbage-eaters in hard hats. "Poor cousin Harry, he's English you know, and has fits. Don't be alarmed, constable, we have a strait-jacket at the hotel." That would be their line, or something like it—and where would Cock Flashy be then, poor thing? At the bottom of the Traun the same evening, likely, with a bag of coal at his feet and Kralta dropping a sentimental tear.

So I played up as seldom before, smiling politely, talking wittily at ease, breathing in the breezes of the distant mountains with every sign of content, coaxing Kralta to buy a monstrous hat in one of the boutiques, drinking in a beer-garden with Willem and shaking my head ruefully as he cheated me at bezique (father's son, no question), laughing heartily at the drolleries of Frosch the gaoler in *Fledermaus* at the little theatre in the evening, remarking at dinner that Austria's contribution to civilisation must surely be the art of cooking cabbage decently,[17] rogering Kralta to stupefaction when we'd retired, and lying awake later with her sleeping boobies across my chest, cudgelling my wits for a way out.

I made the experiment of rising early next morning and

dressing quietly while she was still asleep, slipping out on to the landing—and there was Beefy square-bottomed on a chair, glowering. I bade him a civil good-day and sauntered down into the street, and he simply followed a few paces behind as I strolled to the river and back for breakfast. Willem was already down; he raised an eyebrow, glancing at Beefy, and then asked me if I'd had a pleasant stroll. No alarms, no warning, so they must be sure enough of their grip on me to delegate the task of watchdog to a single ruffian, armed and ruthless no doubt, but still just one man. Interesting . . . and sufficient to raise my hopes a little.

And then, on that second day in Ischl, the whole affair changed, unbelievably, and escape became unthinkable.

It was Wednesday, the day which Willem had appointed for a scout in the direction of Franz-Josef's lodge. It stood on rising ground on the other side of the town, above and beyond the little river Ischl, secluded enough among woodland to give royalty privacy, but an easy walk from the Ischl bridges which span the river by way of a little island lying in midstream.

Willem and I walked through the town and across the bridge to the island, which was laid out as a park, with pleasant gardens among the trees and bushes. We found a quiet spot from which we could look across the river towards the high bank above which the lodge could be seen among the trees. Willem scanned it through field-glasses and then we crossed the farther bridge for a closer look, strolling up the curving road, circling the lodge itself, and back to the road again. Here Willem led the way north, farther up the slope, to a point slightly above the lodge, and took a long slant through the glasses. There were a few folk about, tourists driving and strolling for a look at the royal residence.

"But there won't be a soul this side of the river after dark," says Willem. "Gad, ain't it made for murder, though! Come across from Ischl by day, lie up in the woods—" he nodded to where the trees grew thicker above us "—then swoop down at night, break in, do old F-J's business, and flee any way you like . . . across into the town to your hidey-hole, or back into the woods, or down the Ischl and then the Traun by boat!" He passed me the glasses, chuckling. "But since we shan't give 'em the chance to flee, that don't signify."

He lounged back on the turf, chewing a blade of grass and shading his eyes against the autumn sun while I surveyed the lodge, a white three-storeyed building with a high-pitched roof to one side in which there were dormer windows. Odd little minarets decorated the gable ends, and at what seemed to be the front of the house there was a large square porch with ivy-covered pillars and a flat roof surrounded by a little balustrade. The whole place had an informal, almost untidy look; not very grand for an emperor, I thought.

"I told you he liked to play the simple soul," says Willem. "All ceremony and etiquette at the Hofburg or Schonbrunn, but hail-fellow with the peasants when he's out of town—provided he does the hailing and they knuckle their foreheads like good little serfs. He acts the genial squire, but he's a pompous prig at heart, and God help anyone who comes the familiar with him. Or so I'm told; you've met him, I haven't."

I'd thought him stiff and stupid on short acquaintance, but what exercised me just then was that his lodge, while modest enough, was a sight too large to be guarded by a file of soldiers.

"But not by two clever lads inside the place, who stick close by his nibs night and day, and know the geography," says Willem. "And who know also exactly where the Holnup will try to break in."

I almost dropped the glasses. "How the devil can you know that?"

He gave me his smart-alec smile. "I've never set foot in that bijou residence, but I know every foot of it like my own home. Builders' plans, old boy—you don't think Bismarck overlooks items like that! I could find my way round it in the dark, and probably will."

"But you can't guess which way they'll come—"

"There's a secret stair leading down from the Emperor's bedroom to an outside door—no doubt so that he could sneak out for a night's whoring in town without Sissi knowing . . . although why he should, with that little beauty waiting to be bounced about, beats me," he added, with fine irrelevance. "Anyway, even the servants don't know about the secret stair—"

"But you and Bismarck do, absolutely!"

"Absolutely . . . and it's St. Paul's to the parish pump that the Holnup know, too. Heavens, they're not amateurs! They'd be mad not to take advantage of it, wouldn't you say?"

"And if they don't? Or if it's locked, as it's bound to be?"

He smote his forehead. "Damn! They'll never have thought of that! So they won't bring pick-locks or bolt-shears or anything useful, will they? Ah, well," says the sarcastic brute, "we can tell Bismarck he's fretting about nothing. Oh, come along." He got to his feet, laughing at me. "The thing is, where to take 'em? At the door, or inside, or where? Well, we'll have to think about that. One thing at a time . . ."

We walked down the hill and back across the bridges to Ischl town, and had just reached the spot where the Landstrasse runs into the Kreutzplatz when we were aware of some commotion ahead; people on the Landstrasse were drawing aside to the pavements with a great raising of hats and bobbing of curtsies as a smart open carriage came bowling up the street, its occupant responding to the salutes of the whiffers by making stiff inclinations and tipping his tile. A couple of Hussars trotted ahead, and as they came level with us Willem drew me quickly back into a doorway.

"The Grand Panjandrum himself," says he, "and the less he sees of us just now, the better. Don't want to spoil tomorrow's surprise, do we? Let's grin into our hats 'till he's past." We doffed, covering ourselves, and as the carriage crossed the

Kreutzplatz to polite cheering, Willem laughed. "Tell you what, Harry—he looks more than half like you!"

I don't care to be told that I resemble royalty; it wakes too many unpleasant memories, and in the case of Franz-Josef it was downright foolish, for while he cut a fairish figure, tall, dark and well-moustached and whiskered, he had no more style than a clothes-horse—and I ain't got a Hapsburg lip or the stare of a backward haddock. He didn't have my shoulders or easy carriage, either, and as he'd raised his hat I'd noted that his hair was receding—and dyed, by the look of it. That aside, he hadn't changed much in the fifteen years since I'd seen him. He'd be in his early fifties now, eight years my junior.

"It's a solemn thought," says Willem, as we resumed our walk down the Landstrasse, "that as he drives serenely by, the Holnup lads will be watching." He nodded at the fashionable shoppers thronging the pavements. "Aye, they'll be here, biding their time for tomorrow night, or the next. Too smart to try a shot or a bomb in open day, though—risky, and not near so impressive as cutting his throat in his own bedroom." He slipped his arm through mine. "Little do they know, eh?"

I hardly heard him. Somehow the sight of Franz-Josef had driven it home to me that in a few hours I'd be embarked on the lunatic business of faking a game leg in his coverts, being taken in as his guest, and prowling his blasted house in the middle of the night in the company of this bloodthirsty young ruffian, waiting for assassins to break in. It was like some beastly dream, there in this bustling, sunny resort, with respectable, decent folk strolling by, the women exclaiming at the shop windows, their men pausing indulgently, young people chattering gaily at the café tables— dammit, a pair of *polizei* twirling their moustaches at the next corner . . . and Willem must have had some sixth sense, for his arm tightened on mine and he shot me a quick glance as we walked past them. The urge to wrench free and run screaming for help lasted only an instant; I daren't, and I knew I daren't . . . but, oh Lord, somehow, in the next few hours, I must summon up the courage to try . . . what? The sweat was breaking out on me as we reached the Golden Ship, and Willem called cheerfully for coffee and cake.

And it was all wasted fear, for the die was cast already by hands other than Bismarck's, and rolling in my direction.

We dined early that evening, and for all his artless banter I sensed that Willem was wound tight, as was Kralta. She it was who proposed that we should visit the casino, less from an urge for play, I guessed, than for some distraction from the strain of waiting. Willem said it was a capital notion, and I forced a cheery agreement, so then we waited while Kralta donned her evening finery, and presently we strolled through the lantern-lit gardens to the New Casino, with Beefy acting as rearguard and taking post at the entrance as we passed into the salon.

That feeling of unreality that had gripped me in the streets came back with a vengeance under the glittering chandeliers. It was a scene from operetta, like the Prince's reception we'd seen at the theatre the previous night, a swirl of elegant figures clustered round the tables or waltzing in the ballroom beyond, all laughter and gaiety and heady music, gallants in immaculate evening rig or dress uniform, the ladies splendid in coloured silks, bright eyes and white shoulders and jewels a-gleam in the candle-shine, glasses raised to red lips and white-gloved fingertips resting on stalwart arms, the rattle of the wheel and the voices of the croupiers mingling with the cries of delight or disappointment, the soft strains of "La Belle Hélène" and "Blue Danube" from the orchestra, Ruritania come to life on a warm Austrian evening that would go on flirting and laughing and dancing forever . . . and a bare mile away, the lonely lodge among the dark silent trees with its precious royal tenant all unguarded against the creeping menace that would come by night, and only one desperate adventurer and one shivering poltroon to save the peace of Europe, unless at the eleventh hour that poltroon could streak to safety in the tall timber.

D'you wonder that while I retain a vivid image of the scene in that casino, I haven't the faintest recollection of the play? Not that I'm much in the punting line; running a hell in Santa Fe convinced me that it's money burned unless you hold the bank, but if I'd been as big a gambling fool as George Bentinck I'd not have noticed whether it was faro or roulette or vingt-et-un we wagered on; I was too much occupied keeping down my fears, mechanically holding Kralta's stakes and muttering inane advice, working up my courage with brandy while Willem smoked and watched me across the table.

I know Kralta won, smiling coolly as her chips were pushed across, and suggesting we escape from the noise and crowd into the garden. Willem nodded, and she went off to find her stole and to tittivate while I collected her winnings from the *caissier* and sauntered out of the salon to the entrance, my heart going like a trip-hammer, for I knew it was now or never.

Beefy was on the q.v. at the head of the steps, so I told him offhand that her highness would come presently, and I would wait for her at the little fountain yonder. He scowled doubtfully, and as I went leisurely down the steps to the gravel walk I saw him from the tail of my eye, hesitating whether to wait or come after me. Sure enough, he stuck to his orders, and followed me; I heard his beetle-crunchers on the gravel as I paused to light a cheroot and loafed on idly towards the fountain, glittering prettily under the lanterns a few yards ahead. There were clusters of light everywhere in the gardens, but deep stretches of dark among the trees—let me side-step swiftly into one of these and be off to a flying start, and if I couldn't give that lumbering oaf ten yards in the hundred, even at my time of life, I'd deserve to be caught. And then I'd be in full flight with the length and breadth of Europe before me, Kralta's winnings and my own cash to speed my passage, by train or coach or on foot or on hands and knees if need be—if I've learned one thing in life it's to bolt at the first chance and let the future take care of itself . . . so now I strolled unhurriedly to the fountain, and past it towards the shadows, heard Beefy's exclamation of *"Warten Sie, mein Herr!"*—and as his call ended abruptly in a choking gasp, a tall figure loomed up before me, my arms were gripped either side, and I was fairly heaved off the path and half-carried, half-dragged into the bushes.

I've been collared more often than Bill the Burglar, and these were serious, practised chaps, whoever they were; I had no time to cry out, even if I'd wanted to, which I didn't, for by the sound of it they'd dealt honestly with Beefy, and I wanted no such treatment. They bore me swiftly round a couple of hedges to a little box arbour dim-lit by a lantern overhead, depositing me on a stone bench, and the ghastly thought that they might be the Holnup had barely crossed my mind when the tall figure was before me again, stooping to thrust his face close to mine and astound me with a brisk greeting—in English!

"Evening, colonel. Remember me?"

A hawk face with a long jaw and sharp grey eyes, white hair and trim moustache; I couldn't even begin to place him.

"Hutton, Foreign Office. At Balmoral, thirty years ago. We played tig with Count Ignatieff on the mountain, you recall?"

It came back in an instant—that Russian brute blasting away at me in the bracken, my headlong flight downhill into the path of his murderous *moujik,* the bearded face glaring as he levelled his shotgun, and Hutton appearing from nowhere to put a bullet in him in the nick of time.* He'd been a damned brisk saviour then, and looked no less capable now for all he must have been my age at least. He spoke low, rapping out his words.

"Don't ask, but listen, we've little time. We know all about von Starnberg and the Princess Kralta and how they've brought

* See *Flashman in the Great Game*

you to Ischl. And why . . . yes, we know about the Holnup and their plot to murder the Emperor . . . Bismarck ain't the only one with long ears. We know, and our French colleagues—" he jerked his head at a stocky chap who moved out of the shadows to stand beside him; a bulldog face and moustache with the same keen eyes as Hutton's "—but no one else. Not even Bismarck knows that we know, and so it must remain. Secret . . . 'most secret from on high,' savvy?" That meant the Prime Minister, in politicals' lingo . . . Gladstone. "And higher still," adds Hutton sharply. My God, that could only mean the Queen . . .

"Now, understand this, sir. We know Bismarck's plan, down to the last detail, for safeguarding the Emperor. Starnberg must have put it to you? Very good, tell me what he said, precisely, and quick as you like."

When you've been trained as a political by Sekundar Burnes you talk to the point and ask no questions. In one short minute I'd been given staggering information demanding a thousand "whys," but that didn't matter. What did, was the joyous discovery that I was among friends and safe from Bismarck's ghastly intrigues. So I gave 'em what they wanted, as terse as I knew how, from my boarding the Orient Express, omitting only those tender passages with Kralta which might have offended their sensibilities, and any mention of the Pechmann blackmail: my story was that Willem had backed up his proposal with a pistol. They listened in silence broken only once by a groan from the bushes, at which Hutton snarled over his shoulder: "Hit him again, can't you? And go through the bugger's pockets—every last penny, mind!"

When I'd finished he asked: "Did you believe it?"

"How the blazes could I tell? It sounded wild, but—"

"Oh, it's wild!" he agreed. "It's also gospel true, though I don't blame you for doubting it . . . why the dooce couldn't Bismarck approach you open and aboveboard instead of humbugging you aboard that train? Best way to make you disbelieve 'em, I'd say." He shot me a leery look. "Told Starnberg to go to the devil, did you?"

"By God I did, and let me tell you—"

"But you're still with 'em, so either you've changed your mind or are pretending you've changed it." He was no fool, this one. "Well, sir, it makes no odds, for from this moment you're with 'em in earnest. And that's an order from Downing Street."

Only paralysed disbelief at these frightful words prevented me from depositing my dinner at his feet. He couldn't mean them, surely? But he did; as I gaped in stricken horror he went on urgently:

"It's this way. Bismarck's right. If these Hungarian villains succeed, God help the peace. And he's right, too, that the Emperor can't be warned—"

"It would be fatal!" The Frog spoke for the first time. "There can be no confidence in his judgment. He might well provoke a storm. Bismarck's plan is the only hope."

"It not only preserves the Emperor but deals those Magyar fanatics a fatal blow," says Hutton. "Suppose something arose to make this attempt impossible, they'd just wait for another day— but wipe out their best assassins now, swift and sudden, and they'll not come again!" I could see his eyes fairly gleaming in the shadows. "So it rests with you and von Starnberg—but now you know you have the blessing of our own chief . . . and the French authorities, too, of course," he added quickly, no doubt to keep Jean Crapaud happy.

"M. Grevy approves the plan, and your participation," says Froggy, and smiled grimly. "And your old *copain* of the Legion bids you *'Bonne chance, camarade!'"*

He could only mean Macmahon (who'd never been near me in the bloody Legion, but that's gossip for you), and as I sat rooted and mute at all this appalling news, which had whisked me in a twinkling from the heights of hope to the depths of despair, it struck me that there had been some marvellous secret confabulating in high places lately, hadn't there just? But then, 'tisn't every day that British and French intelligence learn of an idiotic plan by Bismarck to save the Austrian Emperor and prevent bloody war, is it? Gad's me life and blue sacred, they must have thought, Gladstone and Grevy (the Frog-in-chief) must hear about this, and elder wiseacres like Macmahon, and probably D'Israeli . . . and the Queen, God help us, since it's a royal crisis . . . and because they've no notion what to do they convince themselves that Otto's plan is the only course—all the more so because the renowned Flashy, secret diplomatic ruffian extraordinary, former agent of Palmerston and Elgin, veteran of desperate exploits in Central Asia and China and the back o' beyond generally, who's killed more men than the pox and is just the lad for the present crisis, has been recruited to the good cause—never mind how, he's on hand, loaded and ready to fire, your majesty, so don't trouble your royal head about it, all will be well . . . "Indeed, it is most alarming, and too *shocking* that *subjects* should Raise their Hands against their Emperor, whose Royal Person should be *sacred* to them, and the Empress is the *prettiest* and most *charming* creature, and while I could wish that *your* hand, dear Lord Beaconsfield, was at the Helm of the Ship of State in this *crisis,* I dare say that Mr. Gladstone is right, and the matter may be *safely* entrusted to Colonel Flashman, such an *agreeable* man, although my dear Albert thought him a trifle brusque . . ." "Indeed, marm, a somewhat rough diamond, but capable, they say . . ." That would be the gist of it. I could have wept.

For as I sat on the cold bench in the shadows, with waltz music drifting from the casino and my mind numb from the pounding Hutton and this Frog had given it, one thing at least was plain: I was dished. The irony was that in the very moment when I'd eluded Willem and his bullies, running had become impossible. How could I tell Hutton to go to hell with his foul instructions—and have him bearing back to Whitehall (and Windsor and Horse Guards and Pall Mall) the shameful news that the Hector of Afghanistan, hero of Balaclava and Cawnpore, had said thank'ee but he'd rather not save Franz-Josef and the peace of Europe, if you don't mind. My credit, my fame would be blown away; I'd be disgraced, ruined, outcast; the Queen would be *quite shocked*. No, the doom had come upon me, yet again, and I could only cudgel my brains for some respectable alternative to the horror ahead, trying to look stern as I met their eyes, and talking brisk and manly like the gallant old professional they thought I was.

"See here, Hutton," says I, "you know me. I don't croak. But this thing ain't only wild, it's plain foolish. You've got men— well, then, bushwhack these rascals in the grounds, before they get near the lodge—"

"We're seven all told! We couldn't hope to cover the grounds—and if we had more it's odds the Holnup would spot us and cry off to another time."

"But, dammit, man, two men in the house is too few! Suppose they come in force—God knows I'm game, but I ain't young, and Starnberg's only a boy—"

"Never fret about Starnberg! From what I hear he's A1," says Hutton, and laid a hand on my shoulder, damn his impudence. "And I'd back you against odds, however old you are! Now, time's short—"

"But you *must* picket the grounds somehow! If something goes wrong, seven of you could at least—"

"We'll be on hand, colonel, but only at a distance or they'll spot us sure as sin! From this moment we'll have one cover dogging you, every foot o' the way, but more than that we can't do! Now, you'd best rejoin Starnberg and Kralta before they miss you."

"And how the hell do I do that, when you've sandbagged my bloody watchdog? What do I tell 'em, hey? You've blown on me, you gormless ass!"

"Don't you believe it, sir!" He was grinning as he spoke over his shoulder. "How is he?"

"Sleeping sound," chuckles a voice from the dark, and Hutton turned back to me. "Four more unlucky citizens will be assaulted and robbed this fine night, so your cove won't seem out o' place. Damnable, these garotters! Bad as London . . . So your best plan, colonel, is to discover our unconscious friend and raise the alarm, see? How's that for establishing your *bona fides?*" He called it "bonnyfydes"—and why the devil I should remember *that,* of all things, you may well wonder.

"Time to go!" snaps Hutton, straightening up. "Find another victim, eh, Delzons? Off with you, then!" His hand clapped my shoulder again. "All clear, colonel? Not a word about this to Starnberg, mind! You'll see me again . . . afterwards. Good hunting, sir!"

And so help me, he and his lousy Frog accomplice were gone like phantoms into the dark, without another word, leaving me in a rather disturbed state. I'd have cried out after them if I'd been capable of speech; as it was, I had wit enough to see the wisdom of his advice anent Beefy, and after a few seconds' frantic search in the bushes I found the brute, dead to the world, and was waking the echoes with shouts of: *"Helfen! Polizei! Ein Mann ist tot! Helfen, schnell, helfen!"* Thereafter it seemed politic to run towards the casino, repeating my alarm and guiding interested parties to the scene of the crime.

It worked perfectly, of course. Willem was among the first on hand, fairly blazing with unspoken suspicion, which I allayed by explaining that I'd been waiting by the fountain for Kralta when sounds of battery in the bushes had attracted my attention, and on investigating I'd found Beefy supine with two sturdy footpads taking inventory of his pockets. They had fled, I had pursued but lost them in the dark, and returned to minister to Beefy and raise the alarm. And where the blazes were the police, then?

It didn't convince him above half, I'm sure, not at first; I could guess he was wondering why I hadn't taken the chance to vanish . . . and coming slowly to the conclusion that I hadn't wanted to. What sealed the thing was the discovery, a few minutes later, of another unfortunate wandering dazed on the gravel walks and gasping out a tale of armed footpads who'd knocked him down and pinched his watch and purse; half an hour afterwards a third was found unconscious by one of the casino gates, similarly beaten and robbed.

By that time the peelers had arrived in force, shepherding the frightened mob back into the casino, where Beefy and the other victims were being attended to. Plainly a gang of footpads had marked down the casino patrons as well-lined targets, and were making a lightning sweep of the grounds. I made a statement to a most efficient young police inspector, watched closely by a still puzzled Willem with Kralta at his elbow; they were talking *sotto voce*, and if I'd felt like laughing I dare say I'd have been amused at the slow change of expression on Willem's face, for it was clear that she was insisting that here was proof of my sincerity, since not only had I not made for the high hills, I'd absolutely come to Beefy's aid and been first to holler for the law. At last he nodded, but I guessed he was still leery of me—Rudi would have been.

Nothing was said, though, about my "bonnyfydes" as we returned to the Golden Ship, Kralta on my arm murmuring thanks that I hadn't been molested, and Willem snapping impatiently at Beefy, who brought up the rear with his head in a sling. I gathered from their half-heard conversation that Beefy was lamenting the loss of a lock of hair belonging to some bint called Leni which he'd carried in the back of his watch, and getting scant sympathy; Prussians, you know, care not two dams about their inferiors. Neither do I, but I know it's good business to pretend that I do, and looked in on Beefy before retiring to lay a consoling hand on his thick skull; he just gaped like a ruptured bullock.

Being in the throes of fearful depression, I galloped Kralta in a fine frenzy that night, and afterwards fell into a brief nightmare in which Hutton dragged me through the bracken-filled corridors of a great gloomy lodge which turned first into Whampoa's house in Singapore, and then into the Jotunberg dungeons, where Ignatieff was lurking unseen with a shotgun, and Rudi was pursuing me with a blood-stained sabre, and somewhere Charity Spring was roaring: "Stolen your girl's hair, has he? Nothing's safe from the son-of-a-bitch! Aha, but we'll have him presently, *rari nantes in gurgite vasto*,* and be damned to him!" for now I was drowning in the Jotunsee with Narreeman the nautch-dancer strangling me, and then her sneering mask of a face turned into Kralta's, and I woke to find her clinging to me, fast asleep, and my body lathered in sweat.

That was the end of sleep for me. I lay shuddering at the thought of what was to do next day, and even another tupping of the half-drowsing Kralta didn't settle me. To be forced into Bismarck's madness *by my own people* was the crowning unfairness, and I found myself hating Hutton and all his works with a white-hot ferocity. All very well for him, running Gladstone's errands and skulking in safety while poor inoffensive poltroons like me had to contend with murderous maniacs in defence of some useless Hapsburg idiot who knew no better than to give his women social diseases. What galled me more than anything was the knowledge that Hutton and his gang absolutely *enjoyed* their nefarious work—they found two more of his victims plundered insensible in alleys next morning, would you believe it? Pity the traps hadn't caught him red-handed; ten years of skilly and fetters would have done him a power of good.

* Swimming dispersedly in the vasty deep.—Virgil

Chapter 7

One of the lessons that I'd impress on young chaps is this: if you want to pull a bluff, do it with your might, no half-measures. However unlikely the ploy, if your neck is brazen enough, it's odds on you'll get away with it. Take the time I was caught *in flagrante* in a Calcutta hotel by an outraged husband, and sold him on the idea that I was a doctor sounding her chest, or the occasion when they found me climbing through Jefferson Davis's skylight and I pretended I was a workman come to fix his lightning-rod. A moment's guilty hesitation, and I'd have been done for; indignant astonishment at being interfered with saw me through. But I've never done better than Willem von Starnberg in Franz-Josef's woods above Ischl; that was a bravura performance, and would have been a pleasure to witness if I hadn't been writhing in pain after he'd dam' near broken my leg. His father would have been proud of him.

We'd risen well before dawn and made a hurried breakfast—schnapps, mostly, for me, in a futile attempt to steady my nerves—and Kralta was on hand to bid the warriors farewell. Her cheek was like ice when she kissed me, but her lips were hungry enough, and there was moisture in the cold blue eyes and strain showing on the long proud face. She was anxious for me, you see, the besotted little aristo—it's remarkable how even the most worldly of women can be rendered maudlin by Adam's arsenal.

Willem was impatient to be off, and it was more to annoy him than to comfort her that I folded her in a lingering embrace, squeezing her bottom as I assured her that we'd be back in fine trim in a day or two, and then Vienna, ha-ha!

The sun was not yet up, and autumn mist was wreathing over the waters of the Ischl as we crossed the bridges, deserted at that hour, and mounted the slope towards the woods, skirting well to the right of the royal lodge, which lay silent among its surrounding trees; a cock was crowing somewhere, the dew was thick on the short grass, and there was that tang in the nostrils that comes only at daybreak. We were attired as tourist walkers, in tweeds, boots, and gaiters, Willem carrying a rucksack and I a flask and sandwich-case, and it was only when we had reached the higher woods and paused to look back at the lodge, and beyond and beneath it the distant roofs of Ischl town, gilded now by the first rays of the rising sun, that it struck me I was without one necessary item of equipment. When, I asked, was I to be armed for the fray?

"Not yet awhile," smiles Willem. "Remember that presently you're going to be a limping invalid, who's sure to be examined by a doctor, and we don't want him blundering through your clobber and finding the likes of these, do we?" He opened the rucksack to display two revolvers, a Webley and a LeVaux. "I like an English piece myself, but the LeVaux's neat enough for your pocket and fires a .45 slug, guaranteed to give any marauder the deuce of a bellyache. Take your choice."

Without thinking, I indicated the LeVaux . . . and so saved my life, and Franz-Josef's, and heaven knows how many million other lives as well. If I'd chosen the Webley, Europe would probably have gone to war in '83. Think I'm stretching? Wait and see.

"We'll have twenty rounds apiece," says Willem, stowing away the guns. "If we need more . . . then we shall also need the Austrian army." His impatience had gone now that we were under way, and he was in that insufferably jocular mood that his father had affected whenever dirty work was imminent. "Now, 'twill be curtain up in a little while, so let's rehearse our cues, shall we?"

We found a dry fallen tree trunk in the margin of the woods, and he repeated in detail the mad procedure which he'd described on the train, and again at the Golden Ship. It still sounded devilish chancy—suppose Franz-Josef hadn't got up this morning, or didn't invite us to stay, what then? I asked. He shook his head as at a mistrustful child, and was just assuring me patiently that it would all fall out precisely as the genius Otto had forecast, when from somewhere in the woods above us there came the distant sound of a gunshot.

"There, you see!" cries he, springing afoot. "Our royal host is doin' the local chamois a piece of no good!"

"How d'ye know it's him? It might be anyone!"

"It might be the Aston Villa brake-club picnic, but I doubt it! In the Emperor's personal woods?" He swung up his rucksack and plunged into the trees. "Come on!"

We pushed rapidly uphill into the woods, down into a little hollow, and up again over a steep stony place, and now there came two shots in quick succession, much closer and off to our left.

"Wait here!" says Willem, and was off into the undergrowth at a run. I breathed myself against a tree, debating whether to rush blindly downhill away from this fatal nonsense, remembered Hutton and the Queen, and stood there sweating and gnashing my teeth—and here he was again, face alight with unholy joy, slithering towards me over the fallen leaves and needles.

"Eureka! He's there, large as life, havin' a smoke while his loader measures the horns of some dead beast which I suppose he's shot! Couldn't be better!" He caught me by the shoulder. "Now's the hour, Harry my boy! This is where you rick your ankle, and I holler for help! Ready?"

"You're raving mad!" says I, through chattering teeth. "You and Bismarck both—oh, Christ!"

For the swine had fetched me a sudden shattering kick above the ankle, and I went down in agony, fairly writhing on the leaves as I clutched my injured limb and damned him to Hell and beyond. It was as though I'd been shot—and he stepped over me, measured his distance, and kicked me savagely again, in almost the same place.

"If you've hurt yourself, the medico's got to have somethin' to look at, you know!" grins he. "Not so loud, you ass, or they'll think you're dyin'! Groan, and try to look gallantly long-sufferin'!"

I was too dizzy with pain to do anything but curse and weep, and now he was away again, yelling, *"Helfen, mein Herr!"* while I tried to pull myself up by a tree, wrenching at my gaiter-buttons and sock to reveal an ankle that was grazed bloody and already turning blue. God, had he broken it? I nursed the injury with both hands, feeling it beginning to puff and swell, and now footsteps were approaching, Willem's voice raised in concern.

". . . caught his leg between two stones, I think. I don't believe it's broken, but too badly wrenched to walk, I fear. On the first day of our expedition, too!"

"You say your friend is an Englishman?" It was a deep voice, curiously flat and deliberate.

"Why, yes, an Army acquaintance. Neither of us has been to the Saltzkammergut before, you see, and we planned . . . ah, here he is! How is it, Harry? I say, it looks bad!" He turned to his companion. "By the way, I am Count Willem von Starnberg . . . Herr . . . ?" He finished on a question, the cunning young bastard, letting on that he didn't know whom he was addressing, and I gritted my teeth and tried to act up, noting as I did so that it was a good job there were no Highland regiments in the Austrian service, for the Emperor Franz-Josef would have looked abominable in a kilt, with those knobbly knock-knees looking like knuckle-ends between his woollen stockings and his little black *lederhosen*. He wore a shooting jacket and a ridiculous hat with a feather, but there was nothing clownish about the austere frowning face with its heavy whiskers as he stooped to survey my damage. Nothing sympathetic, either, just bovine serious.

"It needs attention," was the royal diagnosis. "Can you walk, sir?"

There must be an actor buried in me, for as Willem bent to help me, and I met Franz-Josef's heavy stare, I fairly gaped wide-eyed and made as though to scramble up.

"My God!" I croaked. "Your majesty! I . . . I . . ." Babble, babble, babble, while Willem looked suitably startled and clicked his heels, and Franz-Josef made another of his lightning deductions.

"You know me?"

Didn't I just, though, begging his pardon, introducing myself with profuse apologies for coming adrift in his coverts, doffing my tile while Willem did likewise, bowing like a clockwork doll while Franz-Josef registered amazement by blinking thoughtfully.

"The officer of Mexico!" says he. "You are he who attempted to save my unhappy brother. I invested you with the Order of Maria Theresa, at Corfu, was it not?"

After that, it was old home week with a vengeance, with Franz-Josef nodding gravely, Willem protesting that we were a hellish nuisance, All-Highest, and wouldn't have dreamed of intruding if we'd only known, Flashy clinging gamely to his tree, and presently even more gamely to the stalwart back of the loader, who was summoned to tote me downhill. I lay there, breathing in his aroma of rifle-oil and cow-dung, wondering what the harvest might be, and Willem walked ahead with Franz-Josef, making deferential noises of gratitude and apology, and to my astonishment making his majesty laugh—say that for the Starnbergs, they could charm birds from the trees when they wanted to, and by the time we reached the lodge the Emperor of Austria was positively jocose, issuing orders to flying minions, and not going off to change his ghastly breeks until he had seen me installed on a couch in a gun-room, with servitors rallying round with hot water and cold compresses, and Willem chivvying them aside while he attended to my bandages himself.

"We're there," he murmured softly. "He knows my family, by name, anyway." I could have said that if he'd known any more of the Starnbergs than that, we'd have been on our way to gaol this minute, but held my peace. "Play up when the doctor comes, mind."

Which I did, with Willem and Franz-Josef, now respectable in a suit, standing by. The sawbones was a plump little cove with gooseberry eyes and trailing whiskers who prodded my injury and pronounced it ugly, but seemed to think I ought to be able to hobble. Capital, thinks I, there'll be no reason to offer us house-room, and we can scuttle back to Ischl and let the Holnup have a free run, but Willem had the answer to that, rot him.

"Your thigh wound, remember," says he, very sober. "A serious injury from my friend's Afghan days," he assured the doctor, "which reacts to any distemper in the limb. Why, Harry, you were laid up for a week in Scotland, I recall, when you'd done no more than stub your toe!"

Observe the guile of it: he knew that if anything appealed to Franz-Josef it was an honourable scar; he was soldier-daft and had himself risked life and limb with extraordinary stupidity during his various campaigns—all of which he'd lost, by the way. So now you find Flashy lying trowserless while the doctor goggled at the impressive scar on my thigh, and the knee wound I'd taken at Harper's Ferry, and even the hole in my buttock where the slave catchers shot me while crossing the frozen Ohio, with Willem murmuring to an impressed Franz-Josef that this wasn't the half of it, you ought to see the rest of the bugger's carcase, not an inch of it whole, I assure your majesty, hell of a life the boy's led, honestly. Or words to that effect.

The Emperor shook his head in respectful wonder, and the

linseed lancer, taking his cue, muttered about secondary reaction and delayed muscular lesions; it might well be, he opined, that even a minor contusion might render a limb temporarily inca-pable. At which Willem played his master-stroke.

"Well, old feller, I can see we'll just have to carry you down to Ischl! Is the thigh very painful? Ne'er mind, I'll whistle up a chair or something, and a few handy chaps . . . if your majesty," says he, with another bow and heel-click, "will be gracious enough to allow my friend to rest here while I make arrange-ments . . . no more than an hour . . . profound apologies . . . great imposition . . . there, there, old chap, just bite on something . . ."

It would have had Scrooge piping his eye. Franz-Josef glow-ered at the doctor and said it would be unwise to move me, surely, and the poultice-walloper agreed that it would be nothing short of bloody reckless. *Richtig*, announced Franz-Josef, then the gentleman stays here, at least until he can walk without diffi-culty, so fall in the loyal attendants.

Willem's protests were pretty to hear, but Franz-Josef wouldn't even listen. Unthinkable that I should be moved in my present state. It would be a privilege to entertain so gallant an officer, to whom his majesty was already indebted for services to the royal family. Count Starnberg must remain also. If my injury permitted, we would give the Emperor the pleasure of our com-pany at dinner. In the meantime, affairs required his attendance elsewhere.

By this time I was beginning to wonder if I'd ever walk again, and it was with some relief that I discovered, after I'd been borne upstairs between two servants and left in a comfortable chamber overlooking the garden, that I could move without the least diffi-culty, and was none the worse except for an uncomfortable bruise. Willem suggested that I should recover sufficiently to hobble by dinner-time. "We're goin' to be afoot tonight," says he, "and it wouldn't do for you to be encountered walkin' if you were meant to be bed-bound, you poor old cripple, you." He was in bouncy fettle, inviting me to admire the way everything had gone exactly according to plan, pacing up and down with his cigarette-holder at a jaunty angle. "A heavy limp, I think, with the aid of a stick. Too late for F-J to turn us out of doors now, what?"

I asked how on earth he'd known so much about my wounds, and received his superior grin. "You can't get it into your head, can you? Bismarck has a genius for detail—why, I know as much about your battle scars as you do!" He reached suddenly to tousle my hair, curse him. "Got yourself scalped by Indians in the wild and woolly west, even! Oh, yes," says the insolent pup, "I've seen a dossier on you that I'll bet contains things you've forgotten—perhaps never knew. You've been about, though—my stars, I hope I'll see half as much by the end of the day." He shook his handsome head, and the admiring look of our first meeting was back again.

"The guv'nor was right—you're the complete hand and no mistake. On that train, there you were, wonderin' what the dooce you'd fallen into, ensnared by a sinister adventuress, menaced by a bravo with a pistol—but did you cry havoc, or bluster, or vow to have the law on us? Well, once—and then mum as an oyster, figurin' chances, listenin' and bidin' your time. I didn't trust you an inch, then; Kralta did, though, and she's no fool, even if she is spoony about you. But it took that business of Gunther gettin' scragged at the casino to convince me—then I knew you must be with us!" He grinned, tongue in cheek. "And it ain't for Franz-Josef or the good o' the peace, is it? It's just for devilment!" He slapped his knee, merry as a maggot. "I like you, Harry, shot if I don't! And we'll have some fun together, just you wait and see!"

He sprang up and tossed his cigarette into the fireplace. "Now then, I'm goin' to take a scout about, get the lie of the land and find out who does what and goes where and when and why. Rub an acquaintance with the aides, if I can, and take a professional interest in this sergeant and his file of sentinels." This with a knowing wink. "You lie and rest your mangled pin, and when I come back we can discuss ways and means, eh?" He chewed his lip and tapped another gasper on his thumbnail, looking keen. "D'ye know, I've a notion tonight is goin' to be the night! Can't tell why—just an instinct. You ever feel that sort of thing?"

"When I was young and green—yes," growls I, to take the bounce out of him. "Sign of nerves, Starnberg. You just wish it was over and done with."

It didn't deflate him a bit. "Nerves yourself!" scoffs he. "If you mean I'm lookin' forward to it, you're right." I believed him, for I'd seen the same bright-eyed excitement at the prospect of slaughter in idiots like Brooke and Custer, and it's the last thing you need when your own fears are gullet-high. "That reminds me," he went on, "time you were properly dressed." He drew the LeVaux from his pocket, spun it deftly, and presented the butt. "Five chambers loaded. I'll give you the other rounds later. Shove it out o' sight for the moment."

Being armed was some comfort, but not much. Like his blasted instinct, it was just a reminder of how close the doom was coming, perhaps only a few short hours away. In the meantime, left to myself, I could only wait, fretting and resting my bogus injury on the sofa, while soft-footed orderlies came and clicked their heels and asked leave to arrange the room and see to the linen and mend the fire and stow away my effects, which must have been sent for to the Golden Ship (trust Willem), and bring me coffee, which I shared with two sprightly youths who were Franz-Josef's aides, come to pay their respects to the wounded guest. I forget their names, but thought of them as Tweedledum and Tweedledee, one fair, one dark, but identical in gaiety, indiscretion, and breezy but deferential attention to me—Tweedledee knew of me by name and fame, and was athirst for reminiscences, but since Tweedledum's interest was merely polite, and I'm an old hand at *not* being pumped, it was child's play to steer the conversation elsewhere.

Thus I learned in short order that Ischl was a confounded

bore, and that it was common gossip that the Emperor was only here because he'd hoped to achieve a reconciliation with Sissi, who was in one of her fits of avoiding Vienna, but had half-agreed to come to Ischl, only she hadn't, more's the pity, for squiring her on horseback would have been a welcome diversion. Never mind, they'd be back in Vienna on Sunday, thank God, and free of the tyranny of the Chief Equerry, who was a muff and a sneak, and of the ordeal of dining with the Emperor, and being used as errand-boys by his secretary, and why the old boy had to spend all day poring over papers when he was meant to be on holiday, beat them altogether. Kept him out of the way, of course, even at luncheon, which was a mercy, since his usual fare was boiled beef and beer at his desk; at least they were spared that. Here, though, my chum Starnberg was a splendid fellow, wasn't he; just the chap to liven up a slow week. And so on, and so on; it would be a dull world if there were no subalterns in it. Quieter, mind you.

They went at last, with noisy jests and good wishes, and I was left to brood until an orderly brought luncheon on a tray—not boiled beef, as I recall, but I was too blue and shaky to make much of whatever it was. I'd barely finished when Willem returned, making a great show of closing the door silently, tiptoeing to sit on my sofa, and speaking in a whisper.

"It's too good to be true! Harry, my boy, I can't believe our luck! Why, it'll be child's play!" He rubbed his hands, chuckling. "I've found the outer door to the Emperor's secret stairway, I'm almost certain! How's that for intelligence work?" He lighted one of his eternal black cigarettes and puffed in triumph.

"I bumped into the sergeant of the guard, accidental-a-purpose. A waxed-moustached old turnip-head who's so damned military he probably rides his wife by numbers—almost ruptured himself comin' to attention when I happened by. I played the condescendin' Junker, commended his turn-out, complimented him on being chosen for such important duty . . ." he waved his holder airily ". . . you know the style. The old fool was so flattered he confessed the job was mostly ceremonial, mindin' the front door, salutin' the Emperor and so on.

" 'But you mount night sentries, surely?' says I. 'One only, *Herr Oberst*,' says he. 'Ah, patrolling, to be sure,' says I. 'By no means, *Herr Oberst*, a fixed post at the sundial corner only.' 'Why there? Can't tell the time at night!' says I. Gad, I was genial! Harry—he didn't know why! Said it was regulations, since God was a boy."

He was so full of himself he couldn't be still, jumping up and pacing to and fro. "That was enough for me. I chatted a moment more, as is my wont, and strolled round by the sundial corner, as he called it. Sentry-box, sure enough—and a few yards farther on an embrasure in the ivy with an old locked door! The window of the Emperor's bedchamber is about twenty feet beyond on the storey above. Well," cries he, "what d'ye think of that for scoutin'?"

Too good to be true, indeed—yet, why not? It fitted . . . if the secret stairway really existed, and I had respect enough for Bismarck's spy *bandobast** to be confident that it did.

"So now," cries Willem, "we know just where to watch!"

"If it is the secret door, and they come that way—"

"It is, and they will!" says he impatiently. "I'm sure of it. But we'll run no risks." He pulled a chair beside the sofa, and sat close. "I've thought it all out, and I'm afraid," says he with a mock-rueful grin, "that you mayn't like it, 'cos you'll miss most o' the sport. Sorry, old chap."

From that moment, you may be sure, I was all ears.

"It's this way. My room's next door here, but we're some way from the Emperor's quarters. Our corridor leads to the main part of the house, which is like so many of these royal places, one room opening on to another and then another, and so on. But then

* organisation (Hind.)

there's another passage to the Emperor's rooms—an ante-room where his orderly sleeps, and then the royal bedchamber over-lookin' the sundial garden. There's a room off the passage for the aides—ah, you've met 'em, couple of society buffoons. So that's the lie o' the land."

He paused to light another whiff. "You see the point—there are only two ways to come at Franz-Josef; either by the secret stair or along the passage leadin' past the aides' room to his quarters. Plug those, and he's secure. Now," says he, leaning close, "I'll lay odds the Holnup will come through the garden in the dead watch, around four, lay out the sentry quietly, jemmy the door, then upstairs and good-night Franz-Josef, all hail Crown Prince Rudolf! But, just in case they enter the house some other way, one of us will lurk by the passage, while t'other is in the garden, coverin' the secret doorway. You follow?"

I followed, and relief was surging through me like the wave of the sea as he went on.

"You at the passage . . . *et moi* in the garden. No, shut up, Harry—it must be so because once the smoke has cleared and the Holnup are laid stiff and stark, I can say I couldn't sleep and was just takin' a stroll and ran into 'em, see? That wouldn't answer for you, with your game leg. Whereas if you're watchin' the passage *inside*, and someone happens along, you can always say you were lookin' for the thunder-closet."

"That means," says I frowning, "that you'll tackle 'em alone—one against perhaps three, perhaps more."

"No more than three, if so many," says he, baring his teeth. "Never fear, Harry, they're dead men." His hands moved like lightning, and there was the Webley in one fist and the Derringer in t'other. "With all respect, old fellow, I doubt if you're as quick with a piece as I, or as good a shot."

"Don't know about that," says I, looking glum while repress-ing an urge to sing Hallelujah. "How many night ambushes have you laid?"

"Enough," says he jauntily. "Cheer up—perhaps they'll come through the house after all!"

"And afterwards—how d'you explain that you went for a night stroll with a gun in your pocket?"

"I didn't. Discoverin' miscreants tryin' to break in with evil intent, I gamely tackled 'em, disarmed one, and . . . Bob's your uncle, as they say."

"I still don't like it," I lied. "We'd be better with two in the garden—"

"No," says he flatly. "One must be in the house . . . you. When you hear a shot, make for your room, and then emerge hobblin' and roarin' for enlightenment—"

"When I hear a shot, I'll be out o' doors before you know it. You may be good, Starnberg, but I've forgotten more about night fighting than you'll ever know. And that, my son, is that." It's always been second nature with me to act sullen-reluctant when I've been denied the prospect of battle and murder; suits my character, you see. In the event that he had to tackle the Holnup alone, the last thing I'd dream of doing would be to hasten to his aid; back to bed and snug down deaf as a post, that would be the ticket for Flashy, and he could have the glory to himself—which, I realised, was what he'd intended all along; I'd been necessary for gaining admittance, and all the rest had been so much gas. Well, good luck, Willem, and I hope you kill a lot of Hungarians.

In the meantime I looked sour, vowing to be in at the death, and he laughed and said, well, so be it, my presence in the garden with my game leg might seem odd, but with the Emperor preserved no one would think twice about it, likely. Then he took a big breath and sat back, delighted with himself and his planning, and fell to admiring Bismarck's uncanny genius, and how it was all falling out precisely as he had forecast. But mostly he was nursing his blood lust, I knew, anticipating the pleasure of shooting assassins—in the back, no doubt. He was what Hickok called "a killing gentleman," was our Willem. Just like dear old dad.

Dinner at five with Franz-Josef would have been a dam' dreary business, no doubt, if I hadn't been so full of inward rejoicing at my reprieve, and consequently at peace with all mankind. I made my appearance limping on a stick, and his majesty combined his congratulations with a dour warning against over-exertion. He was one of these unfortunates who have been created stuffy by God, and whose efforts to unbend create discomfort and unease in all concerned, chiefly himself. It reminded me of a pompous master condescending to the fags; even when he had the words he couldn't get the tune at all.

For example, when he informed me over the soup that he had only poor command of English, he managed to convey that the fault lay not only with his boyhood tutors, but with me for speaking the dam' language in the first place; even his compliment to my German sounded like a reproach. I responded with a wheeze I'd once heard (from Bismarck, as it happens) that a gift for languages was useful only to head-waiters, and Willem played up by saying he'd been told that it was a sign of low intelligence. Franz-Josef rolled a bread-pill gloomily and said that wasn't what his tutors had told him, and he had no experience of head-waiters. After this flying start we ate in silence until Franz-Josef began to question me solemnly about Indian Army camp discipline and sanitary arrangements, with particular reference to care of the feet in hot climates. I did my best, and like a fool ventured Wellington's joke when the Queen asked him what was the aroma from the ranks of the Guards, and Nosey replied: "*Esprit de corps*, ma'am." That was met with a vacant stare, so I guessed he didn't speak French too well either.

The only topics that seemed to bring him to life were horses and game-shooting. He knew his business about the former, and was, I'm told, an expert rider; as for the latter, about which he prosed interminably, I can say only that my abiding memory of Ischl lodge is of rank upon rank of chamois horns covering the walls from floor to ceiling, wherever you went, all shot by the royal sportsman. There must have been thousands of them.[18]

After dinner the real merriment began when we played a game of *tarok,* a sort of whist, and I can testify that to his linguistic shortcomings the Austrian Emperor added an inability to count, and pondered each card at length before playing it. I guess the fun was too much for him, for after a couple of rubbers he went back to work at his desk, and we were free to return to our rooms . . . and wait.

I can't recall many nights longer than that one. Even though I'd been excused active service, so to speak (assuming the enemy didn't come through the house), I was like a cat on hot bricks, and Willem was no better. We played every two-handed game we knew in my room, and he was too edgy to cheat, even. About eight o'clock an orderly brought us tea, when what I needed was brandy, about a pint and a half, and we learned that the Emperor was used to retire to bed about nine, and the establishment closed down accordingly. Sure enough, we heard the tramp of the sergeant and sentry beneath the window, marching round the house, and distant words of command as the sentry was posted.

"Damned old martinet!" mutters Willem, as we heard the heavy tread of the sergeant's return, fading as he went round to the guard-house at the front. "Imagine barkin' orders as if it were a parade. I suppose it's for Franz-Josef's benefit as he says his prayers. The sentry's relieved every three hours, by the way, and you may be sure the Holnup know that, so between three and six will be their best time. We'll be on the watch from ten, though; they'd hardly come before that."

We were standing at the window as he spoke, looking out into the darkened garden, palely lit by the moon in its last quarter, the bushes casting shadows on the turf, and the dark mass of the trees against the night sky with the wind barely ruffling their leaves.

Beneath us there was the sound of a lower window being shuttered, a door banged and we could hear the smack of the bolts thrust home; from somewhere within the house a distant clock sounded the half-hour, and then the only noise was the faint occasional creak of the house itself as it settled for another peaceful night.

I was aware of a faint tapping, and was well pleased to note that it was Willem's fingers playing on the sill. But the handsome face was serene enough now, and when he caught my glance at his restless hand he laughed softly. "Waitin' for the kick-off, eh?" says he. "Or going out to open the battin'. You played at all?"

"If your dossier on me was complete you'd know I took five for twelve against All-England," says I, and he whistled, but when I added that I'd once downed Felix, Pilch, and Mynn in three balls, the ignorant brute had never heard of 'em.* " 'Fore my time," says he. "Grace, now—there's a bat for you." So we talked cricket, while waiting for the attempted murder of the Austrian Emperor. Well, I've known odder conversations on the brink of desperate action.

When the distant chime of ten sounded he slipped away and returned in his night-stalking attire: dark shirt and trowsers with a heavy woollen jersey, light hunting boots, and flask and pistol all stowed away; there was a wicked-looking hunting knife sheathed at his belt.

"You never know what you need until you need it," says he. "Don't fret, I'll be rid of it before any investigation begins." He patted the hilt, and it struck me yet again, watching his quick deft movements, the easy way he held himself, the bright questing eyes, and the confident half-smile on the chiselled face, that there were plenty of fellows I'd rather meet in a dark lane than Willem von Starnberg. He was on a hair-trigger, and enjoying every moment of it.

* See *Flashman's Lady*

"Got your piece?" says he. "Good. I've had a look-see, and the place is like a tomb. What price Ischl for high jinks, eh? I'd rather have Stockholm on a Sunday! Now, I'll take you along to your post, which is in the last of the day-rooms from which the passage runs to the Emperor's billet and the aides' quarters. There's a nice shadowy corner where you can watch the passage entry, and on t'other side of the room there's a flight of stairs leading down to a little hall, where I'll get out by a window." He paused, thinking. "If they come tonight, as I feel they will, you'd best use your judgment when the shootin' starts. A few quick shots will mean it's all over; if there's still firin' after twenty seconds . . . well, 'twill mean there are more of 'em than I bargain for. If they don't come, back to bed with you when the house begins to stir. I'll be out takin' the morning air," he added, with a wink. "All clear, then? All serene-o?"

It wasn't, of course, but I gave him my resolute chin-up look, and got his approving nod. "Best take your stick, in case anyone comes on you unexpected in the small hours, tho' I doubt if there'll be a soul about before dawn. Unless," says he, looking comical, "the Holnup diddle us by coming through the house, in which case . . . well, good huntin', you lucky bastard!"

He moved quickly to the door, peeped out, and slipped into the corridor, motioning me to follow. There was a light burning at the far end, but not a sound in the building save the occasional creak of its timbers. Willem flitted ahead like a ghost, and what we'd have said if someone had popped a head out and found us roaming the darkened house, God knows. We crossed what he'd called the day-rooms one after another; they had lamps burning low, and here and there the waning moon struck a shaft of light through a window, and the embers of a fire glowed in the shadows.

At last he paused, flicking a finger to his left, and I saw a flight of stairs leading down into the blackness. He pointed to his right, and there was the dark opening of the passage leading to Franz-

Josef's room. A lamp gleamed dimly on a table at the passage entry, and now Willem pointed to a shadowy corner to the left of the passage and a few feet from it, where I could see a big leather chair. At his nod I moved quietly towards it; then he blew out the passage light, leaving the room in darkness.

I didn't hear him move, but suddenly I sensed him beside me, his hand gripping mine, and his voice close to my ear; "Good luck, old 'un!," and then a whispered chuckle. "Ain't this the life, though?" Infernal idiot. A second later his shadow was at the head of the stairs, and soon after I heard below the faint noise of a sash being raised and closed again, and good riddance.

And then . . . well, d'you know, there was nothing to do but sit about, a prey to what they call conflicting emotions. I'd run a fair range of them in the past few days, some damned disturbing, a few delightful with Kralta, but mostly bewildering, and now, seated in that great leather contraption, I tried to take stock of what was, you'll allow, an unusual situation. Here was I, in the summer residence of the Emperor of Austria, loaded for bear, waiting for bloody murder to break out in his policies, but the odd thing was that now that the grip had come, I wasn't more than half nervous, let alone scared. I was as well out of harm's way as any man in the place, Willem could bear the brunt—and the aftermath, with everyone behaving like headless chickens, should provide some entertainment. He'd be the hero of the hour (if he lived), but I'd garner some credit if only by limping about looking stern and impressing the excitable kraut-eaters with my British phlegm. A little discreet lying when I saw Hutton again would ensure that favourable reports reached London and Paris (and Windsor, eh?), and after an amiable parting from Franz-Josef it would be hey for Vienna! with a grateful and adoring Kralta.

She was a happy thought as I sat cosily ensconced in the dark, still warm from the dead fireplace. Odd female, handsome enough in her horsy way, with the body of a Dahomey Amazon and appetite to match, but would she have boiled my kettle in the ordinary way of things? Perhaps 'twas the strange circumstances in which we'd met, or the contrast between her icy, damn-you style and the passion with which she performed, that had me drying my chin at my randy recollections: that fur robe slipping to the floor, like the unveiling of a lovely marble statue, the long limbs entwining with mine, the silky hair across my face . . . aye, Vienna beckoned, right enough, and on those blissful imaginings I settled comfortably to my vigil in the hours ahead . . .

. . . to awake with a start, shivering against the cold that had stolen over the darkened room while I slept—for how long? The soft single chime of a clock might mean one o'clock or a quarter, but I had no feeling of cramp, so I couldn't have been far under . . . but what had wakened me? The clock, or the cold, or some other disturbance—and suddenly my hair bristled on my neck as I became aware of a faint scraping sound from the hall below, followed by a rustle and a soft thump . . . Jesus! there was someone moving there, and the scrape had been the raising of the window by which Willem had departed—could he be returning? No, why the hell should he? But who, then . . . and I froze in terror, the sweat breaking out on me like ice, for it could mean only one thing, that the stupid swine's calculations had been all wrong, and the Holnup had never heard of his confounded secret stair, but were slipping into the house burglar-style, intent on their murderous errand, and even now cloaked and sinister figures were at the foot of the stairs, listening, then gliding stealthily forward . . . a stair creaked sharply, and I started half out of my chair, fumbling for the LeVaux, straining eyes and ears against the dark . . . another creak, and a hissing whisper, someone stumbled and cursed, and then to my amazement a voice began croaking softly in drunken song about *liebe kleine Matilde*, only to be hushed by a snarled oath and "*Wo ist die Kerze? Streichholz, Dummkopf!*" followed by a giggling hiccup; a match rasped in the gloom, a faint glow appeared below, and I almost collapsed with relief as slowly up the stairs lurched Tweedledum, holding a candle unsteadily aloft, with Tweedledee clinging to him for support.

They were in dress uniform, and by the look of them had crawled through every pub in Ischl; I've seldom seen tighter subalterns, but Tweedledum at least was plainly alive to the danger of waking the Emperor, for he staggered with elaborate caution, whispering to his mate to be quiet, and must have seen me in my corner if Tweedledee hadn't blown the candle out with an enormous belch. This set him giggling again, Tweedledum dropped the matches, they blundered whimpering in the dark, and would most certainly have come to grief if Tweedledum hadn't insisted that they proceed on hands and knees. They crawled through the furniture more or less quietly, and presently I heard their door close softly, and peace returned to the royal lodge.

But not to me. Perhaps it was the cold, or the unholy scare they'd given me, but as I sat shivering in the dark, envying those drunken pups their beds, I was conscious of a growing unease which was quite at odds with the lustful moonings about Kralta on which I'd dropped off. I couldn't figure it; nothing about my situation had changed, and yet where I'd been fairly tranquil before I was now thoroughly rattled. Very well, I'm a windy beggar whose hopes and fears go up and down like a jack-in-the-box, but this wasn't so much fear as a presentiment that something was wrong, damned wrong, and I couldn't put my finger on it. 'Twasn't a logical foreboding, but pure animal instinct—and thank God for it, 'cos it made me stir restlessly, and my fidgeting changed the course of history.

At the recent alarm I had clutched at the LeVaux in my pocket, and at some point must have drawn it, for now I found I was nervously fiddling its patent safety catch, on and off, and turning the cylinder. That reminded me, with a nasty start, that Willem hadn't given me the promised extra rounds. He'd said it was loaded in five chambers, and in sudden anxiety I probed with my pinky in the dark, trying to feel the tips of the slugs in the cylinders, but couldn't, so I broke the piece open, not knowing that it was one of the new-fangled models with an extractor plate that whips all the shells out together, and squealed with dismay as bullets flew broadcast, clattering on the floor and rolling God alone knew where—and there I was, with an unloaded firearm, my ammunition hopelessly lost in the dark, and nothing for it but to grovel blindly in search of the bloody things, cursing fate and the imbecility of French gunsmiths and their ridiculous patent gadgets, as if anyone needed them.

Frantic scrabbling round the chair brought one bullet to hand, leaving four to find, and since I'd no intention of having only a single shot between me and damnation, I must have light, whatever the consequences. I had no matches—but, stay! Tweedledum had dropped his somewhere, I'd heard them spilling all over the shop, so now I went panting on all fours in quest of them, lost my bearings altogether, fell into the fireplace, struggled out coated in dead ash, fetched my head a shattering crash on a chair-leg, and only found the scattered matches when I knelt on them. In a trice I had one lighted and was kindling the lamp, and a moment later I had scooped up three of the fallen rounds near the chair and was casting about for the fourth.

It was lying close to the fender—at least the case was, but I drew in an astonished breath when I saw that the bullet itself had become detached and lay a few inches away. In fifty years of handling firearms I'd never known the like: what, a slug clamped tight in the brass case (which contained the explosive charge) coming asunder? With a trembling hand I turned the little case to the light: it was empty, and there wasn't a trace of powder where it had fallen.

An icy hand gripped my stomach as I held each of the other whole rounds in turn close to the lamp. Every one bore marks on the edge of the case, as though it had been pried back to remove the slug; indeed, I was able to pull one bullet free and saw to my horror that the case itself was empty.

Willem had removed the charges from all five cartridges, replacing the slugs in them so that they looked like live rounds, and if one hadn't come loose in falling to the floor, I'd never have known that I had, in effect, an empty revolver.

Chapter 8

The discovery that you've been sold a pup is always disconcerting, but your reaction depends on age and experience. In infancy you burst into tears and smash something; in adolescence you may be bewildered (as I was when Lady Geraldine lured me into the long grass on false pretence and then set about me with carnal intent, hurrah!); in riper manhood common sense usually tells you to bolt, which was my instinct on the Pearl River when I learned that my lorcha was carrying not opium, as I'd supposed, but guns for the Taiping rebels. But at sixty-one your brain works faster than your legs, so you reflect, and as often as not reach the right answer by intuition as well as reason.

Kneeling in that cold shadowy chamber, goggling at those five useless rounds gleaming in the dim lamplight, I *knew* in a split second that Willem himself was the assassin, not the guardian, and now that I'd served my turn by helping him to within striking distance of the Emperor, he'd rendered me powerless to intervene in his murderous scheme. But it was a staggering thought—dammit, why should he, a German Junker, a trusted agent of Bismarck, want to kill Franz-Josef, doing the dirty work of Hungarian fanatics like Kossuth and the Holnup? . . . Kossuth, by God! That was the bell that rang to confirm my conclusion, as I remembered him telling me on the train that *his own mother's name* was Kossuth, and that he was part-Hungarian by blood.

Aye, and pure Hungarian, devil a doubt, in heart and soul and allegiance, flown with the wild dream of independence for his mother country, and itching to fire the shot or wield the steel that would set her free—and plunge Europe into civil war.

All this surmised in an instant, and whether 'twas all another great devilment of Bismarck's, or whether Bismarck was guiltless and Willem had duped him as he'd duped me, didn't matter. One thing was sure: I was implicated up to the neck, and as I knelt there sweating my imagination was picturing Willem out yonder, full of spite and sin, disposing of the hapless sentry, humouring the lock of the secret door, stealing up the secret stair knife in hand to the room where his royal victim was asleep . . . or dead already? I glanced in terror towards the passage entry—quick or dead, Franz-Josef was within forty feet of me . . . oh, Christ, how long had Willem been gone? I didn't know. Was it too late to stop him? Perhaps not . . . but that was no work for me, bigod, not if I'd had ten loaded pistols and the Royal Marines at my back; not for Franz-Josef and a dozen like him would I have gone up against Willem von Starnberg, and as for Europe . . . but even as I took the first instinctive stride of panic-stricken flight, I came to a shuddering halt as the awful truth struck me.

I couldn't run! It would be certain death, for if Willem had killed, or was about to kill, the Emperor, I'd be seen as his partner in crime, and while he would have his own escape nicely planned, I'd not have the ghost of a chance of avoiding capture, with the whole country on the look-out. And I'd never persuade them I was an innocent tool, or acting under orders from Downing Street—why, it was odds on I'd be shot on sight or cut down on the spot before I could utter a word in my defence.

I didn't faint at the thought, but only the knowledge that I must act at once enabled me to fight down my mounting panic. Should I raise the alarm? God, no, I daren't, for if Franz-Josef was already a goner, I'd be cooked. The only hope was that Willem hadn't done for him yet, and that I could still . . . and that was when my legs almost gave way, and I found myself fairly sobbing with fear, for I knew I must go out into the ghastly dark, and find the murderous bastard and kill or disable him . . . why, even if Franz-Josef was already tuning up with the choir invisible I might wriggle clear if I could show that I'd flown to the rescue . . . too late, alas . . . oh Jesus, they'd never believe me!

"I'm innocent, gentlemen, I swear it!" I was bleating it softly in the darkness, and time was racing by, and I'd nothing but an empty pistol . . . but suppose Willem was still picking the lock, or waiting for moon-set, or for his Holnup confederates to arrive, or pausing to relieve himself or have a smoke, or for any other reason you like, and I could just steel myself to sally forth and find him, whispering raucously to identify myself . . . well, he might wonder what the blazes I was about, but he'd not shoot before asking questions . . . and I still had the seaman's knife I'd slipped into my boot on the Orient Express, and he'd be off guard (just as his father had been when I'd parted his hair with the cherry brandy bottle)—he might even turn his back on me . . . well, it was that or the hangman's rope, unless they still went in for beheading in Austria.

On that happy thought I put up my empty piece, transferred the knife from my boot to my pocket, and crept as fast as might be down the stairs with my heart against my back teeth. There was the window, pale in the gloom; I slipped over the sill to the ground . . . and realised I'd no notion where the sundial corner was. I forced myself to envisage the house from above . . . there was the Emperor's room, here was I, on t'other side, and there the guardroom by the front porch, so I must make my way cautiously by the back.

There was still faint moonlight, casting shadows from the trees and bushes, and the loom of the house just visible to guide me as I crept along, my fingers brushing the ivy. In my imagination the undergrowth was full of mad Hungarians waiting to leap out and knife me, and once I rose like a startled grouse as an owl hooted only a few yards away. Round one corner, peering cautiously, along the wall towards another—and there was something glittering in the dark off to one side, and I saw that it was the moonlight on a little puddle of rainwater that had collected on what might well be the surface of a sundial. And in that moment, from just beyond the corner I was approaching, came a sound that sent shivers down my spine—a faint clicking noise of metal, and the rustle of someone moving. I tried to whisper, and failed, gulped, and tried again.

"Willem! Are you there? It's me, Harry!"

Dead silence save for the pounding of my heart, and then the faintest of sounds, a foot scraping the ground, and after what seemed an age, Willem's whisper:

"*Was ist das?* Harry, is that you?"

He was still outside! Relief flooded through me—to be followed by a drench of fear at the thought of what I must do. I drew the knife from my pocket, holding it against my thigh, and edged my way round the corner. The ivy was thick on the wall just there, but there was light enough to see a dark opening a couple of yards ahead—the recess of the secret doorway, and just within it the pale outline of a face. I took another step, and the face hissed at me.

"What the hell are you doing here?" In his agitation he lapsed into German. "*Stimmt etwas nicht?* What's up, man?"

Where the inspiration came from, God knows. "The Emperor ain't in bed!" I whispered hoarsely. "He . . . he got up! His aides made a din, and woke him!"

"*Arschloch!*" Whether he meant me or Franz-Josef I can't say, but it was enough to assure me I was right: he was bent on murder, for if he'd been the innocent guardian, why the deuce should he care whether the Emperor was abed or not? The clicking I'd heard must have been his working on the lock . . . Gad, if he decided to give up for the night, I might not have to risk attacking him . . . I could pour out my tale to the Emperor in the morning, denouncing Willem, clearing myself . . . a whirlwind of wild hopes, you see, as I crouched peering at the dim face a yard away, near soiling myself in agitation, and then those hopes were dashed as he spoke again, soft and steady.

"Back inside with you! He's bound to go back to bed presently—and they may still come! Go on, man, be off, quickly!"

And leave you to unpick the lock and do your business, thinks I. There was only one thing for it. I gripped the hilt hard, stepping closer, and as he opened his mouth to speak again I struck upwards, going for his throat, he ducked like lightning, the blade drove past, missing by an inch, his hand clamped on my wrist, and as he twisted and I strove to wrench free, clawing fingers came out of the darkness on my right, fumbling for my throat, a fist smashed against my left temple, and I was hurled backwards and flung to the turf, pinned helpless by a massive body while another seized my legs, and a great stinking paw closed on my mouth—they must have been there, unseen in the gloom, his Holnup accomplices springing into action with the speed and silence of expert bravos. I struggled like bedamned, expecting to feel the agonising bite of steel, but it didn't come; the hands on my mouth and throat tightened, and I felt rather than saw a bearded face snarling into mine in what may have been Hungarian; above us in the dark voices were whispering urgently—Willem seemed to be giving orders, and for an instant the hand lifted from my mouth, but before I could find the breath to bellow a cloth was thrust between my teeth and I was heaved over on to my face and my wrists pinioned behind me.

Meanwhile the debate overhead was deteriorating into agitated bickering, and since some of it was in German and my mind was most wonderfully concentrated, I gathered that Willem didn't know why I'd attacked him, and didn't care, but if the Emperor was up and about they'd best ignore the secret stair and invade the house in force; no, no, says another, the Englander's lying, they always do, and storming the house was too haphazard and the aroused guardroom would be too many for them, to which a third voice said the hell with such timidity, their lives would be well lost if they could only settle Franz-Josef—there's always one like that, you know, full of patriotic lunacy, and good luck to him.

The heavyweight atop of me weighed in with the sensible suggestion that since subduing me had caused enough row to wake the dead, they should give over and come back tomorrow, but before this could be put to the vote he was proved right by a challenge from the darkness, a bawled order, the pounding of boots, and a stentorian command to stand in the name of the Emperor. Willem exclaimed: "*Mist!*," his Webley cracked, there was a yell of pain, and then bedlam ensued, with shots and oaths and screams, the dark was split by flashes of fire, I heard a clash of steel, my incubus arose bawling in several languages and blazing away, and I hastened to improve my position by scrambling up, inadvertently butting him in the crotch. He fell away, howling, and I managed to gain my feet and would have been going like a stag for the safety of the shrubbery if he hadn't staggered into me, bewailing his damaged courting tackle, and I fell full length, only to rise again on stepping-stones of my terrified self, but not alas to higher things, for something caught me an excruciating clout on the back of the skull, and the din of shots and shouting faded as I fell again, this time into merciful unconsciousness.

I suppose I've been laid out, and come to with a head throbbing like an engine-room, more often than most fellows, and can testify that while one descent into oblivion is much like another, there are two kinds of awakening. After a dizzy moment in which you recall your last conscious memory and wonder where the devil you are, realisation dawns—and it may be blissful, as at

Jallalabad or in the cave in the Bighorn Mountains, when I knew that the hell and horror were behind me, and it was bed-time and all well—or you may come round hanging by the heels from a cottonwood with the Apache Ladies Sewing Circle preparing to tickle your fancy, or strapped over a cannon muzzle with the gunners blowing on their fuses.

Having known the last two I can tell you that waking to find yourself bound hand and foot on a camp-bed underground, while alarming, ain't too bad by comparison, and when your smiling captor inquires after your health and offers refreshment . . . well, hope springs eternal, you know. For Willem von Starnberg was bending over me, all solicitude and sounding absolutely light-hearted.

"The guv'nor was right, 'Never forget that fellows like Flashman always come at you when least expected, usually from behind.' Should ha' paid more attention to the old chap, shouldn't I?" He put a hand behind my head, and I yelped hoarsely. "Splittin' to beat the band, eh? No wonder, Zoltan fetched you a dooce of a clip; you've been limp as a dead fish for hours. Care for some schnapps?"

"Where the hell am I? What . . . what's happened?" My voice came out in a quavering croak as he removed the flask from my lips, and as I struggled into a sitting position with his help, my questions trailed off in amazement as I took in my surroundings.

We were alone, in an enormous cavern of what looked like limestone, grey stone at any rate, but with an odd sheen to its towering walls. We were at one end, close by the black mouth of a tunnel from which ran wooden rails bearing a couple of ancient wheeled bogie trucks; the rails ran for about thirty yards into the cave to what looked like a cleft in the floor, and there must have been a bridge once, for I could see that the rails continued on the other side of the cleft before being lost in the gloom. The place was like some cathedral made by nature, huge and empty and utterly silent, and staring up I saw that high overhead there was a fissure in the roof fringed by a tangle of growth from the world outside, and this was the only source of light, glistening dimly on those gigantic smooth curving walls. The floor of the cavern was smooth too, and innocent of loose rocks or rubble, as though some giant housekeeper had swept the great chamber clean.

But the wonder of the place, that made me catch my breath even in my groggy condition, was the little lake that covered almost half the cavern floor on the far side away from the rails. Very well, 'twas only water, a natural bath in the stone, but never was water so still or clear or silent. The surface was like glass, extending perhaps thirty yards in length by twenty across to the far wall, and in its crystal depths, undisturbed by current or eddy, you could make out every detail of the stone bottom ten feet down, as though no water had been there at all. No fish could have swum in it, or weeds grown; it was immaculate, like some enchanted mere of fairy tale, an ice-witch's mirror in the heart of a magic mountain.

Only by the tunnel mouth where I lay were there signs of human occupation: a rough stone fireplace and utensils, palliasses and camp-beds, plain chairs and table, a couple of packing-cases, and a litter of stores and gear. But like ourselves, these worldly things seemed out of place and dwarfed in the awful majesty of the cavern. The cold was fit to freeze you to the bone.

"You're in an old salt-mine in the Saltzkammergut, in the mountains above Ischl,"[19] says Willem. "Jolly little tomb, ain't it? Harkaway!" He had raised his voice, and the echo came back in an eerie whisper, "harkaway . . . away . . . away . . . ," fading ever so softly in the unseen reaches of the cavern. He stood cocking an appreciative ear, very trim in riding boots, breeches, and shooting jacket, and none the worse, it seemed, for the free-for-all shooting match which was the last thing I remembered.

"We're near the surface here," says he, "but God knows how far the tunnels go below. The place hasn't been worked for years. D'ye know, when I was a nipper I pictured salt-mines as hellish places where slaves with red-rimmed eyes waded knee-deep in the stuff. But it's rather grand and spooky, don't you think? Splendid bolt-hole, too, for clandestine plotters like the Holnup. My lads were camped here for a week, but I've had to send 'em off now, thanks to you." He perched on a packing-case, cradling his knee, and gave me his quizzy look. "When did you twig I was the fox at the hen-roost, then?"

"Cut me loose first!" croaks I, but he only grinned and repeated the question, so I told him about finding the tampered cartridges, and he swore and slapped his thigh, laughing.

"I'll be damned! That's what comes o' bein' too clever by half—oh, and bein' in awe of your fearsome reputation! Ironic, ain't it? I gave you a harmless pistol by way of insurance, but if I'd given you a loaded one, Franz-Josef would have been with his fathers by now. Or if you'd come on the scene a minute later, even . . . oh, aye, we had the lock picked and I was about to go aloft when you arrived with your little snickersnee, curse you, and then that damned sergeant and his sentries, and we had to shoot our way clear, and lost two good men—one of 'em your pal Gunther, you'll be desolated to learn. Ah, well, *c'est la guerre!*"

You'd have thought he was describing a rag in the dormitory, chuckling with hardly a sign of irritation. Oh, he was Rudi's boy all right, cool as a trout and regarding me with amusement.

"So there it is!" cries he. "Franz-Josef lives on, two of my boys don't, there ain't a hope of a return match with half a regiment round the place by now, I imagine—supposin' F-J hasn't decamped for Vienna already. The conspiracy is *kaput*, I've had to disperse the best band of night-runners I ever hope to see, and four weeks of dam' good plannin' have gone down the bogs." He jumped down from his seat, and stood before me, hands on hips. "Yes, sir, the guv'nor was right. You truly are an inconvenient son-of-a-bitch. Still . . . no hard feelin's, what? Not on my side, leastways."

Call me a sceptic if you will, but I doubted it. I'd come

within a whisker of cutting his throat, ruined his plot all unwitting, and cost him two men dead—and he didn't mind a bit? No, this could only be cat-and-mouse in the best Starnberg tradition, and his claws would show presently; in the meantime, with my innards turning cartwheels, I pretended to take him at face value.

"Glad to hear it," says I. "Then you won't mind cutting these infernal ropes."

"Certainly . . . by and by," says he. "When my arrangements for departure are complete. Austria's a trifle warm just now, you see, what with two dead desperadoes under the Emperor's window, a sentry with a slit weasand, and those two mysterious visitors, Flashman and Starnberg, vanished none knows whither. It wouldn't surprise me," says the sardonic pup, "if they started lookin' for us, which is why I intend to be over the Italian border by daybreak tomorrow. I've no inclination to grace an Austrian gallows—or rot in a Brandenburg fortress, which is what'll happen if Bismarck ever learns the truth of our little *soiree* yestre'en. He'd have my ballocks for breakfast."

That settled one thing. "So last night was off your own bat! Bismarck had nothing to do with it?"

He stared. "With our gallant attempt to snuff Franz-Josef's wick, you mean? Good lord, no! My word, you do have a low opinion of our worthy Chancellor!" He grinned at my bewilderment. "I see I'll have to explain. Two months ago the Holnup learned that F-J was comin' to Ischl without his usual retinue, and would be a sittin' bird for assassination. Plans were laid for a night attack on the lodge, but Bismarck got wind of it from a spy in the Holnup council, and devised his great plan for guardin' the Emperor, just as Kralta and I told you. What he didn't know, when he entrusted it to me, his loyal agent," he went on, looking waggish, "was that I happen to be a great-nephew of Lajos Kossuth himself, and have been a member of the Holnup since boyhood. And that in choosin' *me* to guard the great booby he was playin' into our hands, makin' our task even easier by

handin' me on a plate the golden opportunity that every
Hungarian patriot has been prayin' for this ten years past. You
may be sure," he added, "that we've identified the spy in our
council, and have left him strictly alone . . . for the time being."

He paused, and just for a moment the bantering manner
dropped from him like a cloak. The boyish face was set and his
eyes were far away as he said softly: "And we were so close.
Another moment—another few seconds—and the blow would
have been struck that would have freed Hungary from the
Hapsburgs forever. *Holnup . . . holnuputan!*"* He gave a deep
sigh, and slowly unclenched his hands—and then he was himself
again, shaking his head at me in mock reproach. "You really have
been an uncommon nuisance, you know."

For some reason, despite my fears, this infuriated me.
"Because I stopped you from committing murder? Why, you
dam' fool, I saved your lousy life, more like! Bismarck would
have had more than your ballocks—he'd have had your neck!"

He regarded me pityingly. "Oh, ye of little faith! D'you think
I'm a half-wit? It was all arranged—once F-J had kicked the
bucket we'd have fetched you out o' the house, quiet-like, tapped
you gently on your great fat head, laid you out beside the royal
corpse with a bloody knife in your hand, and left you to explain
matters when you woke up." He regarded my expression of stupefied horror with cheerful satisfaction. "Of course they'd have
hanged you—if they hadn't finished you off on the spot. But
don't you see, I could then have pleaded injured innocence to
Bismarck, pointing out that it wasn't *I* who brought you into the
business, and that you must have gone berserk, or been a Holnup
hireling all unsuspected, or killed F-J for love of the beauteous
Sissi . . . or anythin' at all. He'd ha' swallowed it. Besides, that
would have been the least of his troubles, with the dogs of war
slippin' all over the parish, and everyone blamin' perfidious

* "Tomorrow . . . the day after tomorrow!"

Albion as usual, and Gladstone havin' apoplexy." He shrugged. "Aye, me, the best-laid schemes . . ."

What was the phrase young Hawkins used in his book? "Surely, while you're above ground, Hell wants its master!" Spoken of the fictitious image of Rudi von Starnberg, but by God it fitted his abominable son even better, sitting there while he lighted another of his blasted cigarettes.[20] Was he mad, perhaps . . . and why had he brought me to this ghastly solitude? It made no sense, for if he'd wanted me dead they could have done for me in the fight at the lodge. Was it possible that his geniality was genuine, and that he didn't mean me harm after all? No, for why was I bound hand and foot? The evil bastard had brought me here to gloat . . . and he must have read my thoughts, for:

"So what now, you wonder?" says he. "Well, Harry, that's a hard one . . . damned hard. You see, the fact is that I like you— and none the less because you've baulked me altogether. Indeed, all the more. And it's just a lost trick in the game, anyway—I'll settle Franz-Josef, one way or t'other, and before long, too. You may count on that. And then . . .'twill all come right, and Hungary will be free soil. But that's by the way."

He seated himself on his packing-case again, blowing smoke-rings and watching them hang motionless in that windless cavern, while my skin crawled.

"The hard thing, though, is that while you're a man after my own heart, just as you were after the guv'nor's, and I'd like to clap hands and part friends . . ." and damned if he didn't sound as though he meant it ". . . you know too much, you see. At the moment, what happened last night is all a great mystery— officially. What do they know, Franz-Josef's people? That someone was tryin' to do him in—the unlocked door and dead sentry tell 'em that. And that it was a Holnup job—the other dead 'un we had to leave with Gunther was a Magyar, and a notorious fire-brand. And that you and I were in the business, some way or other. What then? Whatever they suspect, they can't *prove* a blessed thing against you and me, unless we're fool enough to let ourselves be collared in the next day or two, while the trail's hot and they're still full of zeal. After that, they'll be quite thankful to forget about us, and they can keep the whole unfortunate business quiet. See?"

I saw, all right, and was struck by the sinister significance of the words "you know too much." He continued:

"Which is why I shall lie low in Italy for a spell, before presentin' myself to Bismarck, who'll have no earthly reason to suspect me. *Au contraire*, he'll welcome me with open arms! On the face of it, his great scheme will have worked to admiration, don't you see?" He sat forward, eyes shining. "The Holnup struck, failed, and left two of their number stark and stiff! Bravo, Starnberg and Flashy, cries Otto, couldn't have done better myself! That's what he's bound to think . . . and I shan't disillusion him. If he wonders why we didn't stay to take the credit, I'll say it seemed best to fade modestly away. Oh, he'll swallow it. But . . ." he shook his head solemnly, ". . . suppose *you* were to tell the true story of what happened last night, eh? I'd be embarrassed, Harry. Embarrassed to death, like as not—"

"But I wouldn't say a word!" It came out in a bellow that made the echo ring. "Never, I swear it! My God, no! I wouldn't dream of it! Why the hell should I want to? You can't believe that I'd ever—"

"So you say, in the Saltzkammergut," he interrupted. "But safe in London or Paris? Who knows? Very well, you might keep mum—but I'm certain sure you won't if the Austrian *poliƶei* nab you before you can get out o' the country. And you haven't a hope of doin' that."

"Why not? If you're making for Italy, we can—"

"I can, but you can't. I've a horse up topsides, and I know the country. But I can't risk a passenger. Sorry, old 'un," says he, all manly regret, the hypocritical hound, "but I must take the high road . . . while you take the low." He gestured beyond me, towards the recesses of the cavern.

"You can't mean it! My God, Starnberg . . . Willem—I swear I'll not let on! On my honour! Christ, man, think—who'd believe me if I were fool enough to blab? Bismarck? You know dam' well he wouldn't—never trusted me an inch, the swine! And I'd never peach to the Austrians—you said yourself they can't prove anything! And I could explain, somehow, why I disappeared from the lodge last night—oh, God, I don't know exactly, but I could spin 'em some yarn about how the Holnup abducted me, or anything—"

"I don't doubt that you could!" he agreed. "But would you, when the truth might save your skin? I doubt it. I know dam' well I wouldn't." He paused, reflecting. "Anyway, there's another reason why I can't let you . . . live to tell the tale—even if I could be sure you wouldn't tell it."

"Jesus, man—why?"

He sat a moment, frowning and smiling together, and then flicked away his cigarette and stood up, took a few slow paces, and turned to face me—and, d'ye know, he looked almost wistful.

"Debt of honour, I guess you'd call it," says he. "I feel I owe it to the guv'nor." And as I gagged in appalled disbelief, he went on:

"I've never known, as I told you, what you and he were up to in Strackenz all those years ago. Some stunt of Otto Bismarck's, wasn't it? But I do know that you had the deuce of a turn-up at the last, sabre to sabre, in some castle or other—and 'twas the guv'nor's lastin' regret that it didn't go *à l'outrance*. I don't know what came between you, but I wouldn't mind havin' a quid for every time I heard the old chap say: 'I only wish I'd settled Flashman! He was a strong swordsman, and up to every foul trick, but I was better. Aye, if only I could ha' finished it!' That's what he said."

He turned away to reach in among some gear piled on a case by the tunnel mouth, and when he faced me again he had a dress sabre unsheathed in either hand, the slim blades glittering wickedly in the pale light from the cavern roof.

"So I feel bound to finish it for him," says he.

"But . . . but . . ." I struggled for speech. "You must be crazy! For God's sake, man, there's no need! I've told you I shan't breathe a bloody word! I'll be silent as the grave—"

"That's the ticket!" cries he. "Couldn't ha' put it better myself! And speakin' of graves, you couldn't ask a grander mausoleum than this!" He flourished a point at our ghastly surroundings. "Pretty gothic, what? Oh, shut up, do! Don't tell me you'd not squeal your head off when the traps got you, 'cos it's a lie and we both know it, and it don't matter anyway—I'm doin' this out o' filial piety." He inserted the blade between my ankles and cut the cord. "There now, you can frisk like a lamb and limber up for the fray. Harry be nimble, eh? You'll need to be, I promise."

"Damn you for a fool!" I struggled off the bed. "You can't mean it! Why, it's madness! I've told you I shan't talk, haven't I? You can trust me, I tell you!" I took an unsteady step and tumbled, rolling on the floor. "Loose my hands, rot you—and listen, you ass! Your guv'nor would never have stood for this—we were chums, dammit, comrades, Rudi and I—you said it yourself, he told you I was a man after his own heart—"

"He did. He also advised me to shoot you on sight, so count yourself lucky. Come on, upsadaisy!" He whacked me on the rump with the flat of the blade and I scrambled up cursing. "Now then . . . I'm goin' to untie your wrists, give you a moment to ease the cramps away, and when you're ready you're goin' to pick up that sabre . . ." he tossed one of them on to the bed ". . . and we'll take up where you and the guv'nor left off, savvy?"

"Savvy be damned, I'll not do it! Heavens, man, where's the sense to it? You can't bear me any grudge," I whined, "I didn't try to spoil your beastly plot—"

"Apart from almost severin' my jugular. But I don't hold that against you. All in the way o' business." He tapped his point on my breast. "So is this."

"I'll not fight, I tell you!" I shouted, almost in tears. "You can't make me!"

"True enough," says he. "And I can't run a helpless man through, can I?" His smile became wicked. "Might persuade you, though . . . if you'll just step this way . . ." He prodded me backwards, along by the rails, and perforce I retreated, pleading and blaspheming by turn, while he requested me to "Pass along the bus, please," before seizing my shoulder, spinning me round, and gripping my bound wrists. "Steady the Buffs! Don't want you fallin' and hurtin' yourself . . . yet."

I dam' near swooned. We were on the very lip of the cleft where the rails ended, and I was staring down aghast into a narrow chasm whose smooth walls were visible for only a few yards before they vanished into black nothingness. I swayed giddily on the brink, my crotch shrinking as I tried to rear back from that awful void, but Willem held me in an iron grip, chuckling at my shoulder.

"A soldier's sepulchre, what? That's where your mortal coil is goin', when you've shuffled it off. Can't tell how deep it is, but it looks as though it narrows a bit, some distance down, like those jolly French *oubliettes*, so you'll probably stick fast. You won't mind, bein' dead. On t'other hand, if you won't fight I'll just have to drop you in alive, and the stickin' process might last some time, wouldn't you think?"

That was when I broke. The horror of that gaping shaft, the thought of falling into blackness, the tearing agony of rasping to a flayed, bloody stop between the confining walls, jammed and helpless, to die by inches, rotting in the bowels of the earth . . . I raved, begging him to let me be, promising never to tell, struggling like a maniac until he pulled me away, and I sank to my knees, weeping buckets and babbling for mercy, promising him a fortune if he'd only spare me. He listened in some wonder, and then laughed as though a light had dawned.

"I'll be jiggered!" cries he. "It's the Flashman gambit . . . grovel and whine—then strike when your man's off guard! Didn't I tell you the guv'nor warned me to beware when you started showin' the white feather? Well, you're doin' it a shade too brown, Harry—and t'won't answer, you know. I'm fly to you. 'Sides, I probably have more cash in the bank than you do."

"Help!" I hollered. "Help, murder! Let me be, you lousy bully, you cruel bastard, you! I ain't shamming, you infernal idiot, I swear I'm not! Oh, please, Starnberg . . . Willem, Bill, let me go and I'll never tell! Help!"

"Oh, cheese it, you daft dummy!" He grabbed my neck and pushed me prone, and the cords at my wrists fell away as he cut them through. He stepped swiftly back, as though expecting me to go for him, and watched me warily—he absolutely wasn't sure whether I was bluffing or not. That's what a reputation does for you. Then he wheeled about, strode away to the camp-bed, picked up the other sabre, and sent it slithering and clinking over the stone in my direction.

" 'Play-actor,' the guv'nor called you, didn't he?" says he. "Well, I don't know—and what's more, I don't much care, but I'm gettin' cold, and if you don't take up that tool double quick I'll pitch you down that hole without benefit of clergy, d'ye hear? So get up and come on!"

"You can't mean to butcher me!" I wailed. "My God, man, haven't you any bowels?"

"Ne'er mind about my bowels!" sneers he, casting aside his jacket. "You'll be admirin' your own presently. On guard!"

There's a moment, and I've faced it more often than I care to remember, when you're rat-in-the-corner, all your wriggling and lying and imploring have failed, there's nowhere to run, and your only hope is to do your damnedest and trust to luck and every dirty dodge you know. For a split second I wondered if his last threat had meant that he'd tackle me bare-handed, and if perhaps I was stronger than he . . . but no, in my lusty youth perhaps, but not now against that lithe young athlete, all steel and whipcord. I must just take my chance with the blade.

I picked it up, and somehow the feel of the wire-bound grip steadied me, not much, but enough to face him as he waited, poised on his toes, sleek as a panther, the fine tawny head thrown back and the arrogant smile on his lips—and I felt the tiniest spark of hope.

Whether my blubbering had truly made him wonder or not, I couldn't tell, but one thing was sure—he hadn't fooled me. Oh, he needed me dead for his skin's sake, right enough, but he wasn't thinking of that now, nor of sacrificing me to Rudi's shade, which was so much eyewash. No, what was gripping Master Starnberg was the sheer wanton delight in killing, of adding my distinguished head to his trophy room, of proving his mastery and seeing the fear in the eyes of the beaten opponent at his mercy—I know all about it, you see, for I've enjoyed it myself, but while it's a luxury that a wary coward can afford, it's a weakness in a brave man who's sure of his own superiority, for he forgets what your cold-blooded assassin (and your coward) never forget—that killing is a business, not a pleasure, and you must keep your sense of fun well in check.

Another thing: he was an academic swordsman if ever I saw one, beautifully balanced as he glided forward and saluted, smirking, falling into the sabre guard with an ease that would have done de Gautet's heart good to see. Well, I'd taken the brilliant de Gautet unawares (once), and I doubted if Starnberg was any smarter. So I gripped my hilt tight, like the rawest dragoon recruit, took a hesitant shuffle forward, and played my first card.

"It ain't fair!" I whined. "I've been trussed like a fowl—and I'm an old man, damn you! By gad, if I were your age, you'd think twice, you prancing pimp! Ain't you your father's son, though, taking every mean advantage . . . wait, rot your boots, I ain't ready——"

God, he was quick! One whip of his wrist and his blade was slicing at my neck, and if I hadn't practised my favourite retire, which is to fall backwards, howling, my head would have been on the carpet. I scrambled up, shaken, one hope gone, for I'd intended to move close, mumping piteously, and give him the point unexpected. Now he came in like a dancer, unsmiling and bursting with blood-lust, cutting left and right, the blades clashing and grating, and I had to break ground to avoid being driven back to that awful chasm, side-stepping and tripping over those confounded rails, tumbling down the smooth slope almost to the water's edge.

He bore up, swearing. "D'you do all your fightin' flat on your back, then? Come on, man, get up and look alive!"

"I can't! I've jarred my elbow! A-hh, I think it's broken——"

"No, it's not, you lyin' skunk! You ain't hurt, so pick up your sword and stay on your feet!" And the callous swine pricked me on the leg, drawing blood. I damned his eyes and came afoot, moving cautiously back to the level, and as he cut high and low I gave back again, towards the tunnel mouth. If I could lure him in among the clutter of beds and cases he'd be hampered, and might even stumble . . . but he knew a trick worth two of that and drove me clear of the obstacles—and hope leaped within me, for if I retreated into the tunnel at my back we'd both be fighting in the dark, and I could drop flat and slash at his ankles . . .

"You damned old fox!" shouts he, and with one lightning flurry of his blade he was past me while I cowered and scurried, warding his cuts any old how, and then he was after me again, snarling with laughter as he harried me back into the cavern proper. His sabre seemed to be everywhere, at head and shoulder and flank, and once he feinted low and gave me the point, but I turned it with the forte and in desperation loosed a wild scything sweep which he parried well enough, but paused, eyeing me with some respect.

"Why, you ain't so old, you faker!" cries he. "Though how you troubled the guv'nor, blowed if I know! He must ha' been ill!"

"He was full o' wind and piss, like you!" I panted. "Ran like a whippet—aye, he didn't tell you it ended with him turning tail, did he? No, he wouldn't, not Slimy Starnberg!" I reviled Rudi with every insult I could muster, wheezing hoarsely as he drove me ever back, for I knew 'twas my only hope; my lungs and legs were labouring, and his young strength must prevail unless I could rile him into recklessness. But he was as cool as his father, damn him, chuckling triumphantly as I staggered away, swiping and swearing.

"Bellows to mend, what?" says he. "Best save your breath . . . oh, stop sprintin', can't you? Come on, you old duffer, stand for once and let's see what you're made of!"

So I did, not from choice but 'cos I was too used up to run, employing the rotten swordsman's last resort, the Khyber-knife guard of the Maltese Cross, up-down-across with all your might. No opponent can touch you, but he don't need to, since you'll die of apoplexy from exertion, as I'd discovered back in '60, when old Ghengiz the Mongol and I repelled Sam Collinson's bannermen at the Summer Palace—leastways, old Ghengiz did while I lit out for pastures new.* But there was no Ghengiz now to bear the brunt, and I knew I couldn't last but a few moments more, and then my aching arm and shoulder must fail, and this grinning, handsome sadist would beat down my feeble guard and drive his old steel through my shrinking carcase . . . and it would end here, in this clammy cavern, with the two tiny mannikins hacking away across its floor and the echoes of clashing swords resounding from the great stone arch overhead. I'd be cut down

* See *Flashman and the Dragon*

to death in this forgotten desolation, I who had survived Bala-clava and Cawnpore and Greasy Grass, Fort Raim dungeon and Gettysburg and the guns of Gwalior, slaughtered by this moun-tebank who wasn't more than half a swordsman anyway, for all his academic antics, or he'd have settled an old crock like me ages ago, and the hellish injustice and *meanness* of it all was like gall to my craven soul as I felt my strength ebbing and gave voice yet again to what I dare say will be my dying words one day:

"It ain't fair! I don't deserve this—no, no, wait, for God's sake, not yet . . . a-hhh, I'm done for . . . the doctor was right . . ." And I dropped my sabre, clutching at my heart, face contorted in agony, and sank to my knees.

"What the devil!" cries Willem, as I clasped both hands to my bosom, groaning in unutterable pain, gaping wide to emit a croaking wheeze—and he stopped dead, sabre raised for the *coup de grace*.

"You're shammin', you old sod!" cries he . . . but he came that vital step closer, and I hurled myself forward, my right fist aimed at his groin—and I missed, God damn it to Hell, for my blow caught him on the thigh and sent him staggering but not disabled, and as I grabbed my sabre and let go an almighty cut that should have taken his leg off, the brute parried it and came in hand and foot, eyes blazing.

I turned and ran, shrieking in anticipation of his point in my back, eyes closed in panic, felt myself stumbling down an incline, and plunged flat on my face in freezing water. I was floundering in the shallows of the little lake, and as he came bounding to the margin, sabre raised for a downward cut, I scrambled away until I was knee-deep and out of reach. I daren't go farther, for the cold of that hell-created tarn was fit to freeze Grendel, numbing my feet and calves in seconds, and I knew that immersion would mean death in minutes. He stopped on the brink, measuring the distance, but too wary to come after me, for the water must hinder his feet. He swore, snaking his point at me, and made as downright foolish a statement as ever I heard.

"Come out of that, blast you! You can't run forever!"

"You callous swine!" I yammered. "Go away, you dirty rotter, let me alone, can't you? Oh, Lor', my legs are freezing, you hound!"

"Well, come out, then! I ain't stoppin' you!"

"Damned if I will! You'd cut me down foul, while I was climbing out!"

"Don't be an ass! As if I needed to. Oh, well, freeze or drown, as you please!"

He backed up to the level, and I took a step towards the brink, where my sabre lay.

"Come on, pick it up!" says he. " 'Pon my soul, you're as good as a play, you are!"

"You won't take me unawares?" cries I, crouching furtive-like, extending a wary hand towards my sabre. "You'll give me a moment . . . Bill? Please? My feet are frozen solid . . . won't answer . . ."

"God forbid that the renowned Flashman should die with cold feet!" He laughed impatiently. "Never fear, I'll wait." And as I put a foot on the dry stone, gasping elaborately, he half-turned away in contempt—and I thought, now or never, put my hand on the forte of the blade, grasped it, and launched it spear-fashion with all my remaining strength at his unguarded flank.

For an instant I thought I'd got him, for the sabre flew true as an arrow, but his speed saved him. He'd no time to dodge, but his sword-hand moved like lightning, the blades rang together, and the flying sabre was swept high into the air to fall clattering almost at the mouth of the tunnel. By which time I was on him, fists and cold feet flying, grappling him, and down we went together in a tangle of limbs, Flashy roaring and Willem spitting curses. I took a wild punch at his head and missed, yelping as my knuckles struck the stone, and as I rolled away blind with pain he was on his feet, cutting down at me. His sword struck sparks within an inch of my head, I scrambled on to all fours and came erect—and there he was, extending himself in a lunge that there was no avoiding, and I died in that split second as his point sank home in my unprotected body.

What is it like to be run through? I'll tell you. For an instant, nothing. Then a hideous, tearing agony for another instant—and then nothing again, as you see the blade withdrawn and the blood welling on your shirt, for the pain is lost in shock and disbelief as your eyes meet your assailant's. It's a long moment, that, in which you realise that you ain't dead, and that he's about to launch another thrust to finish you—and it's remarkable how swiftly you can move then, with a hole clean through you from front to back, about midway between your navel and your hip, and spouting gore like a pump. (It don't hurt half as much as a shot through the hand, by the way; that's the real gyp.)

Well, I moved, as Starnberg whirled up his sabre for a cut, and the pain returned with such a sickening spasm that I was near paralysed, and what should have been a backward spring became an agonised stagger, clutching my belly and squealing (appropriately) like a stuck pig. His cut came so close that the point ripped my sleeve, and then the back of my thighs struck something solid, and I went arse over tip into one of the bogie trucks standing on the rails—and the force of my arrival must have jolted its ancient wheels loose from the dust of ages, for the dam' thing began to move.

For a moment all the sense was jarred out of me, and then Willem shouted—with laughter!—and through waves of pain I remembered that the rails ran slightly downwards from the tunnel mouth, and that the bogie must be rolling, slowly at first but with increasing momentum, towards that ghastly *oubliette* where the rails ended.

If I've sinned in my time, wouldn't you say I've paid for it?

There I was, on the broad of my back, legs in the air, leaking blood by the pint with my guts on fire, confined by the sides of the truck, helpless as a beetle on a card as I trundled towards certain death. Bellowing with pain and panic, I grabbed for the top of one side, missed my hold, regained it with a frantic clutch, and heaved myself up bodily with an agonising wrench to my wound. I had a glimpse of Willem shouting in glee—I won't swear he didn't flourish his sabre in a farewell salute, the gloating kite— and as I tried to heave myself clear the confounded truck lurched, throwing me off balance, it was gathering speed, bumping and swaying over the last few yards of track, and as the front wheels went over the edge with a grating crash I tumbled over the side, my shoulder hit the stone with a numbing jar—and my legs were kicking in empty air! I flailed my arms for a hold on the stone, and by the grace of God my left hand fell on the nearside rail, and I was hanging on for dear life, my chest on the stone, my bleeding belly below the brink of the chasm, and the rest of me dangling into the void.

Far below the falling truck was crashing against the rock walls, but I'll swear it made less noise than I did. Feeling my grip slide on the worn wood, I fairly made the welkin ring, striving and failing to haul myself up, getting my numbed right forearm on to the surface, but powerless to gain another inch, my whole right side throbbing with pain . . . and Willem was striding towards me, sabre in hand, grinning with unholy delight as he came to a halt above me. And then he hunkered down, and (it's gospel true) spoke the words which were a catchphrase of my generation, employed facetiously when some terrible crisis was safely past:

"Will you have nuts or a cigar, sir?"

I doubt if the noise I made in reply was a coherent request for assistance, for my sweating grasp was slipping on the rail, I was near fainting with my wound, and already falling in tortured imagination into the stygian bowels of the Saltzkammergut. But he got the point, I'm sure, for he stared into my eyes, and then that devilish, mocking smile spread over his young face . . . and what he did then you may believe or not, as you will, but if you doubt me . . . well, you didn't know Willem von Starnberg, or Rudi, for that matter.

He rested on one knee, laid down his sabre, and his right hand closed on my left wrist like a vise, even as my fingers slipped from the rail. With his left hand he brought his cigarette case from his breast pocket, selected one of his funereal smokes, pushed it between my yammering lips, struck a match, and said amiably:

"No cigar, alas . . . but a last cigarette for the condemned man, what?"

You may say it was the limit of diabolic cruelty, and I'll not dispute it. Or you may say he was stark crazy, and I'll not dispute that, either. At the moment I had no thoughts on the matter, for I was barely conscious, with no will except that which kept my right forearm on the stone, knowing that when it slipped I'd be hanging there by his grip on my other wrist alone . . . until he let go. I know he said something about cigars being bad for the wind anyway, and then: "Gad, but you do give a fellow a run for his money," and on those words he gripped my collar, and with one almighty heave deposited me limp, gasping, and bleeding something pitiful, on the floor of the cave.

For several minutes I couldn't stir, except to tremble violently, and when I had breath to spare from groaning and wheezing and lamenting my punctured gut, which was now more numb than painful, I know I babbled a blessing or two on his head, which I still maintain was natural. It didn't suit him a bit, though; he stood looking vexed and then flung away the gasper and demanded: "Why the devil can't you die clean?" to which I confess I had no ready answer. If I had a thought it was that having saved me, he was now bound to spare me, and I guess the same thing was occurring to him and putting him out of temper. But I can't say what was passing in his mind—indeed, to this day I can't fathom him at all. I can only tell you what was said and done that morning in that godforsaken salt-mine above Ischl.

"It ain't a reprieve, you know!" cries he.

"What d'ye mean?" says I.

"I mean that it's still the Union Jack for you, Flashman!" retorts he—the only time, I think, he'd ever used my surname formal-like, and with a sneer he added words he could only have heard from Rudi. "The game ain't finished yet, play-actor!" Then he snapped something I didn't catch about how if he had let me fall down the cleft I'd likely have found a way out at the bottom. "So you'll go the way I choose, d'ye see? When you're done pukin' and snivellin' you'll get up and take that sabre and stand your ground for a change, my Rugby hero, 'cos if you don't, I'll . . . *Wer ist das?*"

My wail of protest was drowned by his shouted challenge, and I saw he was staring towards the tunnel mouth, suddenly on his guard, crouched like a great cat—and my heart leaped as I saw why.

Someone was standing just within the tunnel mouth, motionless and silent, a dark figure clad in close-fitting shirt and britches and peaked cap, but too much in shadow for the features to be made out. Seconds passed without reply, and Willem started forward a couple of paces and stopped, shouting again: "Who are you? What d'ye want?"

Still there came no reply, but as the echoes resounded from the cavern walls and died away in whispers, the figure stepped swiftly forward, stooped to retrieve my fallen sabre, and straightened again in a stance that left no doubt of his intentions, for he stood like an epee fighter at rest between bouts, left hand on hip, point inclined downwards above the advanced right foot. Willem swore in astonishment and shot a glance at me, lying bemused and bleeding, but I was as baffled as he—and my hopes were shooting skywards, for this mysterious apparition was Salvation, surely, issuing an unspoken challenge to my oppressor, and I was mustering breath to bawl for help when:

"Speak up, damn you!" cries Willem. "Who are you?" The newcomer said not a word, but tilted up his point in invitation.

"Well enough, then!" cries Willem, and laughed. "Whoever you are, we'll have two for the price o' one, what?" And he went in at a run, cutting left and right at the head, but the newcomer side-stepped nimbly, parrying and riposting like an Angelo, so help me, tossing aside the peaked cap to clear his vision—and as the light from above fell full on his features I absolutely cried out in amazement. Either this was all a dream, or the horrors I'd endured had turned my brain, for I was staring at a stark impossibility, a hallucination. The face of the swordsman, fresh and youthful under its mop of auburn curls, was one that I'd last seen smiling wantonly up at me from a lace pillow five years ago: the face of my little charmer of Berlin, Caprice.

It was mad, ridiculous, couldn't be true, and I was seeing things—until Willem's startled oath told me I wasn't. The graceful lines of the figure in its male costume, the dainty shift of the small feet, as much as the pretty little face so unexpectedly revealed, fairly shouted her sex, and he checked in mid-cut and sprang back exclaiming as she came gliding in at speed, boot stamping and point darting at his throat. It was sheer disbelief, not gallantry, that took him aback, for there's no more chivalry in a Starnberg than there is in me; he recovered in an instant and went on the defensive, for that first lightning exchange when she'd turned his cuts with ease and come after him like a fury, told him that suddenly he was fighting for his life, woman or no.

I couldn't believe it, but I didn't care; it was my life in the balance too, and even my wound was forgotten as I watched the shuffling figures and flickering blades, clash-clash and pause, clash-scrape-clash and pause again, but the pauses were of a split second's duration, for she was fighting full tilt with a speed and

energy I'd not have believed was in that slight body, and with a
skill to take your breath away. I'm no great judge, and am only as
good a cut-and-thruster as the troop-sergeant could make me, but
I know an expert when I see one; there's an assurance of bearing and movement that's beyond technique, and Caprice had it.
When Willem attacked suddenly, hewing to beat her guard down
by main force, she stood her ground, feet still and warding his
cuts with quick turns of her wrist; when he feinted and bore in
at her flank she pivoted like a ballet-dancer, facing me with her
back to the lake, and I saw that the girlish face was untroubled;
I remembered fencing against Lakshmibai at Jhansi, the lovely
fierce mask contorted and teeth gritted as she fought like a striking cobra, but Caprice was almost serene; even when she attacked
it was without a change of expression, lips closed, chin up, eyes
unwavering on Willem's, as though all her emotions were concentrated in point and edge.

Once I thought he had her, when her foot slipped, her blade
faltered, and he leaped in, smashing at her hilt to force the sabre
from her hand, the bully-swordsman's trick that I favour myself,
but he hadn't the wit or experience to combine it with a left fist to
the face and a stamp on the toes, and she escaped by yielding to
the blow, dropping to one knee, and rolling away like a gymnast,
cutting swiftly as she regained her feet. At that moment a sudden
spasm of excruciating pain in my side reminded me of more
immediate troubles; my head was swimming with that dizzying
weakness that is the prelude to unconsciousness, and in panic I
clutched at the oozing gash in my side—dear God, I was lying in
a pool of gore, if I fainted now I'd bleed to death. I pressed with
all my might, trying to stem the flow, dragging myself up on an
elbow with some idiot notion that if I could bend my trunk
it would close the wound, and sparing a stricken glance at the
combatants.

Joy was followed instantly by dismay. Willem's left sleeve
was bloody where she'd caught him in rolling away, but she

was falling back now, and he was after her relentlessly, cutting high and low as she retreated; her speed was deserting her, her strength, so much less than his to begin with, was failing under those hammering strokes. He had a six-inch advantage in height, and as much in reach, and he was making it tell. He was laughing again, harsh and triumphant, and as she circled, all on the defensive now, he spoke for the first time, the words coming out in a breathless snarl: "Drop it, you bitch! Give over . . . you're done . . . damn you!"

My heart sank, for her mouth was open now, panting with sheer weariness, and she fairly ran back several steps to avoid his pursuit, halting flat-footed to parry a cut at her head before breaking away again towards the lake. Another wave of giddiness shook me, I could feel myself going, but as he wheeled and drove in and she was forced to halt, guarding and parrying desperately, I summoned the last of my strength to yell:

"Look out, Starnberg—behind you!"

He never even flinched, let alone looked round, the iron-nerved swine, and as she took a faltering side-step that brought them side-on to me, her blade swept dangerously wide in a hurried parry, exposing her head, and he gave an exultant yell as he cut backhanded at her neck, a finishing stroke that must decapitate her—and she ducked, the blade whistled an inch above her curls, and she was dropping full stretch on her left hand like an Italian, driving her point up at his unprotected front. He recovered like lightning, his sabre sweeping across to save his body, but only at the expense of his sword-arm; her point transfixed it just below the elbow, he shrieked and his sword fell, he tottered back a step . . . and Caprice came erect like an acrobat, poised on her toes, her point flickered up to his breast, for a moment they were still as statues, and then her knee bent and her arm straightened with academic precision as she deliberately ran him through the heart.

I saw the point come out six inches through his back, vanishing as she withdrew in graceful recovery. Willem took a step, his mouth opening soundlessly, and then he fell sideways down the incline to the lake, rolling into the shallows with barely a ripple, sliding slowly out from the shore, his body so buoyed by the salt water that his limbs floated on the surface while the crimson cloud of blood wreathed down like smoke into the transparent depths beneath him. Half-conscious as I was, I could see his face ever so clear, and I remember 'twasn't glaring or hanging slack or grinning as corpses often do, but tranquil as a babe's, eyes closed, like some sleeping prince in Norse legend.

The cold stone beneath me seemed to be heaving, and my vision was dimming and clearing and dimming in a most alarming way, but I recall that Caprice tossed her sabre into the lake as she turned and ran towards me, calling something in French that I couldn't make out, and her running shape blurred to a shadow with the light failing behind it, and as the shadow stooped above me the light went out altogether and in the darkness an arm was round my shoulders and fingers were brushing my brow and my face was buried between her bosoms, and my last conscious thought was not of going to find the Great Perhaps, but rather what infernally bad luck to be pegging out at such a moment.

Chapter 9

I don't remember asking the question, but it must have been the first thing I uttered as I came to, for Hutton echoed it, and when I'd blinked my eyes clear I saw that he was sitting by me, trying to look soothing, which ain't easy with a figurehead like his.

" '*Where did she come from?*' " says he. "Still in that salt-mine, are we? Let it wait, colonel. Best lie quiet a spell."

"Quiet be damned." I took in the pleasant little room with the carved wooden eaves beyond the window, the pale sunlight flickering through the curtains, and the cuckoo clock ticking on the whitewashed wall. "Where the devil am I?"

"In bed, for the last four days. In Ischl. Easy, now. You've stitches front and rear, and you left more blood in that cave than you've got in your veins this minute. The less you talk, the better."

"I can listen, curse you." But I sounded feeble, at that, and when I stirred my side pained sharply. "Caprice . . . how did she come there? Come on, man, tell me."

"Well, if you must," says he doubtfully. "Remember, in the casino garden? I said we'd put a cover on you? Well, that was Mamselle. She was behind you every foot o' the way. Didn't care for it, myself. I'd ha' used a man, but our French friend Delzons swore she was the best. Said you and she had worked together before." He paused. "In Berlin, was it?"

"Unofficial. She was . . . French secret department." It was weary work, talking. "I . . . didn't know her . . . capabilities, then."

"Capable's the word. Starnberg ain't the first she's taken off, Delzons says. Good biznai, that. Saved the hangman a job—and Bismarck a red face. What, his star man a Holnup agent! He'll be happy to keep that under the rose. And small comfort to him that that same star man had his gas turned off by a dainty little piece from the beauty chorus. Sabres, bigad!" He began to chuckle, but checked himself. "Here, are you up to this, colonel? I can leave it, you know."

"I ain't complaining," says I, but I closed my eyes and lay quiet. My question had been answered, and I was content to be left alone with my thoughts as Hutton closed the door softly after him.

So *la petite Caprice*, formerly of the Folies, had been my cover. Damned odd—until you reflected, and saw that it wasn't odd at all. Why, even five years ago, according to Blowitz, she'd been A1 in the French secret service, a trained and expert Amazon. I'd known that, in Berlin . . . but of course I'd never given it a thought during those golden hours in that snug boudoir on the Jager Strasse, when I'd been in thrall to the lovely little laughing face beneath the schoolgirl fringe, the eyes sparkling with mischief . . . "I must understand your humour, *n'est-ce pas*? So, *le poissonier* is a thief—that amuses, does it?" The perfect body in the lace negligée silhouetted in the afternoon sun . . . languidly astride my hips, trickling smoke down her nostrils . . . the saucy shrug: "To captivate, to seduce, is nothing—he is only a man" . . . moist red lips and skilfully caressing fingers in a perfumed bed . . .

. . . and the clash of steel echoing in a great stone cavern, the stamp and shuffle of the deadly dance, the reckless gamble of her disarming thrust . . . and the pretty face set and unsmiling as she killed with cold deliberation.

Aye, a far cry between the two, and middling tough to reconcile them. I've known hard women show soft, and soft women turn harpy, but blowed if I remember another who was at such extremes, a giggling feather-brained romp and a practised professional slayer. Thank God for both of 'em, but as I drifted into sleep it was a comforting thought that she wouldn't be the one fetching my slippers in the long winter evenings.

Remember I said there were two kinds of awakening? My drowsy revival with Hutton had been one of the good ones, but next morning's was even better, for while I was still weak as a Hebrew's toddy I was chipper in mind with all perils past, and eager for news. Hutton brought a brisk sawbones who peered and prodded at my stitches, dosed me with jalup, refused my demand for brandy to take away the taste, but agreed that I might have a rump steak instead of the beef tea which they'd been spooning into me in my unconscious state. I told Hutton to make it two, with a pint of beer, and when I'd attended to them and was propped up among my pillows, pale and interesting, he elaborated on what he'd already told me.

"She was on your tail, at a safe distance, from the moment you and Starnberg set off for the lodge, and talked yourselves in—neat scheme of Bismarck's, that. Then when night came, Delzons and I and our four lads joined her in the woods—a skeleton crew, you may say, but ain't we always, damn the Treasury? We picketed the place as best we could, and near midnight Delzons and his Frogs, who were on the side away from the town, heard fellows skulking down from the hill, and guessed they were Holnups come to call. He and his two men sat tight, while Mamselle trailed 'em close to the house—"

"Good God, he let her go alone?"

"She's a stalker—Delzons' fellows call her Le Chaton, French for 'kitten,' I'm told. Some kitten. Anyway, there were three Holnups, gone to ground under a bush, whispering away, and she slid close enough to gather that they were an advance guard, so to speak, and there were others up the hill. Then comes a whistle from near the house, and who should it be but friend Starnberg, *summoning* the three Holnups, if you please. Here's a go, thinks Mamselle, and follows 'em in, to eavesdrop. She must," says Hutton in wonder, "be a bloody Mohawk, that girl. From what she heard, Starnberg was plainly a wrong 'un, but before she could slip back to Delzons to report, you came in view and went for him. The row brought the Emperor's sentries, and all at once there was a battle royal, with more Holnups arriving—we heard it all, but in the dark there was nothing to be done. Mamselle kept her head, though, and when Starnberg's gang brushed off, carrying you along, she stuck to her task, which was to cover you, whatever happened." He paused to ask: "How had you discovered that Starnberg was a bent penny?"

"Tampered cartridges. Ne'er mind that now. What then?"

"She dogged 'em into the hills a few miles, first to a *Steiger's**
hut at the foot o' the mountain, where they rested a spell. Then they put you on a stretcher and went up the mountain to the mouth of the salt-mine. She judged it best not to follow 'em in, but lay up in the rocks nearby, and about dawn the whole crew, as near as she could judge, came out with their dunnage and scattered—but no sign of you and Starnberg, which she couldn't figure . . . neither can I. What was he about?"

"Settling a score. With me. In his own peculiar way."

He frowned. "I don't follow."

"You don't have to. It don't matter." It was none of his business to know about Rudi long ago, or Willem's rum behaviour, killing me one moment, saving me the next. "Nothing to do with this affair, Hutton. A personal grudge, you could call it. Go on."

He gave me a hard look, but continued. "Well, she waited a while. Then she went in. Nick o' time, by the sound of it . . . but you know more than I do about that. She settled Starnberg,

---

* *Steiger,* the foreman in a salt-mine

plugged the leak in you as best she could, and then ran hell-for-leather down the hill, seven or eight miles, to the rendezvous we'd fixed on beforehand. Delzons and I and a couple of our lads went back with her to the mine. I thought you were a goner, but Mamselle put a few stitches in you from the first-aid kit, and after dark we brought you down here to our bolt-hole. She's nursed you these past few days, too. Regular little Nightingale." He shook his head in admiration. "She's a trump and a half, colonel. Blessed if I ever saw a female like her. Smiling sweet and pretty as a peach . . . and she bowled out Starnberg! How the dooce did she do it?"

"Nerve," says I. "And by being a better fencer than he was. Where is she?"

"At the moment, Ischl police station. With Delzons, helping the Austrians trace the Holnup fugitives. Doubt if they'll catch any. No general alarm, you see. Oh, there was a fine hue and cry after you and Starnberg at first. But Delzons and I had our cyphers away to London and Paris soon after, the whole tale, Starnberg and all. That set the wires sparking to Berlin and Vienna." His lean face twisted in a sour grin. "Never knew our Foreign Office could shift so spry, but once they'd telegraphed our Vienna embassy, and the Frogs', and our ambassadors had requested an urgent audience with the Emperor in person . . . well, silence fell. No more hue and cry for you. London directed me to call on the governor of Upper Austria, no less, and assure him of our entire discretion. God knows what Franz-Josef thought of our presumption—and Bismarck's—in saving his life behind his back. But not a word's being said publicly. The Austrian peelers have been advised to treat us and Delzons' people as tourists. So presently we can all go home. Job well done."

He clapped his hands on his knees with finality and stood up, taking a turn to the window. "No question of you making a report. Not officially on service. But I'd be glad of your views on a couple o' things . . ." He cleared his throat. "This Princess Kralta—what about her?"

What with this and that, she'd gone clean out of my mind. "She's Bismarck's mistress, or was. Why, what's happened to her?"

"Nothing. What you've just said explains why. The Ischl police questioned her after the lodge fracas, of course. Known companion of the missing Starnberg. No arrest, though." He gave an amused snort. "From what I've seen of the lady, I'd as soon try to collar the Queen. Very *hoch und wohl-geboren.* Anyway, whatever she told 'em, it brought a couple o' bigwigs post-haste from Berlin yesterday, and I was summoned by the governor and presented to the lady as though she were the Tsar of Russia's aunt. Care to guess what she wanted? News of you." Even poker-faced Hutton couldn't keep the curiosity out of his eyes. "I told her you were indisposed—and she started up, white as paper. 'Not injured?' cries she. I told her you were on the mend. 'Thank God!' says she, and sat down again. Desired me to convey her wishes for your recovery, and trusts you'll call upon her in Vienna, when convenient." He gave the ceiling a jaundiced glance. "Grand Hotel, 9 Karnthner Ring."

Drawing his own conclusions, no doubt. Well, *honi soit* to you, Hutton. I felt better already, for there's no finer tonic than the news that a splendid piece of rattle is turning white as paper and thanking God that you're on the mend. "We have Vienna," by gum—she'd truly meant it, the little darling.

"Hutton," says I, "how long before I'm on my feet?"

"Few days, the doctor says. Once the stitches are out. We can take it, then," says he, "that the lady was not a Holnup accomplice of Starnberg's?"

"Well, Berlin don't seem to think so! Nor the Austrians." I considered. "No . . . I'd say she's a genuine Bismarck agent, and Starnberg hoodwinked her as he did the rest of us, the clever little bastard. If she'd been a Holnup she'd have been out of Ischl long before the traps caught up with her, wouldn't she?"

The truth was I didn't care a rap, and didn't want to know—not when I thought of that voluptuous torso and long white limbs and the golden mane spilling over her shoulders, all waiting in Vienna. What the devil, you don't bed 'em for their politics, do you?

He didn't argue, but asked a few more questions about her which I answered with a discretion that didn't fool him for a moment. I suspect the great long rat was jealous—and not only where Kralta was concerned, for he reverted to Caprice again, with a warmth which I thought quite unbecoming in a Treasury hatchet-man, the lecherous old goat.

"Never seen her like," he repeated, and sighed. "Dear delight to look upon, cold steel within. Mind you, she has her soft side. You should ha' seen her chivvying us up to the mine to bring you down. Fairly shrilling at us to make haste, swore you were dying by inches and we'd be too late. And when she stitched you up she was blubbing. Muttering in French. Quite a taking she was in." He sounded almost piqued.

"Well, you know what women are, ministering angels and all that," says I, pretty smug.

"Aye," says he, pretty dry, and added apropos of nothing that I could see: "She told Delzons she killed Starnberg in self-defence."

I remarked that when a chap was trying to cut your head off, it was a legitimate excuse.

"To be sure. We fished him out o' that pool, you know. Three wounds. One clean through the pump, a cut on his left wrist, and the third through his right arm. Odd, that."

"What's odd about it?"

"You don't truss a man's sword-arm *after* you've killed him. I'd say he was already disarmed when she did him in."

I gave him my best country-bumpkin gape. "Now I don't follow. He's dead and good riddance, ain't he? Well, then, self-defence'll do, I'd say. Does it matter?"

"Not a jot," says he, and rose to depart. "But seeing how she mooned over you later, it struck me she might have been paying him out. On your account." He turned towards the door. "You must ha' known her pretty well in Berlin. About as well as you know that Princess Kralta."

"Hutton," says I, "you're a nosey old gossip."

"Gossip—never. Nosey? That's my trade, colonel."

Well, I'm used to the mixture of huff and perplexity and envious admiration that my success with the fair sex arouses in my fellow man. Seen it in all sorts, from the saintly Albert looking peeved when her fluttering majesty pinned the Afghan medal on my coat, to Bully Dawson, my Rugby fag-master, in a furious bait after I'd thoughtlessly boasted of my juvenile triumph with Lady Geraldine aforesaid. ("What, a high-steppin' filly like her, dotin' on you, damned little squirt that you are!") Most gratifying—and doubly so in Hutton's case. So dear little Caprice had wept over me, had she? Capital news, for if the old fondness still lingered, why shouldn't we resume our idyll of the Jager Strasse, once I was up and doing? Stay, though . . . what about Kralta, panting in Vienna? A ticklish choice, and I was torn. On one hand, there was an exciting variety about Caprice's boudoir behaviour, the merry concubine performing for the fun of it; on t'other, my horsey charmer was wildly passionate and spoony about me—and there was more of her. Much to be said on both sides . . .

In the meantime, Caprice was on hand, and when Hutton gave me the office next day that she purposed to visit me in the evening, I struggled into my shirt and trowsers, cursing my stitches, shaved with care, gave my face furniture a touch of pomade, practised expressions of suffering nobly borne before the mirror while lustfully recalling the soap bubbles of Berlin . . . and paused to wonder, I confess, how it would be, meeting her again.

You see, I don't care to be under obligation to a woman for anything—except money, of course—and this one had saved my life at mighty risk to herself. Furthermore, the harmless jolly little banger of five years ago had emerged as a skilled and ruthless killing lady. On both counts she had the whip hand, so to speak, if she chose to use it—and show me the woman that won't. Well, Caprice didn't; being a clever actress and manager of men, she took what might have been an awkward reunion in her sprightly stride, bowling in without so much as a knock, full of sass and nonsense . . . and 'twas as though five years ago was only yesterday.

"I have not forgiven you!" cries she, dropping her cape and reticule on the table. "Not a word of farewell, not so much as a *billet d'adieu* when you abandon me in Berlin! Oh, *c'est parfait, ça!* Well, M. Jansen-Flashman, what have you to say?" She tossed her head, twinkling severely, and I could have eaten her alive on the spot. "I am waiting, m'sieur!"

"My dear, I've been waiting five years," says I, playing up, "just for the adorable sight of you—and here you are, lovelier than ever!" She made that honking noise of derision that is so vulgarly French, but I wasn't flattering. The pretty girl had become a beauty, the pert gamine face had refined and strengthened, the classroom fringe had given way to the latest upswept style crowned with curls, darker than I remembered—but the cupid's bow lips were as impudent and the blue eyes as mischievous as ever. She was still *la petite Caprice*, if not so little: an inch or two taller and fuller in her tight-bodiced crimson satin that clung like a skin from bare shoulders to wasp waist and then descended to her feet in the fashionable rippling pleats of the time—it hadn't occurred to me that female politicals might dress like evening fashion-plates even when they were in the field, so to speak, and I sat lewdly agog.

"I know that look!" says she. "And I am still waiting."

"But, darling, I couldn't say goodbye—it was Blowitz's fault, you see; he had me on the train to Cologne before I knew it, and—"

"Ah, so Blowitz is to blame! Fat little Stefan overpowered you and carried you off, eh? Some excuse, that!" She advanced with that mincing sway that had never failed to have me clutching for the goods. "Well, it does not serve, milord! I am displeased, and come only to punish you for your neglect, your *discourtoisie*." She struck a pose. "Behold, I wear my most becoming gown—Worth, *s'il vous plait!*—I dress my hair *à la mode*, I devote care to my complexion, a little powder here, a little rouge there, I choose my most costly perfume (mmm-h!), I put round my neck the velvet ribbon *tralala* which so aroused the disgusting Shuvalov—you remember?—I make my person *attrayante* altogether . . . how do you say . . . ? *ravissante, très séduisante—*"

"Alluring, bigod, scrumptious—"

"And then . . ." she bent forward to flaunt 'em and stepped away ". . . then, I place myself at a distance, out of reach." She perched on the table edge, crossing her legs with a flurry of lace petticoat and silk ankles. "And because you are *invalide* you must sit helpless like *le pauvre* M. Tana . . . *non*, M. Tanton . . . *ah, peste! Comment s'appelle-t-il?*"

"Tantalus, you mad little goose!"

"*Précisément* . . . Tantaloose. *Oui*, you are condemned to sit like him, unable to reach out and devour that which you most desire . . . *très succulent, non?*" And the minx stretched voluptuously, pursed her lips, and blew me a kiss. "*Oh, hélas, méchant* . . . if only you were not wounded, eh?"

"Now, that ain't fair! Teasing an old man—and a sick one, too! Here, tell you what—let's kiss and make up, and if you'll forgive me for leaving you flat in Berlin . . . why, I'll forgive you for saving my life, what?"

It had to be said, sooner or later, and when better than straight away, in the midst of chaff? The laughter died in her eyes, but only for an instant, and she was smiling again, shaking her immaculately curled head.

"We will not talk of that," says she, and before I could open my mouth to protest: "We will not talk of it at all. Between good friends, there is no need."

"No need? My dear girl, there's every need—"

"No, *chéri*." She raised a hand, and while she smiled still, her voice was firm and calm. "If you please . . . *non-non, un moment*, let me . . . oh, how to say it? Those two in the *caverne*, they were not you and I. They were two others . . . two *agents secrets*, who did what they must do . . . their *devoir*, their duty. You see?"

What I saw was that this was a Caprice I hadn't known before. Charming and merry as ever, even more beautiful—it made me slaver just to look at her—but with a quiet strength you'd never suspect until she softened her voice and spoke plain and direct, gentle as Gibraltar.

"Let us not speak of it then. It is past, you see, and so are they . . . but we are here!" In an instant she was sparkling again, slipping down from the table, fluttering her hands and laughing. "And it has been so long a time since Berlin, and I was so *désolée* to be left without a word—oh, and enraged, you would not believe! You remember the things I said of Shuvalov, that night of the bath?" She began to giggle. "Well, I said not *quite* as bad of you—but almost. Is there a word in English for angry and sad together? But that is past also!" She knelt quickly by my chair (in a Worth dress, too). "And here we are, I say! Have you missed me, *chéri*?"

As I've said before, damned if I understand women. But if she wanted to forget the horror of that ghastly mine, thank God and hurrah! No doubt she had her reasons, and since gratitude ain't my long suit anyway, and her bright eyes and laughing lips and pouting tits were pleading in unison, I didn't protest.

"Missed you, darling? Damnably—and a sight more than you missed a creaky old codger like me, I'll lay—"

"It is not true! Why, when you abandoned me in Berlin, I was *inconsolable, désolée*—all day! And what is this 'codgeur,' and 'creaky'? Oh, but your English, it is ridiculous!"

"As to the other matter that we ain't to talk about . . . well, I'll just say a ridiculous English thank'ee—"

"And no more!" she commanded. "Or I shall not . . . what did you call it? Kiss and make up?" She gave a languorous wink and put on her husky voice. "Are you . . . strong enough?"

"Try me," says I, reaching for her, but she rose quickly and made a great business of having me put my hands palm down on my chair arms, whereupon she laid her own hands over mine, leaning down firmly to keep 'em pinned, while I feasted my eyes on those superb poonts quivering fragrantly under my very nose, and wondered if my stitches would stand the strain of the capital act performed *in situ*. Then the wanton baggage brought that soft smiling mouth slowly against mine, teasing gently with her tongue, but swiftly withdrawing when I broke free, panting, and tried to seize her bodily, reckless of the darting pain in my flank.

"*Non-non!*" cries she. "Be still, foolish! You will injure your wound! No, desist, *idiot!*" She slapped my hand away from her satin bottom. "It is not possible—"

"Don't tell me what's not possible! Heavens, d'you think I've never been pinked before? T'ain't but a hole in the gut, I can hardly see the dam' thing—"

"Do not tell me what cannot be seen! I have seen it!" For a moment she sounded truly angry, eyes flashing as though on the edge of tears—and then as quickly it had gone, and she was playing the reproachful nursemaid with affected groans and rolling eyes and scathing Gallic rebukes which I accepted like a randy but frustrated lamb, promising to keep my hands to myself, honest injun.

"You behave? Word of honour?" says she, not trusting me an inch.

"I'll prove it," says I. "Give us another kiss, and you'll see."

"*Va-t-en, menteur!*" scoffs she, so I sat on my hands and she consented warily. I knew it was all I was fit for, and made the most of those sweet lips for the few seconds she permitted before she broke away, gratifyingly pink and breathless.

"*Bon,*" says she, and drew some papers from her reticule. "Then I may safely sit by you while you read to me from the present I have brought for you. I coaxed them from an English tourist in the town, pretending an interest in your *culture Anglaise*. His wife, I think, was not amused." She sat on my chair arm, allowing me to put a hand round her waist, and laid the papers in my lap. "What do you say . . . 'for old times' sake,' *non?*"

"Oh, my God!" says I. They were copies of *Punch*. "You cruel little monster! Reminding me of the last time, when you know I'm in no state to explain 'hankey-pankey' to you!"

"*Attention!*" She rapped my wrist. "I know all about *that*, but I do *not* know what is amusing about M. Gladstone dancing in the dress of a sailor, or your policemen being given whistles to blow—ah, yes, or why your *sacré* M. Paunch has such *malice* against us in France, with his bad jokes about Madagascar and *La Chine* and M. de Lesseps, and oh! such fun about Frenchmen playing your blooded cricket—"

" 'Bloody,' dearest, not 'blooded.' And t'ain't ladylike to—"

"Ah, yes, and here—further insult!" She stabbed an indignant fingernail at the page. "France is drawn as an ugly old *paysanne* with fat ankles and abominable clothes—but who is this divine being, so beautiful and elegant of shape in her fine drapery? What does she represent, ha? The Manchester Ship Canal! *Quelle absurdité!*"

"Oh, come, France is mostly a peach in our cartoons. And

we've always made fun of you, ever since Crécy and Joan of Arc and whatnot—but you do the same to us, don't you?"

"*Sans blague!* An example, then?"

"Well, look at Phileas Fogg, a prize muff if ever there was one! That man Verne is never done sniping at us . . . aye, those two British officers in that twaddling book about a comet hitting the earth, what a pair of muttonheaded by-joves they are! Pompous, ill-tempered caricatures, all whiskers and haw-haw and crying 'Balderdash!' "

"And that is not true?" says she, all innocence.

"Course it's not! Stuff and nonsense! Nothing like us!" At which she began to giggle and flicked my whiskers in a marked manner. I could only growl and point out that at least I wasn't in the habit of crying "Balderdash!" or "Haw-haw!"[21]

So we passed a pleasant hour, soon discarding *Punch* and talking about anything and everything except the past few days. I told her about Egypt and Zululand, and she talked of the places she had visited in the course of her work—Rome and Athens and Constantinople and Cairo—but never a word of the work itself. Fashions, food, customs, society doings, men (whom she seemed to find comic, mostly), shops, hotels, and journeys: we compared notes about them all, and even found acquaintances in common, like Liprandi, to whom I'd surrendered, rather informally, at Balaclava, and whom she'd waltzed with at St. Petersburg, and the big Sudanese with tribal cuts on his face who kept the Cigale café in Alex—and Blowitz, naturally, was an amusing topic.

I wasn't sorry, though, when supper-time came. *Tête-à-tête* is all very jolly, but when you know dam' well your voluptuous *vis-à-vis* is a *cul-de-sac,* and she sits on your chair-arm with her udders in your ear and a bare shoulder begging to be nibbled and her perfume conjuring erotic notions, and you daren't stir a lecherous finger for fear of bursting the needlework in your navel and suffering the indignity of having her remove your blood-sodden britches and upbraid you for a forsworn satyr, none of which will do a thing for your future amorous relations . . . well, it's trying, I can tell you. *Le pauvre M. Tantaloose* didn't know what frustration was. Ne'er mind, thinks I, we'll make up for this in Paris presently. Kralta'll keep.

It was quite like old times to sit across the table from her in candlelight, tucking into the cold ham and fruit and Bernkastler, she chattering gaily and I sitting easy and admiring the highlights on the dark curls, and the perfect ivory curves of chin and neck and shoulder. I could have imagined we were back in the Jager Strasse, except for a brief moment when she peeled a plum and presented it to me, laughing, on a fork . . . and I thought of those dainty fingers with their polished nails coiled round a sabre hilt, and of the hidden strength of the slender white arm—but when I looked, the smiling lips and merry eyes were those of the Caprice I knew so well, exclaiming *"Oh-la, gauche!"* when I dropped the fork, and a moment later rising and gleaming at me over the rim of her glass as she proposed a toast to our reunion.

"I've a better toast than that," says I, halting round the table and nuzzling her neck. "To our next meeting, when this dam' scratch of mine has healed." She clinked glasses, but said nothing. I asked when she was going back to Paris.

"Tomorrow, *hélas!* We go one at a time, ever so *discret,* Delzons last of all. Either he or M. Hutton will remain until you are well enough to travel, and then this house will be closed, and the operation will be over." She turned away and put her glass on the mantel, her back to me. "You will return to London?"

"Oh, no hurry. Time for a week or two in Paris, then we'll see." I stepped close to kiss her on the nape of the neck, and she glanced round.

"Why Paris?" says she lightly.

"Why d'you think?" says I, and slipped my hands round to clasp her breasts. She shivered, and then very gently she removed my hands and turned to face me, smiling still, but a touch wary.

"That might . . . be difficult," says she. "I do not think that

Charles-Alain would approve. And I am sure his family would not."

"Charles *who?*"

"Charles-Alain de la Tour d'Auvergne," says she, and the smile had an impish twinkle to it. "My husband. I have been Madame de la Tour d'Auvergne for six months now."

I must have looked like a fish on a slab. "Husband! You—married? My stars above! Well, blow my boots, and you never let on—"

"Blow your boots, you never noticed!" laughs she, holding up her left hand, and there was the gold band, sure enough.

"Eh? What? Well, I never do . . . I mean, I didn't see . . . well, I'll be damned! Of all things! Here, though, I must kiss the bride!" Which I did, and would have made a meal of it, but she slipped away, squeaking at me to mind my wound, and taking refuge behind the table. I bore up, grinning at her across the board.

"Why, you sly little puss! *Le chaton,* right enough! Well, well . . . still, it makes no odds." She looked startled. "Oh, I'll still come to Paris, never you fret—he don't have to know, this de la Thingamabob!"

It was her turn to stare, and then, would you believe it, she went into whoops, and had to sit down in the armchair, helpless with laughter. I asked what was the joke, and when she'd drawn breath and dabbed her eyes, she shook her head at me in despair.

"Oh, but you are the most dreadful, adorable man! No, he would not have to know . . . but *I* would know." She sighed, smiling but solemn. "And I have made my vows."

" 'Strewth! You mean . . . it's no go—just 'cos you're *married?*"

"No go," says she gently. "Ah, *chéri,* I am sorry, but . . . you do understand?"

"Shot if I do!" And I didn't, for 'twasn't as though she was some little bourgeois *hausfrau*—dammit, she was French, and had sported her bum and boobies in the Folies for the entertainment of lewd fellows and rogered with the likes of Shuvalov *pour la patrie,* and myself and God knew how many others for the fun of it . . . and her behaviour this evening hadn't been married-respectable, exactly, dressed to the seductive nines and kissing indecorously.

I remarked on this, and she sighed. "Oh, if you had been well, I would not have come, knowing you would wish to make love . . . but knowing you were *blessé,* and unable to . . ." She gestured helplessly. "Oh, you know . . . I thought we might talk and be jolly, as we used to be, but without . . . oh, 'hankey-pankey.' " She shrugged in pretty apology, and suddenly her face lit up. "Because those were such happy days in Berlin! Oh, not only making love, but being comfortable and laughing and talking— and I wished to see you once again, and remember those times, and see if you had changed—and, oh, I am so glad to find that you have not!" She rose and put a hand to my face and pecked me on the cheek. "But I have, you see. I am Madame de la Tour d'Auvergne now, ever so *respectable.*" She pulled a face. "No more *la gaie Caprice.* I change myself, I change my life . . . and, *hélas,* I must change my old friends. So it is better you do not come to Paris . . . Do you mind very much? You are not angry?"

A number of women have had the poor taste and bad judgment to give me the right about. In my callow youth I resented it damnably, and either thrashed 'em (as with Judy, my guv'nor's piece), or went for 'em with a sabre (Narreeman, my flower of the Khyber), or ran like hell (Lola of the blazing temper and flying crockery). In later years you learn to assume indifference while studying how to pay them out, supposing you care enough. With Caprice, I'd have been piqued, no more . . . if I'd believed her laughable excuse, which I did not for a moment. She, a faithful wife? Come up, love! No, the fact was that Flashy five years on (seen at his worst, mind, flat on his back and beat, and now a hapless invalid) no longer aroused her amorous interest. Well, I could take the jolt to my *amour-propre* the more easily because while she'd been a prime ride and good company, she'd never had the magic that gets beneath your hide, like Yehonala or Lakshmi or Sonsee-array . . . or Elspeth. She was too young for that . . . but old enough to know better than to play the saucy minx, teasing me into a frustrated heat and *then* showing me the door.

Oh, some of the old affection lingered, no doubt, hence the fatuous tale of marital fidelity, to let me down lightly. I could have swallowed it if she'd come right out with it first thing, but she hadn't been able to resist her wanton instinct to set me panting—even now there was a glint of mockery in the ever-so-contrite smile that told me she was enjoying feeling sorry for the randy old fool, well pleased with her beauty's power . . . and doubtless convincing herself that she felt a touch of sentimental remorse, the little hypocrite. Even the best of them like to make you squirm. I had a sudden memory of the salt-mine and that cold steel being driven ruthlessly home . . . and call it sour grapes if you like, but I found myself warming to the thought of Princess Kralta.

"Angry, little one? Not a bit of it!" cries I, beaming like any-thing, and pecked her back. "I'm sorry, o' course—but jolly glad for you! He's a lucky chap, your Charlie—what is he, a dashing hussar, eh?"

"Oh, no . . . but he is a soldier . . . that is, he is a professor of *l'histoire militaire*, at St. Cyr."

"I say! He must be a bright spark! Blackboard-wallahs are pretty senior as a rule."

She confessed that he was older than she (nearly twice her age, in fact) and from an old service family—the usual decayed Frog nobility by the sound of the name,[22] but she wasn't forth-coming at all, and I guessed that the mere thought of the raff-ish Flashy being presented to dear Charles' parents, as an old acquaintance even, filled her with dismay. I found myself wondering how much they knew about her . . . and whether the arrival on Papa d'Auvergne's breakfast table of that splendid photograph of his daughter-in-law, bare-titted among the potted palms and nigger stallions, mightn't enliven his *petit déjeuner*. A passing thought, and cheered me up no end.

"But what do Charles' people think about your working for the secret department? Hardly the thing for a staid married lady, what?"

"They did not approve, of course. But that is past now. We agreed, Charles and I, that I must resign before our marriage—"

"But here you are!"

"Only because this was *une crise*, an emergency, and Delzons was in despair to recruit agents for the occasion. The *département*, like your own in England, must make do with little . . . and I could not refuse Delzons. I owe him too much."

"And Charles didn't mind? Well, he's a sportsman! Of course, it was an important affair, international crisis, and all that."

She hesitated. "He did not know. I am at this moment visiting a school friend in Switzerland."

Better and better. Not the kind of thing to confide to a lover who's just been handed his travel warrant, mind.

"Well, God bless Charles, anyway! I'd like to meet him one o' these days." She didn't clap her hands, so I took them gently in mine and gave her my best wistful sigh, like a ruptured uncle. "And bless you, too, my dear. And since you don't want to talk about t'other thing, in that beastly cave—"

"*Non, non—*"

"Well, then, I shan't, so there. I'll only say that I'm monstrous glad that you visited your school chum in Switzerland, what? And that you came to see me this evening. Quite like old times, eh . . . well, almost." I winked and slid my hands round her rump, kneading away to show there were no hard feelings—and blowed if the sentimental little tart didn't start piping her eye.

"Oh, you are the best man alive! So kind, so *généreux*!" She clung to me, bedewing my shirt, and raised her face to mine. "And . . . and never shall I forget Berlin!" She threw her arms round my neck and kissed me—none of your pecks this time, but the full lascivious munch, wet and wonderful, and if you don't breathe through your nose you die of suffocation. I had to press my stitches hard until she came loose at last, lips quivering, dabbing at her eyes.

"My goodness, what would Charles say?" I wondered, playful-like. "I can't believe professors of *l'histoire militaire* approve o' that sort of thing."

She looked uncertain, and decided to be airy. "*Oh, chacun a son goût*, you know."

"Well, you mustn't shock him. Can't think when I was last kissed thataway. Not since the Orient Express, anyway."

"*Qu'est-ce que c'est?*" A moment's perplexity, and then the penny dropped, and she went pink and took a step back. "Oh! *La princesse* . . . I . . . I did not . . ."

"Ah, you've met her, then?"

"I have seen her, with Delzons. When we were at the police *commissariat*." She was confused, but recovered, smiling brightly. "But of course, she and that other brought you from Germany. She is . . . very beautiful."

"Fine figure of a woman," says I, looking her up and down. "More to the point, she has no conscience where her husband's concerned." I grinned and repeated her own words. "D'you mind very much? You're not angry?"

Just for a moment her eyes flashed, and then she laughed—and riposted neatly by repeating mine.

"Angry? Not a bit of it; I am jolly glad for you. She is perhaps . . ." she made a little fluttering gesture ". . . how do you say . . . more your style?"

"More my age, you mean."

"No such thing!" cries she merrily. "Now, you will take care of your wound, and not make too much exertion—"

"Oh, beef tea and bedsocks, that's my ticket! Don't you over-exert yourself either, or you'll scandalise Charles."

We smiled amiably on each other, and when I'd helped her put on her cape she held out her hand, not her lips.

"*Adieu*, then," says she.

I bowed to kiss her hand. "Au'voir, Caprice . . . oh, *pardon*—Madame. *Bonne chance*."

She went, and as I listened to her heels clicking on the stairs I was wondering where the devil I'd put that photograph. Saving Flashy's life is all very well, but don't ever play fast and loose with his affections. He's a sensitive soul.

Chapter 10

The older you get, the longer you take to heal. The hole in my gut was as neat and handy as a wound can hope to be, and thirty years earlier would have been right in a fortnight, but now it turned angry, no doubt from the strain imposed by my frustrating half-dalliance with Madame de la Tour d'Auvergne, damn her wanton ways. The stitches had come adrift, and had to be replaced by my little medico, I developed a fever which returned me to bed for more than a week, and after that I was no better than walking wounded, for I was weak as a rat and common sense demanded that I should go canny, as Elspeth would say.

She was much in my mind at that time, but then she always is when I've passed through the furnace and am looking for consolation. The thought of that loving smile, the child-like innocence of the forget-me-not eyes, the soft sweet voice, and the matronly charms bursting out of her corset, made me downright homesick, and with Caprice turning me off, the stupid little trollop, I'd have been tempted to set my sights on London if it hadn't been for the prospect of rattling Kralta all over Vienna. I couldn't forgo that, in all conscience; our railway idyll had given me an appetite, and after it was satisfied would be time enough to cry off with the new love and on with the old.

So I bore my captivity into November, glad to be alive, and passing the time pondering on the mysteries of those few short days of strange adventure—barely a week, from the time when I'd been sitting in Berkeley Square gloating over Kralta's picture, to the awful moment when I'd pegged out in that hellish mine, with Caprice clucking over me like an anxious hen and Starnberg's corpse floating in the limpid brine. Reviewing it all . . . I knew *what* had happened, but not *why;* in all the confusion of lies and deceits and *voltes-face,* there were mysteries, as I say, which I didn't understand, and still don't.

On the face of it, Bismarck had concocted a lunatic but logical scheme to save the Austrian Emperor from assassination, and it had succeeded in a way he could never have foreseen, with his trusted henchman proving traitor but being foiled by old Flashy's blundering. Well, lucky old Otto—and lucky Franz-Josef and lucky Europe. (And when we'd gone, no one would ever believe it.) Knowing my opinion of Bismarck, you may wonder that I don't suspect him of some gigantic Machiavellian double-deal whereby he'd invented the tale of a Holnup plot (to hoax simpletons like me and Kralta) so that Starnberg could murder Franz-Josef with Bismarck's blessing, and start another war—he'd done it before, God knows, twice at least, and wouldn't have scrupled to do it again if it had suited his book. But it didn't, you see; he'd built Germany into a European Power, by blood and skulduggery, and had nothing to gain by another explosion. He could rest on his laurels and let nature take its usual disastrous course—as it is doing, if only imbeciles like Asquith would notice. Well, I'm past caring.

At a lesser remove, I couldn't figure Starnberg's behaviour in the mine. Why, having done his level damnedest to kill me, had he saved me from going down that awful chasm into the bowels of the earth? 'Cos he'd wanted to put me away with his own steel? To prolong my agony? Or from some mad, quixotic impulse which he mightn't have understood himself? Search me. Folk like the Starnbergs, father and son, don't play by ordinary rules. I only hope there ain't a grandson loose about the place.

I still wondered, too, why Caprice had cut him down in cold blood, and why she wouldn't talk of it, even. Vanity would have tempted me to take Hutton's judgment that she was dead spoony on me and had done him in for that reason, if she had not since handed me my marching orders. (And on the pretext of fidelity to some muffin of a military historian! I still couldn't get over that. Aye, well, the silly bint would rue her lost opportunities when next Professor Charles-Alain clambered aboard her—in the dark, probably, and wearing a nightcap with a tassel, the daring dog.) My own view, for what it was worth, was that she'd murdered Starnberg because it struck her (being female) as the fitting and tidy thing to do—and gave her the last word, so there. Delzons, her chief, who knew her better than anyone, had a different explanation, which he gave me the day before we left Ischl, and you must make of it what you will.

Hutton had gone back to London by then, after assuring me that Government was satisfied; no official approval, of course, but no censure either; my assistance had been noted, and would be recorded in the secret papers. Aye, I'm still waiting for my peerage.

Delzons had stayed on to close the Ischl house as soon as I was fit to take the open air. Paris was no keener on maintaining bolt-holes out of secret funds than London, and the pair of us transferred to the Golden Ship, myself to complete my convalescence and Delzons to enjoy a holiday—or so he said, but I suspect he was keeping an eye on me to see that I didn't get into mischief. I was glad enough of his company, for he was the best kind of Frog, shrewd and tough as teak, but jolly and with no foolish airs.

It would be late November, when I was healed and feeling barely a twinge, that we walked across the Ischl bridges and up the hill to the royal lodge. The trees were bare, there was a little snow lying, and the river was grey and sullen with icy patches under the banks. The lodge itself was silent under a leaden sky, with only a servant in sight, sweeping leaves and snow from the big porch; it would be months before Franz-Josef returned to add to the collection of heads in that dark panelled chamber where his aides had crawled about, giggling in drink, and I'd had conniptions as I stared at the doctored cartridges.

We circled the place, and Delzons pointed out the spot where he'd lain doggo and Caprice had slipped away to shadow the Holnups. I studied the open ground, dotted with trees and bushes, between where we stood and the lodge, and remarked that a night-stalk would have been ticklish even for my old Apache chums, Quick Killer and Yawner.

"But not for *la petite*," smiles Delzons. "She has no equal. Is it not remarkable, one so delicately feminine, so pretty and *vivace*, so much a child almost, but of a skill and courage and . . . and firm purpose beyond any agent I have seen?" He nodded thoughtfully. "We have a word, colonel, that I think has no equivalent in English, which I apply to nothing and no one but her. *Formidable*."

"She's all o' that." Plainly he was as smitten with her as Hutton had been, but with Delzons it was fond, almost paternal. "Where did she learn to stalk and . . . so on?"

"In the Breton woods as a child, with her three elder brothers." He chuckled. "She was *une luronne*—a tomboy, no? *Oui, un garçon manqué*. Six years younger than they, but their match in all sport, running, climbing, shooting . . . oh, and daring! And they were no *poules mouillées*, no milksops, those three lads. Yet when she was only twelve she was their master with foil and pistol. Some brothers would have been jealous, but Valéry and Claude and Jacques were her adoring slaves—ah, they were close, those four!"

"You knew 'em well, then," says I, as we strolled back.

"Their father was my *copain* in Crimea, before I joined the intelligence. I was to them as an uncle when they were small, and grew to love them, Caprice above all . . . well, a lonely bachelor engrossed in his work must have something to love, *non?*" He paused, musing a moment, then went on. "But then I was posted abroad for several years, and lost touch with the family until the terrible news reached me that the father and three sons had all fallen in the war of '70—he was by then *chef de brigade,* and the three boys had but lately passed through St. Cyr. I was desolate, above all for Caprice, so cruelly deprived at a stroke of all those she loved. I wrote to her, of my grief and condolence, assuring her of my support in any way possible. Thus it was, two years later, when I came home to command the European section of the *département secret,* that she came to see me—*asking for employment. Mon dieu!*" He heaved in emotion, and at once became apologetic. "Oh, forgive me . . . perhaps I weary you? No? Then let us sit a moment."

We settled on a bench by the path overlooking the river, and Delzons lit his pipe, gazing down at the distant snow-patched roofs.

"You conceive my amazement, not only to discover that my little *gamine* had become a lovely young woman, but that she should seek an occupation so unsuitable, *mais inconcevable,* for one so *chaste et modeste.* 'Why, dear child?' I asked. 'I cannot be a soldier like my father and brothers. I shall fight for France in my own way.' That was her reply. As gently as might be, I suggested that there were other ways to serve, that the world of the *département secret* was a hard and dangerous one, and . . . highly unpleasant in ways which she, a convent-reared girl of eighteen, could not conceive. Do you know what she said, colonel? 'Uncle Delzons, I have studied the world from the *tableaux vivants* of the Folies Gaités, and moved among its clientele, who are also hard, dangerous, and unpleasant.' Before I could even express my scandal, for I had known nothing of this, she added—oh, so quiet and demure with that laughter in her innocent eyes—'Also I am fluent in languages, and fence and shoot even better these days.' "

Delzons took the pipe from his mouth, looked at it, and stuck it back. "What could I say? I was shocked, yes—but I saw, too, that beneath the fresh, lovely surface there was a metal that I had never suspected. It is rare, such metal, and essential to the *département secret*. And if I had refused her, I knew there were other sections of the *département* which would not." He laughed ruefully. "The truth was, she was a gift to any *chef d'intelligence*. And so she proved, in small things at first, as translator, courier, embassy *bricoleur*—what you call 'jack-of-all-trades'—and later as secret agent in the field . . . and you know what that means. Yes . . . she was the best."

I said he must have been sorry to lose her, and he grimaced. "She told you? Yes, sorry . . . but I rejoiced also. For six years I had lost sleep, whenever she went into danger. Oh, seldom enough—our work, as you are aware, brings a moment's peril in a year of routine—but when that peril comes . . . No, I am glad she has gone. When I think of the risks she ran—of her facing a man like Starnberg to the death, my heart ceases to beat. If we had lost her . . . my friend, I should have died. It is true, my heart would have ceased forever then."

The usual exaggerated Froggy vapouring, but Delzons wasn't the usual Frog, and I guessed he believed it. I took the opportunity to canvass his opinion.

"Well, you needn't ha' fretted. He was a capital hand with a sabre, but not in her parish." I paused deliberately. "Can't think I've ever seen a neater . . . execution."

His head came round sharply. "Ah! You confirm M. 'Utton's opinion—which I happen to share. The evidence of Starnberg's wounds was conclusive. As you say . . . an execution." His eyes were steady on mine. "But in my report, self-defence. As it must always be when an agent kills . . . in the line of duty."

That reminded me of something Hutton had said. "He told me Starnberg wasn't the first she'd sent down. Were the others self-defence, too?"

He frowned and muttered a nasty word. "I have a great

respect for our colleague 'Utton, but he talks too much." He
sucked at his dead pipe, and continued rapid-fire. "Yes. She has
killed before. Twice. In Egypt, in Turkey. One was a minor diplomat who had found out she was a French agent. The other an
informer whose silence was essential. She was not under my control on either occasion. My responsibility is for Europe. She was
on detachment to another section. I did not seek details."
Abruptly he got to his feet, his mouth set like a trap. "Nor have
she and I ever mentioned the incidents. Shall we walk on,
colonel?"

And this was the girl who had giggled with me over *Punch*. I
fell into step beside him as we walked down to the bridges, his
stick fairly cracking at each stride, but there was a grim grin
under his heavy moustache.

"Oh, M. 'Utton!" cries he. "So talkative, so shrewd! No
doubt he offered you his theory that she slew Starnberg in cold
blood because of a *tendre* for you? *Bon sang de merde!*" He gave a
barking laugh. "Enraged because he had wounded, perhaps slain,
her lover! Perhaps you believe that yourself, because you were
lovers in Berlin—oh, I know all about her 'holiday task' for
Blowitz! What, you do not believe 'Utton's theory? I congratu-
late you!" He calmed after a few steps. "Your *affaire* in Berlin was
an *amour passant*, then. Not of the heart."

Gad, they're a tactful, tasteful lot, the French. "Not on my
side," I told him.

"Nor on hers, whatever the so-shrewd 'Utton may think.
Shall I tell you why she killed Starnberg as she did?"

He had stopped on the bridge, turned to face me. "I told you
her father and brothers fell in the war of '70 against the Germans,
and what she said of fighting in her own way. I did not tell
you how they died. Papa and Jacques were killed in the battle
at Gravelotte. Claude died of his wounds, neglected . . . in a
German hospital. Valéry was in the intelligence. He was captured
at St. Privat on a *mission d'espionnage*. He was shot by a firing

squad of Fransecky's Pomeranians, the day *after* the signing of the armistice, February the first, 1871!" Suddenly the eyes in the bulldog face were bright with angry tears. "They knew the armistice had been signed, but they shot him just the same. Just the same! German chivalry."

It had started to snow, and he was hunched up against the chill wind, staring down at the river.

"So they were gone, all four, it seemed in a moment . . . as the poet says of a snowflake on the water. Did I mention that the diplomat in Turkey and the informer in Egypt were both Germans? No? Well, Caprice does not like Germans. As the Count von Starnberg discovered. But I am keeping you standing in the cold, colonel! Give me your arm, my friend! Shall we seek a café and a cup of chocolate—with a large cognac to flavour it, eh?"

Some clever ass has said that "if" is the biggest word in the language, but I say it's the most useless. There have been so many coincidences in my life, good and bad, that I've learned the folly of exclaiming "If only . . . !" They happen, and that's that, and if the one that brought my Austrian odyssey to a close was uncommon disastrous—and infuriating, because I'd foreseen its possibility—well, I can be philosophic now because, as I've observed before, I'm still here at ninety, more or less, and you can't ask fairer than that.

But that don't mean I'll ever forgive the drunk porter who mislaid my trunk at Charing Cross, because if he hadn't . . . there, you see, "if" almost got the better of me, and no wonder when I think what came of that boozy idiot's carelessness. Shocking state the railways are in.

However, we'll come to Charing Cross all in good time. I'd have been there weeks earlier if (there it is again, dammit) Kralta hadn't been so amorously intoxicated, and the circumstances of our reunion in Vienna so different from what I'd expected. When I took the train from Ischl early in December I was looking forward to a couple of cosy and intimate weeks in which I rogered her blue in the face, sparked her to the opera or whatever evening amusements Vienna offered, wined and dined of the best, saw the sights, took her riding (for she looked too much like a horse to be anything but an equestrian), viewed the Blue Danube from the warm comfort of her bedroom, and back to the muttons again. A modest enough ambition, and would have had me home again by Christmas. Well, I was taken aback, if not disappointed, by what awaited me at the Grand Hotel, and followed in the ensuing weeks.

I'd telegraphed from Ischl to advise her that I'd be rolling in, and when I arrived at the Grand, which was the newest and best-appointed of the leading hotels, she was awaiting me in a suite of rooms that Louis XIV might have thought too large and opulent for his taste. Vienna's like that, you see; in most great cities the new districts are where the Quality hang out, but in Vienna the old sections are the exclusive ones, infested by the most numerous nobility in Europe, living in palaces and splendid mansions built centuries ago by ancestors who plainly felt that even a lavatory wasn't a lavatory unless it could accommodate a hunt ball, with gilded cherubs on the ceiling and walls that looked like wedding cakes. Even new hotels like the Grand were to match, and the whole quarter reeked of money, privilege, and luxury in doubtful taste. It was reckoned to be the richest Upper Ten outside London, and the two hundred families of princes, counts, and assorted titled trash spent ten million quid among 'em per annum, which ain't bad for gaslight and groceries. They spent more, ate more, drank more, danced more, and fornicated more than any other capital on earth (and that's Fetridge[23] talking, not me), and cared not a rap for anything except their musical fame, of which they're wonderfully jealous—not without cause, I'd say, when you think of the waltz.

I'd arranged to arrive in town late, at an hour when Kralta would be cleared for bed and action, but when I reached the hotel close on midnight I saw that I'd been too long in the provinces; the hall was thronged with revellers, the dining salon was full, and an orchestra was going full swing. Even so, I was unprepared for the start I received when I was ushered into her drawing-room: where I'd looked to find her alone, there were thirty folk if there was one, all ablaze in the pink of fashion, and me in my travelling dirt. And she, whom I'd imagined flinging aside her fur robe and flying to my arms, was magnificent in tiara, long gloves, and ivory silk, the image of her photograph, standing amidst her society gaggle, waiting calmly for me to approach, as though she'd been royalty. Which of course she was—European royalty, leastways.

But I couldn't complain of her welcoming smile, with a hand stretched out for me to kiss. "At last, we meet in Vienna!" says she softly, and then I was being presented to Prince This and Baroness That, and Colonel von Stuff and Madame Puff—and this I'll say for them, there wasn't a sneer or a sniff at my tweeds, such as you'd get from Frogs or Dagoes or our own reptilia; Vienna wasn't only polite, it was downright friendly and hospitable, putting a glass in my hand, coaxing me to the buffet, inquiring after my journey, asking how long I'd been in town, exclaiming that I must call or dine or see such-and-such, the men frank and genial, the women gay and easy—some damned handsome pieces there were, too—and Kralta, smiling coolly with her hand on my sleeve, guided me effortlessly through the crowd and out into a secluded alcove—and then she was in my arms, her mouth open under mine, fairly writhing against me, and I was making up for weeks of abstinence and wondering when we could get to work in earnest when suddenly she left off and buried her head on my shoulder.

"Thank God you are safe!" says she, in a choking voice.

"When I heard what that . . . that vile traitor had done to you, I thought I should run mad! Oh, thank God, thank God!"

Thank a nimble little Parisienne cut-throat, thinks I, but all I did was murmur comfort, kissing her again and swearing that I'd been baying the moon at the thought of her, and when could we get shot of her guests? She laughed at that, holding my hands and regarding me fondly, and I found myself marvelling that a woman whose looks didn't compare to half of those on view in her drawing-room could rouse such desire in me—mind you, there wasn't a shape among 'em to match the splendid body in its ivory sheath, or a carriage to set beside that striking figurehead with its long gold tresses coiled beneath the diamond crown.

I had to bottle my ardour for more than an hour, for while the fashionable crowd soon dispersed, four who seemed to be her prime intimates stayed to sup with us. They were an oddish group, I thought: some Prince or other, a distinguished greybeard with an order on his coat, and three females, all extremely personable. One of 'em, a countess, was dark and soulful and soft-spoken, and possessed of the most enormous juggs I've ever seen; how she managed her soup, heaven knows, for I'll swear she couldn't see her plate. T'others were a prattling blonde who flirted out of habit, even with the waiters, and a slender, red-haired piece who drank like a Mississippi pilot, with no visible effect. The Prince was plainly a big gun, and most courteous to me, and Kralta was at her most stately, so it was a decorous enough meal bar the blonde's chatter and coquettish glances, which no one deigned to notice. Good form, the Viennese.

We parted at last, thank the Lord, with bows and nods and polite murmurs, Kralta led the way to her bedchamber, and I was all over her at once, with growls of endearment and a great wrenching of buttons. It was a true meeting of minds, for I doubt if a woman ever stripped faster from full court regalia, and we revelled in each other like peasants in a hayrick, from bed to floor

and back again, I believe, but I ain't sure. And when we were glo-
riously done, and I lay gasping while she wept softly and kissed
the healed scar on my flank, murmuring endearments, I thought,
well, this is why you came to Europe, Flash, and Ischl was worth
it. She said not a word then or thereafter about Starnberg or the
plot, and I was content to let it lie.

I staggered out presently to visit the little private lavatory in
an ante-chamber off the drawing-room, and was taken flat aback
when who should come out of the thunder-house but the Prince,
clad in a silk robe with his beard in a net. What the deuce he was
doing on the premises, I couldn't imagine, but I admired his
aplomb, for I'd ventured out in a state of nature, and he didn't so
much as raise an eyebrow, but waved me in with a courtly hand,
bade me *"Gute Nacht,"* and disappeared through a door on the far
side of the drawing-room. I performed my ablutions in some
bewilderment, and my good angel prompted me to wrap a towel
round myself before venturing out, for when I did, damned if the
door he'd used didn't open, and a massive bosom emerged, followed by the soulful countess in a night-rail fashioned apparently from a scrap of mosquito-net. She gave a start at the sight
of me, murmured *"Entschuldigung!,"* collared a decanter from
the sideboard, and with a sleepy smile and *"Bis später,"* vanished
whence she had come.

Kralta was repairing the damage before her mirror when I
rolled in, much perturbed.

"That Prince and the women—they're out there, large as life!
Who is he, for God's sake?"

"My husband," says she. "You were presented to him."

Well, all I'd caught in the confusing moment of arrival had
been "von und zum umble rumble," as so often happens. I considered, hard.

"Ah! I see. Your husband, eh? And the women?"

"His mistresses," says she, carefully rouging her lip. "It is
convenient that we share the apartment. It is quite large enough,

you see." She began to brush her hair, while I struggled for an appropriate rejoinder, and could think of only one.

"Mistresses, eh? Well, well." She continued to brush calmly, so I added another trenchant observation. "He has three of them."

"Yes. The fair one, Fräulein Boelcke, I had not met before this evening. She talks too freely, don't you think?"

But my conversational bolt was shot. For once I was at a loss—as who would not be, on discovering that while he was bulling a chap's wife all over the shop and probably making a hell of an uproar, the chap himself was virtually next door brushing his teeth or pomading his eyebrows—and even now might be conducting an orgy just across the way with three trollops while the wife of his bosom was smiling tenderly on her bemused lover, kissing him fondly, leading him back to bed, and settling into his arms for conversation and drowsy fondling which must lead inevitably to another outbreak of feverish passion? And it did, even noisier and more protracted than before, for this time she occupied the driving seat, if you know what I mean, and rode herself into a sobbing frenzy they could have heard in Berlin.

I'm an easy-going fellow, as you know, but it struck me as I lay there, urging her on with ecstatic roars and the occasional slap on the rump, and afterwards cradling her to sleep on my breast, that this was a pretty informal household, and would take getting used to. I'm all for cuckolding husbands, and don't give a dam if they know it, unless they're the hellfire horse-whipping sort who'll resent it; indeed, there's nothing like a good gloat in the grinding teeth of some poor muff to whom you've awarded antlers. But when the muff is not only complaisant but approving, and meets you with every politeness at luncheon next day, and his wife is on cordial terms (as cordial, that is, as Kralta could ever be) with the fair trio he's been using as though he were the Sultan of Swat . . . well, it's novel, and I wasn't sure that I cared for it above half.

It took me a few weeks to settle my thoughts on the subject, and reflection was made no easier by the distractions Vienna afforded. I've never wallowed in such sumptuous indulgence in my life; even being a crowned head in Strackenz didn't compare to it. The place was dedicated to sheer pleasure in those days, and I guess I became intoxicated in a way that had nothing to do with drink, although there was enough and to spare of that. Perhaps I was still fagged from my ordeal; at all events I was content to be borne along on that gay, dazzling tide, idling and stuffing and boozing and viewing the capital's wonders by day, consorting with Kralta's vast social circle (which included the Prince and his skirts as often as not) of an evening, and letting her have her haughty head by night.

She was a demanding mistress, and if she hadn't been such a prime mount, and besotted with me to boot, I might have brought her to heel—or tried to. That she was an imperious piece I knew, but now I saw it wasn't just her nature, which was the root of her pride, but the life she led which fostered that almighty growth. Vienna seemed to be at her feet; she was deferred to on all sides, and placed on a social level not far short of imperial, toad-eaten by the flower of society, and ruling it with a tilted chin and cold eye. The style in which she lived argued fabulous wealth, and she spent it like a whaler in port, on the slightest whim; small wonder she liked to call the tune in bed.

Speaking of imperial, I had a taste of that when she took me, with the Prince and his hareem in tow, to a gala ball at Schonbrunn, where the Emperor and Empress condescended to mingle with Vienna's finest. That was a damned odd turn, eerie almost, for a moment came when, with Kralta standing by like a magnificent ring-mistress, I found myself face to face with Franz-Josef and the superb Sissi. He drew himself up to his imposing height, whiskers at the high port, and stared me straight in the eye for a long moment; he said not a word, but held out his hand, and 'twasn't the usual touch-and-away of royalty, but a good strong clasp followed by a hearty shake before he passed on, Sissi following with a smiling turn of her lovely head. That's his vote of thanks for services rendered, thinks I, and the most he can do or I can expect—but I was wrong. There was something more, though whether 'twas his idea or Sissi's I can't say. When the dancing began, and I was restoring myself with a glass of Tokay after whirling Kralta's substantial poundage round the floor, a lordly swell with a ribboned order presented himself and informed me that Her Imperial Majesty would be graciously pleased to accept if I were to beg the honour of leading her out for the next dance.

It was unprecedented, I'm told, to a foreign stranger, and a commoner at that. You may be sure I complied, with a beating heart, I confess. And so I waltzed beneath the chandeliers of Old Vienna, under the eyes of the highest and noblest of the Austrian Empire, with Strauss himself flogging the orchestra, and my partner was that magical raven-haired beauty who had all Europe at her feet, and I didn't tread on 'em once. Afterwards I led her back to Franz-Josef, and received his courteous nod and her brilliant smile.

Well, I've rattled the Empress of China and Her Majesty of Madagascar, to say nothing of an Apache Princess and (to the best of my belief) an Indian Rani, and that's my business, to be written about but not spoken of. But I can tell my great-grandchildren face to face that I've danced with the Queen of Hearts. And she, of course, has danced with me.

We spent Christmas at a castle of Kralta's—or her husband's, I never found out which—high in the snowy Tyrolean mountains, and toasted in the New Year in a luxurious hunting lodge in a little valley whose inhabitants spoke a strange sort of German laced with Scotch expressions—the legacy, I'm told, of medieval mercenaries who never went home, doubtless for fear of arrest. Both places were full of titled guests invited (or commanded, rather) by Kralta, and we drove in sleighs and skated and tobogganed and revelled by evening and pleasured by night, and it was Vienna in the Arctic, with the Prince always on hand, bland and affable as ever with his popsies around him (one of 'em a new bird, an Italian, who'd replaced the garrulous blonde, no doubt on Kralta's orders) and it was all such enormous fun that I was heartily sick of it.

Don't misunderstand me—it wasn't a surfeit of debauchery and the high life, although there does come a time when you find yourself longing for a pint and a pie and a decent night's sleep. And it was only partly that I was beginning to miss English voices and English rain and all those things that make the old country so different, thank God, from the Continent. No, I was beginning to realise what had irked me from the first—being just another player in *their* game, having it taken for granted that I'd be a compliant member of Kralta's curious *ménage,* as though I were the latest recruit, if you know what I mean. I've always been a free lance, so to speak, going my own way on my own terms, and the notion that Viennese society was raising its weary eyebrows and saying: "Ah, yes, this Englishman is new to her entourage; how long will he last, one wonders?," and that Kralta probably thought of me as her husband did of his trollops . . . no, it didn't suit.

The final straw came on a night in the hunting lodge when I'd become so infernally bored that I'd gone to the village for a prose with the peasants at the tavern, and came home in the small hours. Some of the guests were still about in the principal rooms, drinking and flirting and casting (I thought) odd looks in my direction. I went up, and was making for the chamber I shared with Kralta when a soft voice called and I turned to see the Prince's *maîtresse-en-titre,* she of the heroic bosom, standing in an open doorway in a silk night-rail that was never designed for sleeping.

"The Prince is with her highness tonight," says she, with an arch look. Is he, by God! thinks I, and for a moment was seized with an impulse to stride in and drag him off her by the nape of his cuckolded neck—or her off him, more like, the arrogant bitch. Countess Grosbrusts was watching to see what I made of it, so I looked her over thoughtful-like, and she smiled, and I grinned at her, and she shrugged, and I laughed, and she laughed in turn which set 'em shaking, and as she turned into her room, casting a backward glance, I sauntered after, thinking what a capital change for my last night in Austria.

It was the custom at the lodge for the whole troop to gather for a late breakfast in the main salon, so I waited until all had assembled, despatched a lackey to Kralta's quarters with orders to pack my traps and send 'em to the station, strolled down with Lady Bountiful on my arm, and announced to the company that I was desolated to have to leave them that day, as urgent affairs in London demanded my attention (which was prophetic, if you like).

Kralta, seated in state by the fire with her toads clustered round stirring her chocolate for her, went pale; she was looking deuced fetching, I have to say, in a white fur robe which prompted happy memories of the Orient Express. I made my apologies, and her eyes were diamond-hard as she glanced from me to my buxom companion and then to the Prince (who was looking a shade worn, I thought), but she would not have been Kralta if she hadn't responded with icy composure, regretting my departure without expression on that proud horse face. I kissed her hand, made my bow to the Prince, advised him to stick at it, saluted the company, and departed, with a last smile at the splendid white figure seated in state, her golden hair spilling over her shoulders, inclining her head with the regal condescension she'd used at our first meeting. By and large I like to leave 'em happy, but I doubt if she was.

Three days later I was at Charing Cross Station on one of those damp, dismal evenings when the fog rolls inside the buildings and the heart of the returning traveller is gladdened by the sight and smell of it all, London with its grime and bustle and raucous inhabitants, and there ain't a *"Ja, mein Herr,"* to be heard, or a sullen Frog face, and not a plate of *sauerkraut* in sight. I could even listen with fair good humour to the harassed excuses of the Cockney porter carrying my valise as he protested that he didn't knaow nuffink abaht the trunk, guv', 'cos 'Erbert 'ad gorn ter the guard's van for it, and where the 'ell 'e'd got ter, Gawd ownly knew. Sid and Fred were appealed to, search parties were despatched, and 'Erbert was discovered in the left-luggage office, reclining on a lower shelf in a state of merry inebriation. My porter gave tongue blasphemously.

"I knoo the barstid was 'arf-seas over when 'e come on! Din' I say? Din' I? Well, 'e can pick up 'is money if the super sees 'im, an' chance it! Serve the bleeder right, an' all! I'm sorry, guv'! Look, I'll whistle a cab for yer, and Sid an' Fred'll 'ave yer trunk run dahn in no toime!"

It was music to my ears, and I dawdled patiently, drinking in the sights and sounds of home, and even chuckling at the sight of the semi-comatose 'Erbert leaving off his rendition of "Fifteen men onna dead man's chest, yow-ow-ow an' a bottlarum" to assure my porter, whose name was Ginger, that 'e was a blurry good mate an' a jolly ole pal, before subsiding among the piled baggage.

"Stoopid sod!" cried Ginger. "Gawd knaows w'ere 'e's put it! Doan't worry, guv', we'll foind it! 'Ere, Sid, wot trains is goin' aht jus' naow? Can't 'ave the gen'man's trunk bein' sent orf by mistake, can we?"

"Eight o'clock's leavin' shortly f'm Platform Free!" said Sid.

"Jeesus wept, that's the bleedin' boat train! Naow, 'e wouldn't, would 'e? 'Ere, Fred, be a toff an' nip dahn to Free, jus' ter mike shore, an' we'll ferret abaht rahnd the cab-stands an' that—jus' you wait, guv'! We'll 'ave it in arf a tick!"

I continued to loiter as Fred set off for Platform Three, and just then a neat little bottom tripped past, making for the tea-room, and I sauntered idly after it, curious to see if the front view lived up to the trim ankles and waist. No more than that, but it changed my life, for as I strolled along my eye caught sight of "3" above a ticket gate, and I changed course to see how Fred was doing in his quest for my trunk. The train was within a few minutes of leaving, heavy bags were going into the guard's van, and Fred was emerging, shaking his head—and at that moment I caught sight of a familiar face down the platform, and strolled along to make sure. He was carrying a bag, and making for a group of fellows standing by a carriage door. I hove up by him, grinning.

"Hollo, Joe!" says I. "Taken up portering, have you?"

He wheeled round, and absolutely almost dropped the bag in astonishment. "Good God—Flashman!" cries he. "Why—they've found you, then!"

"Found *me*! They can't even find my blasted trunk! Here, what's the matter? I ain't a ghost, you know!"

For he was staring at me as though he couldn't believe his eyes—or eye, rather, for he'd only one ogle, and it was wide in astonishment, which you didn't often see in the imperturbable Garnet Wolseley.

"Stewart! He's here!" cries he, to the men by the carriage, and as they turned to look my heart gave a lurch, and my stick fell clattering to the platform. The man addressed, tall, dark, and grinning all over his face, was striding forward to grip my hand—young Johnny Stewart, a Cherrypicker long after my time, but an old comrade from Egypt.

"Wherever did you spring from?" cries he. "Heavens, I've been turning the town upside down for you—at your clubs, your house, everywhere . . ."

But I wasn't listening. I'd recognised the others at once—Cambridge, commander-in-chief of the Army, with his grey moustache and high balding head; Granville, the Foreign

Secretary; and jumping down from the carriage and hastening towards me with his quick, neat step, hand outstretched and eyes bright with joy, the last man on earth I wanted to see, the man I'd left England to avoid at all costs: Chinese Charley Gordon.

"Flashman, old friend!" He was pumping my fin like a man possessed. "At the eleventh hour! Did you know—oh, but you must have, surely? Where have you been? Stewart and I had given up all hope!"

Somehow I found my voice. "I've been abroad. In Austria."

"Austria?" laughs he. "That ain't abroad! I'll tell you where's abroad—Africa! That's abroad!" He was grinning in disbelief. "You mean you didn't know I was going back to Sudan?"

I shook my head, my innards like lead. "I'm this minute off the train from Calais—"

"The very place we're bound for! Stewart and I are off to Suakim this very night! He's my chief o' staff . . . and just guess—" he poked me in the chest "—who I've been moving heaven and earth to have as my intelligence *bimbashi*! Isn't that so, Garnet? But you were nowhere to be found—and now you drop from the skies! . . . and you never even knew I was going out!"

" 'Twasn't confirmed until today, after all," says Joe.

"If Flashman had been in Town, he'd ha' caught the scent a week ago!" cries Gordon. "Eyes and ears like a dervish scout, he has! How d'ye think he's here? He *knew* by instinct the game was afoot, didn't you, old fellow? My word, and I thought only we Hielandmen had the second sight!" He stepped closer, and his eyes held that barmy mystic glitter that told me God was going to be hauled into the conversation. "Providence guided you . . . aye, guided you to this very platform! Don't let anyone try to tell me there's nothing in the power of prayer!"

If there had been I'd have been back in Austria that minute, or in Wales or Paisley even—anywhere away from this dangerous maniac gripping my sleeve and not letting me get a word in edgewise. I shot a wild glance at the others: Cambridge pop-eyed, Granville smiling but puzzled, Stewart alert and wondering, and only Joe having the grace to frown and chew his lip. I was speechless at the effrontery of the thing, but Gordon, of course, couldn't see an inch beyond what he thought was a priceless stroke of luck, the selfish hound. It was famous, the happiest of omens . . . and at last I found my tongue.

"But I've just arrived—I'm going home!" I protested, and any normal man would have been checked for a moment at least, but not Gordon, drunk with enthusiasm.

"You *were*—and you shall, one o' these days! But you don't think I'm letting you slip now? Not when Fate has delivered you into my hands?" He was all jocularity—and earnest an instant later, gripping my coat. "Flashman, this is big, believe me. Bigger than China, even—perhaps bigger than anything since the Mutiny. I don't know yet—but I do know it calls for the best we've got. It's going to be the hardest thing I've ever tackled . . . and I need you, old comrade." He was a head shorter than I, and having to stare up at me with those pale hypnotic eyes that made you feel like a rabbit before a snake. "See here, I know it's sudden, and here I am springing it on you like a jack-in-the-box—but the Mahdi's sudden too, and Osman Digna, and every minute counts! Let me tell you on the train—too much to explain now—and I don't even know how I'll set about it, only that we've got to set the Sudan to rights before that madman destroys it. It may mean a fight, it may mean a rearguard action, can't tell yet—and neither can they." He jerked his head at the others. "But they're putting the power in my hands, Flashman, and I can choose whoever I wish."

He stepped back, and he was grinning again. "And I have no hesitation in asking leave of His Grace the Commander-in-Chief—" a duck of the head towards Cambridge "—and the Cabinet—" a nod to Granville "—and our chief man-at-arms—" a flourish at Joe, who was trying to interrupt "—to enlist Sir Harry Flashman, and to the dickens with regulations and usual channels! Well, Harry, what d'ye say?"

Before I could speak, Joe got his word in. "Short notice—" he was beginning, and got no further.

"When did he ever need notice? Some notice he had at Pekin, didn't he? Remember, Garnet? Or at Balaclava, or Cawnpore, or Kabul!" He wasn't soft-spoken at the best of times, and in his excitement he was almost shouting, and passengers were turning to stare at us. "He don't need more than a word and a clear road! Do you?"

This was desperate, but the suddenness of it all still had me at a loss for words—that was the effect that Gordon had, you know, when he was in full cry. He was all over you, beating you down by his vanity-fed fervour, blind to everything but his own point of view. Five minutes ago I'd been carelessly eyeing a jaunty backside while Fred or Ginger looked for my luggage—and now I was being dragooned into God knew what horror by this arrogant zealot—and they called the Mahdi a fanatic!

"Hold on, Charley!" I blurted out. "I . . . I'm looking for my traps, dammit! And . . . and I haven't seen my wife yet, or . . . or—"

"Your traps can be sent on!" cries he. "Why, you're all packed! And Wolseley'll make your excuses at home, won't you, Garnet? We shan't be away forever, you know. Besides," cries he merrily, "if I know bonny Elspeth she'll never let you hear the last of it if you don't fall in now! Why, if she were here she'd be bustling you aboard!"

That was the God's truth, by the way. Duty was Elspeth's watchword, especially when it was *my* duty—hadn't she shot me off to India more than once, weeping, I grant you (though what she'd been up to with those grinning Frogs after Madagascar, once I'd been despatched to the cannon's mouth, I didn't care to imagine). But just the thought of her now, not a couple of miles away, and the radiant smile and glad cry with which she'd run to me, lovelier by far than those stale loves I'd been wasting my time on for weeks past, and her adoring blue eyes . . . no, the hell with Gordon, the selfish lunatic, having the impudence to buttonhole me in this outrageous fashion! And I was bracing myself to put my foot down when Cambridge spoke.

"Irregular, I suppose," says he, shaking his fat head—but not in denial. "But, even so . . . well, nothing to hinder . . . if you're sure, Gordon?"

"Of course I'm sure!" He always was, and not about to have his judgment questioned by a mere grandson of George the Third. He was absolutely frowning at them—the Army commander, the Foreign Secretary, and the greatest soldier of the age (who was carrying his bag for him, God love me!).[24] And they were helpless, glancing resignedly at each other and apologetically at me—because he was Gordon, you see. What he was doing wouldn't have washed with them for a moment, if he had been any other man. But then, no other man would have done it.

Granville was raising his fine brows in a why-not fashion. "It rests with Colonel Flashman, of course." There was a silence, and then Joe Wolseley gave me a shrug and a nod. "I'd be only too glad . . . to explain to Lady Flashman, if you . . ." He left it there.

They were all looking at me . . . and I knew it was all up. It was appalling, and beyond belief, and no fate was too dreadful for Gordon, damn his arrogant confidence as he stood there smiling triumphantly . . . but I knew, as I'd known so often, what the answer must be. The Great Christian Hero had tapped my shoulder—and I'd never live it down if I refused. I could have wept at the cruelty of the malign fate that had guided me to Platform Three at that hour—ten minutes later, and the blasted train would have been away, carrying Gordon to Hell or Honolulu for all I cared.

But when the cards are dealt, you must play 'em—and with

style, for your reputation's sake. Flashy has his own way of bowing to the inevitable—and I knew dam' well it would run round Horse Guards and the clubs like wildfire in the morning . . .

"I say—you know Chinese Gordon's gone to the Sudan? Fact—and taken Flashman with him! Met him quite by chance at the station, told Wolseley and Cambridge he must have him along, wouldn't dream of facing the Mahdi without him. They gave him his way, of course, but wondered what Flashman, who's retired, would think of being press-ganged at a moment's notice. D'you know what Flash Harry said, cool as you please? 'Well, the least you can do, Gordon, is pay for my blasted ticket!' "

[This extract from the Papers ends at 8 p.m. on January 18, 1884, with the departure of Major-General Charles George ("Chinese") Gordon for the Sudan, accompanied by a reluctant Flashman. A year later Gordon died in the siege of Khartoum.]

Appendix

THE EMPEROR FRANZ-JOSEF (1830–1916)
AND EMPRESS ELISABETH (1837–1898)

"The last European monarch of the old school," was how the Emperor Franz-Josef I described himself to Theodore Roosevelt, with good reason, for he enjoyed a longer full sovereignty than any other European ruler, from the 1848 revolution, when, as a dashing prince of eighteen, he succeeded to the throne abdicated by his uncle, until the middle of the First World War, by which time he had become the venerable, bald, bewhiskered grandpaternal figure which gazes benevolently out from his best-known portrait, a fine old Austrian gentleman, revered but remote from his subjects and the terrible conflict which he had helped to make. It was a tragic climax to a reign which had been neither successful nor happy; his empire had dwindled in size and power to the brink of extinction, and his personal life had been darkened by misfortunes—his adored Empress had been assassinated, his son had committed suicide, his brother had died before a firing squad, and the murder of his nephew and heir had plunged Europe into war.

If he does not emerge as an attractive figure from his biographies, or from Flashman's brief sketch on short acquaintance, it is still hard not to feel sympathy for Franz-Josef. His own faults may have contributed to his ill luck in love and war and statecraft, but it would have taken a ruler of unusual intelligence and political skill to bridge successfully the long imperial sunset from the end of Europe's *ancien régime* to the age of jazz and democracy and mechanised warfare, and these he simply did not have. He had tried to rule as an absolute monarch presiding over a centralised bureaucracy and suppressing nationalist ambitions (especially those of Hungary) among the ill-assorted races of his unwieldy empire; changing times had forced him into reluctant concessions, but his reactionary nature and passion for the detail of administration, over which he laboured conscientiously, had blinded him to those greater issues which he had neither the vision nor the temperament to understand.

Such virtues as he had were physical rather than intellectual, which befitted the romantic prince of his early days. Tall, handsome, recklessly brave if unsuccessful as a soldier, a splendid horseman and ardent sportsman, he seems to have been amiable and kindly at his best, although one biographer writes of his "haughty and offensive arrogance," and quotes examples. His personal tastes were spartan, his manner dignified and formal, and he was punctilious in matters of protocol, a characteristic which was no help in his marriage.

Franz-Josef's chief recreation was in rural pursuits, shooting above all, and he was never happier than roving the woods above Ischl with his gun, leading the simple life. His other love was the theatre, and its ladies, and the close companion of his old age was an actress, Frau Schratt, to whom he was so closely attached that he became known as "Herr Schratt."

His marriage to Elisabeth of Bavaria, the glamorous "Sissi" or "Sisi," began as a fairy tale and ended in unhappiness and tragedy. We have Flashman's authoritative word for it that she was a rare beauty, although some of her portraits suggest that she was strikingly pretty rather than classically perfect. Franz-Josef fell in love with her at first sight, but he was not a faithful husband, and while his teenage bride never paid him back in kind, she was too lively and spirited to be a docile little Empress. Quite apart from Franz-Josef's infidelities (which did in fact lead to her infection) there were causes enough of disagreement. Sissi detested the ultra-formal etiquette of a hostile court, was disliked by her mother-in-law, developed strong Hungarian sympathies, and had a decidedly eccentric streak in her nature, all of which combined to bring about the imperial couple's estrangement. The adoration in which she was held, especially in Hungary, probably did not help.

She took to wandering about Europe, cruising the Mediterranean and hunting in England and Ireland, a royal gypsy admired not only for her looks and charm but for her generous interest in charitable causes, and for that wayward independence which had so shocked Vienna. She was a fearless horsewoman, an expert gymnast who worked out regularly in a portable gym, a health-and-beauty fanatic who wrote poetry, suffered periodic bouts of ill-health and depression, and all too often gave signs of that instability which led Flashman to doubt her sanity.

Elisabeth bore Franz-Josef three daughters and a son, Rudolf, who is remembered only as the chief actor in the tragedy of Mayerling, where he took his own life and that of his mistress in 1889. Nine years later Elisabeth was stabbed to death by an anti-royalist fanatic at Geneva. She was sixty years old. (See Henri de Weindel, *The Real Francis-Joseph*, 1909; Francis Gribble, *Life of the Emperor Francis Joseph*, 1914; Gordon Brook-Shepherd, *Royal Sunset*, 1987; A. de Burgh, *Elizabeth, Empress of Austria*, 1899; Andrew Sinclair, *Death by Fame*, 1998.)

Notes

1. Henri Stefan Oppert-Blowitz (1825–1903) was Paris correspondent of *The Times* from 1875 to 1902. A Bohemian Jew, born of a good family in what is now Czechoslovakia, he worked as a teacher in France before becoming a journalist almost by accident, and showed that he possessed to a remarkable degree that combination of talents that makes a first-class reporter: immense energy and curiosity, a nose for news, and that mysterious gift of inspiring confidence which makes people talk. He had contacts at the highest level all over Europe, a prodigious memory, a brass neck, and great ingenuity (some said lack of scruple) which together raised him to a unique position in his profession.

   Flashman has drawn him faithfully, and plainly had some affection and considerable respect for the tiny, rotund, charming, bombastic, and rather comic eccentric, whose love of good living, susceptibility to female beauty, delight in extravagant dress, and generous good nature endeared him to many; naturally, he inspired considerable jealousy in his rivals, and was not without detractors to question both his methods and his ability. That Blowitz the brilliant and hard-headed reporter and interviewer was at the same time an incurable romantic with a taste for melodrama and love of the sensational, is obvious from his *Memoirs*, a highly entertaining work made up of material published in his lifetime and episodes dictated in his last year; he kept no diaries, and is said to have taken a note only rarely.

   How far the *Memoirs* are to be trusted is a nice point. Flashman was familiar with them, but is no guide to their reliability; part of his story is identical in outline with one chapter of the *Memoirs*, but since Blowitz is the source in both cases, this means nothing. The enthusiastic Bohemian was never one to spoil a good tale for want of dramatic colouring, and Frank Giles, a later *Times* Paris correspondent, whose biography of Blowitz is admirably fair and meticulously researched, describes the *Memoirs* as a remarkable collection of fact and fiction, and echoes the feeling of a former *Times* proprietor that, at times, "the facts have collapsed under the sheer weight of a powerful imagination." Much of what Blowitz wrote can never be checked, and there is no knowing how great a part his vivid imagination played in what he told Flashman, who seems to have believed him, for what that is worth. I do not hesitate to cite Blowitz in these footnotes, for whatever his failings he was at his best the most superior kind of journalist—a real reporter.

Blowitz's obsession with destiny, etc., his tales of adventures with Marseilles communards, mysterious European royalty, and his kidnapping by gypsies, are to be found in the *Memoirs;* the story that he and his lover threw the lady's husband overboard in Marseilles harbour is told by Prince von Bulow, later German Chancellor, who is not regarded as an invariably reliable source. (See Blowitz's *My Memoirs* (1903); Frank Giles, *A Prince of Journalists* (1962); Prince von Bülow, *Memoirs, 1849–1897* (1932), which contains a fine picture of Blowitz in his working clothes.)   [p. 8]

2. When and where Flashman served in the French Foreign Legion has not yet emerged from his Papers. Several references (like the present one) suggest North Africa, but it is not impossible that he was with the Legion in Mexico c. 1867, when he was aide-de-camp to the ill-fated Emperor Maximilian. "Au jus!" was the cry of the coffee orderlies at reveille, and "the sausage music" is presumably a reference to the Legion's march, "Tiens, voila du boudin." (See also Note 13.)

The authority for Grant's meeting with Macmahon, and their total failure to communicate, is Grant himself. At least they bowed, and shook hands; Grant's aversion to hand-shaking was notorious, as was his taciturnity. (See *From the Tan Yard to the White House*, by William M. Thayer [1886].)   [p. 11]

3. In 1878 Sir Stafford Northcote's Budget, described as "unambitious," increased the duty on dogs and tobacco and raised income tax by 2d; Mrs. Brassey published "The Voyage of the Sunbeam," an account of her round-the-world cruise by yacht; the phonograph ("an instrument which prints sound for subsequent reproduction by electricity") was a popular novelty; and Gilbert and Sullivan's *H.M.S. Pinafore* had its first night on May 25 at the Opera Comique. The great hit of the show was "He Is an Englishman," which became "almost a second national anthem."   [p. 14]

4. As usual with his summaries of international affairs, Flashman's account of events in the Balkans, the Russo-Turkish war, and the Treaty of San Stefano is sketchy and racy, but accurate in its broad essentials. The treaty, reflecting Russia's Panslavic ambition to bring the Balkans under Russian control, was hard on the defeated Turks, and was opposed by Austria and Britain. A conference of the European Powers had been in prospect for some time, but was jeopardised by Russia's objection to a British demand that the San Stefano settlement should be submitted to discussion by the Powers. Largely through the "honest broker" efforts of Bismarck, the German Chancellor, an understanding was reached between Britain and Russia, and the Congress of Berlin was held in June and July of 1878 to revise the treaty and achieve a balance in South-eastern Europe.   [p. 16]

5. Blowitz's opinion of Shuvalov is echoed in von Bulow: "Count Shuvalov was a clever, skilful, amiable and distinguished man, but like so many Russians, he worshipped more than was fitting at the shrine of Aphrodite Pandemos." (Bulow, *My Memoirs*.) (See also Note 7.)   [p. 17]

6. The cartoons of the two English grooms and the crafty fishmonger, and the article headed "Hankey Pankey," are to be found in *Punch* of May 11, 1878; the voluptuous

figure entitled "Harlequin Spring Fashions—really a very little addition to the too-scanty and bespangled costumes Mr. Punch has noticed so often lately," appeared in the previous week. [p. 24]

7. According to von Bülow: "On one of his evening walks in the Friederich-strasse ... which the Berlin police supervised so discreetly, to prevent any unpleasant incident, he [Shuvalov] had made the acquaintance of a too-facile lady, from whose arms it was difficult to entice him." (See *My Memoirs*.) [p. 25]

8. Flashman's version of the Congress of Berlin tallies fairly well with Blowitz's, which does not differ in its essentials from other accounts. From whom Blowitz obtained the advance copy of the treaty is unknown. Waddington, the French Foreign Minister, has been suggested; he was English by blood, though born in Paris, and like Flashman was educated at Rugby, but there is no evidence that he was the source of the leak. What is certain is that Blowitz had an excellent source at the heart of the Congress, and scooped his rivals in day-to-day reporting as well as in obtaining the treaty, much to their annoyance, especially the Germans. He did interview Bismarck (whose under-the-table complaint is authentic), and seems to have bluffed him into withholding the treaty from the German press by himself demanding an exclusive copy. He left the Congress early, pretending to sulk, dictated from memory a substantial portion to his secretary, had the text telegraphed from Brussels by his secretary, and the following day had the satsifaction of an exclusive story in *The Times*. It was one of the greatest scoops in newspaper history, although Flashman is wrong in saying that all the clauses appeared; in fact, seven did not.

There is one important difference between Flashman's version of the Congress and that given by Blowitz in his *Memoirs*. Blowitz says that his information source and go-between was "a young foreigner" who had approached Blowitz for help, and whom he infiltrated into the entourage of an unidentified statesman at the Congress; once installed, he passed information to Blowitz by means of the hat exchange. This seems a highly unlikely story, and it is reasonable to assume that Blowitz, in writing his *Memoirs*, invented it to protect the identities of Flashman, Caprice, and Shuvalov. It is worth noting that von Bulow's story of Shuvalov's infatuation with a courtesan (quoted in Note 7) is consistent with Flashman's version. [p. 38]

9. Sir Garnet (later Viscount) Wolseley confirmed his reputation as Britain's first soldier by his suppression in 1882 of the Egyptian army's revolt against the Khedive. The rebellion was led by Arabi Pasha, an ardent nationalist and anti-European, and after the massacre of more than a hundred foreigners at Alexandria, the port's defences were bombarded by the Royal Navy and Egypt was invaded by Wolseley's force which eventually numbered 40,000. He gained control of the Suez Canal, and when his advance guard was attacked by Arabi at Kassassin on August 28, the Egyptian infantry were routed by a moonlight charge of the British cavalry, in which the Life Guards and the Blues of the Household Brigade ("Tin Bellies," to Flashman) were prominent. Sir Baker Russell's horse was shot under him, but he mounted another, presumably with Flashman's assistance. Arabi's army of about

40,000 was strongly entrenched at Tel-el-Kebir, but after a remarkable night march of six miles in silence, Wolseley's force made a surprise dawn attack, headed by the Highland Brigade, who overwhelmed the Egyptian position. About 2000 of the defenders were killed for the loss of 58 British dead and 400 wounded and missing. Cairo was occupied after a forced march, Arabi was captured and exiled to Ceylon, and the rebellion had been crushed in 25 days. (See Charles Lowe, "Kassassin and Tel-el-Kebir," in *Battles of the Nineteenth Century*, edited by Major Arthur Griffiths, 1896.) [p. 42]

10. One can only take Flashman's word for it that there was a "strong shave" (rumour) in the clubs about Gordon as early as the beginning of October. The situation in the Sudan did not begin to look critical until after the wipe-out of Hicks' command by the Mahdi at Kashgil early in November, and Gordon's name does not appear to have been mentioned in official circles until some weeks later, when Gordon himself was still contemplating service in the Congo. No doubt Flashman's instinct for self-preservation made him unusually prescient. [p. 43]

11. The first official journey of the famous Orient Express began at the Gare de l'Est, Paris, on the evening of Sunday, October 4, 1883. The great train was the brainchild of Georges Nagelmackers of Liege, founder of the *Compagnie Internationale des Wagon-Lits*, and realised his dream of a through express of unsurpassed luxury which should run to the ends of Europe. That first train consisted of the locomotive, two baggage cars, two sleeping-cars, and a dining salon which was to become justly famous; about forty passengers (all male as far as Vienna, where two ladies came aboard), made the inaugural trip from Paris to Constantinople, among them ministers of the French and Belgian governments, several journalists including Blowitz, a Turkish diplomat, Mishak Effendi (identified by Flashman), and Nagelmackers himself. It is interesting, in view of the alias supplied by Blowitz for Flashman in Berlin five years earlier, that on the Orient Express Blowitz shared Voiture 151 with a Dutchman named Janszen. Blowitz got a book out of the trip, which was a memorable one even by his standards, for in Constantinople he obtained the first interview ever granted by the ruler of the Ottoman Empire, Sultan Abdul-Hamid II; in Bucharest he also interviewed the King of Roumania. And being Blowitz, he thoroughly enjoyed the luxury and conviviality of the journey, especially the dining salon. One cannot blame him; as all who have travelled on it agree, there is no train like the Orient Express. (See Michael Barsley, *Orient Express: The Story of the World's Most Fabulous Train*, 1966; Blowitz, *Memoirs*. For the stops and times of Flashman's journey, see *Express Trains, English and Foreign*, by E. Foxwell and T. C. Farrer, 1889.) [p. 60]

12. Whoever "Princess Kralta" may have been, she was obviously a lady of considerable attraction and character. It is possible that Blowitz concealed her real name, since it is a device he employs elsewhere in his *Memoirs;* the only hint he gives of her origin is to describe her mother as "an Oriental flower," but from Flashman's description it would seem that her father at least was European, and Northern European at that. Be that as it may, "Kralta" appears to have occupied an influential position in Continental diplomatic and royal society; the account of her activities

which Blowitz gave to Flashman tallies closely with the *Memoirs*—her acquaintance with Bismarck, his employment of her to discover how Blowitz had got the Berlin Treaty, the melodramatic incident of the candle in the draught which alerted Blowitz to her treachery, and the sensational tale of how, at the German Emperor's request, she soothed the distracted Bismarck with "some kind of diversion"—all these are in the chapter entitled, with Blowitzian panache, "The Revenge of Venus." He does not state bluntly how she "diverted" Bismarck, but the inference could hardly be clearer.

For Flashman's experiences with "Kralta" we have only his own testimony. As to her appearance and personality, he is more detailed than Blowitz, but there are no contradictions between them: both agree that she was imperious and charming, and while Flashman is more specific about what are called vital statistics, he can have had no quarrel with the little Bohemian's romantic raptures. Blowitz was beglamoured on first sight of the Princess at a dinner party, to such an extent that he could not remember who else was present—a most unusual lapse of his remarkable memory. He enthuses about her beauty, radiance, "exquisite elegance," "silky hair" (chestnut at their first meeting, but subsequently "golden"), "melodious voice," "blue eyes which lighted up one of the most fascinating faces I have ever seen," and so on; he even notes the "brilliancy" of her teeth. There is something approaching awe in his description of her crossing a room with "the vague rustle of her silken robes . . . like a rapid vision," and one gets the impression sometimes that he was rather afraid of her. [p. 70]

13. This is the first substantial reference in the Papers to Flashman's sojourn in Mexico in the latter half of the 1860s; hitherto we have known only that he spent time in a Mexican prison, and was an aide-de-camp to the unfortunate Emperor Maximilian, younger brother of Emperor Franz-Josef of Austria. Maximilian, an amiable and well-intentioned prince, interested in botany, was a pawn in the ambitious schemes of Napoleon III of France, who took advantage of civil war in Mexico to send in a French army, ostensibly to collect war debts from the victorious "Liberals" of Benito Juarez, but in fact to establish a puppet empire under Maximilian, who was persuaded to accept the Mexican crown in 1863. He set up a government and was planning social and educational reforms, including freedom for the Indians, but Juarez's forces remained hostile to the imperial regime, and when Napoleon withdrew his forces, partly owing to pressure from the Americans, who were sympathetic to Juarez's republicans, Maximilian was left to his fate. He made a brave fight of it, but was captured by the Juaristas in May 1867, and executed by firing squad in the following month.

What part Flashman played in these events will no doubt be revealed when his Mexican papers come to light. We know that he was in the U.S. with President Lincoln a few days before the latter's death in April 1865, so his Mexican adventures were presumably confined to the next two years at most. The reference to Princess Salm-Salm, the wife of Prince Felix Salm-Salm—a German officer who served in the U.S. Civil War (possibly with Flashman) and was later chief a.d.c. to Maximilian in Mexico—suggests that Flashman was involved in the efforts which both the Prince and Princess made to save the Emperor's life; she was a handsome and fearless lady who has left a spirited account of her adventures in Mexico, and of her later life in European royal circles and in the Franco-Prussian war, in which her husband was killed. Her *Ten Years of My Life* (1868) and the Prince's *My Diary in Mexico* (1874) which she published after his death, give invaluable details of Maximilian's last days.

That the Emperor Maximilian was a cricketer seems to be confirmed by a photograph in a Brussels museum in which he is seen posing at the end of a match with members of the British Legation in Mexico City, *c.* 1865. The editor is indebted to Colonel J. M. C. Watson for a copy of this picture. [p. 84]

14. Flashman seldom elaborates on international affairs, and it is probable that he has summarised, with commendable accuracy, the information given him by Willem von Starnberg touching on the state of the Austrian Empire and its ruler, the Hungarian question, and the relations of Emperor Franz-Josef, the Empress Elisabeth ("Sissi"), and their son, the Crown Prince Rudolf. (See Appendix.) [p. 87]

15. In 1853 Franz-Josef of Austria had escaped with a bad neck wound when he was stabbed by a Hungarian apprentice whose knife was impeded by the Emperor's stiff military collar. Uniform also saved the life of the elderly German Emperor in 1878, when the helmet which he insisted on wearing in accordance with regulations took the blast of a double-barrelled shotgun; he had survived another shooting attempt only three weeks earlier. Tsar Alexander II of Russia was less fortunate; he was killed by a second bomb in St. Petersburg in 1881, only minutes after an earlier device had wrecked his carriage. (See Bulow, and works cited in the Appendix.) [p. 87]

16. The quotation is from "In Ambush," in *Stalky and Co.* [p. 89]

17. Which it still retains. Ischl in Flashman's time had a population of fewer than 3000, and seems to have changed little since then; its lack of size makes it a pleasant little gem among European resorts, tranquil and unhurried in its grand surroundings, and its shops and coffee-houses, with their remarkable range of confections, remain as attractive as ever. It is appropriate that such a Ruritanian setting should have been home to Franz Lehar (after Flashman's day); his villa remains on the banks of the Traun, the Golden Ship was serving excellent cabbage a few years ago, and Frosch and his colleagues were still amusing audiences at the little theatre. [p. 103]

18. Anyone visiting the "Kaiservilla," the royal lodge at Bad Ischl, will probably share Flashman's abiding memory. The lodge today is much as he describes it, and the horns of the Emperor's quarries still adorn its walls in profusion. There is in fact a secret stairway from the Emperor's rooms, remarkably modest chambers simply furnished with, among other items, the plain iron bedstead which he used. It is such an ordinary bedroom that it is hard to realise that this is where the First World War began.

Flashman's brief acquaintance with Franz-Josef illustrates many of the Emperor's characteristics: his passion for the military, his poor grasp of languages other than his own, his rather stuffy formality, his devotion to administrative detail, and the simplicity of his tastes—boiled beef and beer was a favourite meal. He

enjoyed his rubbers of *tarok*, and in his later years especially it was a regular evening pastime. (See Appendix.) [p. 132]

19. There is an old salt-mine in the mountains of the Saltzkammergut above Ischl
which corresponds so closely to Flashman's description that it must surely be the
same one. The strange pool is still there, and the bogies run on rails from the mine
entrance into the great cavern. [p. 147]

20. The quoted line is spoken by Rudolf Rassendyll to Count Rupert of Hentzau in
The Prisoner of Zenda. Flashman claimed that he had told the story of his Strackenz
adventure to Anthony Hope Hawkins (later Sir Anthony Hope) and that the novelist used it as the basis for his famous romance, modelling the Count of Hentzau
on Rudi von Starnberg. [p. 151]

21. Caprice must have charmed at least three copies of *Punch* from her English tourist,
including the most recent issue (October 13) in which France is depicted as a homely
old woman. The cartoon of Gladstone dancing the hornpipe is from a September
number (he was on a cruise with Lord Tennyson) and the alluring figure labelled
"Manchester Ship Canal" is earlier still. *Punch*'s anti-Gallic prejudice runs through
all three numbers. The blimpish British officers cited by Flashman are characters in
Hector Servadac, one of Jules Verne's later science-fiction novels (1877). Police
whistles came into use in 1883. [p. 183]

22. There were many distinguished de la Tour d'Auvergnes, principally Theophile
Malo Corret of that name, a French soldier renowned for his courage and chivalry,
who died in 1800, having consistently refused promotion beyond the rank of captain. He was known as the First Grenadier of France. [p. 187]

23. W. Pembroke Fetridge was the author of *The American Traveller's Guide: Harper's
Handbook for Travellers in Europe*, which first appeared in 1862. Flashman probably
had the 1871 edition. [p. 199]

24. The unique position which Chinese Gordon held in the eyes of officialdom and the
public was demonstrated by the fact that when he left Charing Cross Station for
the Sudan, the Foreign Secretary bought his ticket, the Duke of Cambridge held the
carriage door for him, and Lord (formerly Sir Garnet) Wolseley carried his bag.
(See Charles Chenevix Trench, *Charley Gordon*, 1978.) [p. 213]

THE SUBTLETIES OF BACCARAT

(1890 AND 1891)

"See here, Flashman," says the Prince of Wales, looking hunted and chewing his cigar as though it were plug tobacco, "you must get me out o' this. God knows what Mother would say!"

I couldn't think there was much she hadn't said already. When you're a queen of unblemished virtue, devoted to Duty and the high moral tone, and your son and Heir to the Throne is a notorious wastrel who counts all time lost when he ain't stuffing, swilling, sponging off rich toad-eaters, and rogering everything in skirts, you're apt to be censorious—why, she'd once told Elspeth that she was determined to outlive the brute 'cos he wasn't fit to be king, so there. But in the present instance, so far as I'd gathered from his incoherent growls, I was shot if I could see what he was in a stew about; for once he appeared to be blameless. Yet here he was mangling his weed and twitching like a frightened Falstaff.

We were alone, and he was too fretful to be on his dignity, so I guided him to a chair, soothed him with a stiff b. and s., lit him a fresh smoke, waited courtier-like while he coughed his innards out, and invited him to restate his troubles, as calmly as might be, to sympathetic old Flashy.

"I've just told you!" snaps he, wheezing and wiping his piggy eyes. "It is the most shocking business. They say Bill Cumming has cheated at baccarat!"

That's what I'd thought he said the first time, and wondered if I'd misheard. But he seemed sober and rational, if agitated.

"You mean last night, sir—in the billiard-room?"

"Yes, confound it—and the night before! You were there, hang it all!"

Well, I had been, as an occasional spectator looking in from time to time to make sure my feather-brained wife wasn't slapping down her jewellery and crying "Banco!," but I wasn't having this. I should explain that baccarat is the most imbecile of card games (Elspeth plays it, after all) in which half-wits sit round a large table and the banker deals two cards to the crowd on his right, two to those on his left, and two to himself, the object being to get as near a total of nine with your two cards as may be; if your side gets two deuces, you'll ask for a third card, won't you, hoping for a four or a five, and the banker has the same privilege. If he gets closer to nine, *he* wins; if he doesn't, *you* win. Endless fun, my dear, assuming you can count up to nine, and if it don't rival chess, exactly, at least its simplicity leaves little room for sharp practice. Which was why I couldn't credit what his fat highness was telling me.

"Cheated—at *baccarat*? No, sir, it can't be done," I told him. "Well, not unless you're the banker, and even then, with a four-pack deck, more than two hundred cards, why, you'd have to be the very devil of a mechanic." I considered. "Can't think I've ever seen it tried . . . no, not out West, even. Mind you, they don't go in for baccarat, much . . . vingt-et-un, mostly, and poker—"

"Damn poker!" croaks he. "He cheated, I tell you—and *I* was the blasted banker!"

Come to think of it, so he had been, on both nights, and for a happy moment I wondered if he'd been slipping 'em off the bottom himself, and was trying to shift the blame, in true royal style—but that wouldn't do; he hadn't the spunk for it.

"Let me get this right, sir . . . you tell me Gordon-Cumming *cheated*? For God's sake, who says so?"

"Coventry and Owen Williams. There can be no doubt about it—I saw nothing wrong, but they are quite positive."

Since one of them was a deaf peer, and t'other a Welsh major-general, I didn't put much stock in this. "They say they saw him sharping?"

"No, no, not they—these dreadful Wilson people, the young ones—our host's children, dammit, four or five of them, young Wilson and that impossible fellow Green—and two of the ladies, even . . . they all *saw* him cheat, I tell you!" He thumped his knee, almost eating his cigar. "Why did I ever allow myself to be prevailed upon to come to this infernal house? It will be a lesson to me, Flashman, I don't mind telling you—did you ever hear anything so monstrous?"

"If it's true, sir . . . *How* do they say he cheated?"

"Why, by adding to his stake—putting on counters after the coups were declared in his side's favour—and taking 'em off when he'd lost. They saw him do it time and again, apparently, on both nights, when I," groans he, "was holding the bank!"

The more I heard, the dafter it became. I'm no gambling man myself, much, and have never had the skill or nerve for sharping anyway, but in my time I've seen 'em all: stud games in Abilene livery stables with guns and gold-pokes down on the blanket, nap schools from Ballarat to the Bay, penny-ante blackjack in political country houses (with Disraeli dealing and that oily little worm Bryant planting aces in my unsuspecting pockets, damn him), and watched the sharks at work with cold decks, shaved edges, marked backs, and everything up their sleeves bar a trained midget—and you may take my word for it, the last place on God's earth you'd want to sit on the Queen of Spades or try to juggle the stakes is Grandmama's drawing-room after dinner; you won't last five minutes. As Gordon-Cumming, I was asked to believe, had discovered.

"And no one said anything at the time?"

"Why . . . why, no." He blinked in bearded bewilderment.

"No, they did not . . . the ladies, I suppose . . . the ghastly scene that must have followed . . ." He made vague gestures with his cigar. "But they felt they could not keep silent altogether, and told Williams and Coventry—and they," he fairly snarled, "have told *me*! Before dinner tonight. Why they felt obliged to drag me into the wretched business I cannot think. It's too bad!"

Sheer vapouring, of course. As Prince of Wales, first gentleman of Europe (God help us), he was the bright particular star and pack leader of the genteel rabble assembled at Tranby Croft, Yorks, for the Doncaster races, and knew perfectly well that any serious breach of polite behaviour by a fellow guest, such as cardsharping, was bound to land on his mat. I reminded him of this tactfully, and added that I didn't believe it for a minute. Some foolish mistake or misunderstanding, I said, depend upon it.

"No such thing!" He heaved his guts out of the chair and began to pace about. "The young Wilsons and Green—aye, and that chap what's-his-name—Levett—who is in Cumming's own regiment, for heaven's sake—all avow it. They *saw* him cheat! Coventry and Williams are in no doubt whatsoever. It's too frightful for words!" He gloomed at me, all hang-dog German jowls. "Can you imagine the scandal if it should come out—if it were to reach the Queen's ears that such a thing had happened in . . . in my presence?" He took a step towards me. "My dear Harry—you know about these things—what is to be done?"

One thing was plain—it wasn't Cumming's supposed sleight of hand (which I still couldn't credit) that was putting him in a ferment, but that it had happened in a game presided over by His Royal Grossness, and whatever would Mama say when she heard that he'd been spreading the boards like Faro Jack. Tame stuff, from where I stood, compared to his whoremongering and general depravity, but if it had shaken him to the point where I was his dear Harry, he must be desperate. I'd steered him out of more than one scrape in the past, and here he was again, looking at me like an owl in labour. So, first things first.

"What does Gordon-Cumming say?"

"He denies it outright, of course—Williams and Coventry saw him before dinner, and—"

"You haven't spoken to him yourself, then?"

He shuddered. "No—and I dread it! You think I should not? Oh, if I could avoid it . . . how am I to face him—an old friend, an intimate of years, a fellow officer—a baronet, dammit, a . . . a man of honour . . ."

Aye, that's a word we'll hear more of before this is done, thinks I. "Tell me, sir—these eagle-eyed youngsters . . . how much do they claim Cumming bilked 'em of?"

He goggled at me. "What on earth has that to do with it? If a fellow cheats, what does the amount matter?"

"Something, I'd say. Now, I didn't play either night, but my Elspeth said something about five and ten bob stakes, so it can't have been much of a high game?"

"Heavens, no! A friendly game, to amuse the ladies—why, I set the bank limit at a hundred pounds, both nights—"

"So Cumming can't have won more than a hundred or two, can he? Well, I don't know what he's worth—some say eighty thou' p.a.—but he has a place in Scotland, house in Town, half-colonelcy in the Guards, moves in the top flight, and I've never heard he was short o' the ready, have you?" He shook his head, glowering. "Well, sir—would he risk his good name, his commission, his place in Society—good Lord, everything he counts worth while!—for a few wretched quid that wouldn't keep him in cheroots for a year? Why, sir, it don't bear looking at, even!"

And it didn't. I'm ready to believe evil of anyone, usually with good cause, and especially of Sir William Gordon-Cumming, Bart, whose reputation I'd have been happy to blacken any day (I'll tell you why presently), but this accusation made no sense at all. Quite apart from the mechanical difficulties of the thing, the paltry sums involved, and the ghastly risk he'd have been running, all of which I'd pointed out, there was my knowledge of the man's character, which was that of a top-lofty prig with immense notions of his own dignity, who'd have regarded cheating as shocking bad form, and never mind dishonesty. No, it wouldn't do.

But there was no persuading Bertie the Bounder of that. He was in such a funk about the possible scandal that sweet reason was lost on him, and those two duffers Coventry and Williams had convinced him that the evidence was overwhelming. How, they demanded, when I'd prevailed on the Prince to have 'em in so that I might hear their tale first-hand, could five intelligent young people be mistaken, not on one occasion only, but on several?

"Hold hard a moment," says I. "Let's take it in order. Two nights ago, Monday, you played baccarat in the smoking-room after dinner. I was only in and out while you played, but as I recall you had three card tables pushed together with a cloth over them, to play at. Your highness had the bank—"

"Williams was croupier!" cries Bertie, eager to share the guilt.

"Only on the second night, sir!" says Williams. "There was no croupier on the Monday." Bertie scowled, but couldn't deny it.

"At all events, there were two tableaux of players, one to your right, sir, and one to your left? Where was Gordon-Cumming sitting?"

They consulted about this, and decided he'd been in the left-hand group, or tableau. Mrs. Arthur Wilson, our host's wife, had been first to the Prince's left, then an empty chair (though they couldn't swear it had never been occupied), then Berkeley Levett, then round the corner young Jack Wilson, the son of the house, and Gordon-Cumming next to him, with one of the Somersets beyond. Each staked individually, and took turns at handling the cards dealt to their side.

"How did they place their stakes, precisely?" I asked.

"With counters supplied by his highness," says Coventry,

looking at him as though he were an opium runner. "I think I see the case yonder."

Sure enough, there was a polished wooden box on the table, and Bertie opened it reluctantly to display the leather counters, all stamped with his feathers crest—brown £10 chips, bright red fivers, blue oncers, and so on. Tools of the devil, I could hear the Queen calling them; they travelled with him everywhere.

"I take it everyone staked before his highness dealt?" says I. "Pushing their counter—or counters—forward on the table? Then the cards would be dealt, your highness would declare the bank's score, and then you'd pay out or rake in accordingly—is that so, sir?" Bertie gave a furtive grunt; he was hating this as much as I was enjoying it, I dare say. "Well, then what happened?" They all stood mum, waiting on each other. "Come along, gentlemen," says I, getting brisk. "Who saw whom cheating, and when, and how?"

It was like pulling teeth; they hemmed and hawed, or at least Coventry did, while Williams contradicted him and Bertie ground his teeth and flung his cigar in the fire. At last they got it straight, more or less. On the very first deal, young Jack Wilson had seen Cumming stake £5, and then, looking again when their side won and the Prince was preparing to pay out, had seen to his astonishment that Cumming's stake had magically increased from one red counter to three—£15 where there had been only £5 before. He couldn't be mistaken, because Cumming placed his stake on a piece of white paper which he used for making notes of the play. Young Wilson had thought it damned odd, and later, on the fifth or sixth deal (he couldn't swear which), when their side had won again, he'd seen Cumming drop three red chips, furtive-like, on to the paper where there had originally been only one. He'd collected £20, cool as dammit, and young Wilson had whispered to Levett, seated beside him, the good news that his colonel was working a flanker. Levett had sworn Wilson must be wrong, but had watched himself, and blowed if he hadn't seen Cumming do the same thing again, twice. Once he'd added two £5 chips, and the second time he'd added one, on both occasions after his tableau had been declared the winner.

Described like that, in detail, it sounded impressive, I had to admit, and the Prince regarded me with piggy triumph. "There, you see, Flashman—two men, one in his own regiment, too! And both sure of what they saw!"

"You saw nothing out o' the way yourself, sir?"

"Certainly not. I was occupied with the cards and the bank."

True enough, he would be—but there was something damned strange which they'd evidently overlooked.

"If Cumming *was* cheating," I asked them, "why on earth did he use the brightest chips—the red fivers?" I indicated the open box. "Look at 'em, they stand out a mile! And to make 'em even more conspicuous, he laid them on a white paper! Hang it all, sir, if he'd wanted to be caught he couldn't have been more obvious!"

They couldn't explain it, and Bertie said testily that what I'd said might very well be true, but it didn't alter the fact that he'd been seen padding his stakes, whatever blasted colour they were, and what was to be done, eh?

I said I'd heard the stories of young Wilson and Levett, but what about the other three? Williams said that after the first night's play young Wilson had told his mother what he and Levett had seen; Wilson's sister and her husband, a chap called Lycett Green, had also been informed, and they'd resolved to keep an eye on Cumming the next night, Tuesday. Young Wilson had arranged for a long table to be set up in the billiard room, covered with baize and with a chalk line round the margin beyond which the stakes would be placed—that way, they thought, Cumming wouldn't be able to cheat. I couldn't believe my ears.

"Were they mad?" says I. "They were sure the man was a swindler, yet they were prepared to play with him *again*—and spy on him? And they never thought to tell old Wilson, the father of the family, or anyone senior?"

Coventry looked stuffed at this, and Bertie muttered about the shocking state of Society nowadays, ignorant upstarts who knew no better, and he was a fool to have come within a hundred miles of the confounded place, etc., etc. Williams said that Mrs. Wilson had wanted at all costs to avoid a scandal, and if they hadn't played it would have looked odd, and people might have talked . . . and so on, and so forth.

"Very well, what happened on the Tuesday night?" I asked. "Was he seen juggling his chips again?"

"Twice, at least," says Williams. "He was seen to push a £10 counter over the line after his highness had declared baccarat to the bank." Meaning the bank had lost. "On another occasion he used his pencil to flick a £5 counter, increasing his £2 stake to £7, which," he added gloomily, "was what I, as croupier, paid him."

"But you saw nothing irregular yourself?"

"No . . . tho' I recall that at one hand—I can't tell which— Cumming called out to his highness, 'There is another tenner due here, sir,' and from what I have learned this evening I believe it may have been on an occasion when he . . . when he played . . . ah, wrongly." He was one of your decent asses, Williams, and didn't like to say it plain.

"I remember distinctly telling him to put his stakes where I could see 'em," says Bertie. "But I suspected nothing."

"Who was sitting by him—the second night?"

Coventry gave a start. "Why, my wife—Lady Coventry. But I believe she gave her place up to Lady Flashman for one or two coups, did she not, Williams?"

"Why, so she did," says Williams, turning to me. "I remember now—Cumming was advising your wife about her stakes, Flashman." He gave a ruptured grin. "They were being rather jolly about it, you know; she was . . . well, I gathered she did not know much about the game, and he was helping her."

"I don't suppose *she* saw anything fishy," says Bertie bitterly. I knew what he meant: if Cumming had worn a black mask and made 'em turn out their pockets at pistol-point, she'd have thought it was all in the game.

"Well, there you are, Flashman," says Bertie. He flung down in a chair, a picture of disgruntled anxiety. "You know as much as we do. It's past belief. That Gordon-Cumming, of all men . . ." He gave a despairing shrug. "But there can be no doubt of it . . . can there?" He was positively yearning at Coventry and Williams. "They are certain of what they saw?"

Sure as a gun, they told him, so I intruded the kind of question that occurs only to minds like mine.

"And you're satisfied they ain't lying?" says I, and was met by exclamations of dismay, paws in the air, whatever next?

"Of course they're not!" barks Bertie. "Heavens above, man, would they invent such a dreadful thing?"

"It's about as likely as Bill Cumming cheating for a few sovs," I reminded him. "But there it is, one or t'other—unless Levett and young Wilson were drunk and seeing double."

"Really, Flashman!" cries Williams. "And the other witnesses, on the second night? You'll hardly suggest that Mrs. Wilson or Mrs. Lycett Green were—"

"No, general—but I will suggest that people often see what they expect to see. And I'm dam' sure both those ladies and Lycett Green sat down last night convinced, from what they'd been told, that Cumming was a wrong 'un. Very well," I went on, as they whinnied their protests and Bertie told me I was talking bosh, "have it as you please, I still say Cumming hasn't been nailed to the wall hard enough to satisfy me . . . but he's got a heap of explaining to do, I grant you." I set my sights on Bertie. "And since your highness has done me the honour to ask my advice, I respectfully suggest that you examine these five all-seeing accusers yourself—*and* Gordon-Cumming—before things go any further."

Since this was plain common sense, it earned me a couple of bovine looks and a royal glare and growl, so I begged leave to withdraw and loafed off, leaving the three wise men to blink at each other and resume their chorus of "What is to be done?"— five words which are as sound a motto for disaster as I know. I've heard 'em at Kabul before the Retreat, at Cawnpore, on the heights above the North Valley at Balaclava, and I won't swear someone wasn't croaking them as we laboured up the Greasy Grass slope behind G. A. Custer, God rest his fat-headed soul. No one ever knows the answer, you see, so everyone looks blank until the man in command (in this case Good Prince Edward) makes up his mind in panic, and invariably does the wrong thing.

I took a turn in the empty billiard room, imbibing a meditative brandy and tickling the pills while I considered this unexpected but most welcome bit of mischief, which promised to enliven what had been a damned dull visit so far. I've never been any hand, as you know, at dancing attendance on royalty—unless it's young and female, but especially not Beastly Bert—nor do I enjoy the unsought hospitality of Society parvenus in the wilds of Yorkshire (a sort of English Texas peopled by coarse braggarts and one or two decentish slow bowlers) with nothing to do but watch horses run in the pouring rain. Racing's well enough when you're young and riding yourself, but now that I was in my seventieth year and disinclined to back anything more mettlesome than an armchair,* I found it quite as interesting as a sermon in Gaelic.

So this baccarat nonsense, with its splendid possibilities of scandal, disgrace, and general devilment, looked made to order for diversion, provided it was properly mismanaged—which, with Bertie in a fine funk, Coventry and Williams advising, and myself ready to butter the stairs as chance offered, it probably would be. You may think this a tame enough occupation for one who has assisted at as many major catastrophes as I have, and a poor setting after the camps and courts of the mighty, but I was

* a docile horse

getting on, you know, and as the Good Book says, there's a time for racketing about crying Ha-ha! among the trumpets, and a time for sitting back with your feet dipped in butter watching others fall in the mire.

And I may tell you, not all adventures are to be found 'midst shot and shell, thank God. What happened at Tranby Croft that September week of '90 was as desperate a drama, in its quiet way, as any I've struck, and a mystery which has baffled the wise for twenty years . . . but will no longer, for I was in the thick of it, and can tell you precisely what happened and why, and since I'll be snug in my long home ere this account meets the public eye (supposing it ever does) you may rely on its truth, incredible as it may appear.

In the first place, I'd never have gone near Tranby Croft but for Elspeth. She was a bosom chum of young Daisy Brooke, who was half her age and one of the leading Society fillies of the day, but cast in the same eccentric mould—well, you know what Elspeth's like, and Daisy, who was known as Babbling Brooke, was a sort of mad socialist—even today, when she's Countess of Warwick, no less, she still raves in a ladylike way about the workers, enough said. At the time of Tranby she was a stunning looker, rich as Croesus, randy as a rabbit, and Prince Bertie's mount of the moment—indeed, I ain't sure she wasn't the love of his life, for he'd thrown over Lily Langtry in her favour and remained uncommon faithful to her until Keppel started wobbling her rump at him. I'll say this for him, he had fine taste in bareback riders, as I should know; I'd shared Langtry with him, behind his back, and done my duty by pretty Daisy—as who hadn't? Not La Keppel, though; she was after my time, worse luck, not heaving in view until I'd reached what Macaulay calls the years of chicken broth and flannel, when you realise how dam' ridiculous you'd look chasing dollymops young enough to be your daughter, and seek solace in booze, baccy, and books. Regrettable, of course, but less tiring and expensive.

Anyway, young Daisy Brooke had been first of the invited guests to Tranby, and had persuaded Bertie that the party would be incomplete without her pal Elspeth, Lady Flashman. I had my own jaundiced view of that, born of fifty years' marriage to my dear one, who, I had reason to believe, had not been averse to male attentions in those years when I'd been abroad funking the Queen's enemies. Not that I could be certain, mind you, never have been, and she may have been as chaste as St. Cecilia, but I strongly suspected that the little trollop had been galloped by half the Army List—including H.R.H. the Prince of Wales, *and* William Gordon-Cumming, Bart. True, 'twas only gossip that she and Bertie had been at grips in a potting-shed at Windsor in '59, when I was off in Maryland helping to start the Yankees' civil war, but I'd seen him ogling her on and off ever since.

As to the louse Cumming, he was too tall and fair and Greek god–like by half, and had made a dead run at Elspeth back in the sixties—and him twenty years her junior, the lecherous young rip. No doubt he'd been successful, but I'd no proof; she'd basked in his admiration, right enough, but since she did that with every man she met it meant neither nowt nor somewhat. The thing that set Cumming apart from her other flirtations (?) was that after twenty years' acquaintance she had suddenly dropped him like a hot rivet, even cut him dead in the Row. I never knew why, and didn't inquire; the less I knew of her transgressions (and she of mine) the better—I reckon that's why we've always been such a loving couple. I'd run across Cumming professionally in Zululand, where he was staff-walloping Chelmsford while I was fleeing headlong from Isan'lwana, and we'd met here and there at home, and been half-civil—as I always am to suspected old flames of Elspeth. Wouldn't have anyone to talk to otherwise, and you can't have 'em thinking you're a jealous husband.

By the time of Tranby, to be sure, Elspeth was of an age where it should have been unlikely that either Bertie or Cumming would try to drag her behind the sofa, but I still didn't care to think of her within the fat-fingered reach of one or the trim moustache of t'other. She'd worn uncommon well; middle sixties and still shaped like a Turkish belly-dancer, with the same guile-less idiot smile and wondrous blue eyes that had set me slavering when she was sixteen—she'd performed like a demented houri then, and who was to say she'd lost the taste in half a century? Why, I remember reading of some French king's mistress, Pom-padour or some such, who was still grinding away when she was eighty. Well, there you are.

So I wasn't best pleased when the Tranby invitation arrived; however, I figured that with Daisy on hand to keep Bertie busy, and Cumming reportedly pushing about some American female, I could stop at home with an easy mind. Then at the last minute, blessed if one of Daisy's aged relatives didn't croak, and since it would not have done for dear Lady Flashman to attend their foul house-party unaccompanied, I was dragooned cursing into service. I doubt if our Prince gave three cheers, either; for all the good toadying turns I'd done him, he was still leery of me, and didn't care to look me in the eye. Guilty conscience, no doubt. Until now, that is, when he found himself taken unawares by the makings of a prime scandal, and the prospect of being rit-ually disembowelled by our gracious sovereign when she heard of it, and serve the fat blighter right.

I reflected on these matters as I shoved the ivories round the cushions, and reviewed events since we'd assembled at Tranby two days earlier, which was Monday. It was your middling coun-try house, owned by a shipping moneybags named Wilson—not Society as you'd notice, but his place was convenient to Don-caster, where they were running the Leger on the Wednesday, and if his family and friends were second-run as these things are judged in the impolite world, well, Prince Bertie was a fellow vul-garian, and right at home. There were enough of his regular crawlers, Cumming and the Somersets, to keep him happy, the Wilson gang toadied him to admiration, and as in most bourgeois establishments the rations, liquor, and appointments were first-rate; none of your freezing baronial banquet halls where the soup arrives stone cold after being toted half a mile by gouty servitors and the bed-springs haven't been seen to since Richard the Third's day. It was cosy and quite jolly, the young folk were lively without being a nuisance, Bertie was at ease and affable, and if it was all a dead bore it was comfortable at least.

Elspeth was in her element, flaunting her mature charms on the first evening in a Paris rig-out which drew glittering smiles of envy from the female brigade and an approving grunt and leer from Bertie. She'd had the deuce of a struggle getting into the thing, with me heaving at her stays, but once all was fast and sheeted home she looked nothing like the grandmother she was, with her hair artfully tinted and that milky complexion carefully enhanced, but above all with that happy, complacent radiance which she hasn't lost yet—and she's close on ninety now. Aye, she's always had the priceless gift of pleasing, has Elspeth, and making people laugh—for she's a damned funny woman when she wants to be, a top-hole mimic, and all the more engaging because she plainly hasn't got two brains to rub together. "Never see her but it sets me in humour," Palmerston used to say. That was her talent, to make folk happy.

She charmed Bertie, seated by her at dinner, won admiring glances from the other men with her artless prattle, and to my astonishment even exchanged pleasant banter with Gordon-Cumming. Hollo, thinks I, has the old fire rekindled? Watching her at work, I rather liked the look of her myself, and that night, waking in the small hours to find that plump excellence cuddled up against me, I was amazed to find myself inspired to climb aboard, puffing and creaking, while she giggled drowsily, saying I was a disgrace and would do myself a mischief.

"At our age!" she murmured afterwards. "Whatever would the children say? Oh, Harry lad, d'you mind the Madagascar forest . . . Harry? Harry? My dear, are you all right? Shall I fetch you a glass of water . . . a little brandy, perhaps?" I was thinking, glory, glory, what a hell of a way to die, being in no condition to move, let alone answer, but I remember noting that she hadn't minded a bit, and saying to myself, aye, you'll still bear watching.

Ah, but fond recollection has carried me ahead of events. It was on that night, after dinner, that the Prince had proposed baccarat, and Cumming had supposedly cheated for the first time. I'd no inkling of this, of course, nor yet on the Tuesday evening, when he'd been seen doctoring his stakes yet again, the bounder—they said. Now, on the Wednesday night, the murder was out (among a few people, anyway), and I was in the pool room trying to fathom it—and, I confess, wondering what I might do to jolly the mischief along. Well, you know my style, and between ourselves . . . wouldn't you?

First, though, to the fathoming. So far as I could judge, there was a choice of three explanations—each one so far-fetched as to be nigh impossible.

Odds on with the punters in the know was that Cumming had cheated. It didn't wash with me, much though I'd have liked to believe it. He was a prime tick and arrant snob, a very model of military and social excellence, cool, handsome, lordly, rich, and moustached, wore his handkerchief in his sleeve, looked down his nose at the world, probably was too fastidious to shave in his bath, might well be a former paramour of my beloved, and on all these counts was ripe for any dirty turn I could serve him. But that wasn't the point; however detestable I might think him, the plain fact was that swindling simply wasn't his style. I told myself that even the unlikeliest folk do the damnedest things . . . was it possible that Cumming was the kind of reckless ass who'd play foul in a trifling game, not for gain, but for the sheer mad fun of the thing, to see if he could get away with it? There are such fellows; I've seen 'em. Rudi Starnberg, for one—ah, but he was a villain, in love with knavery. Cumming wasn't, and for all the bone-headed bravery he'd supposedly shown at Ulundi and in the

Sudan, I couldn't see him bucking this tiger. He had too much to lose . . . and while I hate to say it, he was a gentleman.

Then the witnesses were either mistaken or lying. But error must be discounted: two or even three people might improbably be mistaken—but *five?* On two different nights? So all that remained was a conspiracy to disgrace Gordon-Cumming, by five assorted perjurers. Ridiculous, you say . . . well, I don't. I've sworn truth out of England myself all too often, and seen the saintliest specimens lie themselves black and blue for the unlikeliest reasons. I've also known from the age of three that "honour" and "solemn oath" and "word of a gentleman" are mere piss in the wind of greed, ambition, and fear.

Still, you had only to look at the five witnesses to see that conspiracy was too far-fetched altogether. None of 'em even knew Cumming all that well, or had reason to dislike him, let alone plot his ruin. And one of them could be ruled out, flat. Here they are:

Arthur Stanley ("Jack") Wilson, son of the house, a bright young spark who lived off Papa and hoped to be taken for a man-about-town; fairly brainless and possibly capable of being wild, I'd have thought, but hardly vicious;

His sister, Mrs. Lycett Green, middling pretty, inoffensive, ordinary enough and decidedly not Lucrezia Borgia in the making;

Her husband, Lycett Green, a stiffish, old young man, well pleased with himself and his position as master of foxhounds in some northern swamp. In my experience there are dolts, pompous dolts, and M.F.H.s, but they ain't the plotting kind;

Berkeley Levett, a sound muttonhead in Cumming's regiment, and presumably as well disposed to his chief as subalterns ever are, given that Guards officers are usually incapable of any feeling outside their bellies and loins.

Four unlikely conspirators, you'll allow—unless you conceived it possible that Cumming, a noted rake, had ravished Mrs.

Lycett Green before tea on the Monday and provoked the other three into concocting a diabolic plot to avenge her honour—but the fifth witness killed the plot notion stone dead. She was Mrs. Arthur Wilson, our host's wife, as respectable a matron as ever rebuked a cook, nervously gratified beyond measure at the honour of having royalty to stay, and the last person, as Bertie himself had remarked, to wish to have scandal breaking over her roof. If she said she'd seen Cumming jockeying his chips, she meant it.

So there was no explanation, and if I wanted to get to the bottom of the mystery—which I confess was beginning to intrigue me for its own sake—I needed more eye-witness information. It would also be as well to discover if the scandal had leaked at all. On both counts my best source would be the wife of my bosom, who may be tripe-brained but has the eyes, ears, and instincts of an Afridi scout, especially for things that don't concern her.

I made a leisurely patrol, quartering ground and sniffing the wind: the Lycett Greens were nowhere to be seen, but Mrs. Wilson was fretting at her fan and listening absent-minded to Lady Coventry in the drawing-room, and when I looked in at the smoke hole young Wilson and Levett were in deep confabulation, instantly dropped when I appeared, but not before I heard Levett exclaim: "I can't touch it, Jack, I tell you! He's my chief, dash it!" Signs and portents, thinks I, and passed on to the music-room, where one of the females was butchering Yum-Yum to the feigned admiration of the company, and my quarry was ensconced in a corner, fleecing some unfortunate foreigner at backgammon, shaking the dice and her upper works, the abandoned old tart, in a way which plainly put him off his game altogether.

"Another double six, count!" trills she, all rosy triumph. "I declare I never threw so many! Oh, and now a double four! What luck! Why, I am off entirely—oh, dear, and you have a man on the bar still! Oh, what a shame! Harry, come and see—I have a backgammon! Aren't I lucky? No, no, count, I won't have it—put your purse in your pocket! We play for love, not money," says she, looking roguish. "No, no, I shan't take it, really, I assure you! Will you not play another game?"

"After two gammons and a backgammon in five games?" cries the ancient squarehead. "Ah, dear Lady Flashman, against chance and skill I can struggle, but when they are allied with beauty and charm I am overpowered altogether. Am I not right, Sir Harry? But I insist on paying my just debts," says he, planting his sovs in her palm, which gave the old goat the chance to kiss her hand and take a last fond leer at her top hamper, while she purred and protested.

"Och, isn't he the wee duck?" sighs she, jingling her loot as he hobbled away. "Aye, weel, mony a mickle mak's a muckle, as Papa used to say." She slipped it into her bag and broke into civilised speech. "But, you know, Harry, it was *quite* embarrassing, for I threw six and one, and double one, and double six ever so often! I'm sure he believes I use loaded dice!" Loaded tits, more like. "I was *so* glad to see you, for he breathes ever so *hard,* I can't think why, and I could see he *hated* losing, and it was such a bore." She lowered her voice as she took my arm. "Indeed, it's all rather a bore, don't you think? Will we be able to go home tomorrow? Would the Prince be offended? I feel I have had as much of *Tranby company* as I can bear—and I'm sure it can be no fun for you, dearest." The piano gang had begun to perform the last rites on "Three Little Maids," with immense jollity, and as we went out she pulled a face and whispered: "I mean, the Wilsons do their best and are ever so kind and . . . and eager to please— but they are not really *quite* the thing, are they?"

She's God's own original snob, my little Paisley princess—as though her mill-owning father had been a whit better than the Wilsons. But the little skinflint had collared a peerage in his declining years, you see, and she seemed to think that his coronet and cash, with my V.C. and military rank, to say nothing of her own occasional intimacy with the Queen, raised us above the common herd. Which I guess they did, in an odd way—or if not above, apart at least. We ain't top-drawer, but there's no denying we're different.

I told her if she'd had enough of it we could be away on the morning train. "Now that the Leger's run, I doubt if H.R.H. will linger. But I thought you'd been enjoying yourself, old girl, what with cheering on the winners, and sporting your glad rags—and most becoming you look, I may tell you—and being the life and soul, and charming Dirty Bertie . . ."

Mention of her appearance had inevitably brought her to a halt at a mirror in the corridor, and now she gave me a reproach-ful blue eye in the reflection.

"I trust I know what is due to royal rank," says she primly. "And I may tell you that mere polite affability is *not* charming in the odious way you mean it." She patted her gilded tresses com-placently and touched a gloved finger to her plump pink cheek, sighing. "Anyway, I doubt my charming days are gone lang syne—"

"You don't think anything of the sort . . . and neither does Billy Cumming, by all accounts. Oh, I've heard all about that— flirting over the baccarat cards, the two of you!"

Now was there, or was there not, an instant flicker in those glorious eyes before she widened them at me in mock indignation?

"Flirrr-ting! I? Upon my word!" She tossed her head. "The very idea—at my time of life! Flirting, quo' he! Goodness me—"

"I had a touch of your time of life t'other night— remember?" We were alone in the corridor, and I stepped close behind her and gave 'em a loving squeeze. She exclaimed "Oh!" and hit me with her fan.

"*That* was not flirting," says she. "I was a helpless victim—a poor defenceless old biddy, and you should think shame of yourself." She gave her hair a last touch, and turned to peck me on the cheek. "And who says I tried to fetch Billy Cumming, I should like to know? No—stop it, you bad old man, and tell me!"

"Owen Williams—an officer an' a gent, so there! Very jolly over the cards together you were, he tells me."

"He's an auld haver," says she elegantly. "Just because a gentleman helps a lady to make her bets—well, you know I cannae count—"

"Except at backgammon, apparently."

"Backgammon or no, I'm a duffer at cards, as well you know, and I dare say I said something exceptionally foolish, and made him laugh. As for flirting, Harry Flashman, who are you to talk? Do I not remember Mrs. Leo Lade—and Kitty Stevens?" Names from fifty years ago, God help me, still green in her eccentric memory—and I didn't even know who Kitty Stevens *was*! "Uh-huh, that's your eye on a plate, my lad," says she, slipping her arm through mine as we passed on. "What else did that blether Williams tell you?"

Now that was odd; lightly asked—too lightly. "Oh, just that," says I. "I guess he was trying to take a rise out of me, knowing I can't stand Cumming—but *not* knowing that you can't stand him either." I gave her hand a squeeze, reassuring like. "Why, you crossed him off our list years ago."

"Did I? I don't recollect." And that was odder still, for if there's an elephantine memory in London W.1. it resides in the otherwise wayward mind of Elspeth, Lady Flashman (as she had just proved by reference to Mrs. Leo Lade and that other bint, whoever she may have been). Suddenly, I knew that something was up. For all her banter, she'd been on the q.v. from the moment Cumming's name was mentioned: the quick wary glint in the mirror, her artless inquiry about what Williams had said, and the indifferent "Did I? I don't recollect" told me she was keeping something from me. Was it possible that Cumming *had* been trying his lecherous hand again? At her age? Damned unlikely . . . yet then again, Queen Ranavalona had been a grand-mother, and that hadn't stopped *me*. By God, if he had, I'd see to it that he came out of his present pickle with his name and fame in the gutter. But that could wait; I'd another fish to fry at the moment, and as we neared the drawing-room door I paused, assuming a frown.

"Hold on, though—yes, Williams did say another thing . . . Yes . . . At baccarat, last night, did you notice anything . . . well, out o' the way about Cumming's play?"

She looked bewildered—but then, on any subject that hasn't to do with money or erotic activity, she usually is.

"Why, Harry, whatever do you mean?"

"Was there anything remarkable about . . . his placing of the stakes?"

"My stakes, d'you mean? I told you he was helping me—"

"No, *his* stakes! How did he put 'em on the table?"

She looked at me as though I were simple-minded. "Why, with his hand, of course. He just put them . . . down . . ."

"Yes, dearest," says I, keeping a firm grip on myself, "but that's not quite what I mean—"

"—those wee coloured counters with the feathers on them, he just put them in front of him—and mine too, because, you see, he was advising me how to bet, since I did not understand the rules, or how much it would be safe to wager. And I must say," says she, opening the floodgates, "it is quite the *silliest* game, for there's no cleverness in it, and indeed I told him so. 'For how can we tell what to wager,' I said, 'when we have no *notion* of what the Prince's cards may amount to? Why, he may have a count of nine, and then where shall we be?' He laughed and said we must take the risk, for it was a gamble. 'I know *that*,' I said, 'but it would be more fun if we knew *one* of the Prince's cards, and he knew one of ours, for then we could judge how much to put on.' He said we must be like Montrose, and repeated that verse we used to recite at school, you know the one, about fearing our fate too much who will not put it to the touch to win or lose it all, and I said, 'That is all very well, Sir William, but remember what happened to *him*,' and he laughed more than ever . . ."

I love her dearly, far beyond any creature I've ever known, and I can prove it, for never once in almost seventy years of married life have I taken her by the throat. Mind you, it's been a near thing, once or twice.

"—and the court cards, would you believe it, count for nothing! 'Why, then,' I asked him, 'do they have them in the pack at all?' and he said he supposed it was to make weight, whatever that may mean, and I said it was a great annoyance to have to pay out to the bank when we had been dealt two kings, and got another when we asked for a third card, and the Prince's cards were the sorriest *rags*, but they made eight, and that was the better hand, but it seems hard that three kings should be worth nothing at all . . ."

I took her gently by the arm and steered her away from the drawing-room door to an alcove at the end of the corridor, for I could see there was only one way, and that was to come out with the thing plump and plain. "Did you see Cumming at any time add counters to his stake *after* the Prince had declared the result of the hand?"

She took her lower lip gently in her teeth—a tiny gesture of puzzlement which has been turning my heart over since 1839. "You mean after the Prince had said who had won?"

"Precisely."

She frowned. "But, then . . . it would be too late to add to his stake, surely?"

"That's the whole point. Did he, at any time, after the result had been called, place any counters beyond the line?"

"Which line?"

"The line," I replied through gritted teeth, "round the edge of the cloth on the table." It was like talking to a backward Bushman. "The line beyond which the stakes are placed."

"Oh, is that what the line was for? I thought it was just for the look of the thing." She reflected for a moment, and shook her head. "No . . . I cannot think that I saw him putting out more counters, after . . ." As realisation dawned, the forget-me-not eyes opened wide, and her lips parted. "Why, Harry, that would have been cheating!"

"Begad, you're right! So it would . . . but you never saw him do any such thing—with his hands, or a pencil—"

"Gracious, no! Why, I should have checked him at once, and told him it would not do—that he had made a mistake, and must . . ." And at that she stopped short, staring at me, and slowly her alarm changed into the oddest old-fashioned look, and then she smiled—that old teasing cherry-lipped Elspeth pout that used to have me thrusting the door to and wrenching at my breeches. To my astonishment I saw that her eyes were suddenly moist as she shook her head and came close to me, putting a gloved hand up to my whiskers.

"Oh, Harry, my jo, ye sweet old thing!" murmurs she. "Is that why you're tasking me with all these daft questions—because that clavering auld clype Owen Williams has told you that Billy Cumming put his hand on mine once or twice at the baccarat?" She laughed softly, loving-sad, and stroked my withered cheek. "To be sure he did—but only to guide me in placing my wagers, silly! And you're still jealous for your old wife, wild lad that you are—well, I'm glad, so there! Come here!" And she kissed me in a way which any decent matron should have forgotten long ago. "As though I've ever wanted to fetch any man but you," says she fondly, straightening my collar. "Supposing I still could. Now, if you'll give me your arm to the drawing-room, I dare say Mrs. Wilson will be serving tea."

The deuce of it is, when Elspeth turns a conversation topsy-turvy, all wide-eyed innocence, you can never be sure whether it's witlessness or guile. She's always been ivory from her delightful neck upwards, but that don't mean she can't wheedle a duck from a pond when so minded. Knowing her vanity ("Supposing I still could," my eye!) I didn't doubt that she believed my inquiries had been prompted by pure jealousy, to her immense gratification, lovingly expressed . . . still, there was something to do with Cumming that she wasn't telling. Well, perhaps it was something I'd be better for not knowing; one thing seemed clear, for what it was worth: whoever had seen him cheating, she had not.

I left her prattling over the cups to Lady Coventry and on the spur of the moment decided not to visit the Prince to see how his fine frenzy was coming along, but to call on the principal in the case, as promising more information—and entertainment. Faced with ruin and dishonour, Cumming should be an interesting spectacle by now, and a little manly condolence from old comrade Flashy might well lead him to do something amusing. The more mischief the better sport, as the great man said.

He was taking it well, I'll say that, standing before his mantel, every inch the Guardee, rock steady and looking down his aristocratic nose. I guessed he was a volcano ready to erupt, though, and when he'd dismissed his valet I took him flat aback by holding out my hand, avoiding his grip—and seeking his pulse. I do love to startle 'em.

"What the deuce?" cries he, pulling free.

"A touch fast, not much. You'll do." In fact, I hadn't found his pulse. "Seen the Prince, have you?"

"So you've heard! Yes, I have seen his highness." He eyed me with profound dislike. "I suppose you too believe this filthy slander?"

"Why should you think that?" says I, taking a chair.

"Those other idiots do—Williams and Coventry! And the Prince! And when did *you* ever believe good of anyone?"

"Not often, perhaps. But then, they don't often deserve it. In your case, as it happens, I'm probably the only man in this house who is *not* convinced that you played foul."

His sneer vanished in astonishment, and he took a pace forward, only to stop in sudden doubt. "You're not? Why?" Leery of me, you see; many people are.

"Because it makes no sense." I told him my reasons, which you know, and with every word his expression lightened until he was looking almost hopeful, in a frantic way.

"Have you said this to the Prince? What did he say, in heaven's name?"

I shook my head. "Didn't persuade him—or Coventry and Williams. Can't blame 'em altogether, you know; the evidence is pretty strong, on the face of it. Five witnesses—"

"Witnesses?" cries he. "Damned imbeciles! Two idiot women, a parcel of boys who know nothing—what's their word worth?" Almost in an instant the cool Guardee was gone, and he was standing before me, fists clenched and eyes wild, voice shaking with fury. Strange how a man can show a calm front and a stiff lip when all the world's agin him, but drop a sympathetic word and all the rage and indignation will come bubbling out, because he thinks he's found a friend to confide in.

"How can they *believe* it?" he stormed. "My God, Flashman, how can they? Men who've known me twenty years and more— trusted friends! As though I would . . . *stoop* to this . . . this damned infamy! And for what?" There were tears in his eyes, and if he'd stamped and torn his hair I'd not have been surprised. "For a few paltry pounds? By heaven, I'll throw it back in their faces—"

"Not if you've any sense, you won't," says I, and he stared. "Might be taken for an admission of guilt. You won it fair and square, did you? Then you keep it." Sound advice, by the way.

"That's the whole point, though," I added, sitting forward and giving him my eye. "Now, Cumming, don't start tearing the curtains, but tell me, straight out . . . did you cheat?"

He was breathing hard, but at that he stiffened, and answered straight. "I did not! On my word of honour."

He was telling the truth, no question. Not because he said so, but because of what I'd seen and heard from the moment I'd entered the room. I don't claim to be an infallible judge of my fellow man (and woman); I can be deceived, and put no faith in oaths and promises, however solemn. But I've been about, and if I knew anything at all, Gordon-Cumming's demeanour, in and out of anger, rang true.

"Very good. Now, these witnesses—are they lying?"

That set him away again. "How the blazes should I know? The whole thing is abominable! What's it to me whether they're lying or not? Pack of idiots and prying women! Who cares what they say! Let me tell you, Flashman, their foul charges don't matter a straw to me—they're worthless! But that men like Williams and . . . and the Prince, whom I counted a friend—that they should turn against me . . . that they can bring themselves to believe this vile thing—my God, and that you, of all people, should be alone in having . . . having faith in me . . ."

I dare say he didn't mean it to sound like an insult, but it did, and I found myself liking him even less than usual. He had gulped himself silent with outrage, so I resumed.

"You haven't answered. Are they lying?"

"I neither know nor care!" He paced about and stopped, glaring at the wall. "Oh, I suppose not! The damned fools must *think* they saw something wrong, but who knows with ignorant young asses like those? What do they know of card play, even, or how such games are conducted? Tyros and schoolboys—that dummy Levett! That he should think for a moment—"

"Stop vapouring, and keep your head," I told him. "Dammit, man, I'm trying to help you!" I wasn't, but there. "If you want to come out of this, you'd best stop ranting, and *think*. Now, then— they weren't lying, you believe. So they were mistaken. How? That's the thing—what was there in your play—the way you staked—that made 'em think you were diddling them?" I offered him a cheroot, and struck a match. "Now, settle down, and think that over."

He puffed at the weed in silence, made to speak, thought better of it, and then shrugged helplessly.

"How can I tell what they think they saw? Minds like theirs . . . stupid women and scatterbrains like young Wilson—"

"That won't answer. See here—from what I've learned, they claim that on two or three occasions you had a £5 stake in front of you, and then hey, presto! it was £15—*after* the hand had been declared. Now, how could that be? Think, man—unless they were seeing things, you must have added another two red chips to the one already there. Did you? Could you? No, don't start bellowing—think! If you weren't cheating—how came those extra chips to be there?"

He stood nursing his brow, and turned to me a face that was haggard with frustration. "I don't know, Flashman. It can't have been so . . . I swear I never added to my stake after the . . ." And suddenly he stopped, and his eyes and mouth opened wide, and he gave a choking gasp. "Oh, my God! Of course! The *coup de trois*! That's it, Flashman! The *coup de trois*!" And he let out a great wailing noise which I took to be relief. "The *coup de trois*!"

"What the hell's the *coup de trois*?"

"My system!" His eyes were blazing. "Why didn't I think of it at once! I was tripling up—don't you see? Look here!" He lugged a handful of coins from his pocket, spilling 'em all over the shop, and planked one on the table. "There—that's my £5 stake. I win—and am paid a fiver from the bank . . ." He clapped down a second coin. "I let 'em lie, and add *another* fiver . . ." down went a third coin ". . . and that's my stake for the *next* hand—£15! It's how I always play! Stake a fiver, win another, add a third! The *coup de trois*!" He was laughing in sheer triumph. "Why, it's as old as the hills! Every punter knows it—but not those green monkeys, Wilson and Levett! They see a fiver staked, look away, look back again *after* the coup's been declared *and the bank has paid out*—and see three fivers—my original stake, my winning, and

the third which I've added for the *next* coup, *perfectly properly!*"
He let out a huge gasp of relief and subsided into a chair. "And
because they're ignorant novices, brought up on old maid and
halma, they think it's foul play!"

"The only thing is," says I, "that they're sure you added the
extra chips *after* the coup was declared, but *before* the bank paid
out—and that you accepted payment of £15."

"Then they're wrong, that's all! It's a question of . . . of timing, can't you see?"

"They say that on one coup you jockeyed your stake and
demanded an extra tenner from the bank—"

"Stuff and nonsense!"

"—and that once you flicked a chip over the line with a
pencil—"

"That is a lie!" He was on his feet again, white with anger.
"Dammit, man, can't you see sense? Don't you see what has happened? Some young fool sees my *coup de trois,* thinks it's a fraud,
tells the other young fools, and because they're as dense as he is—
aye, and as eager to believe the worst—they see all manner of
things that ain't there! Flicking chips with pencils—bah!" In his
excitement he took me by the arm. "Don't you see, Flashman?"

In fact, I did, and was feeling much let down. For what he
said made some sort of sense . . . perhaps. Half-baked lads like
Levett and Wilson, knowing nothing of such systems as the
coup de trois employed by seasoned gamesters like Cumming,
might well misinterpret his actions. It was, as he said, a question
of timing, and in an ill-regulated drawing-room game, with no
croupier on the first night, and the bank paying out any old how,
it was possible that they might have thought Cumming was still to
be paid when in fact he'd already got his winnings and was letting
'em lie, with an additional fiver, for the next coup. Now, if the
thing were explained to them, they'd surely be bound to give him
the benefit of the doubt—for Bertie would leap at the explanation

as a lifeline, and for decency's sake they'd have to admit that they might have been mistaken.

If there had been a cat handy I'd have kicked it. What had promised to be a splendid scandal looked like fizzling out like the dampest of squibs, and this damned baronet would walk away without a blot on his escutcheon . . . or so it seemed to me just then. From the first, you see, I'd feared that there might be a simple explanation, and here was a plausible one, rot it. It was all most damnably deflating—and worse because I'd guided him to his bloody loophole of escape.

"Don't you see?" cries he again, impatiently. "Heavens, it's as plain as daylight now! You must see that! It's obvious to any-one above a half-wit—even a muttonhead like Williams can't fail to see it! Am I right?"

I put on my judicial face and said that he probably was. "Well, thank God for that!" cries he sarcastically, and if anything had been needed to convince me he was telling the truth, it was his sneering tone. Not a hint of doubt that his explanation mightn't wash, no palpitating hope of its acceptance—only cold fury that he, the soul of honour, had been disgracefully traduced, and that his peers had believed it. Two minutes since he'd been in an agony of despair, but now Sir William Gordon-Cumming, Bart, was back in the saddle, bursting with injured self-righteousness and the arrogant certainty of his kind. And, you'll note, not a whisper of gratitude to your correspondent.

"The Prince must be told at once! He's a man of sense—unlike those clowns Coventry and Williams. I don't doubt they persuaded him against his will, but when I put it to him he'll see the right of it." He was at his dressing-table, flourishing his silver-backed brushes, improving his parting, with a dab or two at the ends of his pathetic Guardee moustache, and shooting his cuffs, while I marvelled at the human capacity for self-delusion. He was full of exultant confidence now, and it never crossed his shallow mind that others might be less ready to take his view of the matter. I've said his explanation was plausible, but it wasn't near as cast-iron as he thought. Much would depend on how it was presented . . . and how ready they were to believe it.

"It may be a lesson to them against jumping to conclusions! And on such flimsy evidence—the babbling of those whippersnappers! And *my* character, *my* good name, *my* record of honourable service, were to count for nothing against their damned gossip, the confounded little spies!" He was striding for the door, in full raging fettle, when he suddenly wheeled about. "No, by heavens, I'll not do it!" He snapped his fingers, pointing at me. "Why should I?"

"Why shouldn't you do what?" was all I could say, for his anger had dropped from him like a shed cloak, and he was smiling grimly as he came slowly back to me.

"Why should I humble myself with explanations? I'm the injured party, am I not? I'm the one who has suffered this . . . this intolerable affront! I have been insulted in the grossest fashion on the word of a pack of mannerless brats, and two elderly fools who, I have no doubt, persuaded His Royal Highness against his better judgment and honourable instincts." Drunk with vindictive justification he might be, he wasn't ass enough to impugn Saintly Bertie. He gave a barking laugh. "Lord, Flashman, in our fathers' day I'd have been justified in blowing their imbecile heads off on Calais sands! Am I to crawl to them and say, 'Please, sir, I can *prove* your informants—ha, inform*ers*, I should say!— have been utterly in the wrong, and will you kindly tell 'em so, and condescend to forgive me for having conducted myself like a man of honour?' Is that what I'm supposed to do?"

Talk about women scorned; their fury ain't in it with a Scotch baronet's wounded self-esteem. Had I ever, I wondered, encountered such an immortally conceited ass with a truer touch for self-destruction? George Custer came to mind. Aye, put him and

Gordon-Cumming on the edge of a precipice and I'd not care to bet which would tumble first into the void, bellowing his grievance.

"What," says I, keeping my countenance with proper gravity, "do you propose to do?"

"Not a damned thing! You—" stabbing me on the chest "—since you've thrust your spoon into the dixie, can do it for me! You can be my messenger, Flashman, and have the satisfaction of showing them what asses they've made of themselves! You've got the gift o' the gab, don't we know it?" says he, with a curl of his voice if not of his lip. "You can explain about the *coup de trois* and the rest of it—because I'm damned if I will! It's not for me to make a plea to them—let 'em come to me! I'll accept their apology—Coventry and Williams, I mean, and those three gutter-snipes! Not the ladies, of course—and certainly not His Royal Highness, who has been most disgracefully imposed on, I'm sure of that. Yes," says he, head up and shoulders square, with exultation in his eye, "that's the way to do it! So off you go, old fellow, and don't spare 'em!" Seeing me stand thoughtful, he frowned impatiently. "Well—will you?"

Would I not? I've told you my score against Gordon-Cumming—a natural detestation of his supercilious vanity, his unconcealed dislike of me, above all the suspicion that he'd ploughed with my heifer, and now, if you please, the arrogant bastard was appointing me his message-boy. Throw into the scale his overweening certainty that he'd cleared himself, and must be grovelled to in consequence, and you'll understand (if you know me at all) that I would not have missed the chance to sink the swine, not for my soul's salvation.

For it was in my hands, no error. His *coup de trois* excuse had put the whole affair on a knife-edge. If it were shrewdly urged, the three wise men, and the witnesses, might be disposed, for the sake of avoiding a horrid scandal, to swallow it. Well, by the time I'd done with it, they'd spew it all over the floor.

So I consented to act as his go-between, and left him grinding his teeth at the prospect of accusers confounded and honour restored. No time, we agreed, must be lost, so I made for the Prince's apartments, and whom should I meet on the way but the three leading witnesses, plainly just come from a royal audience: Master Wilson bright with excitement, Lycett Green tight-lipped, and young Levett plainly wishing himself in the Outer Hebrides. No change on that front, thinks I, and the air of gloom in H.R.H.'s sitting-room, most of it cigar smoke, confirmed my conclusion.

"That fellow is impossible!" Bertie was croaking, and I gathered he meant Lycett Green. "Not a shadow of doubt, according to him. Oh, it's intolerable! What can we do but believe them?"

"As your highness says." Coventry sounded like a vicar at the graveside. "That being so, we are bound to take . . ." he frowned as he dredged his vocabulary ". . . ah, measures . . . in regard to Sir William."

"Lycett Green won't keep quiet if we don't," says Williams.

"Self-righteous ass!" snaps Bertie. "No, that's not fair . . . he's a decent man, no doubt—I only wish he weren't so infernally adamant." He scowled at me. "Well?" I said I'd seen Gordon-Cumming.

"And much good that will have done! I've seen him myself—and it was heart-breaking! I tell you, the man almost had tears in his eyes! One of my closest friends, I'd ha' trusted him with my life—but how can I credit his denial in the face of . . . of . . ." He flourished a paw in the direction of the door. "They're so *sure*! Even Levett, poor devil—heavens, we could hardly drag it out of him!" He sat down, groaning, drew on his cigar as though it were poisoned, and regarded me dyspeptically. "What did Cumming have to say to you?"

"Denied it, absolutely. I suppose he gave your highness his explanation?"

That brought him bolt upright. "What explanation?"

I hesitated, with an artistic frown, and shook my head. "I don't know quite what to make of it myself . . . I confess that I . . ." At that I stopped, waiting for him to demand what the devil I was talking about, which he did, with considerable vigour.

"Well, sir . . ." I began, half-apologetic, and then I gave him the *coup de trois* story, plain and matter-of-fact, but with dark doubt hovering over every word, and was gratified to see Coventry's face growing long as a coffin, Williams frowning in disbelief, and the light of hope fading from Bertie's bloodshot ogles.

"D'you believe it?" cries he, and I maintained the manly silence that damned Gordon-Cumming as no words could. "But is it possible?" he insisted.

"Possible, sir?" I made a lip and shrugged. "Aye, I dare say it's . . . possible . . ."

"But even if it were true," broke in Williams, "and you plainly don't think it is, it still does not explain all the . . . the irregularities. The pencil, that sort of thing." He met Bertie's despairing eye. "I regret to say it, sir, but it sounds to me like the feeble excuse of a desperate man. And I'm sure," he added, "that that is how Green and the others will regard it."

Coventry heaved a draughty sigh. "Indeed, it only confirms my belief that Sir William . . . ah, that the witnesses . . . the charges . . ."

"That he's a cheat and a liar!" cries Bertie. He growled down his temper, gnashed on his cigar, and faced us. "Very well, then. God knows we've done our best to sift the thing—and that's our conclusion. He's played foul and been caught out. Now," says he, and for the first time that night he sounded royal, "how is it to be hushed up?"

They stood mum, so I put in my oar again. " 'Fraid it can't be, sir . . . unless you and Williams are prepared to risk a court martial."

If I'd said "are prepared to steal the Crown Jewels and make a run for Paraguay," I couldn't have provoked a finer display of consternation, but before Bertie could explode, I explained.

"You and he both hold the Queen's commission, sir. I'm retired, of course. But as serving officers, aware of dishonourable conduct by a brother officer, you're obliged to bring it to the attention of your superiors. Since your highness is a field marshal, I'm not sure who your superiors are, exactly . . . Her Majesty, of course. Or I dare say the colonel of Cumming's regiment would do . . ."

I was drowned out by a prolonged fit of princely coughing, the result of outraged smoke going down the wrong way, which gave him time to digest my warning, and emerge mopping and wheezing to announce hoarsely that he didn't give a tinker's dam for courts martial, or words to that effect, and not a whisper was to be breathed to military superiors or anyone else, was that clear?

"It must not come out!" he croaks. "At all costs it must be confined to . . . to ourselves. The scandal . . ." He couldn't bring himself even to contemplate it. "A way must be found!" He sat down again, thumping his knees. "It must!"

Which left us back at the starting-gate, three of us racking our brains and Flashy looking perplexed but inwardly serene, for all I was waiting for was a lead. At last Coventry gave it.

"If some accommodation could be found," says he, "which would signify . . . ah, disapprobation of Sir William's conduct, while satisfying the . . . ah, resentment of his accusers, and of course ensuring that no word of this deplorable affair ever—"

"Oh, talk sense, Coventry!" barks Bertie. "They want his head on a charger! Green made that plain enough—and how you're to contrive that in secrecy I cannot imagine!"

"How d'you punish him without exposing him?" wonders Williams, and I saw it was time for the Flashman Compromise which had been taking shape in my mind over the past minute or two. I made a judicial noise to attract their attention.

"I wonder if Lord Coventry hasn't pointed the way, sir," says I. "Suppose . . . yes, how would it do? . . . if Cumming were to sign a paper . . . you know, an undertaking sort of thing . . . pledging himself never to touch a card again. Eh?" They stood mute as ducks in thunder. "Stiff penalty for a man in his position, what? I'd be surprised if that didn't satisfy Green and his pals. And in return," I tapped the table impressively, "they would pledge themselves to silence—as would we, absolutely. That would settle things—without a breath of scandal."

There was a hole in it a mile wide, but I knew Bertie wouldn't spot it: my last five words were all that mattered to him. He was pointing like a setter, Coventry was in his customary fog, but Williams burst out:

"Cumming would never do such a thing! Why, it would be tantamount to a confession of guilt."

"Not a bit of it, Owen!" says I. "He ain't admitting a thing— and if he were, 'twould only be to us, and his accusers, who think he's guilty anyway. No one else would ever know." I turned to Bertie, his cigar now in tatters. "I'm sure he'll agree, sir—what other choice has he? Public disgrace . . . and worse than that," I went on, fixing Coventry and Williams with my sternest look, "would be the shameful burden of knowing that greater names than his had been tarnished by the publication of his dishonour."

That did the trick: Bertie started as though I'd put a bayonet into his leg, and from Williams' expression I knew that if I'd said: "Tell Cumming that if he don't do as he's told, and preserve our precious Prince from scandal, God help him," I could not have been plainer. Coventry, naturally, was appalled.

"But . . . such a document, supposing Sir William should consent to sign it, in return for a pledge of silence . . . would it not bear a . . . an odour of . . . of conspiracy?"

"Certainly not," says I. "It would be a simple promise never to play cards again, signed by him, duly witnessed by His Royal Highness—and by the accusers. Nothing smoky about it. They would give their word of honour to His Highness never to speak or write of the matter hereafter. And that would be that, tight as a drum."

Bertie hadn't said a word for several minutes, and when he did it was clear what was preoccupying him. "Could we be sure those people would keep silence?"

"Once they'd given their word to the Prince of Wales?" says I, and that seemed to satisfy him, for he sat in silence a moment, and then asked the other two what they thought of the scheme. They puffed doubtfully, of course, Williams because he feared that Cumming would refuse to sign, and Coventry out of general anxiety. Would Lycett Green and Co. agree, he wondered, and Bertie let out a muffled snarl.

"They'll agree!" says he grimly, which settled that, and they passed on to the wording of the document, which was simple enough, and then to considering how it might best be put to the guilty party. Bertie wondered if I should take part with Coventry and Williams, but modesty forbade.

"I'm no diplomat, sir," says I. "Too blunt by half. His lordship and Owen will do it ten times better without me. Besides," I added, blunt honest old Flashy, "the fact is he don't like me. Dunno why, but there it is. No point in putting his back up, so the less I'm mentioned, the better."

D'you know, Williams absolutely shook his head in sympathy, and Bertie went so far as to give my arm a clap before I withdrew. He was even more demonstrative an hour later, when I was summoned to his presence just as I was on the point of turning in, and found him sitting on the edge of his bed in his dressing-gown, glass in hand, cigar at the high port, plainly dog-weary but content at having laboured well in the vineyard.

"Well, he's signed!" cries he jovially. He picked up a paper and held it out: just a few lines, with a forest of names at the foot, led by "W. Gordon-Cumming" and the Prince's scrawl. "Not without the deuce of a struggle, Owen Williams tells me. Swore it was tantamount to a confession, but gave in when they told him it was that or ruin. Help yourself, Flashman," indicating decanter and humidor, "and sit ye down. Gad, I don't care if I never have such an evening again—after dinner, too, shan't sleep a wink." He swigged comfortably. "D'you know, I did not half believe he'd put his signature to it—but you knew, downy old bird that you are!" He was positively twinkling.

"Well, sir, he really didn't have much choice, did he? All things considered, he's come off dam' lightly."

"That's what Lycett Green thinks, tho' he'd the grace not to say so. Oh, aye, they've all put their names to it, as you see." He peered at the paper, shaking his head. "I must say, it's a damning thing for an innocent man to sign . . . and yet . . ." He screwed up his little eyes at me. "D'you think there's the least possibility he's telling the truth?"

"Look at it this way, sir—would you have signed it, knowing yourself innocent? Or would you have damned 'em for liars and offered to put 'em through every court in the land? Or taken a horsewhip to 'em?"

And think what Mama would have made of that, I might have added. He looked solemn, wagging his head, and then demanded, almost peevishly:

"What the devil possessed him to *do* it—to cheat, I mean? Was he off his head, d'you think? You know, temporarily deranged? One hears of such things."

"Dunno, sir. And I doubt if he does, either."

He shook his head and rumbled a few philosophies while we sipped and smoked. He was enjoying his relief, and when we parted he was at his most affable, pumping my fin and calling me Harry again. "I'm obliged to you . . . not for the first time. This—" he tapped Cumming's paper "—was a brainwave, and the sooner it's safely bestowed, the better. Not the sort of item we'd care to see in the morning press, what? Well, good-night to you, old fellow, thank'ee again . . . aye, and thank the Lord we'll hear no more of it!"

And if you believe that, sweet prince, you will indeed believe anything, thinks I. For if there was one stone cold certainty, it was that we would hear more, abundantly more and running over, of the Great Baccarat Scandal of Tranby Croft. Bertie, blind to everything but the need to keep it from the Queen's ears, and asses like Coventry and Williams, might suppose that the vows of silence sworn by all and sundry would prove binding—honour and all that, you know. I knew better. At least a dozen folk, two of 'em women, were in the secret, and the notion that they'd *all* hold their tongues was plain foolish. It was bound to get out—as I'd determined it should from the moment I'd stood in Gordon-Cumming's presence, weighed him up, and realised what a prime subject he was for shoving down the drain. All it needed after that, as you know, was an inspiration, and careful management; now, nature could take its course.

Which it did, and if it took longer to leak out than I'd expected, the resultant row was worth the delay. It's still not established who blew the gaff, but my firm belief is that it was Bertie himself, unlikely as that may seem. But the fact is that the Yankee papers named as their source none other than Elspeth's chum, Daisy Brooke aforementioned (it was they who christened her Babbling Brooke), and since she was warming the princely mattress in those days, it's odds on that he whispered the scandal to her, more fool he. Daisy swore 'twasn't so, and threatened to sue, but never did.

Whoever blabbed, it was all over the clubs and messes before Christmas that Cumming had cheated, chaps were cutting him dead, and he was demanding retractions and apologies and not getting them. So there he was, reputation blasted, and nothing for it, you'd have thought, but to order a pint of port and a pistol for breakfast or join the Foreign Legion.

He did neither. To the shocked murmurs and secret glee of Society, the delight of the public, and I've no doubt the terror of the Prince of Wales, he brought an action for slander against his five accusers from Tranby.

The trial came off in June of '91, and it's one of the regrets of my life that I was not present, if only to see stout Bertie in the witness-box, squirming under the inquisition of saucy jurors who didn't know their place, unlike the judge and counsel who grovelled to him something servile, and did everything but tote him in and out of court in a palankeen. The proceedings lasted a week, and by all accounts it was one of the finest legal circuses ever seen, with the judge as ringmaster and nothing lacking but an orchestra and chorus girls. Knowing our revered Lord Chief Justice of the day, the ancient Coleridge, I wasn't surprised, for he was a jolly old buck with a tremendous fund of good stories; once made a speech lasting twenty-three days, they tell me, and was responsible for the three-mile limit, in case you're interested.

You may be sure I was sorely tempted once or twice to view the spectacle, but decided reluctantly to keep clear—when you've had a hand in engineering a disaster it's best to stand well out from under to avoid falling debris. I knew Bertie and Co. wouldn't advertise my part in the affair, which was deplorable enough without the notorious Flashy being dragged in, and sure enough they didn't. One or two who knew I'd been at Tranby quizzed me, but I took a stern and silent line—you know, shockin' biznai, old comrade, beyond belief, state o' the Army, damnable altogether . . . that sort of thing.

Aside from the verdict, which I'll tell you presently in case you don't know, the great sensation was the storm that burst over the head of our unfortunate Heir Apparent. God forbid I should ever feel sorry for the fat bounder, but even I was astonished at the way the press and pulpits laid into him; you'd have thought he'd been kidnapping nuns and selling 'em to the Port Said brothels. And all because he'd been playing baccarat! "Woe to the

Monarchy!" wailed one rag, another spoke of a "chorus of con-
demnation," and the rest expressed shock and disgust, denounced
his taste for the "lowest type of gambling," and recoiled from the
spectacle of "the future King of England officiating at a gam-
blers' orgy." Even *The Times* went wild with terms like "regret,"
"concern," and "distress," a Scotch journal decided that "the
Prince is evidently not what he ought to be," but the leader I liked
best was the one that said the British Empire was humiliated and
the rest of civilisation was pointing the finger at us.

As to the trial itself, you can go to the official record if you've
a mind to, but I flatter myself you won't learn much that I haven't
told you. The lawyers went back and forth over every blessed
moment of those three nights, every shift of those damned counters, every syllable of who said what to whom, and what expressions they wore, and what they thought and why, over and over,
and I dare say at the end of it the jury were as fogged as the
public. The biggest guns of the day fought the case: Clarke,
the Solicitor-General, no less, who appeared for Cumming, was
reckoned the shrewdest mouthpiece of the day, while the defendants were represented by two of the best hatchet-men in the
business, Charles Russell and young Asquith—you know the latter as the buffoon who infests Number 10 Downing Street at the
moment, and my recollection of him is as a shining morning face
to which I once presented a prize at the City of London School,
but for all that he was accounted a sharp hand in court, while
Russell was a human hawk, and looked it.

Reading the press reports, I concluded that the evidence
given didn't differ much from what I myself remembered of
events, and in nothing essential. Owen Williams had drawn
up a précis of what had happened at Tranby, in which various
holes were picked: there seemed to be uncertainty over the order
of the interviews on the Wednesday evening, and some vague-
ness as to who had suggested presenting the damning document
to Cumming—which wasn't surprising, since it had been yours

truly, and they were keeping me out of it. Elspeth likewise: I'd been worried that she might be called as a witness, since on the first night she'd sat as an onlooker, and on the second had for a time taken Lady Coventry's place next to Cumming, but either they'd forgotten about her—or more likely they'd remembered, and had realised that the last thing the trial needed was her driv-elling brightly in the witness-box. Like several others of the party, she wasn't even mentioned.

None of which mattered to the case. Cumming, in evidence, repeated his flat denial of the charges, claiming that he'd lost his head and signed the paper only because he'd been persuaded that there was no other way to avoid a public scandal. He got in a sly thrust at Bertie by suggesting that H.R.H. had been chiefly con-cerned to cover his own ample rear—which, as I knew, was gospel true.

The five accusers stuck by their stories pretty well, although Clarke, who was obviously a complete hand at confusing the issue with trivial questions, claimed to find all kinds of discrepancies in their testimony; he also hinted, ever so delicately, that a couple of them might have been tight, had great fun about Lycett Green's being a master of foxhounds, and took a nice injured line of sur-prise that in view of Cumming's pledged word, stainless char-acter, and so forth, they weren't prepared to admit they'd been mistaken. His final speech was four times as long as that of Rus-sell, who simply went straight at Cumming's throat: why hadn't he demanded to be brought face to face with his accusers, as any honest man would have done? He also reminded the jury that the five accusers weren't alone in thinking Cumming guilty; the Prince, Williams, and Coventry thought so too.

In all that I read, I could put my finger on only one flat lie: the defendants' denial that there had been any arrangement to keep watch on Cumming's play the second night. Well, I ask you! You're told a man has been cheating, and *don't* keep an eye on him next time? Pull the other one, Walker; you watch him like a lynx.

According to Owen Williams, they'd told him they'd agreed to watch, but now, in the witness-box, they were claiming they'd done no such thing. Their reason was plain enough: they didn't want to be thought of as spying on a fellow guest, and there was some fine wriggling under cross-examination—one of 'em, I think it was Lycett Green, absolutely said: "Knowing the man had cheated, I looked, but not with a view to watching," which is as fine a piece of humbug as I could ha' thought up myself. Not that it made a ha'porth of difference: they'd seen what they'd seen, and held by it.

By the morning of the seventh day, with the cases of both sides completed, the thing was on a knife-edge: half the Town was positive Gordon-Cumming was the biggest cheat since Jacob, while t'other half held that Clarke had shown up the five accusers for unreliable idiots (if not vindictive parvenus) whose evidence wasn't worth stale beans. Perambulating from the Park to the Temple during the day, I heard Cumming damned and defended in the clubs, but the farther east I walked, the more I encountered a truly British phenomenon: among the com-monalty, the anti-Cummings wanted to see him done down for precisely the same reason that the pro-Cummings hoped he'd win: because he was a toff. The lord-haters were full of righ-teous indignation about the pampered rich rioting and gaming while honest folk went hungry, so to Hell with Cumming and the Prince of Wales and the lot of 'em; on the other side were the forelock-tuggers who thought it "a bleedin' disgrice that a proper gent wot 'ad fought for Queen an' country" should be defamed by the likes o' them nobodies. No wonder the foreigners can't understand us.

No doubt because I hoped to see him sunk to perdition, I could imagine several excellent reasons why the jury should find in his favour and award him thumping damages. Foremost in my mind still, you see, was the conviction that he couldn't have cheated; spite and prejudice aside, it wasn't in the man's nature.

But it was up to the jury now, and no doubt all hung on the direction they would receive from the venerable Coleridge. The early editions were carrying his summing-up at length, and I studied it eagerly in the corner of a Fleet Street pub, with a pie and pint to keep me company.

The day's proceedings had begun with a protest from that ass Owen Williams, demanding to make a statement against the Solicitor-General, Clarke, who, says Williams, had accused him of an "abominable crime—of sacrificing an innocent man." Coleridge couldn't remember what exact words had been used, but told Williams that counsel could say what they dam' well liked in Court, and would Williams kindly keep quiet and give him, Coleridge, some judging-room, or words to that effect. After which Williams presumably retired, gnashing, and Coleridge addressed the twelve good men and true.

It must have been a sight to see, for he apparently played the wise, simple old codger, peering over his glasses while he told the jury what brilliant chaps Clarke and Russell and Asquith were: he didn't say they were too clever by half, exactly, but he thought it no bad thing that "the humble jog-trot" of his summing-up should intervene between their fireworks and the verdict.

Having put the wigged brigade in their place, he told the jury something that was news to me: that cheating at cards was an offence for which you could be nailed in court. He then went on to remind them that Clarke had said Cumming wasn't interested in soaking his accusers; they would bear that in mind if the question of damages arose. (A hundred to eight he'll tell 'em to find for Cumming, thinks I.) And another thing: whether they disapproved of gambling or not was beside the point, which was simply this: did Cumming cheat or not?

He rambled on, fairly reasonably it seemed to me, about the actual play, and the witnesses' testimony, and caused some mirth by describing Cumming's system of betting as sounding like *"coup d'état."* Well, he knew it couldn't be *coup d'état,* but it was some French expression or other . . . oh, *coup de trois,* was it? Ah, well . . . On he went, honest old Coleridge, as gentle and benign as could be, drawing the jury's attention to various points, reminding them that it didn't matter a hoot what *he* thought, it was up to them, and all he could do was raise questions for them, which they must answer. Only once did he rouse himself, to have a brief bicker with Clarke for seeming to turn up his nose at the social standing of some of the accusers. It wasn't Lycett Green's fault that his father was an engineer, was it? And if young Jack Wilson was a shiftless layabout, what was wrong with that? And if the Wilsons toad-ate the Prince, why, who did not?

Clarke said he hadn't called Lycett Green's father an engineer, and Coleridge said, well, if he hadn't, his junior had. No he hadn't, either, says Clarke, but Coleridge ignored him and said he didn't see why a chap should be laughed at because his father was an engineer, and if a chap liked hobnobbing with the Prince, where was the harm, eh? It wouldn't prejudice him against Gordon-Cumming, anyway, and *that* was the point.

Furthermore, this stuff about Gordon-Cumming losing his head didn't impress the bench. Cumming had had lots of time to think before he signed the paper, and knew what he was doing. He hadn't asked to be confronted by his accusers, either; pretty rum, that seemed to Coleridge. And he hadn't returned his winnings—put 'em in the bank, 238 quids' worth. Well, well . . .

Having read this far, I felt the odds were shifting in the direction of the defendants, but you still couldn't tell. Then the silly old buffer got on to a new tack: the Prince of Wales. Well, Coleridge couldn't see the throne toppling simply because the Prince had played baccarat. The Prince had a busy public life, opening things and making speeches and listening to speeches, and a hell of a bore it must be, in Coleridge's view, so if he wanted to enjoy himself of an evening, why not? Some people might say why not read the Bible instead of playing baccarat, but it was a free country, wasn't it?

Sound stuff, in its way, interspersed with quotations from Shakespeare (including a bit of Henry V at Agincourt on the subject of honour), and other authors with whom he didn't doubt the jury were familiar, and a few Latin tags to remind them that this was serious work—and then, at the end of his summing-up, when they must have been sitting in a restful fog, he left off playing the genial, philosophising old buffer and delivered the thrust that settled the case once and for all.

Would an innocent man, he wondered, sign a document stating he had cheated, simply to prevent its being known that the Prince of Wales had played baccarat? Would a man allow himself to be called a card-sharp rather than have it known that the Prince had done something of which many people might disapprove? No, Coleridge couldn't swallow that.

The jury retired . . . and that, blast it, was as far as the report went, so I set off for home, and it was in the gentle even-fall that I came on a newsboy hollering "Verdict!" on the corner of Bruton Street, and there it was in the stop press: the jury had taken only thirteen minutes to find for the defendants.

So that was Cumming ruined. The twelve good men had declared him a cheat and a liar.

I confess it took me aback—splendid news though it was. How the devil had a jury of Englishmen, brought up to give a man the benefit of the doubt, come to that conclusion? Still, they'd been in court, and I had not—and they'd reached their decision double quick, hadn't they just, in hardly more time than it would take to call for votes round the table. No doubts, apparently, and certainly no arguments.

Strangely, where opinion had been evenly divided before, it swung violently to Cumming after the verdict. One learned journal opined that you wouldn't have hung a dog on the evidence that he'd cheated, and I heard it said on every side that the thing should never have come to trial at all: it should have been settled at Tranby, and would have been but for ill-advised zeal on the part of the Prince's friends to save him from scandal.

The irony was that in spite of all the reverential treatment and may-it-please-your-royal-highnessing he'd received in court, the trial did Bertie more damage than any other incident in his well-spotted career. The press, as I've said, damned him from Belgrade to breakfast, and when he issued a statement (with the blessing, they say, of the Prime Minister and the Archbishop of Canterbury) protesting that he had a horror of gambling, and did his utmost to discourage it, he was seen for the windy little hypocrite he was, and hooted in the streets.

Cumming was finished socially and professionally, of course, and had the sense to resign, marry his American girl, and retire to Scotland; if I knew him at all, any shame he felt would be nothing to his rage against the society that had branded him, and the prince who'd betrayed him, and I dare say he's brooding in his Highland fastness this minute, armoured in righteous wrath, despising the world that cast him out. Small wonder, for I can tell you now, at the end of my little tale . . . Gordon-Cumming was railroaded. He didn't cheat at baccarat.

I learned this within twenty-four hours of the verdict, but there was nothing to be done, even if I'd wanted to. No one would have credited the truth for a moment; I didn't myself, at first, for it beggared belief. But there can be no doubt about it, for it fits exactly with the evidence of both sides, and the source is unimpeachable—I've lived with her seventy years, after all, and know that while she may suppress a little *veri* and suggest a touch of *falsi* on occasion, Elspeth ain't a liar.

We were at breakfast, which for me in my indulgent age was Russian style (sausage, brandy, and coffee) and for her the fodder of her native heath: porridge, ham, eggs, black pudding, some piscine abomination called Arbroath smokies, oatcakes, rolls, and marmalade (God knows how she's kept her figure), while we read the morning journals. Usually she reads and prattles together, but that morning she was silent, absorbing the Cumming debacle. When she'd laid her eye-glasses aside she sat for a while, stirring her tea in a thoughtful, contented manner.

"Rum business, that," says I. "D'ye know, old girl, it's beyond me. Granted he's a poisonous tick . . . I still can't believe he cheated."

"Neither he did," says she.

"What's that? Oh, I see . . . you don't think it likely, either. Well, I don't suppose we'll ever know for certain, but—"

"Oh, but I do know," says she, laying down her spoon. "He did not cheat at all. Well, I think not, on the first night, and I know he did not, on the second." She sipped her tea, while I choked on my brandy.

"What d'you mean—you *know?* You don't know a thing about it! Why, when I asked you, that night at Tranby . . . remember, whether he'd been jockeying his stakes, you didn't know what I meant, even!"

"I knew perfectly well what you meant, but it would not have been prudent to say anything just then. It would not have suited," says she calmly, "at all."

"You mean . . . you're saying you *knew then* he hadn't cheated?" In my agitation I overset my cup, coffee all over the shop. "But . . . how could you possibly . . . what the blazes are you talking about?"

"There is no need to fly at me, or take that crabbit tone," says she, rising swiftly. "Quick, put a plate under the cloth before it stains the table! Drat, such a mess! Here, let me 'tend to it, and you ring for Jane . . . oh, the best walnut!"

"Damn Jane and the walnut! Will you tell me what you mean!" She had the cloth back, clucking and mopping the table with a napkin. "Elspeth! What's this rot about Cumming not cheating? How do you know, dammit?"

"It's a mercy your cup had gone cold . . . oh, how vexing! It'll have to be French polished." She peered at the wood. "Oh, dear, why did I not wait till you were settled—guid kens I should know by now what you're like in the morning." She discarded the napkin with dainty distaste and resumed her seat. "Sir William Gordon-Cumming did not cheat. That is what I mean." She sighed, in a Patient Griselda sort of way. "The fact is, you see . . . I did."

Lord knows what I looked like in that moment, a cod on a slab likely. She lifted a swift warning finger.

"Now, please, my love, do not raise your voice, or rage at me. It's done, and there is no undoing it, and the servants would hear. If you are angry, I'm sorry, but if you'll just bide quiet and hear me out, you may not be *too* angry, I hope." She smiled at me as though I were an infant drooling in my crib, and took a sip of tea.

"Now, then. It was I who added counters to his stakes, just once or twice, and not *nearly* as often as they said—why, I was quite *shocked* when I read in the papers last week, the kind of evidence they were giving, even Mrs. Wilson—dear me, if there had been *that* much hankey-pankey with the counters the whole world must have seen, the Prince and everyone! The way folk deceive themselves! But I suppose," she shrugged, "that the General Solicitor or whatever they call him was right, and they saw what they wanted to see . . . only they didn't, if you know what I mean, for it wasn't Billy Cumming cheating, it was me . . . or should it be I? Anyway, I only did it now and then . . . well, three or four times, perhaps, I'm not sure, but often enough to make them think *he* was cheating, I'm glad to say," she added complacently. "And you should not be angry, I think, because he deserved it, and I was right."

It's hard, when your life has contained as many hellish surprises as mine, to put 'em in order of disturbance—Gul Shah appearing in that Afghan dungeon, Cleonie whipping off her eyepatch, meeting Bismarck in his nightmare castle, waking to find myself trussed over a gun muzzle at Gwalior, and any number of equally beastly shocks, but I've never been more thoroughly winded than by those incredible words across the breakfast dishes on Wednesday, June 10th, 1891 . . . from *Elspeth* of all people! For a moment I wondered if she was making a ghastly joke, or if that pea-brain had given way at last . . . but no, I knew her artless prattle too well, and that she meant every damned word and there was no point in bellowing disbelief. I forced myself to be calm and sit mum while I downed my brandy and poured another stiff 'un before demanding, no doubt in an incredulous croak:

"You're telling me that *he didn't* cheat . . . but *you did*—and that you were laying a plant on him?" Seeing her bewildered, I translated: "Making him look guilty, dammit! For the love of God, woman—*why?*"

Her eyes widened. "Why, to punish him! To pay him out for his bad conduct! His . . . his black wickedness!" All of a sudden she was breathing fiery indignation, Boadicea in a lace dressing-gown. "And so I did, and now he is disgraced, and a pariah and a hissing, and serve him right! He should be torn by wild horses, so he should! He is a base, horrid man, and I hope he suffers as he deserves!" She began to butter toast ferociously, while I sat stricken, wondering what the devil he'd done, horrid suspicions leaping to mind, but before I could voice them she gave one of her wordless Caledonian exclamations of impatience, left off buttering, tossed her head, and regained her composure.

"Oh, feegh! Harry, I beg your pardon, getting het-up in that unseemly way . . . oh, but when I think of him . . ." She took a deep breath, and spooned marmalade on to her plate. "But it's by with now, thank goodness, and he's paid for a villain, de'il mend him, and I'm the happy woman that's done it, for I never thought to have the chance, and long I bided, waiting the day." As always when deeply moved she was getting Scotcher by the minute, but now she paused for a mouthful of toast. "And then, at Tranby, when I heard that Wilson loon whispering to his friend, and understood what was what, I soon saw in a blink how I might settle his hash for him, once for all. And I did that!" says she, taking a grim nibble. "Oh, if only I could make marmalade like Granny Morrison's . . . there's no right flavour to this bought stuff. Would you oblige me with the honey, dearest?"

I shoved it across in a daze. The enormity, the impossibility of what she said she'd done, her fury against Cumming for heaven knew what unimaginable reason—I still couldn't take it in, but I knew that if you're to get sense out of Elspeth you must let her babble to a finish in her own weird way, giving what assistance you may. I clutched at the nearest straw.

"What did Wilson whisper? To whom? When?"

"Why, on the first night, when the Prince said, 'Who's for baccarat, everyone?' and they went to play in the smoking-room, and Count Lutzow and I and Miss Naylor and Lady Brougham went to watch." She frowned at the honey. "Is it very fattening, do you suppose? Oh, well . . . So the Prince said, 'Shall you and I make a jolly bank together, Lady Flashman?' but I said I did not know the rules and must watch till I got the hang of it, and then I should be honoured to help him, and he said, quite jocose, 'Ah, well, one of these days, then,' and Count Lutzow found me a chair next to that young fellow with the poker up his back, like all the Guardees, what's his name—?"

"Berkeley Levett, you mean? Elspeth, for mercy's sake—"

"Like enough . . . he might have been Berkeley Square for all the sense I could get from him . . . so then they played, and after a wee while, the Wilson boy—the one they call Jack, though his name is Arthur, I think, or is it Stanley?—anyway, I heard him whisper to Levett, 'I say, this is a bit hot!' which I thought odd, when it wasn't at all, I was quite chilly away from the fire, and without my shawl . . . but a moment later I saw he meant something quite otherwise, for he whispered again, that the man next to him was *cheating*—and I saw he meant Billy Cumming . . . Harry, dear, would you ring for hot water? The pot has gone

quite cold—I'm sure they don't make delft as they used to, or perhaps the cosy is getting thin—they stuff them with anything at all
these days, we always had a good thick woollen one at home that
Grizel knitted, but they do tend to smell rather, after a while . . ."

Husbands tend to lose their reason rather, after a while, too,
so lest you should suffer likewise I'll relieve her account with a
précis: she had heard Levett say Wilson must be mistaken, and
Wilson had told him to look for himself. Lady Flashman, scent-
ing mischief breast-high, had also fixed her bonny blue gimlets
on the suspect, seen him drop red counters on his paper after
coups had been called, and heard Levett mutter, "By jove, it *is* too
hot!"—but unlike the two young men she had concluded *that
Cumming was playing fair*. Simple she may be, but she has her
country's instinct for anything to do with money and sharp practice, and her unerring eye had spotted what they had missed . . .

"For I was positive, Harry, that he did not drop his counters
until *after* the Prince had paid the wagers, and what he was doing
was laying his wager for the *next* coup. Well," says she earnestly,
"that was not cheating, was it? But they *thought* it was, you see.
They did not understand that he was playing that French system
of his, the coup de thingamabob which was mentioned in court
last week—I did not understand it myself till I read about it in the
papers and realised he was telling the truth when he said he did
not cheat. But at the time, of course, I did not know about the
French coup thing . . . and while I did not think he was cheating,
how could I be sure, when *they* thought he was, and I supposed
they knew more about the game than I did? In any event," she
concluded cheerfully, "it did not signify whether he had cheated
or not, so long as they *thought* he did. Do you see, my love?"

Heaven forfend that I should ever fail to grasp something that
was clear to her, but as I gazed into those forget-me-not eyes
fixed so eagerly on mine I had to confess myself somewhat
buffaloed, and begged her to continue, which she did at length,
and gradually light began to dawn. Later that night, after the

game, Count Lutzow (the cabbage-eating poont-fancier whom she fleeced at backgammon two nights later) had come to her like Rumour painted full of tongues, with news that a scandalous crisis was at hand: Sir William Gordon-Cumming had been seen cheating, and watch was to be kept on him the following night. How Lutzow had heard this, God alone knows, for according to what was said in court young Wilson had confided his suspicions to no one on the Monday night except Levett and, later, his mother: but there you are, Lutzow had got wind of it somehow. Sly bastards, these squareheads. Of course, he swore dear Lady Flashman to silence . . .

I could hold in no longer. "But dammit all, girl, why didn't you say something then? You believed he hadn't cheated, and that Wilson and Levett were mistaken . . . and yet you let 'em lay a trap for him on the following night—for that's what it was—"

"I should think I did!" cries she. "It was then I saw my chance to be revenged on him. Whether he'd cheated or no' the first night, I could make sure he was *seen* to cheat on the Tuesday, when every eye would be on him. It was ever so easy," she went on serenely. "I begged Lady Coventry to give me her place beside him, and—forgive me, dearest, and do not be *too* shocked—I put my knee against his, and smiled 'couthie and slee,' to fetch him, for he always had a fancy to me, you know, and men are so *vain* and *silly*, even an old dame like me can gowk them . . . well, it was no work at all to have him put his hand on mine to guide me in making my bets, and I saw to it that he kept it there, and made a flirt of it, our hands together whenever we wagered . . . and that is how counters came to be on his paper when they should not have been—"

This was too much. "Of all the nonsense! Don't tell me you can palm a gaming-chip—as if you were Klondike Kate! Why, it would take a top sharp, a first-rate mechanic—"

"Harry," says she quietly, and held out her hand, the empty palm towards me. "Take my hand, love . . . yours on the back of mine, so . . . and now we lay them down . . . and then we take them away . . ."

So help me God, there was the little round lid of the mustard pot on the cloth which had been bare. I gaped, struggling for speech.

"My God . . . where on earth did you learn that?"

"Oh, ever so long ago—from that friend of yours in the 11th Hussars, what was his name? Brand? O'Brien? It's the simplest sleight of hand, really—"

"Bryant! That damned toad!"

"Please, Harry, do not thunder! He was the cleverest conjurer, you remember—"

"He was a low, conniving blackguard! D'you know he once laid a plant on *me*, made me out a cheat and swindler in front of Bentinck and Disraeli and half the bloody country . . ." A dreadful suspicion struck me: had the loathsome Bryant been another of her fancy-men? "When the blue blazes did you know him?"

"Oh, how can I remember? 'Twas years and years since, about the Crimea time, I think, when we were acquainted with Lord Cardigan, and O'Brien or Brand was one of his officers, and showed me ever so many diverting tricks—surely you mind how I used to amuse Havvy and wee Selina with them? No, well, you must have been from home . . . At all events," says she reasonably, "if O'Bryant once embarrassed you with his jiggery-pokery . . . would that be the time Papa sent you away to Africa? My, he was a dour man when he wanted to be . . . Well, you can see it was not hard for me to do the like by Billy Cumming, was it?"

There is a tide in the affairs of men when you simply have to chuck it—as, for example, when you learn that the wife of your unsuspecting bosom is a practised thimblerigger who has used her flash arts to ruin an innocent man. For it must all be true: she could never have invented anything so wild—and it fitted the facts and solved the mystery. And while no normal being would even have thought of such a thing, or had the audacity to attempt it, Elspeth has always been that alarming mixture of an idiot and a bearcat for nerve. Being a poltroon myself, I blurted out the first thing that came into my head.

"But, dear God—suppose you'd been caught?"

"Fiddlesticks! Have I not just shown you? And who," she looked droll, "would ever suspect dear old Lady Flashman? Once, perhaps, I was a wee bit gallus, when he was playing with his pencil, and I took his hand as though to write something between us . . . and pushed a counter over the line. And the silly gommerils all swore in court that *he* had done it! Why, I was as safe as Coutts'!"

D'you know, looking at that angelic smile, and contemplating what she'd done, I was almost scared of her, for the first time in fifty years. My Elspeth, whose kindly, feckless good nature I'd taken for granted, had confessed with shameless satisfaction to a crime that would have shocked Delilah. If she'd burned Cumming at the stake she couldn't have done worse by him . . . and suddenly I found myself thinking of Sonsee-Array and Narreeman and the Dragon Empress and the Amazons and Ranavalona (I've known some fragile little blossoms in my time) and their genius for finding a man's tenderest spot and twisting till he squeals . . . and realising that my gentle helpmeet was their sister under her cream and roses skin. Well, *ex Elspetho semper aliquid novi*, thinks I, who'd have believed it, and thank God she's on my side. But what, in the name of all that was wonderful, could Cumming have done to drive her to such a monstrous revenge?

"I don't care to say!" was her astonishing reply when I demanded to be told (not for the first time, you'll note). Her smile had vanished. "It was too . . . too *outré* for words!"

Her vocabulary being what it is, that might mean anything from farting to high treason. I felt an icy clutch at my innards, of rage against Cumming for whatever atrocious offence he might have given her, and of fear that I might be expected to do something dangerous about it, like offering to shoot the swine. But I couldn't leave it there. Having told her appalling tale with happy abandon, she was now plainly uneasy at my question, frowning and looking askance. "Please do not ask me," says she.

I knew roaring and pounding the table wouldn't serve, so I waited, pushed back my chair, and patted my knee. "Here, old lady," says I, and after a moment she came round and seated herself on my creaking thigh. "Now then, you're bound to tell me, you know, and I shan't be a bit angry either, honest Injun. You can kick twenty Cummings into the gutter, and I'll lose no sleep, 'cos I know my girl wouldn't do such a . . . such a thing without good cause. But I must know *why* you paid him out—and why you didn't tell me all about it that night at Tranby." I gave her a squeeze and a kiss and my quizziest Flashy smile. "We've never had any secrets from each other, have we?" I'll fry in Hell, no doubt about it.

"I couldn't tell you then," says she, nestling against my shoulder. "I feared you would be angry, and might . . . might tell people . . . no, no, you would not do that, but you might have done something, I don't know what, to . . . to interfere, and spoil it, and prevent him meeting his just deserts, the dirty beast!" Only Elspeth can talk like that with a straight face; comes of Paisley and reading novels. Her mouth was drooping, and there were absolute tears in her eyes. "You see, I knew what I had done was dreadful and . . . and dishonourable—and you are the very soul of honour!" She said it, God help me. "The *chevalier sans peur et sans reproche*, that's what the Queen called you, I heard her—"

"Bless me, did she?"

"—and if I had told you at Tranby, why, you would have been in such a fix, on the horns of Tantalus, whether to speak out, which I knew you wouldn't ever do, for my sake, or else be an . . . an accomplice in my dishonourable deed! And that would not have done!" She dabbed her eyes with her sleeve. "So I had to be silent, and deceive you, and I'm so sorry for that, dearest, I truly am—but not for what I did to Billy Cumming, and if you blame me, I can't help it! Oh, Harry, I have so wanted to confess it all to you, so many, many times, but I was bound to wait until the trial was over, you see, for then it would be too late!" She had her arms round my neck, eyes piteous in entreaty. "Oh, Harry, my jo, can you forgive me? If you don't, I think I'll die . . . for I only did it for love of you and . . . and your honour!"

You understand now why I said that Elspeth must be allowed to babble to a conclusion if you're to reach sense at last. Well, we were getting on.

"Dear lass," says I, trying not to wince with my leg cracking under the strain, "whatever does my honour have to do with it? And for heaven's sake, *what did Gordon-Cumming do*—to make you hate him so, and serve him such a ghastly turn?"

At last it came, in a whisper, her head bowed.

"He . . . he called you a coward."

I dam' near let her fall on the floor. "What was that?"

"A coward!" Her head came up, and suddenly she was fairly blazing with rage. "He said it to my face! He did! Oh, I burn with shame to think of it, the vile falsehood! The evil, wicked story-teller! He said you had run away from the Seekhs or the Zulus or someone at that place in Africa, Isal-something-or-other—"

"Isan'lwana? God love us, who didn't?" But she was too angry to hear me, raging on in full spate about how the *bra\zen rascal* had *dared* to say that I had fled headlong, and escaped in a cart while my comrades perished, and had *skulked* in the hospital at Rorke's Drift (all true, except the bit about the hospital—a fat chance anyone had to skulk with the roof on fire and those fearsome black buggers coming through the wall), and she had been so *distraught* by his *slanders* that she had removed from his presence, *nigh weeping*, and if she had been a man she would have *slain* him on the spot.

"To hear him *lying* in his jealous teeth, the toad, defaming *you*, the bravest, gallantest, *best* soldier in all the world, as everyone knows, that have won the V.C. and done ever so many heroic deeds, the Hector of Afghanistan and the Bayard of Balaclava it said in the papers, and I cut them out *every one,* and keep them, and didn't I see you fight like a lion against those disagreeable folk in Madagascar, and you brought me away safe and sound, and had followed to the ends of the earth all for my sake, and rescued me, that didn't deserve it, and you the dearest, kindest *valiant knight,* so you are . . ." At which point she buried her face in my neck and howled for a spell, while I moved her fine poundage on to a convenient chair and massaged my numbed limb, marvelling at the mysterious workings of the female mind. She continued to cling to me, uttering muffled anathemas against Cumming, and at last came to the surface, moist and pink.

"I would not have told you if you had not pressed me," gulps she, "for it *soils* my *lips* to have to repeat his *sinful* lies. He tried to dishonour you, and I was resolved to dishonour *him* by hook or crook, if it took a *lifetime,* and if what I did was dishonourable, too, and underhand and sly, I don't care a *docken*! He's a cur, and that's what he is, and now every dog on the midden kens what he is!"

It ain't easy for a sonsy matron with blonde curls to look like the wrath of God, but she was managing uncommon well. She sniffed, defiant and soulful together.

"Now you know the kind of woman you married. And if you spurn me it will break my heart—but I would do it again, a thousand times!" I'll swear she gritted her teeth. "No one—no one!—speaks ill of my hero, and that's the size of it!"

And that, dear reader, is why William Gordon-Cumming was cast into outer darkness: because he'd blown on Flashy's honour. Ironic, wouldn't you say? It had been his bad luck that where an ordinary wife would have treated his insults with icy disdain, or at most urged her husband to call on the cad with a horsewhip, my eccentric lady had nursed her vengeance for years before ruining him with a stratagem so dangerous (never mind its warped lunacy) that my blood still runs cold to think of it, twenty years on. Social ruin aside, the crazy bitch could have gone to gaol for criminal conspiracy—not that that would enter her empty head, or deter her if it had. The only qualm she'd felt was that if I learned the truth of the disgraceful way she'd engineered Cumming's downfall, I might recoil from her in virtuous disgust—which only goes to show that after fifty years she knew no more of my true character than I, apparently, did of hers.

And she'd done it all for a mere word: coward (a true word, if she'd only known it). Aye . . . and for the love of Harry. Well, I ain't the most sentimental chap, as you know, but as I thought about that, and considered her while she dried her tears . . . dammit, I was touched. Not many husbands are given such proof of loyalty, and fidelity, and devotion carried to the point of insanity—not that I'm saying she's mad, mind, but . . . well, you're bound to agree there's something loose up yonder. Still, barmy or not, the little darling deserved every comfort I could give her, and I was about to embrace her with cries of reassurance . . . when a thought crossed my mind.

She was watching me with pink-nosed anxiety. "Oh, Harry, can you forgive me? Oh, why do you look so stern? Do you despise me?"

"Eh? Oh, lord, no! What, despise you? Good God, girl, I'm proud of you!" And I hugged her, slightly preoccupied.

"Are you sure? Oh, my darling, when I see you frown . . . and I know that what I did was ignoble and . . . and unladylike, and not at all the thing, and how could you be proud of me—oh, I fear that you *disdain* me! Please, dear one, tell me it's not so!" She put her hands either side of my face, imploring at point-blank, which ain't helpful when you're trying to think. I forced myself to sound sincere and hearty.

"Of course I don't disdain you, you little goose! What, for snookering Gordon-Cumming so cleverly? I should say not! It was the smartest stunt since Torres Vedras, and—"

"Torres who?"

"—and nothing ignoble about it, so don't fret your bonny head. He's well served." Damned right; nothing's too bad for the man who tells truth about Flashy. But that was by the way . . .

"Oh, Harry!" She was all over me, arms round my neck, fairly squeaking with joy. "Then you are not angry, and I'm truly forgiven? Oh, you are the best, the kindest of husbands . . ." She kissed me for all she was worth. "And all is truly well?"

"Absolutely! Couldn't be better. So you mustn't cry any more—make your pretty nose red if you do. Now, what about that tea you were going to ring for?"

She kissed me again and fled from the room, calling for Jane, but in fact to make repairs to her appearance—as I'd known she would when I mentioned her nose. I wanted a moment to reflect.

Cumming was down the drain: excellent. Elspeth was none the worse for her idiotic behaviour; indeed, she'd done me proud in her misguided way, championing my "honour," as she conceived it: excellent again. She's solved the Tranby mystery, too, albeit her explanation was as staggering as it was undoubtedly true. On only one little point had she been reticent, and it was exercising me rather.

The whole world knew I was one of the few who'd escaped the Isan'lwana massacre in '79, but that was no disgrace since there were no living witnesses to my terrified flight, and if Cumming chose to make the worst out of it, much good it would do him, with my heroic reputation. But that was by the way, since I'd gathered that he'd confided his opinion to Elspeth alone: the point was, *when* precisely had he done so, and in what circumstances? I didn't doubt he'd called me a coward, you understand, but it ain't the kind of thing a fellow says by way of social chat over the tea-cups, is it? "Ah, Lady Flashman, delightful weather, is it not? And did you enjoy *The Gondoliers?* Such jolly tunes! No, I fear the dear Bishop's health is not what it was . . . by the by, did I never tell you, your husband's a bloody poltroon who ran screaming from Isan'lwana? Oh, you hadn't heard . . . ?" No, hardly.

In my experience, which is considerable, observations like "coward" are usually made *fortissimo* at the climax of a first-rate turn-up between a lady and gentleman most intimately acquainted . . . a lover's quarrel, perhaps? You'll recall that Cumming was among those I'd suspected of dancing the honeymoon hornpipe with my dear one in days gone by; it had been no more than my normal suspicion of her, and had gone clean out of my head during the Tranby scandal, but now it was back with a vengeance. Yes . . .'twould be about ten years since she'd dropped Cumming's acquaintance abruptly, and my lurid imagination could conjure up the scene in some silken nest of sin around South Audley Street, circa 1880, Cumming all moustachioed and masterful in his long combinations and my adulterous angel bursting proudly out of her corset as they slanged each other across the crumpled sheets of shame. God knows I've been there often enough myself, when passion has staled to moody discontent, sullen exchanges wax into recrimination, the errant wife makes odious comparisons to the lover's disadvantage—and that's the moment when Lothario, cut to the quick, speaks his mind of the cuckolded husband. "Your precious Harry's not so much of a man, I can tell you . . ." followed by a shriek of indignation and the crash of a hurled utensil . . . aye, that's how it would have been, devil a doubt; try as I might, I couldn't picture it any different: Cumming *must* have been the little trollop's lover, to call me a coward to her face. If this wasn't proof, nothing was.

I sat brooding darkly, remembering the straw sticking to the back of her dress after she'd been in the woods with that randy redskin Spotted Tail; Cardigan with his pants round his ankles and her in bare buff when I blundered boozily out of the cupboard where I'd been asleep; the shiny black boots that had betrayed her assignation with that smirking swine Watkins or Watney or whatever the hell his name was; her preening herself in her sarong before that oily pirate Usman who'd diddled me at cricket . . . and heaven knew how many others of whom I'd feared the worst. Time and again I'd been torn by jealous unproven suspicion, and resolved to have it out with her . . . and shirked at the last 'cos I'd rather not know. Well, not this time, bigod; I felt my anger rising as I remembered her protestations that she'd only done the dirty on Cumming to avenge my "honour"—ha! Like as not her true reason for wreaking vengeance on him was because he'd kicked her out of bed . . . But if that were so, she'd never have said a word to me about laying a plant on him, would she? Oh, lord, were my foul imaginings getting the better of me yet again; was I judging her by my own murky lights? So many times I'd faced this same hideous question: Elspeth, true or false? It was high time I had an answer, and I was going red in the face and growling as she came tripping back into the room, plump and radiant, no sign at all of her recent distress.

"Jane is bringing fresh tea, and some of those little German biscuits, and oh, you're not angry with me, dearest, and all is—" She stopped short in dismay. "Why, Harry, whatever is the matter? Why are you scowling so? Oh, my love, what is it?"

I had risen in my jealous wrath. Now I sat down again, marshalling my words, while she viewed me in pretty alarm.

"Elspeth!" says I . . . and stopped short in turn. "Ah . . . what's that? Bringing tea, is she? Well, now . . . ah, what about a pot of coffee for the old man, eh? Scowling? No, no, just this leg o' mine giving me a twinge . . . the old wound, you know . . . Here, you come and sit on t'other one, and give us a kiss!"

As the black chap said in Shakespeare's play, 'tis better as it is.

Appendix

It hardly seemed worth while to give footnotes to Flashman's account of the Tranby Croft affair, since almost all of them would have led the reader to the same authority, W. Teignmouth Shore's *The Baccarat Case: Gordon-Cumming v. Wilson and Others,* 1932, in the Notable British Trials Series. It contains a full transcript of the trial, with notes and comments, and is the best and fullest work on the subject. Other books which touch on the case and related matters include Margaret Blunden, *The Countess of Warwick,* 1967; Piers Compton, *Victorian Vortex,* 1977; Philippe Julian, *Edward and the Edwardians;* and an anonymous work, *The Private Life of the King,* 1901.

Teignmouth Shore published his book "to win justice for the memory of a man much wronged," and nailed his colours to the mast with his opening quotation from *Truth,* which asserted after the trial that a dog would not have been hanged on the evidence that convicted Gordon-Cumming. It was an opinion shared by many, and if Flashman is to be believed, they were right.

His view of the verdict aside, Mr. Shore makes several points of interest. He describes the outcry against the Prince of Wales as outrageous, and one has to agree that whatever the faults of the future King Edward VII, he hardly deserved the storm which burst over his hapless head from a press which knew a ripe scandal when it saw one, and was only too glad of a royal scapegoat.

Mr. Shore wondered if any newspaper "of high standing" in 1932 would have been so censorious. Perhaps not; he did not live to see the 1990s. At the same time, the Prince showed lamentable judgment when the cheating allegation was first brought to his notice, and Mr. Shore is plainly right when he suggests that the sensible thing would have been to insist on accused and accusers thrashing the matter out on the spot. There was indeed a remarkable lack of common sense in the way the affair was handled, and in the pathetic belief that it could be kept quiet. Obviously (as Flashman confirms) panic struck not only the Prince and his advisers, but Gordon-Cumming also, or he would never have signed the damning document.

Mr. Shore is scathing on the conduct of the trial, "the Court being turned by consent of the judge into a theatre, and a shoddy theatre at that."

Whether Flashman's sensational disclosure finally settles the controversy is for his readers to decide; it fits the known facts, and if it seems unlikely, that is perfectly in keeping with the rest of The Baccarat Case.

An entertaining experiment, which I have made myself, is to insert a cover over the introduction to Mr. Shore's book, and over the last page which carries the verdict, and invite someone who knows nothing of the case to read the trial and pronounce Sir William Gordon-Cumming guilty or not. The reactions are interesting.

FLASHMAN AND THE TIGER

(1879 AND 1894)

Chapter 1

You think twice about committing murder when you're over seventy. Mind you, it's not something I've ever undertaken lightly, for all that I must have sent several score of the Queen's enemies to their last accounts in my time, to say nothing of various bad men and oddsbodies who've had the misfortune to cross me when my trigger-finger was jumpy. More than a hundred, easy, I should think—which ain't a bad tally for a true-blue coward who'd sooner shirk a fight than eat his dinner, and has run from more battle-fields than he can count. I've been lucky, I suppose—and devilish quick.

But those were killings in the way of business, as a soldier, or in my many misadventures in the world's wild places, where it was me or t'other fellow. Murder's different, you see; it takes more courage than I've ever had, to think it out, and weigh the consequences, and keep your hand steady as you thumb back the hammer and draw a bead on the unsuspecting back. You need to be in a perfect fever of fear and rage, as I was when I threw de Gautet over the cliff in Germany in '48, or when I sicked on that poor lunatic steward to shoot John Charity Spring, M.A., on the slave-ship off the Cuba coast. That's always been more my style, to get some idiot to do the dirty work for me. But there comes a time when there's no scapegoat handy, and you have to do the business yourself—and that's when you sweat at the thought of the black cap and the noose at the end of the eight-o'clock walk. It makes my teeth chatter on the glass just to write about it—aye, and suppose you bungle it, and your victim turns on you, full of spite and indignation? That can easily happen, you know, when you're an old man with a shaky wrist and a cloudy eye, too stiff in the joints even to cut and run. What business have you got at your time of life to be trying to slaughter a man fifteen years younger than you are, in the middle of civilised London, especially when he's a high-tailed gun-slick with a beltful of scalps who can shoot your ears off with his eyes shut? For that's what Tiger Jack Moran was, and no mistake.

So you understand why I say it takes a deal of thought before you determine to go after a man like that with fatal intent, knowing that your speed and cunning have been undermined by a lifetime of booze and evil living and your white hair's coming out in handfuls. Dammit, I wouldn't have tackled him in my prime, when I had size and strength and viciousness to set in the balance against my yellow belly. But there I was, a hoary old grandfather, full of years and dignity and undeserved military honours, with my knighthood and V.C., as respectable an old buffer as ever shuffled down St. James's with a flower in my buttonhole, pausing only to belch claret or exchange grave salutes with Cabinet Ministers and clubmen. ("Why, there's old General Flashman," they'd say, "dear old Sir Harry—wonderful how he keeps going. They say it's the brandy that does it; grand old chap he is." That was all they knew.) But there I was, I say, at a time when I ought to have had nothing to do but drink my way gently towards an honoured grave, spend my wife's fortune, gorge at the best places, leer at the young women, and generally enjoy a dissolute old age—and suddenly, I had to kill Tiger Jack. Nothing else for it.

What brought the beads out on my withered brow more than anything else was my recollection of our first meeting, so many years before, when I'd seen for myself what an ice-cold killing villain he was—aye, and it was in a place where sheer cool nerve and skill with a gun were the narrow margin between escape and horrible death. You'll remember the name: Isan'lwana. I can see it still, the great jagged rock of the "Little House" rearing up above the stony, sun-baked African plain, the scattered lines of our red-coated infantry, joking and cat-calling among themselves as they waited for the ammunition that never came; the red-capped Natal Kaffirs scurrying back to take their positions on the rocky slope; a black-tunicked rider of Frontier Horse leaping the gun limbers bellowing a fatuous order to laager the wagons, which went unheeded and was too late by hours; Pulleine fumbling with his field-glasses and shouting hoarsely: "Is that a rider from Lord Chelmsford?"; a colour-sergeant frantically hammering at the lid of an ammunition box; the puffs of smoke from our advanced line firing steadily at the Zulu skirmishers; the rattle of musketry over the ridge to the left; the distant figures of Durnford's men on the right flank falling back, firing as they came; a voice croaking: "Oh, dear God Almighty!"—and it was mine, as I looked nor'east over the ranks of the 24th, and saw the skyline begin to move, like a brown blanket stirred by something beneath it, and then all along the crest there was the rippling, twinkling flash of thousands of spear-points, and a limitless line of white and coloured shields with nodding plumes behind them, rank after rank, and down the forward slope came the black spilling tide of Ketshwayo's impis, twenty thousand savages rolling towards our pitiful position with its far-stretched line of defenders, Death sweeping towards us at that fearful thunderous jog-trot that made the earth tremble beneath our very feet, while the spears crashed on the ox-hide shields, and the dust rolled up in a bank before them as they chanted out their terrible bass chorus: "*Uzitulele, kagali 'muntu!*"—which, you'll be enchanted to know, means roughly: "He is silent, he doesn't start the attack."

Which was a bloody lie, from where I was standing petrified, and the horrible thing was, I wasn't even *in* the Army, but was there by pure chance (how, exactly, I'll tell you another time). Much consolation that was, you can imagine, as that frightful black horde came surging across the plain towards our makeshift camp beneath Isan'lwana rock, the great mass in the centre coming on in perfect formation while the flank regiments raced out in the "horns" which would encircle our position. And there was poor old Flashy, caught behind the companies of the 24th as they poured their volley-firing into the "chest" of the Zulu army, cheering and shouting for the ammunition-carriers, and Durnford's bald forehead glinting in the sun above his splendid whiskers as he pulled his men back to the donga and blazed away at the left "horn" sweeping in towards them.

For one brief moment, as I cast a frantic eye behind me to pick out the quickest line of retreat to the Rorke's Drift track, I absolutely thought it might be touch and go. You see, while we were most damnably trapped, without proper defences, in spite of the warnings old Paul Kruger had given to Chelmsford about laagering and trenching every night in Zulu country,' and while we were only a few hundred white soldiers and loyal niggers against the whole Zulu army—well, a few dozen Martini-Henrys, in the hands of men who know how to use 'em, can stop a whole lot of blacks with clubs and spears. I'd been with Campbell's Highlanders at Balaclava, when they broke the Ruski cavalry with two volleys, and I still bore the scars of Little Big Horn, where Reno's troopers held off half the Sioux nation (the other half were killing Custer and me just down the valley, but that's another story).* Anyway, as I watched the 24th companies on the Isan'lwana slope, pouring their fire into the brown, and the artillery banging away for dear life, cutting great lanes in the impis, I thought, bigod, we'll hold 'em yet. And we would have done, but the ammunition boxes hadn't been broken out, and just as the great mass of Zulus, a bare furlong from our forward

* See *Flashman and the Redskins*

troops, seemed to be wavering and hanging back—why, the 24th were down to their last packets, and the yelling and cheering turned to desperate cries of:

"Ammunition, there! Bring the boxes, for God's sake!"

Our fire slackened, the 24th took a step back, the Natal Kaffirs came pouring away from the left under the lee of the hill, flinging their arms aside as they ran, the order "Fix bayonets!" rang out from the ranks immediately to my front, and the Zulu regiments rallied and came bounding in in a great mad charge, the rain of throwing spears whistling ahead of them like hail, and the stabbing assegais coming out from behind the white shields as they tore into our disordered front line, the roar of " *'Suthu!* *'Suthu!"* giving way to their hideous hissing " *'S-jee! 'S-jee!"* as the spears struck home.

Time for the lunch interval, thinks I; let's be off. Once they were at close quarters, there wasn't a hope, and by the look of it, through that hell of smoke and gunfire and fleeing men, with Kaffirs rushing past, and the gunners and wagon-men frantically trying to inspan and flee, the surviving remnants of the 24th weren't going to hold that huge press of Zulus more than a matter of minutes. Thus far in the battle, being only a well-meaning civilian, I'd made a tremendous show of trying to get the wagons to laager in a circle, so that we could make a stand if our forward troops gave way—it was the sensible thing to do, and it also kept me at a safe distance from the fighting. So I was well placed beside an inspanned cart when the dam burst, and the Nokenke regiment of Ketshwayo's army (that's who the historians tell me it was, anyway; I only know they were appalling bastards with leopard-skin head-dresses, screaming fit to chill your blood) came tearing up the hill.

I was into that wagon in a twinkling, bawling to the driver to go like blazes, and blasting away over the tailboard with an Adams six-shooter in each fist. I wish I'd a pound for every time I've looked out at a charging barbarian horde with my guts dis-

solving and prayers babbling out of me, but that one took the biscuit. They came racing in, huge black-limbed monsters with their
six-foot shields up, eyes and teeth glaring over the top like spec-
tres, the plumes tossing and those disgusting two-foot steel blades
glittering and smoking with blood. I saw three men of the 24th,
back to back, swinging their clubbed rifles, go down before the
charge, and the Zulus barely broke stride as they ripped the
corpses up with their assegais (to let the dead spirits out, don't
you know) and rushed on. I blazed away, weeping and swearing,
thinking oh God, this is the end, and I'm sorry I've led such a misspent life, and don't send me to Hell, whatever Dr. Arnold says—
and my hammer clicked down on an empty chamber just as the
first Zulu vaulted over the side of the wagon, howling like a
dervish.

I screamed and closed with him, seizing his right wrist as
the spear-point swung at my breast, my hand slipping on that
oily skin; I drove a knee at his groin, butting him for all I was
worth and trying to bite his throat—all I got was a mouthful of
monkey-skin collar, and God, how he stank! A shot crashed right
beside my ear, and the Zulu fell away, his face a mask of blood.[2] I
never even saw who had shot him, nor did I pause to inquire, for
as I reeled away to the side of the wagon, here came a gun-team
thundering past, with an artilleryman crouched on one of the
leaders, lashing at the beasts and at the Zulus who raced alongside
trying to spear him from the saddle. Behind the team the gun was
bouncing over the ground, with some poor devil clinging to the
muzzle, his feet trailing in the dust, until a Zulu, leaping behind,
dashed his brains out with a knobkerrie.

You don't think twice at such moments; you truly don't. I had
one glimpse that still stays in my memory—of that rock-strewn
slope, covered with charging Zulus spearing the last knots of
defenders; of men screaming and falling; of a sergeant of the 24th
rolling on the ground locked with a black warrior, while the others paused to watch; of a bullock lumbering past, bellowing, with

an assegai in its flank; of bloody corpses, red-coated or black-skinned, sprawled among the dusty ruin of broken carts, ration boxes, and fallen equipment; of hate-filled black faces and polished black bodies—all that in a split second, and then I went over the side of that cart in a flying dive on to the gun that was racketing past, clutching frantically at the hot metal, almost slipping down between barrel and wheel, but somehow managing to stay aboard as it tore onwards, bouncing left and right, towards the little saddle of ground that runs from Isan'lwana hill.

How I survived the next minute I don't know. I clung to the gun, keeping low, hearing a spear glance clanging from the metal; a club caught me a blow on the shoulder, but I stuck like a leech, and the gun must have picked up speed, because the closest Zulus were suddenly lost in the dust-cloud, and for a moment we were clear of the immediate pursuit, the driver still holding his seat on the leader and yelling and quirting away as the team topped the crest and went careering down the far slope towards the Rorke's Drift track.

The slope was thick with fugitives, white and black, a few mounted but most on foot, going pell-mell down to the broken ground and distant scrub with only one thought in mind—to get away from the merciless black vengeance behind us. They seemed to be making for a deep ravine about half a mile to the left, where it seemed to me they were sure to be caught by the left "horn" of the Zulu army as it came circling in; I struggled up astride the gun and bawled above the din to the driver to bear right for the Rorke's Drift road. He cast a terrified glance over his shoulder, pointing frantically and shaking his head; I looked, and my heart died. Already, round the far side of the Isan'lwana hill, the vanguard of the Zulu right "horn" was streaming down like a black lance-head to cut the track; I could make out the green monkey caps and plumes of the Tulwana regiment. Five minutes at most, and the ring of steel would have closed round Isan'lwana, and God help anything white that was still inside.

There was nothing for it but the ravine, and we rushed down the slope at breakneck speed, the driver lashing the exhausted horses, and Flashy going up and down astride that damned barrel like a pea on a drum. I stole a glance back, and beyond the scattered groups of running fugitives I could see the first ranks of the Zulu "chest" coming over the hill; this won't do, my lad, thinks I, we'll have to move a deal faster if we want to see Piccadilly again. The gun lurched under me, sickeningly, there was a yell of alarm from the driver ahead, and by God the right rear-wheeler had broken a trace and was veering madly off to the right, head up and snorting; she stumbled and went down as the second trace parted, and I shot off the gun as it slewed round, hit the ground with a fearful jar, and went rolling arse over elbow, tearing the skin off shoulder and knee on the rock-hard earth before I fetched up winded within a yard of the fallen horse.

I had a hand on its mane as it thrashed up again, hooves flying, and you may be sure I wasn't the only one. Half a dozen fugitives had the same notion, and one, a sergeant gunner, was half-aboard the beast. "Mine, damn you!" roars he. "She can't take two!"

"Right you are, my son," says I, and knocked him flying. I got a limb across that heaving bare back—and that's all I ever need.³ Thank God I've never seen the mount I couldn't master; I wound my hands into the mane, dug in my heels, and went head down for the ravine, just as the gun I had lately left went careering into it—team, driver, and all. It was a deep, narrow cleft— Christ! was it narrow enough to jump? I tensed myself for the leap, gave her my heel at the last moment, and we went soaring over; there was a horrible instant when we seemed to hang on the far lip, but we scrambled to safety by our eyebrows. I heard a scream behind me, and turned to see a big grey failing to make the same jump; she fell back into the ravine, with her rider crushed beneath her.

The ravine, and the bank I had just left, looked like Dante's

Inferno; they were fleeing down it among the rock and thorn,
towards the Buffalo River five miles away, and those black devils
were on the far lip—" '*S-jee!* '*S-jee!*'" and the assegais flashing up
and down like pistons. I looked to my right front, where the
Tulwana were streaking across the track; there was still a gap
between them and the ravine, and I went for it hell-for-leather,
the horse slithering on the loose rocks and me clinging like grim
death. She was only an artillery screw, but there must have been
a hunter ancestor in her somewhere, for she outraced that Zulu
pincer with a hundred yards to spare, and I was able to hold her
in as we shot into the safety of the scrub, with the screams and
gunshots fading into the distance behind us.

That was how I made my strategic retreat, then, from the
massacre of Isan'lwana—the greatest debacle of British arms
since the Kabul retreat nearly forty years earlier.[4] Oh, aye, I'd
been in that, too, freezing and bleeding on that nightmare march
which never reached the Khyber. But I'd been a thoughtless boy
then; at Isan'lwana I was an older, much wiser soldier, and I knew
I was a long way from safety yet. I couldn't tell how many others
had won clear (about fifty, in fact, against a thousand who fell
under the assegais), but I could guess that the next stop along the
line for Ketshwayo's merry men would be Rorke's Drift, eight
miles away on the Buffalo. They'd gobble up the picquet there,
and be over the Natal border by sundown; it behoved Flashy to
bear away north, and try to cross the river well beyond the reach
of the impis. The trouble was, even I didn't know how fast Zulus
can travel with the blood smell in their nostrils.[5]

It was about the middle of the afternoon when I came out of
the scrub and boulders, into a little kraal perhaps ten miles from
Isan'lwana. I reckoned I was clear of pursuit, but my beast was
tuckered out, and I could have jumped for joy at the sight of an
army wagon among the huts, and a burly red-cheeked sergeant
puffing his cutty while he watched the native women tending a
cooking-pot close by. It was a stray ammunition cart belonging to

a flying column sent out north the previous day; they'd had a brush with some Zulu scouts last evening, and there were two or three wounded on blankets laid across the ammunition boxes. The cart was taking them down to Rorke's Drift, the sergeant said.

"Not today you ain't," says I, and told him briefly what had happened to most of Chelmsford's force. He goggled and dropped his pipe.

"Cripes!" says he. "Why, the rest of our column was makin' for Isan'lwana this mornin'! 'Ere, Tiger Jack's got to 'ear about this! Major! Major, sir—come quick!"

And that was when I got my first sight of Tiger Jack Moran. He came out of one of the huts in answer to the sergeant's cry, and as soon as I clapped eyes on him, thinks I, this is a killing gentleman. He was perhaps forty, as big as I was, but leaner, and he walked with a smooth, pigeon-toed stride, like a great slim cat. His face was lean, too, and nut-brown, with a huge hooked nose, a bristling black moustache, and two brilliant blue eyes that were never still; they slid over you and away and back again. It was a strong face, but mean; even the rat-trap mouth had an odd lift at one side which, with the ever-shifting eyes, made it look as though he knew some secret joke about you. For the rest, he wore a faded Sapper jacket and a wideawake hat, with a black sash round his hips; when he turned I saw he had one of the new long-barrelled Remington .44 revolvers reversed through the sash over his right rump—a gunfighter's gun, with the foresight filed away, if you please. Well, well, thinks I, here's one to keep an eye on.

"Chelmsford's wiped out, you say?" The blue eyes looked everywhere but into mine; I wouldn't have trusted this fellow with the mess funds in a hurry. "The whole command?"

"Half of it, anyway," says I, guzzling away at a plate of salt and mealies the sergeant had given me. "Chelmsford himself's off in the blue with Number 3 Column, and if he's wise he'll stay there. Ketshwayo's army must be cayoodling round Rorke's Drift by now, thousands of the brutes. There's no hope that way—if it comes to that, I doubt if there'll be anything white and living between Blood River and the Tugela by sunrise tomorrow."

"You don't say," says he. "And you got away, eh? You're not Army, though?"

"Not at the moment. I'm retired, but I imagine you've heard of me." I didn't like his manner above half, with his slippery eyes and half-smile. "My name's—"

"Silence!" He threw up a hand, and his head jerked round, listening. The sergeant and I held our breath, listening with him. I couldn't hear a thing, beyond the noises of the kraal; the fire crackling, the soft shuffling of one of the nigger women, a baby crying in one of the huts. Just hot silence, in that baking sun, and then Moran says sharply to me:

"You came on that horse—how long did it take you?"

"Two hours, perhaps—look here—"

"Inspan that wagon!" he barked at the sergeant. "Look alive, now! Get that damned black driver—sharp's the word! We'll have 'em on top of us before we know it!" And before I could protest he had swung away and was running between the huts, jumping on to a great boulder, and looking back the way I had come, shading his eyes.

You don't waste time arguing with a man who knows his business. I felt the hot prickle of fear down my spine as I helped the sergeant get the beasts inspanned—they were horses, thank God; bullocks would have been useless if we were going to have to cut out as fast as Moran seemed to think we must. He jumped down from the rock and came striding back towards us, his head turning left and right to scan the ridges either side of the village, his hand twitching nervously at his right hip.

"Get those three wounded lying down! And get aboard yourselves—driver, start that rig moving!" He glanced at me, that sly grin turning the corner of his mouth. "I'd climb in, mister, if I were you. Unless my shikari's instinct is playing me false, your black friends are closer than you think, and I don't—"

Then it happened, and if I hadn't seen it with my own eyes I'd not have believed it—and I knew Hickok in his prime, remember, before his eyesight went, and John Wesley Hardin, too.

The sergeant, in the act of climbing over the tailboard, let out a hell of a shriek; I glimpsed his face, red and staring, and his arm flung out to point, and then his eyes stared horribly, and he slumped down into the dust, with a throwing assegai between his shoulders, his limbs thrashing wildly. I turned, and there, not twenty yards away beyond Moran, standing on the boulder he'd just left and poised in the act of throwing, was a Zulu warrior. I could still tell you every detail of him (that's what shock does to you)—the great black body behind the red and white shield, the calf-skin girdle, the white cow-tail garters, the ringed head with its nodding blue plume, even the little horn snuff-box swinging from his neck. It was a nightmare figure—and now there were two more, either side of him, leaping between the huts, scream-ing " 'S-jee!" with their assegais raised to hurl at us.

Moran had spun on his heel at the sergeant's scream, and I swear I never saw his right hand move. But the Remington was in his fist, and the boom-boom-boom of its triple explosion was almost like one echoing shot. The Zulu on the rock jerked upright, snatching at his face, and toppled backwards; the fore-most of the two running towards us pitched headlong, with half his head blown away in a sudden bloody spray, and the third man stumbled crazily, dropping his shield and rolling over and over to finish a bare two yards from us, sprawled on his back. There was a hole where his right eye had been. And Moran's pistol was back in his sash.

"Twins, by the look of 'em," says he. "Did you know the Zulus think they make the best scouts?[6] Well, don't stand gawp-ing, old fellow—there'll be plenty of live ones on the scene presently. Mind the step!" And he was over the back of the mov-ing wagon, with me tumbling breathlessly after him, shocked out of my wits by the speed and terror of it all. I'd say from the moment the sergeant fell to our jumping into the wagon had been a good five seconds—and in that time three men had died, thank God, and the man beside me was chuckling and pushing fresh shells into his revolver.

He was right about the live ones arriving, too—as our wagon wheeled out of the village on to a great empty stretch of plain beyond it, we could see black figures gliding in among the huts on the far side, and by the time we were a furlong out on the plain itself, with the driver lashing like fury and the wagon rolling dangerously from side to side, they were breaking cover in pursuit. There must have been more than twenty of them, and I don't recall a more fearful sight than that silent half-moon of racing black figures, each with his mottled red and white shield and fistful of glittering spears, their white hide kilts and garters flying as they ran.

"Udloko, unless I'm mistook," says Moran. "Good regiment, that. Let's add to their battle honours, what?"

He had got a Martini from one of the wounded men who were lying pale and silent behind us in the jolting wagon, and now he snuggled the butt into his shoulder, keeping the barrel clear of the rattling tailboard, and let off four shots as fast as he could eject and reload. He hit three more Zulus—this at a range of two hundred yards, from a wagon that was bucking like a ship at sea, and at moving targets. I tell you, I was stricken between terror and sheer admiration.[7]

"Damnation!" says he, after his missed shot. "Bet he felt the wind of it, though." He saw me staring, and grinned. "Don't be alarmed, old boy; just pass up the cartridge packets and I'll have our gallant foes discouraged in half a jiffy, just see if I don't!"

But when I applied to the wounded for more cartridges, damned if there was a round among them.

"Well, we're sitting on half a ton of the things," says Moran, cool as you please, and tapped the ammunition boxes. "Let's forage, shall we?" So we broke open a case—and it was carbine ammunition, quite unsuitable for Martinis. I swallowed my innards for about the twentieth time that day; all the boxes carried the same stamp. And there, still loping across the sun-scorched plain behind us, not apparently having lost any distance, were the twenty Zulus, looking as fit as fleas and a dam' sight more unpleasant.

"Now, that's vexing," says Moran, laying down his rifle and unlimbering his Remington again. He spun the chamber. "Six shots—hm'm. Well, let's hope none of the horses breaks a leg, what?"

"For God's sake, man!" My voice came out in a dreadful squeak. "They can't keep up this pace forever!"

"Who—the horses, or Ketshwayo's sporting and athletic club?" He gripped the tailboard and weighed the distance between us and our pursuers. "I think, on the whole, I'd put my money on the blacks. More staying power, don't you know? By George, can't they run, though!"

"But, my God, we're done for! They're gaining on us, I tell you—"

"Quite," says he. "Better think of something, eh? Unless we want our hides stretched over some damned Udloko war-drum, that is. Let's see, now." He stood up in the swaying wagon, clutching a support, and peered ahead under the canvas cover, resting a hand on the shoulder of the terrified nigger driver who was rolling his eyes and letting his team rip for all it was worth. "If I remember right, this blasted plain ends in a deep gully about a mile ahead—there's a crazy kind of bridge over it . . . we came across it on the way up. It took the wagon, all right—but very slowly. 'Fraid by the time we get across our friends will be calling on us—an' six shots won't go far among that crowd, even if I make every one tell—which I would, of course. Wait, though!" And he dropped down on one knee, pushing one of the wounded men aside and ferreting among the ammunition boxes.

I was hardly listening to him; my eyes were fixed on that line of steadily-running black figures, coming on inexorably in our wake. They were losing distance, though, it seemed to me—yes, there must be nearly a quarter of a mile between us now—but our beasts were tiring, too; they couldn't keep up this speed much longer, dragging a heavy wagon behind them. When we reached the bridge, would there be time for the wagon to make its careful way across, before they caught up? . . . I scrabbled at Moran's arm, yammering hopefully, and he grinned as he straightened up from his search among the boxes, holding up a large packet of waxed brown paper in one hand.

"There we are, sonny boy," says he, chuckling. "Thought I remembered it. Blasting powder—and a darling little primer! Now, watch your Uncle Jack!"

I don't want to live through another five minutes like those last agonising moments while we sped across the plain, slower and slower with every yard, straining our eyes back at those distant black figures behind. Even when we reached the gully, a great rocky cleft that stretched as far as one could see on either side, like a volcanic crack, with a rickety plank bridge spanning its thirty feet, there was the time-consuming labour of getting the wounded out and across. The nigger driver and I managed it between us, and sinful hard it was, for two of 'em had to be carried the whole way. Moran, meanwhile, coaxed the team on to the swaying bridge, until the wagon was fairly in the middle of it; then we outspanned the horses and led them across, glancing back fearfully. There they came, those black fiends of the pit, a bare hundred yards away, sprinting full lick now that they saw we were halted and apparently stuck. They set up a great yell of "*Suthu!*" as they tore in towards the bridge, and Moran, who had been working in the wagon, jumped down and ran across to the little cluster of boulders where we had laid the wounded.

He dropped down beside me, looking back at the wagon; it was perhaps thirty yards off, with the waxed brown packet of gunpowder sitting on top of the ammunition boxes, and the tiny white primer fixed to the side of the packet. With a rifle, I might have hit it myself; all he had was a hand-gun.

"Well, here's luck," says he. "One shot'll have to do it."

He was right, I realised, and my mouth was parched with fear. If he missed the primer, his shot would hit the powder packet, but that wouldn't explode it. It would just knock it over, and the primer would go God knew where. And the first Zulu was racing on to the bridge, shield aloft in triumph, with his hideous legion shrieking at his heels.

"Gather round, dear boys," murmurs Moran, cocking his pistol. "Get yourselves nice and comfy round the bonfire . . . Christ!"

His head jerked up, the colour draining from his face. It may have been a puff of wind, or perhaps the Zulus swarming past the wagon on that shaky bridge had disturbed it—but the front flap of the canvas cover suddenly swung across, momentarily hiding the tiny white target. It flapped again—for a split second the primer was visible—the first half-dozen Zulus were past the wagon and within three strides of the solid ground, assegais gleaming and knobkerries brandished—howling black faces— another flap of the canvas—the crash of Moran's revolver—and with a roar of thunder the wagon, the bridge, and everything on it dissolved in a great blast of orange flame. I was hurled flat, my ears deafened and singing; a piece of timber clattered against the rock beside me. I came dizzily to my feet, to stare at the empty ravine, with a great black cloud billowing in the air above it, a few shreds of rope and timber dangling from the far lip, and on this side, lying in the dust, a single assegai.

Moran reversed his revolver in his hand and pushed it into the back of his sash. Then he tilted his hat back and flicked his forefinger at its brim.

"*Bayete*, Udloko," says he softly. "I *do* like a snap shot, though. Give the gentleman a coconut."

That was in '79, my first acquaintance with Tiger Jack, and it was to last only a few more feverish hours which I'll describe at length some other day, for they don't matter to the Tiger's tale, which is strange enough without Rorke's Drift to interrupt it. That was a nightmare in its own right, if you like—worse than Little Hand or Greasy Grass, for at least at those I'd been able to run. Why, at the Drift there wasn't even room to hide, and it'll make a ghastly chapter of its own in my African odyssey, if I can set it down before drink and senility carry me off.

Enough for the moment to say that Moran and I were *driven* absolutely into that beastly carnage. You see, with our wagon blown to pieces he and I lit out on two of the draught screws, leaving the wounded in a dry cave, Moran intent on fetching help for them, Flashy merely fleeing in his wake—and as dark fell we blundered slap into an impi, for the hills were full of the brutes by now. Then it was head down and heels in, nip and tuck for our lives through the Zulu-infested night with the fiends howling at our heels, and suddenly Moran was yelling and making for a burning building dead ahead, with all hell breaking loose around it, Zulus by the hundred and shots blazing, and there was nothing for it but to follow as he went careering through scrub and bushes, putting his beast to a stone wall, and then a barricade where black bodies and red coats were hacking and slashing in the fire-glare, bayonet against assegai, and my screw took the wall but baulked at the barricade, which I cleared in a frantic dive, launching myself from a pile of Zulu corpses, landing head first on the smoking veranda of what had been the post hospital, going clean through the charred floor, and being hauled half-conscious from the smouldering wreckage by a huge cove with a red beard who left off pistolling to ask me where the dooce I'd come from. I inquired, at the top of my voice, where the hell I was, and between shots he told me.

That, briefly, is how I came to join the garrison at Rorke's Drift—and all the world knows what happened there. A hundred Warwickshire Welshmen and a handful of invalids stopped four thousand Udloko and Tulwana Zulus in bloody shambles at the mealie-bag ramparts, hammer and tongs and no quarter through that ghastly night with the burning hospital turning the wreckage of the little outpost into a fair semblance of Hell, and Flashy seeking in vain for a quiet corner—which I thought I'd found, once, on the thatch of the commissariat store, and damned if they didn't set fire to that, too. Eleven Victoria Crosses they won, Chard with his beard scorched, Bromhead stone-deaf, and those ragged Taffies half-dead on their feet, but not too done to fight— oh, and talk. As an unworthy holder of that Cross myself, I'll say they earned them, and as much glory as you like, for there never was a stand like it in all the history of war. For they didn't only stand against impossible odds, you see—they stood and *won*, the garrulous little buggers, and not just 'cos they had Martinis against spears and clubs and a few muskets; they beat 'em hand to hand too, steel against steel at the barricades, and John Zulu gave them best. Well, you know what I think of heroism, and I can't abide leeks, but I wear a daffodil as my buttonhole on Davy's Day, for Rorke's Drift.[8]

But that's not to my purpose with Tiger Jack. He was in the thick of it, though I didn't even glimpse him from the time we jumped the barricades, until next morning, when the impis had drawn off, leaving us to lick our wounds among the smoking ruins. It was only then that we learned each other's name, when Chelmsford, who'd been traipsing out yonder with his column, rode in. When everyone had done cheering, he spotted me, and made me known to Chard and Bromhead, and that was when Moran, who was sitting by on a biscuit box cleaning his Remington, came suddenly to his feet, and for once the sliding blue eyes stared straight at me in astonishment. Presently he came over.

"Flashman? Not Sir Harry . . . Kabul, and the Light Brigade?"

I'm used to it; not the least irony of my undetected poltroonery is the awe my fearsome reputation inspires. They always stare, as Moran did, if not so intently. For a moment he even paled, and then the thin mouth was half-smiling again, and his eyes shifted away.

"Well, think o' that," says he, and chewed his lip. "I'd never have recognised you. By Jove—" and he gave a queer little laugh "—if I'd only known."

Then he turned on his heel and walked away, with that quick, feline stride and the Remington on his hip, out of my life for the next fifteen years. When he walked back in, it was in a place as different from Rorke's Drift as anything on this earth could be. Instead of a smoking, blood-stained ruin, there was the plush and gilt of the circle bar at the St. James's Theatre, instead of the Sapper jacket and .44 revolver there was an opera cloak and silver-mounted cane, and instead of dead Zulus for company there was Oscar Wilde. (I make no comparisons.)

It was pure chance I was at that theatre at all—or even in London, for it was still winter, when Elspeth and I prefer to snug up cosily at our Leicestershire place, where the drink and vittles are of the best, and we can snarl at each other comfortably. But she had insisted we go up to Town for the Macmillan christening°— being Scotch herself, and fancying that she occupied a place in Society, she was forever burdening other unfortunate Caledonians with her presence—and I didn't mind too much; I'd heard rumours from friends in the know that there was to be a monstrous increase in death duties at the next Budget, and being in my seventy-second year by then, with a fat sum in the bank, it seemed sensible to squander as much among the fleshpots as we indecently could.

So to Town we went, and in between brandy-soaked evenings with old comrades and hopeful prowlings after a new generation of loose women, I allowed myself to be talked into escorting my grand-daughter to the theatre to see Mrs. Campbell drivelling abominably in *Mrs. Tanqueray*. I'd much have preferred going to watch Nala Damajanti and her Amazing Snakes at the Palace, or the corsetted fat bottoms and tits in George Edwardes' show, but being a besotted grandparent I'd have let my little Selina coax me into watching three hours of steady rain and been happy. She was a little darling, and the apple of my bleary old eye—how my son, as unpromising a prig as ever saddened a father's heart by becoming a parson, could have sired such an angel, I've never been able to fathom. I call her little, but in fact she was one of your tall, stately beauties, with raven-black hair (like mine, once), eyes flashing dark as a gypsy's, and a face that could change from classical perfection to sparkling mischief in an instant. She was just nineteen then, a lovely, lively innocent, and I watched her like a jealous hawk where the Society boys were concerned—I know what I was like when I was their age, and I wasn't having the dirty young rips lechering round my little Selly. Besides, she was officially affianced to young Randall Stanger, a titled muttonhead in the Guards, and their forthcoming nuptials would be quite an event of the Season.

She was chattering happily as we came out after the third act, and caught the eye of the bold Oscar, who was holding forth languidly to a group of his fritillaries near the bar entrance, looking as usual like an overfed trout in a toupé. He and I had known each other more or less since the days when I was being pursued by Lillie Langtry; as I went past now, trying not to notice him, with Selly on my arm, he nudged one of his myrmidons and said *sotto voce*:

"Strange, how desire doth so outrun performance," and then, pretending just to notice me: "Why, General Flashman! In London out of season? That can only mean that all the hares and foxes have left the country, or the French are invading it." His group of harumphrodites all tittered at this, and the fat posturer waved his gold-tipped cigarette, well pleased with his insolence. I looked at him.

"Quoting Shakespeare, Oscar?" says I. "Pity you don't crib him more often. Get better notices, what? My dear," says I to Selly, "this is Mr. Wilde, who writes comic material for the halls. My grand-daughter, Miss Selina Flashman."

"Your grandchild? Incredible!" drawls he. "But delightful—beautiful! Why, if dear Bosie were here, instead of indulging himself so selfishly in Italy, he would write verses to you, ma'mselle—verses like purple blooms in a caliph's garden. I would write them myself, but my new play, you know . . ." He pressed her hand, with his fruity smile. "And I see, dear Miss Flashman, that you are discriminating as well as beautiful—you have had the excellent taste to choose as your grandfather one of the few civilised generals in the British Army." He waited for her look of surprise. "He never won a battle, you know. May I present Mr. Beasley[10] . . . Mr. Bruce . . . Mr. Gaston . . . Colonel Moran . . ."

He turned her with a flutter of his plump hand to his toadies, and gave me his drooping insolent stare. "Do you know, my dear Sir Harry, I believe I have a splendid idea. I might—" he poked his gilded cigarette at me "—I might confer on you an immortality quite beyond your deserts. I might put you in a play—assuming the Lord Chamberlain had no objection. Think what a stir that would create at the Horse Guards." He gave a mincing little titter.

"You do, Father Oscar,"[11] says I, "and I'll certainly confer immortality on you."

"How so?" cries he, affecting astonishment.

"I'll kick you straight in the tinklers—assuming you've got any," says I. "Think what a stir that'll create in the Café Royal." I turned to Selly, who was out of earshot, listening to what one of Oscar's creatures was saying. "Come, my dear. Our carriage will be—" And that was the moment when I found myself looking at Moran.

He was on the fringe of Oscar's group—and so out of place among that posy of simpering pimps that I wonder I hadn't noticed him earlier. But now recognition was instant, and mutual. His hair had gone, save a grey fringe about the ears, the splendid moustache was snow-white, and the lined brown face had turned boozer's red, but there was no mistaking that hawk nose and the bright, shifting eyes. Dress him how and where you liked, he was still Tiger Jack.

He was looking at me with that odd quirky little smile at the corner of his thin mouth, and then the blue eyes turned from me to Selina, who was laughing happily at what someone was saying, fluttering her fan before her white shoulders, teasing the speaker innocently. Moran looked at her for a moment, and when his eyes came back to mine he was grinning—and it wasn't a nice grin.

Now all this happened in an instant, while I was recognising him, and realising that he had recognised me. There was a second's pause, and then as I was about to move forward and greet him he stepped quickly back, murmuring an excuse to Selly and the others, and slipped into the bar. I didn't know what to make of it, but it seemed damned odd behaviour; however, it didn't matter, and Selly was taking my arm and murmuring farewells, so I exchanged another disgusted glare with Wilde and led her away. She had noticed, though—sharp little creature that she was.

"Why did that gentleman—Colonel Moran—hurry off so suddenly?" says she, when we were in the carriage. "I'm sure he knew you."

"He did," says I. "At least, we met once—in a war."

"But then, so many of these people seem to behave . . . most curiously," says Selly. "Mr. Oscar Wilde, for instance—is he not a very strange person, gramps?"

"That's one way of putting it," says I. "And don't call me 'gramps,' young woman; I'm grandpapa."

Now, why the blazes should Moran have avoided me? Lots of fellows do, of course, but he had no earthly reason that I could think of. We'd met only once, as you know, and been comrades-in-arms after a fashion—indeed, he'd saved my life. It seemed odd, and I puzzled over it for a while, but then gave it up, and was snoozing in my corner of the carriage and had to be roused by a giggling Selina when we reached home in Berkeley Square.

Moran wasn't alone in giving me the cold shoulder at that time, though. Only a couple of days after the theatre I was cut stone dead by someone a deal more important—the Prince of Wales, no less, shied violently away from me in the United Service card-room, and hightailed it as fast as his ponderous guts would let him, giving me a shifty squint over his shoulder as he went. That, I confess, I found pretty raw. It's embarrassing enough to be cut by the most vulgar man in Europe, but when he is also a Prince who is deeply in your debt you begin to wonder what royalty's coming to. For if ever anyone had cause to be grateful to me, it was Beastly Bertie; not only had I done my bit to guide his youthful footsteps along the path of vice and loose living (not that he'd needed much coaching), I'd even resigned Lily Langtry in his favour, turned a deaf ear to rumours that he and my darling Elspeth had behaved indecorously in a potting-shed, and only three years earlier had plucked him, only slightly soiled, out of the Tranby card scandal. If that wasn't enough, he was still using a cosy little property of mine on Hay Hill to con-duct his furtive fornications with the worst sort of women, duchesses and actresses and the like. Well, thinks I, as I watched him rolling off, if that's your gratitude you can take your trol-lops elsewhere; I'd a good mind to charge him rent, or corkage. I didn't, of course; a bounder he might be, but it don't pay to offend the heir to the Throne.

Such rubs apart, I passed the next few weeks agreeably enough. There was plenty of interest about town, what with a Society murder—a young sprig of the nobility called Adair get-ting himself shot mysteriously in the West End—and a crisis in the government, when that dodderer Gladstone finally resigned.

I ran into him in the lavatory of the Reform Club—not a place I belong to, you understand, but I'd been to a champagne and lobster supper in St. James's, and just looked in to unload. Gladstone was standing brooding over a basin in a nonconformist way, offensively sober as usual, when I staggered along, middling tight.

"Hollo, old 'un," says I. "Marching orders at last, hey? Ne'er mind, it happens to all of us. It's this damned Irish business, I suppose—" for as you know, he was always fussing over Ireland; no one knew what to do about it, and while the Paddies seemed to be in favour of leaving the place and going to America, Gladstone was trying to make 'em keep it; something like that.

"Where you went wrong," I told him, "was in not giving the place back to the Pope long ago, and apologising for the condition it's in. Fact."

He stood glaring at me with a face like a door-knocker.

"Good-night, General Flashman," he snapped, and I just sank my head on the basin and cried: "Oh, God, what a loss Palmerston was!" while he stumped off, and took to his bed in Brighton.[12]

However, that's by the way: I must return to the matter of Colonel Tiger Jack Moran, who had gone clean out of my mind after that fleeting glimpse of him at the theatre, until a dirty night at the end of March, when I was sitting up late reading, Elspeth having taken herself off to bed with the new serial story. The house was still, the fire almost out, and I was drowsing over the paper, which was full of interesting items about the Matabele war, and the Sanitation Conference in Paris, and news of an action by the Frogs against my old chums the Touaregs at Timbuctoo, in which large numbers of sheep had been captured,[13] when Shadwell, the butler, came in all agog to say that my granddaughter was here, and must see me.

"At this hour?" says I, and then she came fluttering into the room in a rush of pink ball-gown, her lovely little face staring with woe, and fairly flung herself on my chest, crying:

"Oh, grandpapa, grandpapa, what shall I do? Oh, gramps, please help me—please!"

"In God's name, Selina!" says I, staggered. I waved the goggling Shadwell out of the room, and sat her down, all trembling, in a chair. "My dear child, whatever's the matter?"

For a moment she couldn't tell me, but could only sit shuddering and sobbing and biting her lip, so I pushed a tot of brandy into her, and when she had coughed and swallowed she lifted her tear-streaked face and caught my hand.

"Oh, gramps, I don't know what to do! It is the most dreadful thing—I think I shall die!" She took a great sobbing breath. "It is Randall—and . . . and Colonel Moran! Oh, what are we to do?"

"Moran?" I was dumfounded. "That fellow we saw at the theatre? Why, what the dooce has he to do with you, child?"

It took some more sips of brandy, punctuated by wails and tears, to get the story out of her, and it was a beauty, if you like. Apparently Moran was well known in gaming circles in Town, and made a practice of inveigling young idiots to play with him—that solved the mystery of why he'd been in Oscar Wilde's company; there was never any lack of rich and witless young gulls round Oscar. And among the spring lambs he'd fleeced was Selina's intended, Randall Stanger; by what she said, Moran had got into him for a cool few thou'.

"In God's name, girl, if it's only money—" I was crying out in relief, but it was worse than that; fatally worse. The half-wit Randall, afraid to tell his lordly Papa, had set out to recoup his losses, using regimental money, heaven help us, and had lost that, too. Which was black ruin, and disgrace, when the thing was detected, as it would be.

However, I'm an old hand at scandals, as you may guess.

How much? I asked her briskly, and she bleated out, picking her fan to pieces: twelve thousand. I swallowed hard and said, well, Randall shall have it from my bank tomorrow—he can pay off Moran, and put whatever is necessary back into his mess funds double quick, and no one'll be the wiser. (What the blazes, I'm not a charitable man, but the young fool was going to be my grandson-in-law.)

Would you believe it, she just wailed the louder, shaking her head and sobbing that it wouldn't save him—nothing would.

"Colonel Moran *knows*—he knows where Randall has got the money from, and promises to expose him . . . unless . . ." She buried her face in the cushions, bawling fit to break her stays.

"Unless what, confound it? What does he want, except his money?"

"Unless . . . unless . . ." says she, gazing at me with those great tear-filled eyes. "Unless . . . I . . . oh, gramps, I must die first! He will expose Randall unless I . . . submit . . . oh, God! *I'm* his price! Don't you see? Oh, what am I to do?"

Well, this was Act Two of "The Villain Still Pursued Her" with a vengeance, wasn't it just? Not that I disbelieved it for an instant—show me melodrama, and I'll show you truth, every time. And I didn't waste effort clutching my brow, exclaiming "The villain—he shall rue this day!" I could even see Moran's point of view—I'd played Wicked Jasper myself, in my time, twirling my whiskers at Beauty and chivvying 'em into bed as the price of my silence or good will. But this was my own grand-daughter, and my gorge rose at the thought of her at the mercy of that wicked old roué. She must be saved, at any cost.

"When do you have to answer him?" I asked.

"Next week," she sobbed. "He will wait only a few days— and then . . . then I must be . . . ruined!"

"Does Randall know?" I asked, and she shook her head, snivelling into her handkerchief. "Well, don't let him know, understand? No one must know—above all, not your grandmother. Let me see—first thing is an order on my bank for the twelve thousand, so that this idiot you're going to marry can square his accounts—"

"But Colonel Moran—" she wailed, beating her little fist.

"I'll see to him, never fear. Now, Selly, all is going to be well, d'you see? Absolutely well—and you don't have to worry your pretty head over it, you understand me?" I took her hand and put my arm round her shoulders and rubbed my old whiskers against her brow, as I'd done since she was a baby, and she wept on my shoulder. "Now—you dry your eyes, and let's see your best smile—no, your best one, I said—there, that's my princess." I wiped a tear from her cheek, and she flung her arms round my ancient neck.

"Oh, gramps—you are the dearest grandpapa! I know you will make it right!" She sniffed in my ear. "Perhaps . . . after all, if you offered him more money . . . he is such a greedy, odious person. But you will find a way, won't you?"

That, of course, remained to be seen, and when I'd packed her off to bed, and sent word round to her fond parents' house that she'd be staying the night with us, I sought enlightenment in brandy. I find it helps. Moran, thinks I to myself; evil, lecherous skunk. I thought of that shifty eye and wicked mouth—aye, he fitted the part he'd written for himself. Trying to ruin virginity, was he—and my little Selly's at that, damn him. Well, now, if I was in his shoes (as I had been, of course) what would make me forego my dirty designs? Threats of violence?—well, they'd have worked on me, but they wouldn't on Moran, that was certain. He was all cold steel and courage, that one; I'd seen him. Money, then? Aye, I could have been bought off—I had been, in the past. So—Flashy's bank account was in for another rough shaking. Well, if needs must, so be it—I couldn't see any other way.

Not that I was resigned to tamely paying up, you understand; if I could find a way of foiling the swine I'd do it, but I plied my wits through a bottle and a half by next afternoon, without striking paydirt. However, until I saw Moran himself, there was nothing to be done, so I sought out his direction by discreet inquiry, and early evening found me round at his rooms, off Bond Street, sending in my card. I was ushered up, and there was the man himself, very much at his ease, in a most luxuriously fitted den, all leather and good panels and big game trophies on the walls. Chinese carpet, too, rot him; his price wasn't going to be a cheap one.

"Well, well," says he, setting his back to the mantel, very lean and cool. "I half-expected you'd be round, if not quite so soon."

"All right, Moran," says I, giving him my damn-you stare, and keeping my tile on. "What's the game?"

"Game, my dear chap? The only game I'm interested in is big game, what? Reminds me—have you seen that rubbish in *The Times* sporting columns—review of some book on shikar'?" He sauntered forward to his desk, and picked up a paper. "Here we are—'No beast, perhaps, is more dangerous than the buffalo.' What tosh, don't you agree? Why, what buffalo that ever walked could compare with a wounded leopard, eh? Or a tiger, if it comes to that. But maybe you've another opinion?" He gave a short laugh, and the blue eyes slipped quickly over me. "What d'ye think of my collection, by the way? Only the best of it here, of course—rather fine, though. That ibex head, for example, and the snow leopard beside the window—"

"My only interest in your collection," I growled, "is that it isn't going to contain my grand-daughter."

"No?" says he, lightly. "Thought she'd look rather well, mounted—wouldn't you think? Don't do anything foolish," he added sharply, as I started to plough forward, snarling at his filthy insolence. "You're past the age when you can lift your stick to anyone—not that you could ever have lifted it to me."

My rage was almost choking me as I glared at him, standing so easy behind his desk, mocking me.

"Listen, you foul kite," says I. "You'll drop this vile . . . affront you've put on my girl, or by God it'll be the worse for you! I'll make this town too hot for you, so help me, I will! You think I'm helpless, do you? You'll find out other—"

"Drop it, you old fool," snaps he. "D'you think you can bluster at me? Think back to Isan'lwana and ask yourself if I'm the man to be brow-beaten. Yes—that makes you think twice!"

He was right there; I stood seething helplessly.

"Damn you! All right, then," for I knew it had to come to this, "what's your price?"

He laughed aloud. "Money? Are you seriously trying to buy me off? You've a poorer opinion of Miss Selina's charms than I'd have thought possible in a rake of your experience."

"Blast your lousy tongue—how much?"

He took a cigar from his pocket, lit it coolly while I boiled with anger, and blew out the match.

"You haven't got that much money," he drawled. "Not—" he blew smoke across the desk at me "—if you were Moss Abrahams in person. Oh, don't think it wouldn't give me great pleasure to beggar you—it would. But I'll enjoy your plump little granddaughter even more—oh, so much more! She'd be very much my meat in any circumstances—but the fact that she's yours—" he poked his cigar at me, grinning "—oh, that makes her a prize indeed!"

This was beyond all understanding. I gaped at the man, dumfounded.

"What the devil d'you mean? That she's my grandchild—what has that to do with it, in God's name? What have I ever done to you? I don't even know you, hardly—and you saved my skin in Zululand, didn't you?"

"Aye," says he. "If I'd only known, though—who you were! Remember, I told you at Rorke's Drift? But I didn't know—by

God, if I had, you'd never have come over the Buffalo alive!"
And for once the eyes were steady, glaring hate at me. I couldn't
fathom it.

"What the blazes are you talking about? Good God above,
man, what the devil have you got against me? I've never injured
you—or if you think I have, I swear I don't know about it! What
is it, damn you?" He said not a word. "And whatever it is, what's
my Selina to do with anything? Why should you want to harm
her, you bastard? An innocent—dear God, have you no decency?
And I? What have I done—?"

"You don't know, do you?" says he, softly. "You truly don't.
But then—how should you? How would you remember—out of
all the vile things you've done—why should you remember . . .
me?"

This was beyond comprehension; I wondered was the fellow
a lunatic. But mad or not, there was that in his baleful stare that
terrified me—for Selly as much as for myself.

"Shall I remind you?" says he, and his voice grated like
gravel. "You think we met for the first time in Zululand, do you?"
He shook his head. "Oh, no, Flashman. Cast your mind back . . .
forty-five years. A long time, eh? D'you remember an African
slave-ship, called the *Balliol College,* trading into the Dahomey
coast? A ship commanded by a human devil called John Charity
Spring, M.A.? A ship on which you, Flashman, served as supercargo? D'you remember?"

Did I not? I'd never forget it.

"But . . . but what has that to do with—you? Why, you can
only have been a child in those days—"

"Aye—a child!" he roared, suddenly, crashing his fist on the
desk. "A child of fourteen—that's what I was!" His face was
crimson, working with fury, but he mastered himself and went
on, in a rasping whisper:

"You remember an expedition upriver—to the village of
King Gezo, who sold niggers to Spring? You remember that

death-house, built of skulls, and the human sacrifices, and those savage Amazon women who were Gezo's bodyguard? D'you remember? Oh, yes, I see that you do. And d'you remember the bargain that monster Spring struck with that monster Gezo—half a dozen Amazon women to be sold into slavery in exchange for a case of Adams revolvers which you—" his finger stabbed out at me "—demonstrated for that black fiend?"

As clear as day I could see it—the hideous Gezo leaping up and down on his stool, slobbering in excitement, with those great black fighting-women ranged by his throne; I could feel the Adams kicking in my fist as I blew holes in the skull wall for his edification.

"Six women in exchange for a case of revolvers and—what else?" Moran's face was terrible to see. "What turned the scale in that infamous bargain—d'you recall? Again, I see you do." His voice was barely audible. "Gezo demanded that Spring's cabin-boy be left with him—as a slave. And Spring, and you, and the rest of that hell-ship's crew—you agreed, and left the child behind." He straightened up from the desk. "I was that boy."

It was beyond belief. It couldn't be true, not for a minute . . . but even as the denial sprang to my lips, my wits were telling me that no one—no one on earth, could have known the details of that shameful transaction of Spring's, unless he'd been there. And yet . . .

"But that's moonshine!" I cried. "Why, I remember that boy—a snivelling little Cockney guttersnipe with a cross-eye . . . nothing like you! And, damnation, you were educated at Eton— I looked you up in *Who's Who*!"

"Quite true," says he. "And like many a public school boy before me—and many since—I ran away . . . don't tell me you never drove some panic-stricken little fag to do the same at Rugby. Oh, yes, I ran—and thought it would be a fine thing to go for a ship's boy, and seek my fortune. I was a good enough actor, even then, to fake a Whitechapel whine—the genteel Captain

Spring would never have shipped a little gentleman as cabin-boy, now would he?" The sneer writhed at the corner of his mouth. "But he was ready enough to drug him with native beer and sell him as a slave to that unspeakable savage, in exchange for a gaggle of half-naked black sluts! Oh, aye, you were all willing enough for that!"

"It's a lie!" cries I. "It was all Spring's idea—I knew nothing of it! Why, I even pleaded with him, I remember—but it was too late, don't you see—?"

"Pleaded?" he scoffed. "When did you ever plead for anything except your own miserable self? What did you care, if a white child was left to the mercy of that . . . that gross black brute?" His eyes were darting about the room as he spoke, and his hand was shaking on the desk-top. "Two years I endured there—two years in that rotting jungle hell, praying for death, kicked and scourged and tortured by those animals . . . aye, you can stare in horror, you that left me to it! Two years—before I had the courage to run again, and by God's grace was picked up by Portugee slavers, who carried me to the coast. Portugee scum, mark you—they saved me from the fate I'd been doomed to by fellow Englishmen."

"But I'd no hand in that! I tell you, it was no fault of mine! By God, it must have been frightful, Moran—I don't wonder you're . . . well, upset . . . perfectly appalling, on my word . . . but it was all Charity Spring's doing, don't you see? I'm clean innocent—you can't bear me a grudge for what that scoundrel did! Why, he'd kidnapped me, in the first place—"

"Spring's long gone to his account," says he, and laughed harshly. "So have several others. Oh, yes, I marked you all down for settlement." For a fleeting second he met my eye. "You remember Sullivan, the Yankee bucko mate? I got him in Galveston in '69.[14] And the surgeon—what was his name? An Irishman. He went in Bombay. I took 'em as I found 'em, you see—and while I was making my own career, in the Indian Army, I often thought about you. But I never had the chance—till now."

There was a moment's silence, while I stood like a snared rabbit, too stunned and scared to speak, and he went on.

"But you're too old to be worth killing, Flashman. Oh, it would be easy enough—you've seen me, and you possibly know I'm rated the best big-game shot in India, if not the world. If General Flashman were found with his head blown off on his Leicestershire estate—who'd ever suspect the eminent and respectable Colonel John Sebastian Moran?" He sneered and shook his head. "Poor sport. But little Miss Selina—there's a worthwhile quarry, if you like. I saw how to strike at you, the night I saw her at the theatre. And you, you foul old tyke, can do nothing about it. For if she shrinks from me at the last—well, young Stanger's name will be blasted, and her hopes with it—and yours. A splendid scandal there'll be." He leaned against the mantel again, his thumbs in his weskit, and gloated at me. "Either way, you'll pay—for what you did to me. Personally, I think the young lady will save her lover's honour at the expense of her own—I hope so, anyway. But I don't much mind."

This was appalling—for the fellow *was* mad, I was sure, eaten up with his hatred and lust for vengeance. And he had marked down Selly, to strike at me . . . and he was right, she'd sacrifice herself to shame to save Stanger—and if she didn't, his life and hers would both be ruined. I could have wept, at the thought of her frail, tender innocence at the mercy of this crazy, murderous ogre—I absolutely did weep, begging him to accept any price, offering to ransom her as high as twenty thousand, or thirty (I called a halt there, I remember), promising to use my influence to obtain him patronage, or a title, literally pleading at the swine's feet and drawing his attention to my white hairs and old age—and he simply laughed at me.

So I raged at him, threatening, vowing I'd be his ruin somehow—I'd kill him, I said, even if I swung for it, and he just jeered in my face.

"Oh, how I wish you'd try! How I would admire to see that! Go home and get your pistol and your black mask, and collect a gang of bullies—why don't you? Or cross the Channel with me, and we'll shoot it out on the sands! I can just see that! You pathetic old corpse!"

In the end he kicked me out, and I slunk off home in a rage of such fear and frustration and misery as I've seldom felt before. I was helpless—he couldn't be bought, he couldn't be moved, he couldn't be bullied or bluffed. He was even invulnerable against the last resort of violence—oh, he might be near sixty, but his hand was still rock-steady and his eye clear, and even if there had been such a thing as a hired gun in the Home Counties, what chance would he have stood against the lightning skill I'd seen proved on Ketshwayo's Zulus? No—Moran held all the aces. And Selina, my precious little darling, was doomed. I went home and drank myself blind.

You may think, for a man who puts a fairly low price on maiden virtue, that I was getting into a rare sweat at the thought of her being deflowered by Moran. But your own flesh and blood is something different; she wasn't like the women of my youth—most of whom had been a pretty loose set, anyway. She was sweet and gentle and from a different stable altogether—the thought of Moran subjecting her brought me out in a sweat of horror. Damn Stanger, for his idiocy, and damn Gezo, for not cutting Moran's whelp throat when he had the chance. Careless old swine. But there was no use cursing; I had to think, and if necessary (shocking thought) to act. And after an unconscionable amount of drink and heart-searching, I realised that I was going to have to kill Moran.

Maybe it was senile decay that brought me to this awful conclusion; I don't know. I've been desperately driven in my time, and done some wild things, coward and all that I am; I can only say that it seemed worth the risk for Selina's sake. Risk? Certainty, where Moran was concerned—and yet, need it be so certain? Granted he was the deadliest hand with a gun I'd ever seen—he was bound to turn his back sometime. And London wasn't Zululand, or Abilene of the old days; no one *expects* to be shot in the back on Half Moon Street. A man in disguise, on a dark April night, if he shadowed his victim carefully, and bided his time, might get off the necessary shots and then slide into cover—our bobbies ain't used to that sort of thing, thank God. It was desperate, but it was possible—I'd had more experience of skulking and shooting from cover than I cared to think of, and— but, dear God, I was an old man, and getting feeble, and half-fuddled with drink, and scared blue into the bargain. I sat there, maudlin, drivelling to myself and looking at Selly's picture.

Then I put the bottle away, and went upstairs and rooted through my old clothes, and found myself opening a certain drawer. There they were: the old German revolver with which I'd shot my way out of Fort Raim dungeon; the Navy Colt that I'd blazed away with, eyes shut, at Gettysburg; the Khyber knife I'd got from Ilderim Khan in the Mutiny; the scarred old double-action Bulldog, and the neat little Galand pocket pistol—it had four rounds in it, too, confound it.[15] Well, if I ever summoned up the nerve to draw a bead on Moran, I'd sure as hell not have the chance to use more than four rounds. He'd be blasting back after just one—happy thought, though: maybe he didn't travel heeled. Not many London clubmen do—by Jove, if he was unarmed, that would be famous! And then a quick hobble round the corner, into the dark—why not?

It was at this point, as I said at the beginning of my story, that I decided murder is a chancy thing for a septuagenarian coward. I teetered on the brink, fearfully, and then I thought, what the devil, even if Palmer gets his Old Age Pension bill through, I still won't qualify, because it specifically excludes drunkards from benefit.[16] Selly's worth it, says I, snuffling to myself. And so the die was cast.

Once I'm committed, I don't do things by halves. I would have to settle the business at night, in the best disguise I could find, so I sorted out some of the motley garments I'd brought back from my travels and set about turning myself into an elderly down-at-heel of the kind that slinks round the West End streets, picking up cigar butts and sleeping in areas. It wasn't difficult—in my time I've impersonated everything from a bronco Apache to a prince consort, and with my grey hairs I was halfway there.

So that was easy; the next thing was to decide where I was going to dry-gulch Moran. I had a week at most at my disposal, so for three or four nights I set off stealthily after dark, dressed in an ancient pea-jacket and patched unmentionables, with a muffler and billycock hat and cracked boots, Galand in one pocket and flask in t'other, skulking round Conduit Street to see what his movements were. I was in a putrid state of funk, of course, but even so I felt downright ridiculous—hanging about waiting to murder someone, at my time of life.

For two nights I never saw hide nor hair of him, and then on the Tuesday he broke cover, shortly after six, and I trailed him to a cab on Bond Street and lost him—for I couldn't take a cab in pursuit; dressed as I was, any self-respecting cabby would have taken his whip to me, and if I'd tried to run after him I'd have been lying on the pavement wheezing my guts up inside ten yards. So that was another wasted night, but on the Wednesday he decided to walk, jauntering out of his rooms in full evening fig and strolling all the way to St. James's, where he spent four hours at the Bagatelle—dealing 'em off the bottom, no doubt. Then he took a cab home, and I was dished again.

This was desperate, I decided. There hadn't been a chance, so far, to do him more mischief than curse, and nights spent hanging around street-corners had sapped my resolution abominably, as well as giving me the cold. I was having the deuce of a job getting in and out undetected at home, too, and to make matters worse I had a distraught Selly on my hands on Thursday morning, wanting to know what was to be done. She'd had a note from the swine; it simply said: "Well? M."

The poor creature was nearly distracted with fear, and it was all I could do to stop her having hysterics, which my wife would certainly have heard. But one thing the sight of her distress did for me: I resolved that if Tiger Jack Moran was still alive on Friday morning, it wouldn't be for want of effort on my part. If the worst came to the worst I'd stalk him home that Thursday night and kill him on his own front-door step and take my chance. (That's what being a doting grandparent can do to you.)

I was late on my beat that night, though, on account of being dragooned into standing up with the Connaughts at the Army's football challenge match at Aldershot in the afternoon[17]—two sets of hooligans hacking each other in the mud—and it was near eight before I got on post in my rags, huddled in a doorway nipping at my pint flask of spirits with a quaking heart. But just on nine Moran came out, in opera hat and lined cloak, swinging his long cane jauntily. He strolled by within a yard of me; for a moment the gaslight fell on that fierce hawk profile and sprouting moustache, and I felt my innards turn to jelly, and then he was past. One odd thing I noticed; under one arm he carried a flat case. But I was too taken up with considering the loose, fit stride of the man, and the graceful way he carried himself—he looked as dangerous as they come—to worry about trifles.

I thought he might be for the clubs again, but to my surprise he turned up Oxford Street, sauntering calmly along, and then made north. I couldn't figure why he hadn't taken a cab; as it was, I had to move sharper than I cared to keep him in view, and when we got off Oxford Street, and people were scarcer, I had to hang back for fear of being spotted, hurrying to catch up whenever he rounded a corner. This was new territory to me, but I remember we had crossed Wigmore Street, and then I stopped with my heart racing, as he paused beside the entrance to a darkened arch and looked back; he glanced up and down the street—there was hardly a soul about—and then he turned under the arch and disappeared.

Meanwhile I was having minor fits. I couldn't begin to guess what he was up to, but I knew it was now or never. I couldn't hope for a better chance than this, in a network of streets which were as near to being deserted as central London ever is, with my quarry moving down a dark alley. I hurried forward as fast as I could, reached the archway with my lungs bursting, peered cautiously round the corner, and was in time to see him entering a doorway under a single guttering gas-flare at the other end. I waited a few seconds, and then stole forward, the butt of the Galand greasy with sweat in my hand.

I reached the doorway on tiptoe and paused. It was open. I strained my ears, and heard his feet creaking on stairs—up, up, up, turn, and up again. I didn't hesitate—I couldn't; if I waited, there was no certainty he'd come out again this way, and if I was to follow him I must do it while his own footsteps would drown out the sound of mine. I took one last pull at my flask for luck, and went through the door; the light filtering in showed me the foot of the stairs, and then I was sneaking up, into the stuffy darkness, gun out, keeping close to the rickety banisters.

It's a strange thing, but however funky you may be—and I'll take on all comers in that line—once you're moving there's a kind of controlled panic that guides your feet; I went up those stairs like an elderly ghost, holding my breath until I nearly burst, and crouched on the first landing. I heard his feet across the top landing, and then recede as though he'd gone into a room—then silence.

That was the worst part. Up there, on the top floor, was not only as dangerous a man as I'd ever met, but a top-hole shikari, a night-bird, a trained and skilful hunter who could catch the sound of grass growing. I felt the bile come up in my throat with fear—but I was armed, wasn't I, and he probably wasn't, and I'd been a pretty useful night-skulker in my time, too. I'd make no more noise going up than down—and I thought of Selina, and went on up, slow step after slow step, until my head was on a level with the top landing. I peeped over the top step—and that was as far as Flashy was going, no error.

Directly ahead of me was what seemed to be a closet, with the door ajar, and to its left was an open door. Through this I could see clear across a room to the window on the far side, and there, with the street-light beating in on his crouching figure, was Tiger Jack. He was down on one knee, peering through the glass, and keeping himself to the side, under cover. He had put off his hat, and his bald dome shone like a beacon.

It was only now, with a queer shock of surprise, that I found myself wondering what the devil he was about—creeping into an empty house in the middle of the night and staring out of windows. By God, it was fishy, and then as I watched I saw him fumble with the case he'd been carrying, pick up his cane, and unscrew its top. There was a scraping sound, and then a soft snap; he reached out and eased up the sash of the window, and gently pushed something out through the gap—and my bowels did a cartwheel as I saw that what his cane had become was the barrel of a rifle!

Petrified, I could only watch—and then I saw that he was surveying a window on the other side of the street; a lighted window, with a man's silhouette clear on the blind. Moran gazed at it steadily—he was watching for movement, of course, and then he brought his made-up rifle up to his shoulder, with his right arm stretched out to the side as he flexed the fingers of his trigger-hand.

Suddenly I realised that this was the moment—the moment that would never occur again. I didn't know what the hell he was up to, or who his mysterious victim might be—any devilment was nuts to Moran, and it didn't matter a dam. What did, was that he was within twenty feet of me, with his back turned, and every nerve concentrated on his deadly task. Your bird, old Flash, thinks I, and I brought up the Galand, cocked it with the trigger back to make no sound, rested my gun-wrist on the top step, and drew a dead bead on the back of that great bald head.

It isn't often that I've had cause to bless my trembling nerves—or my unsteady boozer's hand. But by God they saved my neck then. For even as Moran brought his right hand to the stock of his rifle, and settled into his aim, my faltering trigger-finger got a fit of the shakes; my aim wavered, and I paused, sweating—and in that moment I learned that, old as I was, I was a better shikari than Moran would ever be. For in that second's pause I realised something that he hadn't noticed; I can't explain it—call it sixth sense, or a coward's instinct shaped and refined over a lifetime—but in that second I realised that we were not alone. There was someone else in the room with him—to the left, in the space hidden from me, watching him, and waiting.

I lay still as death, my hair rising on my scalp—and then as Moran hung on his aim there was a plop like a cork exploding from a champagne bottle and a distant crash of glass. I nearly had a seizure as a hidden voice bawled: "Now!" and as Moran swung from the window there was a scramble of feet and two dark shapes hurled themselves on him, fists swinging like billy-ho, and the three of them went down in a swearing, yelling tangle. There was a cry from the street, and a piercing whistle from the room where Moran was locked in combat with those two fine chaps, and then more whistles shrilled from below, there was the crash of a door being hurled back, feet racing on the stairs—and General Sir Harry Flashman, V.C., K.B., K.C.I.E., was into that closet like an electrified stoat, hauling the door to behind him and silently gulping another precious mouthful from his flask to prevent apoplexy.

It sounded like the Household Brigade coming up the stairs, pounding past my hiding-place into the room where the others were still wrestling and cursing away; that's it, Tiger, thinks I, kick the bastards' shins and good luck to you. Then the sounds faded, and I heard a murmur of voices, too indistinct to be made out. I didn't mind, crouched in my cupboard with my heart clattering against my ribs, but then curiosity got the better of me as usual, and I pushed my door open a crack to listen. A high-pitched, nasal voice was talking, and sounding well pleased with itself:

". . . who else did you suppose it was, inspector? Well, well—permit me to introduce Colonel John Sebastian Moran, formerly of the Indian Army, and the deadliest game shot in either hemisphere. Tiger Jack, as I believe he was once known—but now himself bagged at last."

Then Moran broke in, and he was cursing like a steamboat pilot with his toes in the mangle, until an official voice told him to hold his tongue, and after some more confused cussing and conversation which I didn't catch, the high-pitched chap was heard again:

"I believe a comparison of the bullet fired tonight, with that which was found in the body of Ronald Adair, who was murdered last month, will prove instructive, inspector. It will be for you to decide, but it seems to me that a charge of murder must certainly lie . . ."

I went giddy at the words, and the rest of them were lost in the gurgling of my flask as I clapped it to my lips. Murder! I could have danced and sung in my closet! They'd got the old swine—I didn't understand it, of course, or why he should have murdered the chap Adair whose death had been all through the papers, but what did it matter? Tiger Jack was for the Newgate polka, by the sound of it—and Selly was saved, for even if he tried to blacken young Stanger now, out of spite, who'd mind the yelping of a convicted felon? And I was out from under, too—I broke into a cold sweat at the thought of how close I'd been to squeezing my trigger; it could have been me that they were hauling downstairs now with the darbies on, full steam for the condemned cell.[18]

I almost cried from relief in that stuffy closet as I heard them clattering down and out to the Black Maria; the street door slammed, I listened, but there wasn't a sound. Very cautiously I peeped out; all was still as sleep, so I tiptoed carefully down to the first landing, and leaned on the banisters to still my racing heart and get my breath back. Selly was safe, Moran was scuppered, and—

The creak of a door overhead gave me such a start I nearly pitched headlong into the stairwell—dear God, there was someone still up there!

"But of course, my dear fellow, you shall hear all about it—come along." It was the high-pitched voice again, and at the sound of it I was scuttling frantically down the last flight, into the lane, and wheezing at high speed towards the arch when I came to a shuddering stop—plumb ahead, in the archway, was the unmistakeable silhouette of a police constable, feet planted, guarding my only escape. If I'd had the wind left I'd have squealed aloud—then I saw his back was to me, unsuspecting. But behind me, in the empty house, voices were descending the stairs; in two seconds they'd be in view, and I was trapped, helpless, in the alleyway between them and the Law!

I suppose, if I'd had time for reflection, I could have told myself that I was doing no wrong, had committed no offence, and could have faced anyone with a clean conscience. Aye, but there was the pistol in my pocket, and the likelihood that those interfering bobbies would have wanted to know who I was, and what business I had there—God, what a to-do there would be if it was discovered that the celebrated Sir Harry Flashman was creeping about disguised as a scarecrow, with a shooting iron in his pocket, at the scene of an attempted murder! How could I hope to explain—avoid scandal . . . oh, anyway, when you go about feeling as permanently guilty as I do, you don't waste time over niceties. At all costs I must avoid detection; there was only one thing for it—I was dressed like a soup-kitchen derelict, and in a twinkling I had poured the rest of my flask down my coat-front, sprawled down against a convenient grating, and was lying there wheezing like an intoxicated grampus, trying to look like a stupefied down-and-out who has crept in to doss for the night, when the footsteps turned out of the house and came towards me.

If they've any sense they'll just pass by, thinks I—well, don't you, when you see some ragged bummaree sleeping it off in the gutter? But no, curse their nosiness, they didn't. The footsteps stopped beside me, and I chanced a quick look at 'em through half-closed lids—a tall, slim cove in a long coat, bare-headed and balding, and a big, hulking chap with a bulldog moustache and hard hat. They looked like a poet and a bailiff.

"What's this?" says the bailiff, stooping over me.

"A tramp," says the poet. "One of the flotsam, escaping his misery in a few hours of drunken slumber."

"Think he's all right?" says the bailiff, rot him, and blow me if he wasn't fumbling for my pulse. "Going at full gallop," says he, and blast his infernal impudence, he put a hand on my brow. "My goodness, but he's feverish. D'you think we should get help for him?"

"You'll get no thanks beyond a flood of curses if you do," says the poet carelessly. "Really, doctor, even without close examination my nose can tell me more than your fingers. The fellow is hopelessly under the influence of drink—and rather inferior drink, at that, I fancy," says he, stooping and sniffing at the fumes which were rising from my sodden breast. "Yes, American bourbon, unless I am mistaken. The odour is quite distinctive—you may have remarked that to the trained senses, each spirit has its own peculiar characteristics; I believe I have in the past drawn your attention to the marked difference between the rich, sugary aroma of rum, and the more delicate sweet smell of gin," says this amazing lunatic. "But what now?"

The bailiff, having taken his confounded liberties with my wrist and brow, was pausing in the act of trying to lift one of my eyelids, and his next words filled me with panic.

"Good Lord!" he exclaimed. "I believe I know this chap—but no, it can't be, surely! Only he's uncommonly like that old general . . . oh, what's-his-name? You know, made such a hash of the Khartoum business, with Gordon . . . yes, and years ago he won a great name in Russia, and the Mutiny—V.C. and knighthood—it's on the tip of my tongue—"

"My dear fellow," says the high-pitched poet, "I can't imagine who your general may be—it can hardly be Lord Roberts, I fancy—but it seems likely that he would choose to sleep in his home or his club, rather than in an alley. Besides," he went on wearily, stooping a little closer—and damned unnerving it was, to feel those two faces peering at me through the gloom, while I tried to sham insensible—"besides, this is a nautical, not a military man; he is not English, but either American or German—probably the latter, since he has certainly studied at a second-rate German university, but undoubtedly he has been in America quite lately. He is known to the police, is currently working as a ship's steward, or in some equally menial capacity at sea—for I observe that he has declined even from his modest beginnings—and will, unless I am greatly mistaken, be in Hamburg by the beginning of next week—provided he wakes up in time. More than that," says the know-all ignoramus, "I cannot tell you from a superficial examination. Except, of course, for the obvious fact that he found his way here via Piccadilly Circus."

"Well," says the other doubtfully, "I'm sure you're right, but he looks extremely like old what's-his-name. But how on earth can you tell so much about him from so brief a scrutiny?"

"You have not forgotten my methods since we last met,

surely?" says the conceited ass, who I began to suspect was some kind of maniac. "Very well, apply them. Observe," he went on impatiently, "that the man wears a pea-jacket, with brass buttons, which is seldom seen except on sea-faring men. Add that to the patent fact that he is a German, or German-American—"

"I don't see," began the bailiff, only to be swept aside.

"The duelling scars, doctor! Observe them, quite plain, close to the ears on either side." He'd sharp eyes, all right, to spot those; a gift to me from Otto Bismarck, years ago. "They are the unfailing trade-mark of the German student, and since they have been inexpertly inflicted—you will note that they are too high— it is not too much to assume that he received them not at Heidelberg or Gottingen, but at some less distinguished academy. This suggests a middle-class beginning from which, obviously, he has descended to at least the fringes of crime."

"How can you tell that?"

"The fine silver flask in his hand was not honestly acquired by such a seedy drunkard as this, surely. It is safe to deduce that its acquisition was only one of many petty pilferings, some of which must inevitably have attracted the attention of the police."

"Of course! Well, I should have noticed that. But how can you say he is a ship's steward, or that he has been in America, or that he's going to Hamburg—"

"His appearance, although dissipated, is not entirely unre- deemed. Some care has been taken with the moustache and whiskers, no doubt to compensate for the ravages which drink and evil living have stamped on his countenance." I could have struck the arrogant, prying bastard, but I grimly kept on playing possum. "Again, the hands are well kept, and the nails, so he is not a simple focsle hand. What, then, but a stew- ard? The boots, although cracked, are of exceptionally good manufacture—doubtless a gratuity from some first-class passen- ger. As to his American sojourn, we have established that he drinks bourbon whisky, a taste for which is seldom developed outside the United States. Furthermore, since I noticed from the shipping lists this morning that the liner *Brunnhilde* has arrived in London from New York, and will leave on Saturday for Hamburg, I think we may reasonably conclude, bearing in mind the other points we have established, that here we have one of her crew, mis-spending his shore leave."

"Amazing!" cries the bailiff. "And, of course, quite simple when you explain it. My dear fellow, your uncanny powers have not deserted you in your absence!"

"I trust they are still equal, at least, to drawing such obvious inferences as these. And now, doctor, I think we have spent long enough over this poor, besotted hulk, who, I fear, would have furnished more interesting material for the meeting of the Inebriation Society than for us. I think you will admit that this pathetic shell has little in common with your distinguished Indian general."

"Unhesitatingly!" cries the other oaf, standing up, and as they sauntered off, leaving me quaking with relief and indignation— drunken ship's dogsbody from a second-rate German university, indeed!—I heard him ask:

"But how did you know he got here by way of Piccadilly?"

"He reeked of bourbon whisky, which is not easy to obtain outside the American Bar, and his condition suggested that he had filled his flask at least once since coming ashore . . ."

I waited until the coast was clear, and then creaked to my feet and hurried homeward, stiff and sore and stinking of brandy (bourbon, my eye!—as though I'd pollute my liver with that rotgut) and if my "besotted shell" was in poor shape, my heart was rejoicing. It had all come right, for little Selly and me, and as I limped my way towards Berkeley Square I was in capital fettle. I was even whistling to myself as I loitered past the end of Hay Hill, and then my roving eye chanced to fall on a certain lighted window, and I bore up short, thinking hollo, what's this?

For it was *my* window, in the chambers of my salad days,

which as I've told you I had placed at the convenience of the Prince of Wales for the entertainment of his secret gallops. I remembered seeing in the morning's paper that he had been due at Charing Cross that evening from France; by George, thinks I, the randy little pig can't wait for his English muttons, for all that he must have been panting after half the skirt dancers of Paris this month past. No sooner home than he's in the saddle again. I was shaking my head sadly over such scandalous conduct, when along comes a cab round the corner from Grafton Street, pulling up at the very door to my Hay Hill place—it was pretty late by now, and all quiet, very discreet. Aha, thinks I, here's his little macaroon; let's see who it is this time, so that we can tattle at the club in the morning.

So I shuffled close, just as a heavily-veiled lady got out, without paying the cab, which rattled off at once. *That* proved it, and as she crossed the pavement and passed into the entry I was abreast, glancing in. She pulled off her veil, and shook her hair, just as I passed, and for a split second I saw her face before she hurried on. And I staggered, as though from a blow, clutching the railings and sinking to the pavement. For there was no mistaking; it was my own grand-daughter, little Selina.

I've been hit hard in my time, but that nearly carried me off. My own grand-daughter—going up to that pot-bellied satyr! I sprawled there against the railings, dumfounded. Selina, the wide-eyed, tender innocent—mistress to the revolting Bertie! No, no, it couldn't be . . . why, only that morning she'd been pleading with me to save her from the embraces of Moran; she'd seemed almost out of her wits—by George, though, well she might be, if she was the Prince of Wales's secret pet! She couldn't afford to compromise herself with half-pay adventurers like Tiger Jack, not if she was to keep in favour with her royal lover. And she couldn't be mixed up in scandals over her fiancé's pilfering regimental funds, neither. She had *had* to get Moran silenced (with my money, she hoped) if she was to stay topsides with Bertie. No wonder she'd wailed on my bosom, the designing, wicked little hussy. And I'd been in a lather about her honour—her honour! My own grand-daughter.

That, of course, was the point. She *was my* grand-daughter, and what's bred in the bone . . . oh, but she'd hocussed me properly, playing shrinking Purity, and I'd been ready to shell out half my fortune—and I'd come within an ace of committing murder for her. That was the far outside of enough—I stared up at that lighted window, bursting with outrage—and then for all my fury I found I was grinning, and then laughing, as I clung to the railings. Say what you like; consider that sweet, innocent, butter-melting beauty and the mind behind it—oh, she was Flashy's little grandchild, all right, every inch of her.

"Wot's all the row, then?" says a voice, and there was a burly, bearded copper shining his bull's-eye on me. "Yore tight," says he.

"No, guv'nor, not a bit," I wheezed. "Just resting."

"Don't gimme none o' your sauce," says he. "This 'ere's a respectable neighbour'ood—the likes o' you can do yer boozin' some place else, you follow? Nah then, 'op it."

"Yuss, guv'nor," says I. "Just goin', honnist."

"Orta know better, a man yore age. Look at yerself—proper disgrace, you are. Don't you old rummies never learn?"

"No," says I. "We never do." And I set off, under his disapproving eye, across Berkeley Square.

Notes

1. Paul Kruger (1825–1904), later President of the South African Republic, claimed that if Lord Chelmsford had taken his advice on Zulu fighting, Isandhlwana need not have been lost. "Oom Paul" spoke from experience; he had himself been caught by the speed of a Zulu attack, and survived only after hand-to-hand fighting inside his laager (square of wagons). (See J. Martineau's *Life of Sir Bartle Frere*, 1893.) In fairness to Chelmsford, the failure to laager was Colonel Durnford's; Rider Haggard, who knew Durnford well, advances an interesting theory on his tactics in *The Tale of Isandhlwana*, but agrees with Kruger that laagering would have saved the day.
[p. 298]

2. In connection with Flashman's defence of the wagon with his revolvers, it is interesting to note that one of the Zulu warriors, a son of Chief Sirayo, later described how he had seen one of the British force, "a very tall man," keeping up a spirited revolver fire from an empty wagon. "We all said what a very brave man he was . . . he kept his ground for a very long time." This admittedly does not sound like Flashman, and Mackinnon and Shadbolt, in *The South African Campaign of 1879–80*, are probably correct when they identify the hero as Captain Younghusband of the 24th Regiment.
[p. 300]

3. This was not the only incident of its kind at Isandhlwana. The editor is indebted to Colonel John Awdry of Fovant for drawing his attention to the experience of General (formerly Lieutenant) Smith-Dorrien, one of the survivors of the battle. During the rout Smith-Dorrien came on a man who had been kicked by his horse and could not mount; Smith-Dorrien helped him into the saddle and gave him a knife, and the rider, having promised to catch a horse for Smith-Dorrien, promptly fled from the battlefield. If Flashman's account of his own evasion were not so precise, one would be tempted to identify him with Smith-Dorrien's fugitive. (See *The Man Who Disobeyed*, by A. J. Smithers.)
[p. 302]

4. The battle of Isandhlwana (the place of the Little House or Little Hand) was fought on January 22, 1879, when 1600 British and native troops of Lord Chelmsford's force invading Zululand were overwhelmed by 20,000 warriors of the impis of King Cetewayo (Ketshwayo). What Flashman was doing there is a mystery.

Earlier in the present volume he refers to a visit paid to South Africa in connection with a mine (whether gold or diamond he does not say) belonging to a relative of Lady Flashman's, and there is evidence elsewhere that later he took part in an expedition through unexplored territory in the interior, but how he came to be involved in Chelmsford's operations is still unexplained. Usually in his memoirs he is careful to give full military and political background to his activities, but in this case he treats Isandhlwana, and the equally famous defence of Rorke's Drift, as mere incidents in his story, and clarification must wait on further study of the Flashman Papers, or possibly of *Dawns and Departures of a Soldier's Life*, should the missing volumes of that work come to light. There, it may be, will be found some account of the preliminaries to the Zulu War—the border friction between the Transvaal Dutch and Cetewayo's people, Britain's annexation of the Transvaal and failure to settle the border question, the decision to send in Chelmsford's three columns, the establishment of the base at Isandhlwana, and Chelmsford's departure thence with part of his force in the hope of gaining a quick victory over the Zulu army, while Major Pulleine was left to defend the Isandhlwana camp, only to be wiped out by a Zulu attack which was entirely unexpected.

Why Flashman treats this notable imperial disaster, and its sequel at Rorke's Drift, so cursorily is plain enough. His chief concern in this extract (which came to light more than twenty years ago as a separate fragment in that packet of his Papers dealing with the Indian Mutiny) is to tell the story of his dealings with the notorious Colonel John Sebastian ("Tiger Jack") Moran, and he does not hesitate to pass by great events with little more than a glance. Thus his description of the Isandhlwana fighting is sketchy and highly personal. Reading it, one might suppose that hardly any time elapsed between the first appearance of the Zulus and their final assault on the camp, but in fact there was much intervening activity. Following Lord Chelmsford's departure at dawn, various detachments had been sent out from Pulleine's camp under the Isandhlwana hill as advance pickets and to deal with small groups of Zulus who had appeared; the largest of these detachments, Colonel Durnford's, encountered a powerful impi and was forced to beat a fighting retreat towards the camp, where Pulleine was already under attack. How Flashman came to be within earshot of Pulleine and have a view of Durnford, whose retreat had begun some miles away, one can only guess; no doubt he moved at his customary high speed, and it is likely that in his recollection of his panic-stricken confusion he has unwittingly "telescoped" events and time. His description of the battle's climax accords with other accounts, but he does not mention that the Zulu advance was held up and badly mauled at various points before the final overrunning of the British position. The encircling "chest and horns" tactic was entirely successful, and those of Pulleine's force who escaped the main action were hunted down the ravine to Fugitives' Drift on the Buffalo River. (See Rider Haggard's account written for Andrew Lang; Colenso and Durnford, *History of the Zulu War*, 1881; Sir Reginald Coupland, *Zulu Battle-Piece*, 1948; Donald L. Morris, *The Washing of the Spears*, 1965; C. T. Binns' *The Last Zulu King*; Mackinnon and Shadbolt; and the personal narrative of C. L. Norris-Newman, the only journalist to travel with

Chelmsford's force, *In Zululand with the British*, 1880. An interesting memoir of Zululand during the war is the journal of Cornelius Vjin, a trader who was in Zulu hands for much of the time, *Cetshwayo's Dutchman*, 1880.) [p. 303]

5. Flashman was right that the Zulus would attack Rorke's Drift, but wrong in supposing that they would invade Natal. Isandhlwana had been the most disastrous battle defeat suffered by British troops against native forces in the nineteenth century—although it was to be matched by the wipe-out of a brigade by Afghan tribesmen at Maiwand a year later—but it had been a costly victory for the Zulus, who were finally beaten at Ulundi in July, 1879. [p. 303]

6. For interesting information on Zulu superstitions, see Frazer's *Golden Bough*. In fact, Moran was somewhat out of date; the practice of sending twins first in battle appears to have died out earlier in the century, in King Chaka's time. [p. 306]

7. The pursuing Zulus were certainly soldiers of the Udloko regiment, part of the Undi corps who formed the right wing of the impis at Isandhlwana. Their red and white shields were distinctive. The Martini-Henry was a single-shot weapon, but a good rifleman could fire six rounds in half a minute. [p. 307]

8. The siege of the little Buffalo River station at Rorke's Drift began only a few hours after Isandhlwana, and lasted through the night until the following morning. The garrison was about 130 strong, and was commanded by Lieutenant John Chard of the Royal Engineers and Lieutenant Gonville Bromhead of the 24th (Warwickshire) Regiment, largely recruited in Wales, and later renamed the South Wales Borderers. The attacking Zulu force, consisting of the Udloko, Tulwana, and 'Ndluyengwe regiments, was at least 4000 strong. Both sides fought with the utmost bravery from late afternoon until the climax of the battle at midnight, the Zulus trying to break into the perimeter hastily improvised of mealie-bags and biscuit boxes, and being met by the volleys of the defenders' Martini-Henrys. Savage close-quarter fighting took place at the barricades, and in the hospital, which caught fire at about six o'clock, when the wounded had to be evacuated; by midnight the perimeter had shrunk to sixty-five yards in front of the storehouse. Following as it did on the disaster of Isandhlwana, the defence of Rorke's Drift became, deservedly, a Victorian legend. Seventeen of the defenders died, and at least 400 Zulus. Eleven Victoria Crosses were awarded.

Flashman's account makes it clear that he and Moran must have reached the Drift about eight or nine o'clock, while the hospital was still burning, and entered the perimeter after jumping the stone wall and the mealie-bag barricade which had been built to defend the hospital at the western end of the post. The "huge cove" with the red beard was presumably Chaplain George Smith, but Flashman is probably mistaken in describing him as "pistolling," since the Chaplain was foremost in the vital work of carrying ammunition. (See Michael Glover, *Rorke's Drift*, 1975, an excellent account of the siege and its background, and other works cited in these Notes.) [p. 312]

9. *The Times* of Monday, February 12, 1894, carried under the name Macmillan a notice of the birth of a boy the previous Saturday; he was subsequently christened Maurice Harold. [p. 313]

10. Either Flashman's memory or his hearing has played him false. Oscar Wilde attended a performance of Pinero's *The Second Mrs. Tanqueray* at the St. James's in February, 1894, in the company of Aubrey *Beardsley*, whom he wished to present to Mrs. Patrick Campbell. (See *The Letters of Oscar Wilde.*) His new play, which he mentioned to Selina, would be either *An Ideal Husband*, which was in manuscript at that time, or *The Importance of Being Earnest;* both were produced in the following year. [p. 315]

11. "Father Oscar." Flashman was needling deliberately; he obviously knew that Wilde was sensitive about being no longer in the first flush of youth, and hated being called "Papa" or "Father." (See Lord Alfred Douglas's *Oscar Wilde and Myself*, 1914.) [p. 315]

12. W. E. Gladstone resigned as Prime Minister, and retired from politics, on March 3, 1894. [p. 318]

13. The appearance of this item in the press establishes the date as March 29, 1894. Elspeth's serial may have been *Under the Red Robe*, by Stanley J. Weyman, which appeared in instalments in the *Illustrated London News* early in this year. [p. 318]

14. Elsewhere in his memoirs (see *Flash for Freedom!*) Flashman has suggested that Sullivan was killed by Charity Spring aboard the *Balliol College* slave-ship in 1848, during a fight with an American warship; presumably the mate was only badly wounded, and recovered to fall a victim to Moran twenty years later. [p. 326]

15. Flashman made reluctant use of an astonishing variety of weaponry during his adventurous life, but although he makes frequent references to Adams revolvers there is no evidence that he had any particularly favourite side-arm. Those listed here appear to have been kept for sentimental rather than for practical reasons. The most interesting item is "the scarred old double-action Bulldog," since it was just such a weapon that he used at Little Big Horn; he had borrowed it from Custer himself, and may even have accidentally shot the General with it in the heat of battle. But that gun he flung away in panic, and the mystery remains—how (and why) did he acquire another like it? Only two of Flashman's side-arms appear to have survived: his Khyber knife, bequeathed to Mr. Paget Morrison, the custodian of his papers, and a Tranter revolver from Cartwright of Norwich, engraved with the owner's name, now in the possession of Mr. Garry James of Los Angeles, California. [p. 329]

16. Colonel Palmer's old age pension proposals of 1894 did in fact exclude anyone convicted of a crime in the previous fifteen years, or of drunkenness in the previous ten. [p. 330]

17. In the Army Cup Final played on April 5, 1894, the Black Watch beat the Royal Artillery, 7–2. The Duchess of Connaught, apparently supported by General Flashman, presented the cup. [p. 331]

18. Apart from a few minor discrepancies, Flashman's account of Colonel Moran's movements and arrest on that Thursday night corroborates the celebrated narrative of Dr. Watson, who has described the Colonel's capture in "The Adventure of the Empty House" (see *The Return of Sherlock Holmes*, by Sir Arthur Conan Doyle). It will be remembered that Moran was apprehended by Holmes and Watson in the

act of trying to murder the former (who had rigged up a dummy to draw his fire); Moran's motive was revenge (and no doubt fear that Holmes would identify him as the murderer of the Hon. Ronald Adair, whom Moran had killed some days previously).

Flashman, of course, had no inkling of all this at the time, as his story shows. He was not to know that Moran, after retiring from the Indian Army, had turned his uncanny marksmanship to account by becoming a professional assassin in the employ of Holmes's arch-enemy, Professor Moriarty, or that the Colonel eked out his contract fees by card-sharping, as in the case of Stanger and Adair. After his arrest by Holmes and Watson, Moran was charged with the Adair murder, but presumably escaped the gallows, since Dr. Watson was still referring to him as "living" in 1902 ("The Adventure of the Illustrious Client"), and even suggested that he was alive in 1914 ("His Last Bow"). (See *The Annotated Sherlock Holmes*, volume 2, by William S. Baring-Gould. This distinguished work confirms the date of Moran's arrest given by Flashman—April 5, 1894.)

The main discrepancy between the Watson and Flashman versions is interesting rather than important: Watson says that Moran fired from the ground floor of the empty house, while Flashman places him in an upper storey. The error is probably Watson's. There has been much controversy among Baker Street addicts about angles of fire, the laws of optics, parabolas, etc. (see Baring-Gould), but to a rifleman it is obvious that Moran would have preferred a direct horizontal shot to an upward one, and this seems to have been the opinion of the artists who illustrated Watson's account: the celebrated Sidney Paget, in the *Strand Magazine* of October, 1903, shows Moran looking straight across from his window, and the drawing of the American illustrator Joseph Camana in 1947 has both marksman and target on the same level.

Both Watson and Flashman are mistaken about Moran's age. Watson says he was born in 1840; Flashman, by stating that Moran was fifteen years his junior, implies that the date was 1837. But since Moran himself states that he was fourteen in 1848, we must accept that he was born in 1834, which is in keeping with Watson's description of him as "elderly" and a "fierce old man" in 1894.   [p. 336]

A NOTE ABOUT THE AUTHOR

George MacDonald Fraser was born in England and schooled in Scotland, served in a Highland Regiment in India, Africa, and the Middle East, and now lives with his family on the Isle of Man. In addition to The Flashman Papers and several other novels, he has written the screenplays for Richard Lester's *The Three Musketeers* and *The Four Musketeers*, and the James Bond film *Octopussy*.

A NOTE ON THE TYPE

Pierre Simon Fournier *le jeune,* who designed the type used in this book, was both an originator and a collector of types. His services to the art of printing were his design of letters, his creation of ornaments and initials, and his standardization of type sizes. His types are old style in character and sharply cut. In 1764 and 1766 he published his *Manuel typographique,* a treatise on the history of French types and printing, on type-founding in all its details, and on what many consider his most important contribution to typography—the measurement of type by the point system.

Composed by
Creative Graphics, Inc.,
Allentown, Pennsylvania

Printed and bound by
R. R. Donnelley & Sons Company,
Harrisonburg, Virginia

Designed by
Soonyoung Kwon